Synopsis

Are you working harder for less?

Ever wonder why?

Otherworlders Rantor and Torvald think they know why,
and are out to tell anyone who will listen.

But Ifford Furze, a retiring offworld entity with an inferiority complex about his appearance and genetic heritage, frankly couldn't care less if the Fed is a mechanism for the covert transfer of wealth. He's been ordered here by the 'home planet' to study mainstream economics at the Otto Von Bismarck School of Banking, Business, and Co-Operative Inter-Dependent Pre-Eminent Hegemony and has no interest in theories, or in changing the worlds.

He just wants to stay out of trouble and be left alone to read his mystery novels and munch his Krunchie-Krunchies in peace and quiet.

So how does Ifford end up being a wanted entity?
(Or - does he?)

And do Rantor and Torvald really have a plan that will save his bacon - when he finds himself with nowhere to run and nowhere to hide?

READ WHAT THE CRITICS ARE SAYING
ABOUT THIS BOOK.

"KIND OF A ROMP – if you don't mind a rather farcical plot."

"PACKS QUITE A WALLOP -- uniquely, unforgettably egregious."

"A NOVEL OF IDEAS – someone else's ideas."

"COMPELLING – I couldn't wait
to put it down."

"A VERITABLE *TOUR DE FORCE*, TOUCHING – AND
SURPASSING - all that is most execrable in the realms of both fiction
and non-fiction. Oxymoronically, this, in itself, constitutes a major
achievement – of sorts. Not just any old writer could have pulled it off
by design, let alone as the present author apparently did, without effort
and entirely unintentionally."

"RECOMMENDED for insomniacs;
induces sleep."

"FORTUNATELY, only once in a very great while does a book such as
this one come along. In fact, happily, I can't think of
another quite like it."

"TIME-TRAVEL, *sub-rosa* parallel jurisdictions, trauma-based mind
control, the Fed as a mechanism for the covert transfer of wealth
from the working classes … I ask you now.
What an imagination."

"OCCASIONAL INTERLUDES OF MILDLY ENTERTAINING,
BLACKLY HUMOROUS DIALOGUE and/or description
sandwiched between very long sections of
dreary, boring, incoherent, and ill-informed sermonizing."

"IT IS BOOKS LIKE THIS that make one wonder what these worlds
are coming to. After reading it, I wanted to have my memory erased."

"So bad IT'S GOOD. My nomination for this year's
Darwin Award in fiction."

"STANDARD conspiracy theory drivel. Don't waste your time on it."

"WHETHER THE PLOT is pure fiction or has any basis in fact, whether the putative author exists as a real entity or not, the book brings to mind E.A. Poe and other unstable imaginations."

"A CONFUSED and confusing book. It is hard to tell where the author is coming from – or where he's trying to take us."

"A CRY for help."

"I CAN certainly understand why the book was self-published."

"THE BAD NEWS is that I had to read the book in order to write this review of it. The good news is that I'm done."

"THE BOOK IS BOTH so-so and original.
But the parts that are even so-so are not original, and the parts that are original are not even so-so."

"MOST of the quotations at the chapter heads were just made up. Had to have been."

"IF THE INTENT WAS to popularize any of the ideas and alleged 'information' presented in this absurd mish-mash of 'theory' and conjecture, the author has failed, having only discredited it all as so much uneasy speculation on the part of those who, apparently, have nothing better to do with their time."

"I GOT CURIOUS and did a little investigating. At least the story *behind* the book is mildly interesting. Turns out the author, when the book was written, was working as an espresso puller at a Starbuck's in downtown Honolulu and living in a cheap dive in Chinatown. Homesick for the mainland, the author got the idea of self-publishing this book in hopes of selling enough copies to make one-way plane fare to Frisco or L.A. As this review goes to press, the author still resides in Honolulu."

But really . . .

Why take the word of establishment intellectuals – on anything ?

So, introducing . . .

Our Mysterious Anti-Hero...

Who is, or was, or will be, or might have been, Ifford Furze?

"Ifford Furze is a pathetic excuse for a human being. Literally. Wherever the hell he is now. He probably has NO idea how much trouble he's caused here in this strand, by writing those stupid memoirs of his. And who knows, what with the Ripple Effect, whether it will even be confined to this probability strand, or even to this Dimension. He's a jerk. And don't quote me. Not even anonymously."
(Name withheld) Administrative Assistant to a member of the Federal Reserve's Open Market Committee

"Ifford was my son. At least, I'm pretty sure he was. Or still is, maybe. My only son – that I know about, anyway. I just talked to him on the phone a few times, but he seemed like a real nice boy."
Gladys X, retired cocktail waitress

"Ifford? He was sweet. And cute. Really, really cute. You don't happen to have his email address, do you?"
Raquelle Angelina Nelson, model

The Dark Secrets of Money and Banking...

"Banking was conceived in iniquity and was born in sin. Bankers own the earth. Take it away from them but leave them the power to create deposits, and with a flick of the pen they will create enough deposits to buy it back again. However, take it all away from them, and all the great fortunes like mind will disappear, and they ought to disappear, for the world would be a happier and better world to live in. But if you wish to remain the slaves of the bankers, and pay the cost of your own slavery, let them continue to create deposits."

Sir Josiah Stamp, past President of the Bank of England

~ ~ ~ ~ ~ ~ ~ ~ ~ ~ ~ ~ ~ ~

"Think," Torvald mused, "As you commented earlier, Florence – just consider the immense wealth – the sweat equity, so to speak - that has, over the past century and more, been surreptitiously appropriated, or transferred, from the working class to the hidden banking aristocracy and their cronies - primarily by the legalized/institutionalized plunder of inflation   - inflation resulting, of course from the continuous creation, by the banking cartel called the Fed, of illusory 'deposits' – 'deposits' that are nothing more than book-keeping entries or worthless paper and metal slug 'money' ... and then think of what this nation - and its standard of living - might be like if the country had an *honest* banking system, and a *real* unit of account, with which to measure – and store -- the value of a man's labor -- rather than so much Monopoly money, the 'value' of which, if it can be said to have any, is constantly shifting - downward. Imagine, if the wealth created by the people with their labor had been allowed, for these past several generations, to remain in the possession and control of those whose labor created it -- the working masses whose labor has created -- and continues to create -- all wealth, all capital ..."

And the Labyrinth that is the Law ...

The law was simple, but hath been industriously rendered
perplex.
Algernon Sidney

Been down so long, seem like up to me ...
Furry Lewis

~ ~ ~ ~ ~ ~ ~ ~ ~ ~ ~ ~ ~ ~ ~

"So, are you saying," queried Rantor, "That the current 'government' is in fact *a private corporation* ... that its law is *private law, masquerading as public law*... that *all of our transactions with it are in commerce,* in a fictional 'hover zone,' in an equity/ admiralty/maritime jurisdiction ... and that the people – one by one, individually and unwittingly - bring themselves into nexus with and obligation to this 'corporation' 'voluntarily' b*y contracting with it*?

"YES!" burbled Riggs, in his enththusiasm choking a bit on his latte. "YES! And to follow the rabbit to its hole is to understand that, behind all the subterfuge, legal jargon, and complexity, the power at the top of the commercial/governmental heap is 'the bank.' We have 'government of the banks, by the banks, for the banks' ... is to understand that 'the bank' is behind every single war this nation and its people have EVER been involved in, from the very, very beginning ... is to understand that 'the bank' IS 'the government,' here. Every single bit of what is marketed to us as government has nothing to do with any Republican Form, created by Law by the 'People at large' via any democratic Law-making process. We know that by simply looking at the 'funny money.' So, YES! EVERYTHING we see is nothing more than *a commercial shell marketed to us as 'government.'* The irony – and tragedy - is that it appears to have been this way from the beginning."

So then," asked Rantor, "Would you say that all the reference to the Constitution and constitutional Law is window dressing – a false front *to sustain the misconception held by almost all of us that we do have a legitimate constitutional government in place?*

"Um-hmm. And the evidence is everywhere. It's the mystery of a thousand thousand clues in plain sight."

9

Which together
form the subject matter of …

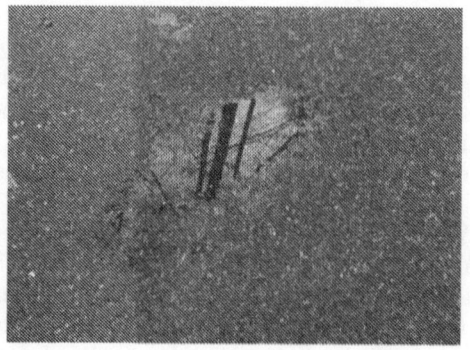

Gangstas
in Pinstripe Suits

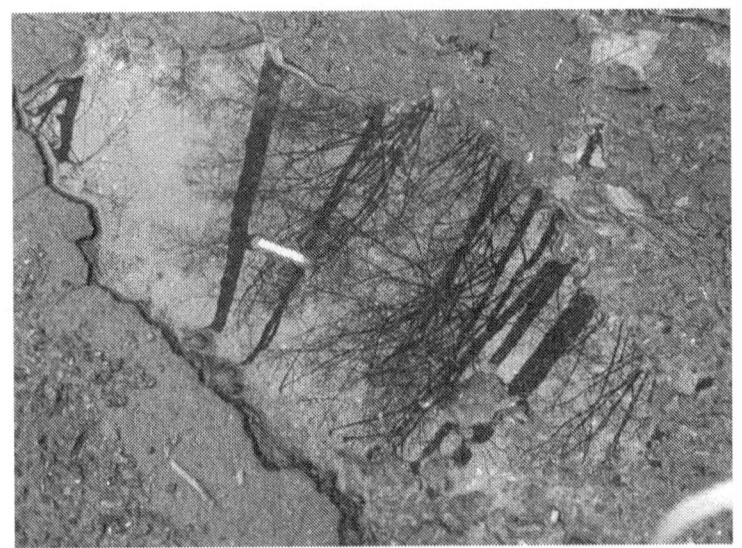

By

J. C. Wiater

Acknowledgements:

The quotations in Part I, Chapter 12, were taken from the Introduction (by Max Lerner) to *The Prince and the Discourses* by Niccolo Macchiavelli, published in 1950, a Modern Library College Edition by Random House, Inc.

The Part II chapter-head quotations from Delmore Schwartz are all from his poem, *The Heavy Bear That Goes With Me*.

The song excerpts in the final chapter of this book are from *I Can See Clearly* Now, by Johnny Nash.

All photographs, drawings, and cover art are by the author, except the world map on page 5, which is in the public domain.

Many source materials were used, some but not all of them referenced in the book and website lists at the end of the book, but the author assumes responsibility for any errors or inaccuracies.

Dedicated to
The exploitees
Who are working ever more for ever less

And to the 'thinking few'
Present and future
That they may
One day
Wake up ...

... And smell the coffee.

It is not enough to have a good mind.
The main thing is, to use it well.

Rene Descartes

In one of Planet Earth's infinitely many probable reality
strands, the following events,
or something very like them,
did, or may, occur ...

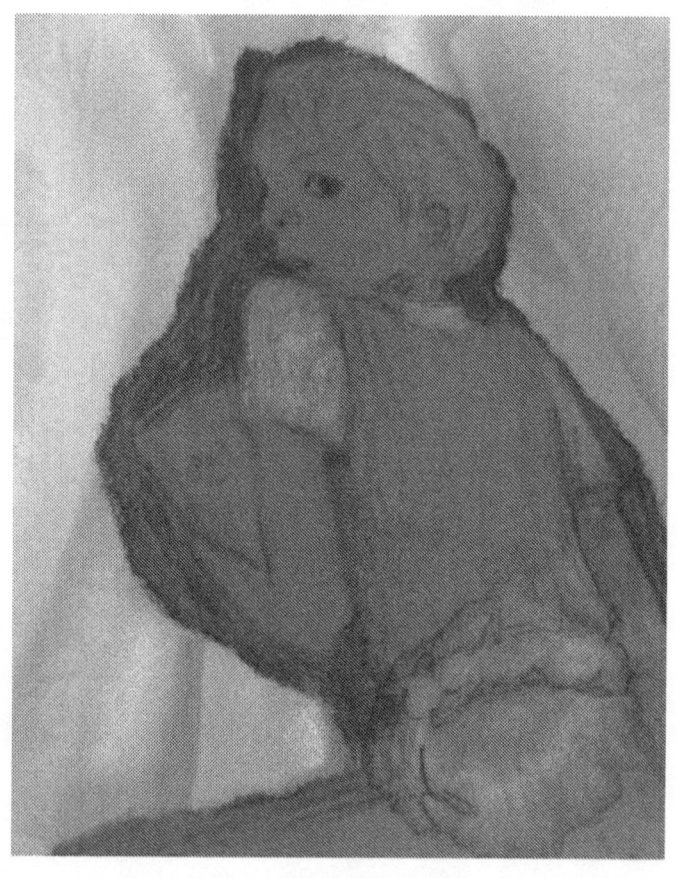

PART ONE: ONLY A HYBRID

"The mind of the Englishman does not readily accept anything he cannot see, or even sometimes anything he can see which is unprecedented in his experience, so that like the West American farmer, confronted for the first time by the sight of a giraffe, his impulse is to cry out angrily, 'I don't believe it!'"

Nesta Webster

Had anything been wrong, [I] would certainly have heard.

W.H. Auden,
'The Unknown Citizen'

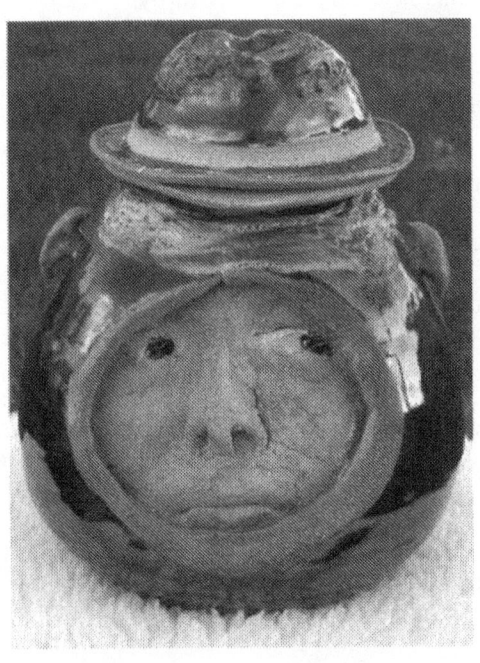

CHAPTER ONE: I GET A NEW ROOMMATE

Evil hiding among us is an ancient theme.

John Carpenter

I was idly knocking about the old domicile one mid-winter's night after dinner, knowing deep down that I should hit the books for a couple of good, solid hours of study before turning in at my usual sensible hour of 10, but rather resisting my fate, when I was startled by a sudden forceful rapping at the door.

Startled, I say, because I did not get many visitors - at any rate, no visitor had been announced - and this didn't sound at all like the porter's usual respectfully discrete - at times so discrete as to be scarcely audible - scrabbling.

"Who's there?" I called, a trifle warily.

"Your new roommate," came the *basso profundo* reply. "Open up!"

"Gracious!" I said, or perhaps squeaked, through the door, the blood beginning to pound a bit in the ears. "Are you sure? No one told me I was getting a new roommate."

I had rather been enjoying my solitude these last couple of weeks in the aftermath of the wafting away of Calvin, and the faint hope had begun to stir that I might continue on unmolested by the turbulent vibrations of another sentient being in these chambers for the rest of the school year.

"It says here, Suite 2-C in the Warburg Hall. Ifford Clarence Furze. That's you, isn't it? C'mon, man - open up!" And he actually rattled the handle!

"Surely, if I had been assigned a new roommate, someone would have mentioned it. And why didn't the doorman ring me up to announce you?"

16

"He's asleep, friend. I didn't have the heart to disturb the old man. And I looked in your mailbox on my way up. There's a pink slip in there that probably is your official notice of my arrival. What about it, Furze? Do I sleep in the hallway tonight, or what? Would you consider tossing me out a blanket? Or do you think you can risk unbolting the door?"

His tones of sarcasm were unmistakable. And it was true that I had neglected to check my mail that afternoon, and had not even gotten around to listening to my phone messages. Reluctantly, I turned the lock and opened the door a cautious couple of inches.

I don't mind admitting that the entity I beheld standing before me caused the knees to tremble and the visage (I'm sure) to go all pale and ashen. I clung to the door like a drowning man to a spar of driftwood and gulped audibly. In the utter silence of that moment, it sounded dreadfully loud - almost a sort of series of rapid clicks. I wondered a bit hysterically if everything was quite all right with the old larynx, or whether I might not, in my anxiety, have dislocated it, or some such thing. I made a mental note to remember to get it checked at the student health center on the morrow.

An extremely tall and burley reptilian stood there, not six inches away from me, a sardonic smile playing on what would have been his lips, if he'd had any lips. What he had was a sort of a muzzle, like a dog's, but hairless, and scaly. Eye contact with this fellow did a sort of violence to the soul. Particularly horrifying were the pupils - positively sub-zero, they were, two glistening deep-chocolate vertical slits - narrow, smooth-edged, bottomless crevasses, they seemed, soul-less chasms in a plain of gold-flecked, rust-brown irises.

My willowy frame undulated markedly once or twice; wincing under the impact of those eyes, I averted the gaze and, acting wholly on that animal instinct for survival which takes the helm in times of crisis, shakily attempted to shut the door in his face. He was too quick for me, however, and, salesman-like, deftly inserted a huge shoe between the door and its jamb, so to speak, a good-humoredly contemptuous smile-cum-sneer still wreathing his snout.

"Calm down, Ifford," he said, in a theatrical oily tone obviously meant to soothe. "Haven't you ever seen a reptoid before?" He pushed the door open and entered - very swiftly and gracefully, for his size, and considering that he was carrying two large, bulging canvas valises. His long tail writhed about like a python in its death agonies, coming perilously close to end tables and lamps.

"Careful with the tail, if you don't mind," I said. "They charge us for any breakage. And some of these things are my own. Antiques - or practically, anyway."

He had been surveying the room, and he did not cease his inventory to glance at me or respond in any way to my request, but the tail subsided to a tense, spasmodic twitching of its tip.

"What is this? An old *Leave It to Beaver* set, or what?"

"One of my hobbies is collecting '50s memorabilia," I responded stiffly, gnashing my teeth inwardly, and rather wishing there were a lethal weapon handy. I mean, the fellow had absolutely no sense of *comme il faut*.

"I suppose I can get used to if I must," he conceded in a *noblesse oblige* sort of tone, fiddling absently with the slender, whip-like end of his remarkably long tail.

"So glad to hear it," said I, with what was meant to be a withering sarcasm, which my new roommate seemed not to notice, being apparently one of those thick-skinned types oblivious to innuendo.

"It's just that I find it depressing," he went on. "All this ratty old stuff."

To tell the truth, it had come increasingly to have the same effect on me. I had even wondered if the shabby, and - face it - tacky, decor had contributed at all to Calvin's decline. He had spent less and less time in our rooms as his saga had ground on to its inexorable climax.

"Well," I sighed after a moment, resigning myself to the cruel turn my fortunes had apparently taken, "Let me show you where your bedroom is."

He grumbled over the fact that his was the room which gave onto the passageway between two buildings rather than onto the open quadrangle with its lawns and cobbled pathways and big old maple and chestnut trees; however, to my relief he did not attempt to bully me into an exchange of rooms, but heaved his bags rather gloomily onto the bed and began to unpack and put away his things. I noticed that one entire suitcase seemed to be filled with books.

I said I would go out to the kitchenette and heat some water for coffee, to which he grunted what I took to be an assent. As I was preparing the coffee, my thoughts turned, with a stifled cry of inner anguish and a sort of tremolo of the strings pulsating in the background, to Calvin Rorschak, my recently departed roommate, on whose merits I found myself ruminating for the first time with a belated appreciation.

Not that Calvin was departed in the sense of having gone to his eternal reward; no, Calvin had been rescinded, you might say - yanked back to the home planet by an aggrieved father and a solicitous mother, doubtless acting under the duress of royal edict. He had been a gentle, rather ethereal soul, totally out of his element at the Otto Von Bismarck School of Banking, Business, and Co-operative Inter-dependent Pre-Eminent Hegemony. Increasingly, as the semester had progressed, he had withdrawn from school activities, finally cutting his moorings entirely and drifting dreamily away from the uncongenial discipline of class attendance, the writing of papers, and the heavy load of assigned readings on politico-economics, banking, and the stratagems of planetary and galactic inter-dependent pre-eminence.

I think the entities on Calvin's planet were evolved from koala-like creatures. At any rate, he had looked rather like a koala - short, chunky, and slow-moving, with quite a heavy dusting of reddish body hair all over, from what I had been able to see - he had been a modest fellow - I had always wondered about his buttocks - and a broad, flattish nose under a pair of big, saucer-shaped sky-blue eyes as utterly devoid of expression as a cat's.

For relaxation, Calvin had liked to settle in the crook of a branch in one of the big chestnut trees in the quad, nibbling on leaves, I guess, or sucking the sap out of twigs, or whatever, and reading the poetry of Christina Rossetti, Ogden Nash, and Shel Silverstein. As the quarter had progressed, he had spent more and more of his time perched in his favorite tree, reading, chuckling, sighing, and nibbling, until finally, some equally fuzzy relative or trusted family retainer had appeared one day, helped him pack his things, and had escorted him back, I assume, from whence he came.

I had been somewhat relieved to see him go, I'll admit, just because I enjoyed having the rooms entirely to myself; but now I found myself regretting his loss. This new roommate, whatever his name was, and whatever hole (or eon) he'd crawled out of, seemed to portend the sort of character-building opportunity I preferred, if at all possible, to avoid.

I put the coffee things on a tray and carried them out to the dining nook, where I found my new roommate sitting at the table reading a book.

"Well," said I, cheerily, "We've got regular and de-caf - it's just instant, of course, though it is instant espresso, or so the label claims - and sugar and just the powdered cream, at the moment, I'm afraid, and the hot water's in this insulated jug, so - help yourself."

"No biscotti or croissants?" he. responded churlishly, without looking up from his book. I chuckled, thinking it his idea of a joke - a sort of ice-breaker, you know - but, a glance at the scaly furrowed brow and the petulant line of the lips told me he was utterly sincere. (I was to learn that he was absolutely incapable of any sort of guile or self-disguise).

Thinking to myself somewhat bitterly that the fellow really did seem to have the manners as well as the appearance of a Komodo Dragon, I said, "I'm sorry - not at the moment." In a somewhat martyred tone, which he totally failed to notice.

After a lengthy awkward silence in which he slurped and read and I stirred and sipped, I attempted to get the social ball rolling. We were, after all, going to be living together.

"What's that book you're reading?"

"The Creature from Jekyll Island," he answered, looking up at me with an almost agreeable expression on his reptilian map, and scooting forward on his chair eagerly, his tail beginning to twitch back and fourth in a gesture I was soon to recognize as an index of escalating emotional intensity.

"I don't recognize the title," I said. "It can't be one of our required texts. Is it on one of the 'read for additional credit' lists? Or are you doing a term paper on it?" But my little attempt to lighten the general mood fell flat. When it came to a sense of humor, my new roomie seemed to have a deeply negative balance.

"Are you kidding?" he snorted derisively. The fellow was all tact and suavity. "Any professor who used this book in his class would get the old heave-ho in very short order. They know which side their bread's buttered on."

"Hmmmm ..." I kept it non-committal. Ifford Furze is known for his ability to pour oil on the troubled waters and sooth the savage beast. This fellow positively seemed to cry out for domestication. Or sedation. Or even, God knows, lobotomy. I wasn't sure what he was driving at, but I wasn't at all eager to throw faggots on his flame. It was growing late, and I was feeling the strain of the evening's calamitous events. I was eager to draw the interview to a close and retire to the privacy of my bedchamber and the consolations of my latest mystery novel and my private stash of Grandma O'Houlihan's Crunchy Chocolate Morsels (which I was not about to bring out and share with this lout).

"Yes, well - you know, I'm afraid I don't even know your name ..."

"Rantor," he growled with a little scowl. I wasn't sure whether it was a name or an imprecation, but decided to give him the benefit of the doubt and consider it the former. Actually, he seemed put out that I hadn't taken up his conversational gambit. I began to wonder if he might not be one of those who burn to impart a message of great importance to all mankind.

"Yes, well, Rantor," I said soothingly, "You will have to tell me all about it one day soon, but for now" - here I yawned convincingly, so much so that he followed suit, displaying a fascinating mouthful of very sharp and gleaming white teeth, hundreds of them, it looked like - " I really must toddle off to bed. I have an 8 o'clock class on Mondays, Wednesdays, and Fridays, *malheureusement*. By the way - why haven't you a key?"

"I'm to get it from the porter."

"All rightie, then. Good night. Sleep well."

He muttered something into his book, to which he had sulkily returned, and I, after beaming somewhat inanely at the top of his scaly, wedge-shaped head, turned and gratefully fled the presence.

"Glennie"

CHAPTER 2: REPTOIDS AND ASTEROIDS

Evil is easy, and has infinite forms.

Blaise Pascal

The next day, as might be expected, Rantor was much on my mind. He had told me at breakfast that he had left his old digs after what sounded like a frightful quarrel with his roommate, whom he did not describe beyond telling me that he was 'as dumb as a box of rocks' and 'completely brainwashed.'

Naturally, I felt that none of this boded well for our future cohabitation, given that he made it clear by his demeanor and general attitude that he already had me pegged as being also as dumb as the proverbial rock-box. Distinctly troubled and in need of the opportunity to tell all to someone of a gentle and sympathetic cast of mind, I hastened after my last class to a little hamburger joint not far from campus, where my girlfriend and I meet every Friday for lunch, to hash over the week's events and lay plans for the week-end.

Before I introduce you to Glendith, I suppose I should tell you that she, like I, is a hybrid being, conceived in a test tube and gestated in a tank. We both do have pictures – acquired on the black market, as it were - of our alleged respective mothers … in fact, we both carry pictures of them, she in a locket about her neck and I in my wallet. But we of course have never actually met them, contact being not officially sanctioned – by which I mean, forbidden - interest in such matters being considered wasteful and inefficient.

We were both raised in group homes, on the same planet actually, but we never met until we came to Earth to study. According to what we have been told, we both have Earthling mothers and - well, some other kind, shall I say, of father, and we resemble one another physically - rather small and slender, with large heads, large slanting eyes, and fine, wispy, white-blond hair. On me the effect is rather gargoyle-like, unfortunately, in a space-age sort of way, but on her it looks great, and she attracts her share of admiring glances as she walks about campus. Some Earthlings regard offworlders as exotic, and word has it that some types of females are in hot demand at the various strip clubs in town.

We both desperately wish we were full-blooded humans from Earth, and to 'pass' as a real Earthling, in any interaction, however brief, with any other entity, but especially an Earthling, is blissfully exhilarating for us. Almost as euphoric as winning the lottery.

Perhaps because we had no real family life, we both long to stay on Earth, marry - although not necessarily one another - and raise large families. However, there is a good chance that we are both sterile. (We are, you see, what might be called experimental models.)

23

My eyes misted over a bit and I felt quite emotional, for me, as I saw her, good old familiar Glennie, sitting in our usual booth, leafing through an *Entities!* magazine and sipping a cherry Coke through a straw. She wore, taking it from top to bottom, a classic page boy hair-do, her gold, heart-shaped locket containing the picture of her mother, a plain simple cream-colored angora long-sleeved sweater, a plaid pleated skirt in reds and blues and creams and greens, with some thin black lines in there, too, and saddle shoes with fuzzy white ankle socks.

In case you're wondering about the get-up, what with its being so retro and all, I will clue you in re the important biographical datum that the decade of the '50's here on Earth is our 'thing,' Glennie's and mine - *Leave It to Beaver; Father Knows Best; Our Miss Brooks; I Love Lucy; Ozzie and Harriet; Have Gun, Will Travel; The Twilight Zone; Gunsmoke;* Jerry Lee Lewis; Elvis Presley; *The Ed Sullivan Show* - and so on. The odd thing is that even though we both long, in a tepid sort of way that is a bit hard to describe, to be passionate and emotional, we really are not. It apparently isn't in our nature, and even our fervor for the '50s is a very cool and deliberate sort of enthusiasm, more chosen and methodically cultivated than felt. We want to want the '50s - or anything at all, for that matter, I suppose. Glendith put it in a nutshell as we were walking to our dorms after lunch one Friday afternoon. "What's to feel?" she said, with an eloquent shrug of her thin little shoulders and a weary, rather cynical side-long glance at me out of her beautiful eyes - one thing I will say for Glendith, she really does have beautiful eyes.

To a large extent, I sometimes think, we are simply living life because we think we must, and as we think we must. I wonder at times if we are our own creatures in any way at all.

But this is beginning to smack of self-pity, an ever-present danger among us hybrids, according to our parent-surrogate care providers - sort of a genetic weakness or some such and something they warned us always to be on our guard against. But you have to admit that it is an odd thing to live with, knowing that you have been engineered as a sort of an experiment.

I ordered our Giganto-Burgers and then slid into the booth opposite Glennie. Before I could impart my news, she started right in telling me about a conversation she'd just had with an acquaintance of hers, an Earthling - or so he claims - named Jacko. He's the Public Affairs Director for the smaller of the two public radio stations run by the local government-funded university. Glennie's majoring in information-shaping and delivery, and a requirement for one of her classes involves doing volunteer work at some radio or TV station. Jacko does not seem to rate Glennie's intellect too highly; at least, that's what she believes. For whatever reason, he does not, in general, seem to regard her as worth talking to; but occasionally, she gets him in the right mood, and he talks to her, an event that invariably leaves her all a-bubble and a-glow. Glennie is a data junkie, feeding a later-stage information dependency - especially, she delights to feast upon suppressed information, and Jacko's supra-pharyngeal ganglion is a very questing and fertile nerve-center, the, in my opinion rather prolix, not to say questionable, emanations of which keep my darling endlessly amazed, aghast, and agog. She loves a good story, does Glennie.

Today, as usual, she couldn't wait to tell me all about it.

"I had the most interesting conversation with Jacko this morning, Iffy. He says that about 12,000 years ago, a planet that had been in orbit between Mars and Jupiter either blew up, somehow, or was blown up - that was the origin of this solar system's asteroid belt. He says that some of this material is in an elliptical orbit around the sun and only comes by every 12,000 years, because of the pattern of its orbit. He says that these orbiting asteroids are due to return in 5 to 14 years, and that they will collide with Earth, probably wiping out all higher life forms."

"Well, at least we shall be spared, then. Where did he get all this information?"

"I'm not sure. He says he's doing independent research, and cracking codes, and things. He says the government of the planet knows of this impending event but isn't letting the people in on it. For obvious reasons. That's why they're building the underground bases at Jilted Bride's Lake, Tehohohachapi, Sweetness and Light, under Marble Mountain, and so on. They're survival centers.

"So the ruling elites just plan to save themselves?"

"No; he says they plan to keep a nucleus population of 144,000 Earthlings – I'm not sure why that exact number - from the major races, black, brown, and white, for a maximally diverse gene pool."

"Hummm. Makes sense, I suppose, in a twisted, Strangelovian sort of way."

"He says a sort of Golden Age actually will - or could - come about, a few years after the collision, when all the dust and debris have settled. There will be lots of ice extending down into the present temperate regions, like where we are, because all of the debris in the atmosphere will have the effect of lowering the Earth's temperature, but he says conditions will be idyllic at the equator once the dust settles. Initially, of course, the impact, or impacts, will create incredible winds, and earthquakes, and tsunami as high as the Olympian Mountains, and all sorts of other effects."

"So, what do you think, Glennie? Should we be making plans to flee the planet?"

"I don't know. There are so many theories. What do you think?"

"You know what I think - I think Jacko is a disinformation agent, preying on innocent and susceptible minds like your own, sent out by the power-mad evil planners to sow the seeds of fear and confusion. You have to admit that his job at the station is a slot they'd be apt to want to fill with one of their people." I am always teasing her, saying that volunteering at that station has turned her into a conspiracy theorist. Which actually, to a certain extant, it seems to have done.

"I just don't think Jacko's a spook, Iffy."

Glennie, I suspect, has a bit of a crush on Jacko. She has a tendency to spring to his defense. He is certainly taller and huskier than I, and of course, much more humanoid. Though he definitely wouldn't be my cup of tea, if I were on the other side of the gender gap.

"You know the old saying - 'Everyone's a spook but me and thee, and sometimes I wonder about thee.' Even thee, dear Glennie."

"And what about thee, dear Iffy?"

"For me to know and you to find out, M'Dear. But I've got some news, too. There has been a blessed event. An inscrutable Fate has seen fit to provide me with a new roommate."

"Oh? When did this happen?"

"Just last night. I'm still reeling from the impact of the blow."

"As bad as all that? What's this guy like, anyway?"

"Seems to be a sort of Caliban minus the refinement and cultivation. About as large as an underground base, but scaly, with a prognathous jaw, enough teeth to open a shop, and an attitude."

"A reptoid? But there's only a handful of them on campus."

"Yes. Hard-core affirmative action cases."

"What's his name?"

"Ranto, or Rantor, is what I think he said. He has a rather snarly way of talking - replete with *basso profundo* cross currents and undercurrents that tend to impede the flow of intelligible sound."

A reflective look bloomed on the beloved's map as she thoughtfully bit off another hunk of burger.

"I might know this fellow, Iffy. There's this reptoid that keeps coming around the station, trying to talk Jacko into letting him do a program on the Federal Reserve System. I'm pretty sure his name is Rantor. Does he have these sort of creepy eyes, like rusted steel? And this really long tail that seems to live a life of its own? That he holds onto and sort of twiddles the end of, and picks his teeth with, when he's thinking? And kind of a perpetual frown?"

"I'd call it a glower, but, yes - there cannot be two such. This plane of existence is not loath to mete out cruel fates and unpleasant characters in prodigal amounts, but even here there are limits. Is Jacko going to let him do a program?"

"He's thinking about it. He told the guy to go ahead and put something on tape. Jacko's afraid it's an arcane subject that'll just put people to sleep - he's already got such a tough time slot, 3 to 6 a.m. on Saturday and Sunday mornings. It's all the station will give him, you know. But the reptoid - Rantor - says it's very important, and really interesting once people realize how relevant the issues are to their day-to-day lives."

I remembered my fleeting intuition last night that Rantor was one of these birds who live and breathe to proselytize. Given what I'd seen of him so far, it made sense. They're usually intense, humorless types as intent upon their monomania as a dog upon its dinner. And what was that book he'd been reading - *The Legacy of Jekyll Island*? - it had sounded like a mystery novel or sci fi thriller, but it seems to me now that I think of it that Jekyll Island was the place the chaps repaired to a century or two ago to hammer out the basic architecture of the Federal Reserve System.

Glendith and I munched our way through our what remained of our Giganto-Burgers and slurped our cherry Cokes to the syrupy dregs in meditative silence, for the most part, she no doubt pondering the asteroids reputedly hurtling our way, and I, of course, mulling over the whole roommate question, pro and con, yea and nay. It was a landslide victory for the nays, but the question was - how to implement the decision of the body politic.

"Rantor"

CHAPTER 3: REPTOID MEETS GIRL

Evil is the stone on which the good sharpens itself.

Dorothy Auchterlonie

Before we'd parted that afternoon, Glennie and I arranged that she would come over to the old homestead on the morrow for tea and crumpets. She was eager to have a look at the new roommate and ascertain whether he and the reptilian she'd seen at the radio station were in fact one and the same turbulent individual. The name Rantor, it seems, is a common one among reptoids.

That evening, I casually questioned Rantor re his plans for the Saturday and was informed that he planned to pass it as he usually did, in his room, reading. I decided to say nothing about Glennie's scheduled visit lest I scare him off or provoke some sort of scene - heaven only knows over what - I had just more or less slid right into the habit of treating the fellow with the utmost caution, as if he were a beaker of liquid nitroglycerin.

The next day, winter's gloomy early twilight found old Ifford loitering a bit edgily about the place, running the feather duster over end tables and window ledges, gazing out at the frost-bitten landscape and just generally killing time, waiting for the call from the porter informing me of Miss LaFour's arrival. This came as expected within a few minutes of the appointed hour, we hybrids being generally punctual and reliable to a fault, and while I was waiting for her to make her way up, I went over to Rantor's closed bedroom door and tapped respectfully.

He neither rose to open the door for me nor invited me in, but just bellowed, "What is it?" in a peevish tone which suggested that he was annoyed at being interrupted in his reading.

I shouted back, "A friend of mine is dropping in for tea - and crumpets, scones, croissants, lemon curd - pretty much the whole nine yards, should be quite a sumptuous repast - and we'd like you to join us. What do you say?"

There was a brief pause, as though he were examining the scheme for flaws - *caveat emptor*, et cetera - and then he roared, almost convivially, "Sure. Why not? I'll be out in 15 minutes or so, as soon as I finish this chapter."

Just then Glennie rang the bell, and I went to open the door for her. We went right out to the kitchenette to heat the water and arrange the delicacies on a platter. I had spared no expense when shopping that morning, and it really looked quite beautiful - and considering what it cost, it jolly well should have - glistening raspberry reds and lemon yellows scattered amidst a landscape of flaky pastry rolled and twisted into various elegant shapes and dusted with powdered sugar. I had even bought a few marzipan fruits which we placed artistically here and there amongst the pastries. It made me wish I had a camera.

At the sound of the whistling tea kettle, Rantor emerged from his lair, looking a bit drowsy and rumpled, as though he had been reading in bed and had fallen asleep over his book. He had taken no special pains with his toilette, that much was clear, and I darted a quick glance at Glennie to gage the impact thus far. The reptoid was so massive, really, and so far removed, evolutionarily speaking, from all that was near and dear, that my impulse as he lumbered towards us was still to look for cover, or the nearest exit. But Glendith looked as cool and collected as Grace Kelly waiting in a white satin evening gown to be introduced to Cary Grant.

"Rantor, come over here and meet a good friend of mine," I called to him, striving for a sort of cheery and off-hand lord-of-the-manor effect. "This is Glendith LaFour. Her friends, among whom we hope you will be numbered, old roommate of mine, call her Glennie. She and I hail originally from the same piece of rock out there in the inky void. Glennie, this is the new roommate I told you about yesterday. Rantor...? I guess I don't know your last name, do I, old man?"

"Just Rantor will do," the lizard replied in his guttural tones. "Pleased to meet you, Glennie." And he actually extended to her his large, scaly paw. The fellow was passingly acquainted with the conventions of civilized society after all, by the gods!

"Likewise, I'm sure," replied Glendith, taking his big mitt in hers and giving it a vigorous pumping. We hybrids are constantly struggling by word and deed to give the lie to this image we have somehow acquired here on *Gaia* of being total wimps with no more verve and spirit than a box of Kleenex.

"Interesting last name you have," replied the reptile. "Are you by any chance a clone?"

Glennie's poise faltered seriously - looked, in fact, about ready to throw in the towel altogether and call it a day. She was a bit pink in the face and seemed unable to frame a reply, so I attempted to bail the poor girl out.

"Actually, old man, she is. One of only twelve. A limited edition. An experimental model - very successful, I think ..." here I smiled and cast an encouraging look Glennie's way, hoping to buck the old girl up, but

31

she, still gazing as she was, very pink and flustered, at the toes of her saddle shoes, did not seem to catch it - "But she is, I assure you, the only Glendith La Four on Planet Earth. An original on this planet."

I don't know whether he perceived his *gaffe* or not - probably not - but the hulking brute had gone straight for the jugular. Glennie is painfully sensitive about being a clone - mortified is not too strong a word to apply. I will confess here that I intended to keep her secret on these pages, which is why I represented her as being, like your narrator, and as if that were not bad enough, only a hybrid. Actually, it is a picture of the hybrid female from whom she was cloned that my poor Glennie carries in a locket around her neck.

Since most clones harbor similar poignant feelings and existential *Angst*, it is part of the unspoken social code never to bring the subject up in mixed company. It's a bit like asking a girl if she's having her period just now or going into the particulars of one's latest bowel movement at the dinner table. Poor Glennie! Once again I found myself wishing I had at hand the means of reducing this atavism to an evaporating mist hovering over a dusting of powdery ash on the floor. But I wasn't packing my piece, and anyway, so direct an approach would have repercussions.

The thing to do was to propel us past this painful hiatus, and I, radiating for all I was worth the hostly vibrations of casual affability, suggested, therefore, that we waste no more time, but sit right down, before the tea got cold and the crumpets stale, and commence doing away with the evidence - which we did, Rantor - apparently oblivious, somehow, to the embarrassment he had inflicted - showing great gusto, loading his plate with quite a representative (and costly!) assortment of the available goodies and lacing his tea - brewed strong, the English way, which is how I like it - liberally with cream - real cream, this time - and sugar.

In order to give Glennie some time out of the limelight to take a few deep breaths and re-group, I brought up, as we munched and slurped, the only thing I could think of.

"What was that book you were reading over coffee the other night, Rantor? - something about Jekyll Island, wasn't it? At first I thought it must be a thriller of some sort - R.L. Stevenson revisited, you know - but then I seemed to remember that Jekyll Island was that place the banking fellows went off to in order to draft their banking reform legislation - isn't that right? And a jolly good thing it was they did, from what I hear - or the planet would be in even direr straits than it is now."

"A good thing, you say? I suppose that's what they're teaching you in your school of pre-eminent hegemony, or whatever it's called - your school of power politics. The pen is mightier than the sword, all right, but if it's really power you're after, the raw stuff and plenty of it, go into banking. Right?"

"I thought you were studying at the Otto Von Bismark School, too. Aren't you?" Suavely choosing to steer a course around the avalanche of steamy opinion.

"No, I'm studying engineering. But I'm interested in economics and banking practices."

"You haven't by any chance been talking with Jacko over at KROK about doing a show on the subject, have you?"

"As a matter of fact, I have. How did you know that? Minoring in intelligence? Have a little web of spies out as part of an assignment for one of your classes? We are all aware of the thirst of our controllers to know EVERYTHING."

Goodness, he was a nasty fellow. Just when I started to feel a bit less repulsed, he always resumed slathering on the unpleasantness with a renewed zeal. I noticed that Glennie seemed to have reassembled the inner being and was following the proceedings with an amused smile playing about her tiny mouth. We hybrids for the most part have these tiny little noses, mouths, and ears. It's one of our identifying characteristics.

Swallowing the urge to pummel the gargantuan about the head and shoulders, I managed to say, in, I hoped, not too strangled a tone, "Not to worry, Rantor. My web of intelligence operatives is still in the planning stages. A distant dream, and all that. No, it's just that a friend of mine - one of those present in fact, Glennie, here - does a little work for Jacko now and then, and informs me that she's seen a fellow of roughly" (I laid savage emphasis on the 'roughly') your description loitering about the place and importuning him for a piece of the air."

There was a pause, broken only by a breathless sort of muted giggle from Glennie's general vicinity - an odd little production that seemed to have emerged despite her best efforts at censorship.

Rantor swiveled the old bean to gaze on the girl intently for a moment or two with furrowed brow, and then said, "You're the one with the saddle shoes and bobby sox, aren't you? I knew you looked familiar, but I couldn't quite remember where I'd seen you."

She thrust a slender leg out from under the table and waggled a saddle shoe, saying, very brief and to the point, "Bingo!" - but softening the mild sarcasm with a little smile, accompanied by a glance from beneath lowered lids. Actually, with her large blue-green eyes shining with amusement - most of us hybrids have these pale, watery blue eyes, but Glennie has these jewel-like, almost turquoise orbs, most distinctive - and her complexion still suffused with a rosy glow, she looked quite lovely, I thought - almost like a doe-eyed Earthling of the Aryan persuasion just come in from an afternoon's ice skating with her beau, was the general effect.

"Well, since you seem to be an insider, how about telling me what Jacko really thinks about letting me do a program on the Fed?"

"Jacko doesn't talk to me very much. I'm hardly what you'd call a confidante. He hasn't told me much more than what he told you. Basically, he doesn't think it's a very important issue, and he's afraid his listeners, who - you know - thrive, I guess you could say - on a high-protein diet of heavy-duty crisis, scandal, and cover-up in the worlds of government and big business, will find it pretty tame stuff and rather soporific. Especially at that hour. But he's willing to listen to your tape."

"How come you're working for him? You got some information you're trying to get out?"

"Heavens, no. I'm majoring in information-shaping and delivery, is all. A class I'm taking requires some volunteer work in the media, and I chose KROK, mainly because it's on campus, and I don't have to take the bus to get there. But it is a very interesting place to work. I'm always learning something new."

"So Ifford's gonna be a banker, and Glennie's gonna concoct and administer information. Quite the pair of radicals."

"You'll have to hold up that end of things, I'm afraid, old man. Between the three of us, we'll make a little microcosm, touching all the bases - the good, the bad, and the ugly," I suggested, still striving doggedly, if at this stage of affairs a trifle grimly, for the light, careless tone of a Depression era matinee idol.

"Well, Ifford, since you're majoring in banking, maybe you can tell me a little about what they're teaching you at the Otto von Bismarck School."

I should explain here that it is my cherished habit and firm policy NOT to employ the gray matter on the weekends, getting more than enough of that sort of workout during the week, it being more or less compulsory at the Otto Von Bismarck School. But - anything for a friend, is my motto, and besides, I did not want to risk a darkening of the reptilian brow.

"Sure - why not? As best I can, anyway. What is it you'd like to know? Fire when ready, old boy."

"What's with all these English-isms, anyway? - 'Old man, old boy, old chap' - you auditioning for a part, or what?"

"No, I'm afraid that's the way I really talk. There's a decidedly English influence on the home planet. We all of us speak English English. Some of us more than others, of course." I neglected to mention that one of my idols is Bertie Wooster, as created by that redoubtable writer of humorous fiction, P.G. Wodehouse. The information is personal, and the literary allusion would doubtless have been over his head.

"Glennie doesn't seem to."

"She, if I may take the liberty of speaking for her, has made a concerted effort to re-cast herself in the American mold. She loves all things American - don't you, Glennie?"

"Pretty much. Especially from the '50s and early '60s."

"Well, that explains it, " said Rantor. "So, Ifford - tell me about the Fed, for starters. Why, according to The Otto Von Bismarck School, was the Federal Reserve Act passed, back in 1913?"

"Well, hmmmm ... I guess that the people had had it up to here with the chaos of unregulated banking - runs on the bank, bank failures, depressions, and so on - and so some of the more far-seeing legislators and members of the banking community decided to spearhead a movement for banking reform. Actually, the citizenry were involved, too - there was a citizens' committee for banking reform based in Chicago, if I am remembering correctly. And some of the more progressive intellectuals and economists supported the movement, as well, many of these also being headquartered at the University of Chicago.

"And, um, let's see ... oh yes, Paul Warburg - I'm sure you know who he was, pretty much the father and guiding spirit of the Federal Reserve System - devoted much effort to the good cause, writing articles, lecturing - you know, educating people. A real public-spirited reformer. At heart a retiring sort, the kind who'd much rather stay home and potter about amongst the African violets and delphiniums - but one of those birds who felt the call to public service so strongly that he overcame his basically reclusive leanings and sallied forth - the shy warrior, one biographer called him - to become the man, more than any other, responsible for getting the Federal Reserve Act passed. You probably know that the benighted public, and some of the more reactionary legislators, put up quite a struggle."

"Then Torvald's right," mused Rantor, as if to himself - the first time I'd ever known the fellow to muse, introspect, or pause in reflection. Who was this Torvald? I wondered, but before I could give voice to the question, the reptoid surged relentlessly on.

"So, tell me," he asked next, in his patronizing, I-shall-humor-this-benighted-idiot tone which I found almost fully as annoying as the test of the emergency warning signal that is broadcast on the tube every Saturday at noon, "Why was there so much secrecy surrounding the trip the seven took to Jekyll Island? If they were public-spirited reformers out to better the lot of humanity, why did they have to sneak around?"

I was not exactly sure who these seven were, but I did not ask. I was sure, you see, that had I done so, he'd have told me.

"Well, you know how people - entities, I mean - are, Rantor. I speak not of those present, of course, but of the unwashed masses. Stubborn, superstitious, fear-ridden children in adult bodies, alas. They had somehow conceived an exaggerated mistrust, almost amounting to paranoia, of the Wall Street bankers, and were sure to put the kibosh on any plan put forth by them - the Money Trust, as I believe they were called."

"Well, OK - so what about the Fed's track record? What were its objectives, and how well has it succeeded in meeting them?"

"I'm not sure, to be frank, that I can remember all of its objectives. I could always go and look it up in one of my textbooks, if you really have a thirst that must be slaked. Just, basically, to stabilize the economy, provide an elastic currency, make things run more smoothly - that sort of thing."

"OK, so, looking at the record of history, Ifford, what kind of a grade would you give the Fed, in terms of how well it's delivered the goods? The Federal Reserve Act was passed in 1913. So, with the Fed's firm hand at the throttle, this country has gone through stock market crashes in 1921 and 1929, the Great Depression of '29 to '39, and boom-bust cycles ever since. Oh, and here's a biggie - what about the over 1,000% inflation, which has destroyed over 90% of the dollar's purchasing power? And the inexorable decline in the national standard of living, as evidenced by all these homeless families they have here these days, living in cars and campgrounds and family members' back yards. What do your professors and textbooks have to say about these problems - if the Fed has been that good for the country - for its people, I mean?"

"Well, the economy is very, very complex, Rantor, old man. I'm not sure any of us would have done much better. These men are doing the best they can, you know - but they're not gods. But that the system works well, or well enough, seems hardly in doubt. I mean – it's even being exported to other worlds, as I understand. You must have heard of the IMMM – the Fed's planetary outreach endeavor?"

"The Inter-Galactic Missionary Marketing Ministry? Yes, I've heard of it. Well - another thing that puzzles me, Ifford, old man, has to do with this inflation. Where does that lost purchasing power of the dollar go? Does it just sort of evaporate into thin air, or what?"

"Actually, I don't know. That's an interesting question. I mean - it's just gone - isn't it? No one benefits. It's just - one of those unfortunate facts of life - like death and taxes. We all know that the Fed tries to keep the rate of inflation as low as possible."

"Just out of curiosity," he doggedly persisted, "What have they taught you regarding pre-20th Century economic history?"

"Not very much. They basically say that it was pretty much a chaotic, disorganized mess that left the country more or less crying out for regulation."

"And you just took their word for it?"

"Well, of course I did. Wading through all that banking and economic history can be pretty boring, you know. I don't think any of us is studying banking because we find it passionately absorbing. And the required readings and other work keep us busy enough. If they tell us we can omit close scrutiny of the 19th Century, we're more than happy to take their word for it. I mean - why would they lie?"

"Why would they LIE?" repeated the odious amphibian in the most theatrically incredulous tones imaginable, wagging the old bean from side to side slowly, and casting his gold-flecked eyes heavenward as if to say 'Give me strength', 'What next, O Lord,' 'What fools these mortals be,' and so forth and so on.

I mean - a bit insulting - what? - and here I'd been thinking that I'd acquitted myself quite well under his intense cross-examination, and had even imagined old Professor Forthwith standing on the sidelines, as it were, rubbing his palms together in satisfaction and beaming his approval. I glanced at Glennie, hoping to receive - I don't know - a conspiratorial glance, or an exasperated one, or a warm one, or some sort of subtly-communicated pro-Ifford sentiment - but the old girl was sitting with saddle shoes propped on the rung of her chair and the pink tip of her tongue peeking out from the corner of her little mouth in concentration as she steadied her plate with one hand and used her fork with the other to slice a marzipan strawberry into as many very thin slices as possible. It was impossible to tell if she'd been following the repartee closely, or off in dreamland the whole while, or what. I saw, at any rate, that no help could be expected from that quarter, so I girded the loins, took a deep breath, and turned my somewhat resentful gaze once again at the scaly behemoth, who was taking advantage of the lull in the proceedings to demolish an almond cream croissant of, it seemed to me, a particularly poignant and fragile beauty.

"Rantor, old man," I began slowly, in tones fairly a-drip with wounded dignity, "I'm afraid I don't quite get your drift. Your point eludes me. I was following you for a while, but the scent has grown cold. What, if you don't mind spelling it out for me, is the significance of the martyred heavenward rolling of the eyeballs?"

There followed what I believe is referred to as a pregnant pause, while Rantor seemed to struggle to assemble, or reduce, his thoughts into a coherent utterance or two. Finally, he spoke.

"Ifford," he said, gazing at me earnestly with those unsettling chocolate and amber eyes, a buttery croissant crumb bobbling on his upper lip as he spoke, "I scarcely know where to begin. There's so much to say. All things considered, I think it might be best if I were to turn you over to Torvald. He's better at this sort of thing than I am."

"Just as long as you will personally guarantee my safety, old man. Who or what is this Torvald, anyway? And what sort of thing IS this sort of thing?"

"Torvald"

CHAPTER FOUR: MY RE-EDUCATION COMMENCES

I know that most men, including those at ease with problems of the greatest complexity, can seldom accept even the simplest and most obvious truth if it be such as would oblige them to admit the falsity of conclusions which they have delighted in explaining to collegues, which they have proudly taught others, and which they have woven, thread by thread, into the fabric of their lives.

Leo Tolstoy

Glennie stood tranquilly under the streetlight, hands thrust deep into her pockets, watching me as I strode towards her. She had donned the foul weather gear, the whole nine yards as they say here - boots, her cashmere muffler in the red, white, and blue stars and stripes of the American flag, and, the *piece de resistance*, found one happy day in a thrift store, a long navy blue coat of thick luxuriant wool, belted around the middle and reaching past mid-calf. The bulky winter garb made the girl herself appear even smaller than usual; she looked rather like a child who had been playing dress-up in her mother's clothes. A light snow was falling, and the small, dry flakes lay without melting on her hair and shoulders. As I came up to her, I surprised us both by placing my hands on her shoulders and giving her a little kiss on the lips; nothing deep, passionate, or searching, for we hybrids are for the most part not like that, tending, as I believe I have mentioned, rather to the off-hand and low-key end of the emotional spectrum. This was more a little brush, the barest and briefest of contacts - sort of a trial run, you might say.

Even so, the old girl looked taken aback, the eyes saucer-like, the mouth slightly ajar, et cetera. Clearly, she had not been mentally prepared, and I made a mental note to lay a little groundwork the next time - though of what that might consist, I had as yet no clear idea.

Resolving to give the matter some thought at my earliest convenience, I gave a gay, careless laugh, took both her hands in mine, beamed into her eyes, and said, "Well! You're looking lovely his evening, I must say! Just brushed the teeth, have you - and scrubbed the face, and arranged the coiffure, straightened the seams and brushed the lint off the pea jacket, and what not?"

"Ifford, what's WITH you?" she queried. She wore the most annoying little frown of puzzlement. I mean, can't a fellow ever be in a gay and insouciant mood without occasioning alarm?

"You haven't been - drinking, or - or anything like that, have you?" She disengaged her hands from mine, and I took a quick step back, fearing somehow that her intention was to lay a motherly hand on my brow, or feel for the fevered pulse.

"No, of course not," I said, frowning and taking hold of her arm as we began walking together towards The Ragged Edge - a very good, if, in the matter of appearance, somewhat bedraggled little coffee house, where the espresso is never bitter and the pastries never day-old, and where we were to meet Rantor and the mysterious Torvald for after-dinner coffee and conversation. It was only the next day, the Sunday, and already Rantor was placing me as promised in the competent hands of Torvald.

We walked on through the falling snow in silence for a few minutes, and then Glennie said, "Iffy? Has Rantor been making you feel sort of bland and uninteresting? Is that it?"

Ever since she'd taken the psychology class, she had not been the same girl. A veritable Sherlock Holmes of the intra- and inter-personal, she had become, piecing together one's entire emotional history, major traumas, complexes, and inner anguish from the way one said, 'How do you do, nice day isn't it?'

Those who say all they want is to be understood, really understood, by one sympathetic significant other just don't know what it's like - to be so unremittingly, so thoroughly and methodically, so inexorably understood. Or at least considered. It gets a little old at times, I can tell you. There is at least a certain privacy in being misunderstood.

Perhaps she was right about Rantor. But personally, I doubted it. However, it seemed, at least, as good a theory as any other, and it did please the old girl to be right about these things; so I gave a sigh, and said, in an off-hand way that, yes, I supposed that could be it. I was rewarded by a small, pleased smile that blinked very quickly on and off. She glanced up at me - snowflakes on her very eyelashes, I swear! - and said casually, "You know, I like you just fine the way you are, Iffy."

One thing about Glennie - she's a kind soul. If the other eleven are like her, I'd say the mad scientists back home had better stick with the original blueprint.

Well, we chugged on through that eerie muffled silence and unnatural nighttime brightness of the snow, finally rounding the ultimate corner, to behold with glad eyes the seedy and disheveled exterior of The Ragged Edge. With its peeling paint and its pathetically sagging door, it looked indeed like a once-beautiful woman well past her prime but still struggling gamely to hold her own. But its windows, steamily covered on the inside with condensed moisture, shone forth warmly, and we were glad to come in out of the cold. We entered gratefully and stood looking around the place for the familiar hulking form and glittering eye.

We saw him way in the back, waving energetically - he had been lucky enough to nab one of the better tables, a large round thing with a semi-circular padded booth, a bit set off from the other tables and, blessedly, at the farthest remove from the blaring speakers. We hybrids are more delicately nurtured, apparently, than the vast majority of the natives on this planet, and our nerves are painfully abraided by much of what passes here for music.

As we made our way towards the reptile, I perceived with some dismay that his companion appeared to be an off-planet entity of the type known as the 'Nordic Blond.' These birds, both male and female, tend, in the looks department, to be generally of movie-star quality - tall, blond, slender, and dazzlingly good-looking - and the present specimen was no exception to the rule, resembling a fair-haired version of a young Greek god who pays regular visits to the work-out gym and the tanning salon, and perhaps even has rejuvenating things done to the complexion. As was only to be expected, Glennie's face bore the highly interested expression of a Golden Retriever whose master has just picked up the leash and red rubber ball and is heading for the door.

Introductions were made - the chap's name was of a kingly magnificence - Zebulon Torvald Glendenning, no less - or it might have been Torvald Zebulon Glendenning - hands were shaken with manly firmness, and comments on the weather exchanged; then, remembering that the place had no table service, we trouped *en masse* to the counter and placed our orders, self opting for a double hazelnut latte with plenty of foam, and a particularly exquisite apple tart made, I believe, on the premises and featuring - in addition to the slices of very tart apple - an excellent puff pastry, a scattering of walnuts and chocolate chips, and thin drizzles of a buttery cream cheese icing applied as a finishing touch back in the kitchen by some minimum-wage cross between a haiku poet and an action painter.

We carried all back to the table, and scooted into place, and sipped, and nibbled, and then - well, push had come to shove, hadn't it? I mean, I really don't know what had possessed me to agree to this meeting, when I could so easily have put it off by pleading a numbing load of schoolwork, or a stabbing pain in the left ventricle, or any number of things: that I had, haunting the by-ways of the brain, a sestina that would give me no peace until I succumbed and committed it to paper; that I needed to catch up on the hand laundry; that I had an antimacassar badly in need of mending. The possibilities were endless. And yet here, somehow, I sat.

One thing of which I was sure, as I sat gloomily forking in the buttery mouthfuls, was that I had no interest whatever in whatever it was these two had to impart, and that I simply must learn to say no. Perhaps that makes two things. Anyway: the main point was that we hybrids tend to be entirely too accommodating, too complaisant - or is it compliant? - and that many a time and oft I have found myself in similar sticky situations, enmeshed in the coils of a Fate which could easily have been averted if I had only had the moral fiber and quickness of wit to say, thank you so much, what a pity, and all, but I regret that I have a previous engagement. Or even - if it became absolutely necessary to be this brutally honest - then: I'm sorry but I'm not interested; why don't you go along without me?

But I had been my usual pliant self, and so there we sat. I was quite caught up in the foregoing dark ruminations. I'm not sure what was occupying the minds of Glennie and Rantor, or that of the Norse god, but the thoughts of all must have turned inward for a spot of reflection on what had passed so far and a consideration, perhaps, of how best to proceed; whatever it was that was occurring in the inner recesses, there passed a brief interlude of silence, as all sat and stared pensively, more or less in separate unison, into the foam atop the espresso.

In the end, it was Torvald who started the conversational ball rolling by asking me how I liked my classes at the Otto Von Bismarck School. These fellows went straight to the point and, once there, settled in for the duration, it seemed.

Well, fine, said I; I mean, banking was not a subject over which the average bloke could easily wax rhapsodic, but the school had a good reputation, and that was the main thing, wasn't it? I mean, I didn't know about him, but in my case, the object of all this schooling was not so much the fine-tuning of the soul and sensibility as the achieving of a competitive edge when it came to this matter of making a living - what?

I thought it best to get my cards right out on the table - you know – alert the chap, right off the bat, that Ifford simply is not one of those political, or theoretical, or philosophical, types who gladly gab on into the night, assailing one another freely with obscure studies and subtle considerations which cast doubt on the other fellow's conclusions and render moot his most cherished precepts regarding the meaning of it all. No, Ifford is the sturdy, practical sort who wishes only to tend his own pea patch, stay well-fed and warm, and leave the mapping out of the intangible underpinnings to those who feel at home dealing in airy nothings.

"Funny you should bring that up, that matter of making a living," my interlocutor ploughed on, it having been, he averred, the very subject loitering amongst, or amidst, his own neurons and synapses. Though that might not have been exactly how he phrased it.

Do tell, how fascinating, please go on, thought I, in, I will freely admit, an excess of venomous sarcasm. But of all this black emoting I, being like most hybrids - those hailing from our planet, at least - very well bred, betrayed not an iota, it being my policy to maintain, when all else fails, a discrete silence. Resolutely keeping on the old map, therefore, an expression of the utmost conviviality and alert interest in the proceedings, I merely said something noncommittal like, Hmmmmm? and proceeded with the interment of my apple tart.

Torvald next wanted to know if I had given any thought to the issue of the declining standard of living. It certainly made that matter of making a living more problematic, especially for the lower strata. Did they treat of these matters, he wondered, at the Otto von Bismarck School? What was I being told by my professors? And what did I make of it all?

This, if I may again editorialize freely, is precisely what I most emphatically do not like about such interludes as the one in progress - they require one to think, which, say what you will, is no small matter or easy task. I may, I trust, speak freely on these pages. In connection with my endeavors at The Otto Von Bismarck School, I am obliged - even though I do have the great advantage of being endowed by Nature, or my genetic engineers, with a near-photographic memory - to exercise the brain lavishly and without stint Monday through Friday, incessantly throughout the day and often even on into the night, when those more fortunate than I are pleasantly whiling away the hours before the tube, or purchasing trinkets at the mall, entirely untroubled by the need to, in any way, shape, or form, think. I believe I have already alluded to the fact that, as a way of coping with the heavy demands made upon my brain, it has become my custom to arrange things in such a way that - though I may have to work - and think - like one possessed during the week, my week-ends are blissfully free of the need for any save what I may perhaps designate as the recreational or volitional thinking - which movie to see, which restaurant to go to, which is the more attractive actress or the better wine.

But we hybrids are ever-obliging. It must be something deep within our genes - an inserted item, perhaps. Dutifully, therefore, even though this was a Sunday and although inwardly agonizing, I smiled pleasantly at my inquisitor, cast the eyes heavenward as I habitually do when employing the gray matter, and revved the mental engine, vigorously canvassing the memory banks and engaging the discriminative intellect. In short, I cogitated for all I was worth - but without much result.

"Well," said I, emerging empty-handed from the deep wells of thought. "Well, well, well! I'm sorry to say that I seem to have drawn a blank. *Nihil*. My classes so far have dealt for the most part quite narrowly with business and banking practices. What I know about the contemporary economic picture is mostly just what I've picked up from the print media and telly.

"So I know, oh ... that wage increases tend to lag a bit behind inflation, and that the planet's in a pickle with the burgeoning population and dwindling natural resources and the rising crime rate, not to mention terrorism, and the demand for ever-more services from government and the crisis of rapidly rising health care costs and the salination of farm land and dropping water tables and global warming and what have you. It's a very complex picture and I'm sure the problem you asked about, the declining standard of living, has many causes, not just one or two. And that there's probably not much that can be done about these thorny problems - or this government of, by, and for the people would be doing it in order to win the gratitude and support of the voters at the next election." (I *had* taken a class in American Government.)

Here Torvald and Rantor exchanged meaningful glances and knowing smiles, which rather made me feel that I had been set up and was - to put it bluntly - being toyed with. To my own surprise, I felt a little *frisson* of what practically amounted to anger.

"Look here, you two," I was rather amazed to hear myself saying, with an entirely uncharacteristic intensity of feeling, "Why don't you just abandon the Socratic stuff and come out with it. I know you've got a point of view which you're dying to impart, so - what's holding you back? Why so mysterious? Out with it, man - let's have it. I'm all ears. Enlighten me. Bring me up to speed."

Glancing at Glennie to catch the impact on her of my manly self-assertion, I noticed that the old girl wore a positively happy and expectant look, a bit like the actress in that play about being afraid of

46

Virginia Woolfe which was put on last spring by the Karl and Groucho Marx School of Creative Writing and Dramatics here on campus. I remember this very fragile blonde girl with big eyes, a bit like Glennie, actually, who, when the inner tensions and hidden dynamics of those onstage were heating up and threatening to break their chains and go on the rampage, chose a brief moment of charged silence to clap her hands and squeal, Oh! Violence! Violence! It was a shocking moment which had stayed with me; but it surprised me considerably to see that Glennie, my somber and sedate Glennie, was apparently capable of a similar giddy excitement when witnessing things gladiatorial.

Rantor, too, seemed gladdened by the turn things had taken, and looked over at Torvald with the eagerly expectant look of a schoolboy a-waiting his gumdrops on treat day. The expression on his face seemed to say, Oh, boy, here comes the good part. His attitude towards his friend apparently verged on the worshipful.

Torvald cleared his throat, and hesitated what seemed a very long while before speaking. Finally he said, "I'm sorry, Ifford, if I seemed to be playing cat-and-mouse with you. I really was - am - interested to know what you think. It's like raw data to me. I'm always interested to find out the beliefs that are being inculcated, and the best way to do that is to talk to people."

"The inculcees, you mean?" I responded a trifle bitterly. I mean - did he actually expect that to make me feel better? I considered interjecting here a pointed comment about laboratory rats and guinea pigs and having some idea now about how they must feel, and might have done so, but was given no opportunity to speak, the Nordic boy wonder scarcely even pausing to come up for air, but plowing on regardless, like one of those all-terrain vehicles which they employ in the military.

"My point of view, since you asked for it," - had I? - "On the declining standard of living here in this country is that it has by no means naturally evolved or just happened, but that it is in fact part of a larger, a very cohesive and well-thought-out, plan. That it has been very deliberately brought about, and that it's not by any means as low as it's going to get."

"Plan? Come, now. Whose plan? I mean, who would plan such a thing? And who could possibly bring off such a large-scale plan, even if they wanted to? Who could possibly benefit from such a plan? And all this talk against government ..."

Frankly, I was beginning to wonder if this chap wasn't one of those conspiracy theorist fellows you hear so much about. Plan? I ask you, now!

There followed another exchange of meaningful glances between reptoid and demigod, making me again feel that I was not regarded by them as being quite up to their level of play. Once again the problem seemed to be, how to bridge this chasm that yawned between us; how to communicate with one of such doubtful intellect, and so deeply mired in ignorance and wrong thinking to boot. Another long pause ensued. Then Torvald spoke.

CHAPTER 5: THE (un)WILLING SUSPENSION OF DISBELIEF

Every man who attacks my belief diminishes in some degree
my confidence in it, and therefore makes me uneasy; and I am
angry with him who makes me uneasy.

Samuel Johnson

"So - you are thinking that we are conspiracy theorists, and that our theories are ..."

"Well - yes, actually - to be perfectly candid - that they are specious, now that we have opened the topic for frank discussion. I don't mean to be offensive, really I don't ..." - I had, you see, been mulling it all over a bit, as I trudged my daily rounds - "But, frankly, it seems to me, you know, that all of this government cloaks and daggers lore, much of it, anyway, is more the stuff of the movie theatre and the ten penny thriller than real life, and to be exaggerated in the same way that movies and novels in need of the compelling plot and high dramatic interest tend to exaggerate and distort reality. Don't get me wrong - that there occurs the occasional bit of chicanery and corruption here and there in government, I have no trouble believing; but anything like ... an organized, on-going, over-arching, multi-generational conspiracy on the part of those in the spheres of government and/or the banking or corporate world - it frankly just seems too much to swallow - either that such a thing could be possible to carry out, unbeknownst to the general public, over decades, or that any such thing is currently in place, in progress - right here and now."

"Actually, Ifford, most people feel as you do. In fact, I myself used to be more or less of the same opinion."

"Yes, well ... now, at any rate, you and Rantor seem to believe the political situation here to be grim, and increasingly grimmer - here in what is still considered to be one of the more people-friendly, so to speak, countries and governments on this planet - and even, perhaps, in the known Universe ... and frankly - well - I'm sorry, you know, but I just don't buy it."

"What, if you don't mind my asking, are your problems with that view?"

"Well, for starters, why would your government harm its own citizens? I mean, governments in general are formed to help, not harm - right? Public servants, and all that? Surely those holding the reins of power are not of the same class of beings as those fiends who populate the lurid pulp fiction - the Batman and Superman comics and so on. You and Rantor almost make them sound like that. Bad guys on a grand, almost a mythic, scale. I mean - you in this country are widely known to have one of the better governments going ... and then," - I was warming to my subject, you see - "As regards all of this alleged government corruption - for one thing, if it were so, surely the media would be onto it, what with all of them, as we know, always panting to be first with a hot story ... and then - well, what's it all in aid of? All of this alleged government corruption? I mean - why have corrupt government in the first place? Wouldn't it be far easier to just have, you know, a fair, honest, open, and above-board sort of government that wouldn't have to go to all the trouble and expense - and risk - of surveilling and oppressing and deceiving and harassing the public? I mean - it's got to be a pretty big job. And enormously expensive ... so, why even bother? To me, it just doesn't compute. Frankly, it's hard to believe that such a thing would even be possible - with so many people involved, and spanning generations, if you and your scaly chum are to be believed. And then, as I've already mentioned - surely the media would be telling the public if this were happening - wouldn't they? The Fourth Estate, aren't they called? The watchdog media? Always eager to be the first channel or news magazine to break a hot story?"

For ad libbing it, I thought I had done rather a good job. I sat there feeling modestly triumphant, and rather expecting - oh, perhaps an admiring word or two ... and certainly, some hemming and hawing, what I think is called extemporizing, from the glamour boy. I will have to look it up, that word. But I think it might apply here. At any rate, I rather thought I might have trumped the fellow, and I sat sipping my latte, waiting. I glanced at Glennie to see what effect, if any, my virile self-assertion had had on her. But her expression was an inscrutable one.

"I think, Ifford," Torvald replied after a moment spent, I assumed, processing my objections, and struggling to come up with a defense of his position, "That a good way to approach this, for starters, might be from the abstract and theoretical angle. What I will ask of you is what I believe is referred to in some circles as a 'willing suspension of disbelief.' Not a permanent one, mind you. We're not moving into any realm of faith or metaphysics. I'm just asking you to try a few new ideas on for size, and to" - here he switched metaphors in mid-stride - "simply savor their taste for a while before spitting them out. And you, too, of course, Glennie." And he turned upon my Glendith so radiantly charming a smile and so direct and prolonged a gaze that I almost felt that, had there been a referee present, he would have blown his whistle and given a penalty. I mean, there *are* unwritten rules, and the girl *was* *MY* girlfriend. At least, as far as the two of them knew. But then, it was only a look, albeit an exceedingly, if not excessively, moist and friendly one. Glennie, for her part, soaked it up, blushing and looking pleased and flattered.

As much to put an end to this lengthy drinking in of one another's essence as out of any other motive, I spoke. "Torvald," said I, "I cannot of course speak for Glendith, but as far as I'm concerned, if it's a willing suspension of disbelief you want, then it's a willing suspension of disbelief you shall have. But not this evening, I'm afraid. Tomorrow morning, at that time when it's always darkest - before the dawn, you know - Ifford must roll out of bed and toil through the snow and ice to a monumentally dry and boring lecture on the intricacies of banking as practiced on the blue planet. To come through such an experience without permanent damage to the *mens* and *corpore*, I have found that one must be well-fortified with plenty of vitamins, a positive attitude, a double espresso, a saintly patience, and a good night's sleep. As regards the latter, it is already past my customary bedtime. And though I have spoken to them at length about the matter, they flatly refuse to delay the onset of the proceedings for me on those mornings when it has been necessary to sleep in a little. And I believe Glennie, too, has an early class. Therefore, we had best be shoving off."

"Yes, it is getting late - and we all do have classes tomorrow morning ... but I've got it all right on the tip of my tongue, Ifford, what I'd like to say, for you to think about ... in reply to the objections you just raised. So if I can beg your indulgence for just a few minutes more, I'd be glad if you'd let me put my thoughts out on the table - for you to think about - with an open mind, that willing suspension of disbelief that I mentioned ..."

"Oh - all rightie, then. Fire away. Just please, if you don't mind - try to give me the short version."

Inwardly gnashing the teeth, rending the garments, and casting the eyes heavenward, don't you know - but it was simply not in my repertoire to be so discourteous as to turn the fellow down. And being,

51

after all, a banking major and therefore an old hand at enduring what have to be among the most tedious and boring lectures the academic world has to dish out, then surely, as it seemed to matter so very much to them, I could manage to get through a few more minutes of their take on it all.

CHAPTER 6: I AM EXPOSED TO THE CONCEPT OF LEGALIZED PLUNDER

Man can live and satisfy his wants only by ceaseless labor; by the ceaseless application of his faculties to natural resources. This process is the origin of property. But it is also true that a man may live and satisfy his wants by seizing and consuming the products of the labor of others. This process is the origin of plunder. Now, since man is naturally inclined to avoid pain - and since all labor is pain in itself - it follows that men will resort to plunder whenever plunder is easier than work. When plunder becomes a way of life for a group of men living in society, they create for themselves, in the course of time, a legal system that authorizes it and a moral code that glorifies it.

Frederick Bastiat

"Great! I'll try to be brief." The chap wore the please expression of a state lottery winner, more or less combined with the eager look of a dog whose master is preparing its dinner. It seemed easy enough to make these two happy. Just agree to listen to their theories.

"Well! If you go back and study history - real history, I mean, and not the standard spun and altered, sanitized 'history' that has been crafted for public consumption - you find that ever since men have organized themselves, or been organized, into governments, a certain type of smart and unprincipled individual has sought to gain positions of control in or of those governments. Why, you might ask. Or, actually, seem to be asking. Who might do such a thing, and why? A reasonable enough question. And the answer, briefly, Ifford, has to do with plunder. It seems to be part of human nature to not want to have to work for a living - to want to get the necessities and luxuries of life, money, and goods, as many of them as possible, as easily as possible - the easy life that we all dream of. Many, throughout the passage of the generations, have found that the easiest way to attain wealth is simply to take it from someone who has created it by his labor and industry. We all know there are the petty con men out there, trying to avoid hard work by cleverly using guile and deception to ..."

"... Part the sucker from his buck?"

"Exactly. As the saying goes. Well, as history clearly shows, and the founders of this country knew so well, there also are those con-men who think, and operate, on a grander scale, as well as more subtly, and across generations - you can just look at the Mafia to prove to yourself that large, organized covert criminal enterprises can have continuity over generations; and recall the anti-trust legislation passed early in the last century here - the existence of which pretty much *ipso facto* proves that big businesses will conspire - work together covertly, if you're more comfortable with that phrasing - to interfere with the healthy competition of the free market in order to keep prices - and profitability – high."

"And that these covert joint efforts to interfere with the functioning of the free market economy are tolerated over pretty extensive periods of time by those in power in government ..." Rantor added dryly.

"Yes, good point, Rantor - and parenthetically I will mention here that – as I'd like to talk about in more detail when we have more time - in fact big government, like any *concentration of power*, is useful to power and wealth seekers – because those in positions of control in those centers of power can be bribed and otherwise influenced, can be gotten control of, and government's purposes subverted – its powers used to aid rather than combat or destroy such unfair practices – unfair, that is, both to their competition and to the buying public."

"And," Rantor continued, "History teaches nothing if not that government, if not for sale, is definitely for rent or lease if the price is right. And big, centralized government – enhancing and concentrating government's powers – is what best suits the purposes of those who wish to use those powers - government's *monopoly on the legal right to use force*, and *its extensive infrastructure* - to benefit themselves at the expense of the general public. Hence the steady move from limited and fragmented powers, in the original government created by the country's founders, to the modern monolithic corporate state into which that government of limited powers has morphed. "

"Yes. Bourgeoned," supplied Torvald.

"Ballooned," Glennie for some reason tacked on.

"Yes, yes, yes. Blossomed. Bloomed," I agreed impatiently. I mean – was this the monthly meeting of some sort of synonym society? How much more surreal could things get, over a mere cup of coffee?

54

"Indeed," intoned Torvald wisely, "And if those in positions of power in government can be bribed or otherwise influenced to turn a blind eye to such activities – price-fixing, monopolistic collusion - and such enterprises – organized crime – does not that fact logically argue that what those in government can be rewarded - bribed - for tolerating, they can be willing, if the rewards are sufficient, to undertake to do themselves? As an example, just look at how hugely the current Vice President and his business firm are profiting from the latest 'war' in the Mid-East – being awarded all sorts of no-bid war-related contracts. Clearly a flagrant conflict of interest, and yet a situation blandly accepted by all branches of government, both parties, and the 'watchdog' media. We have that old problem of, who will watch the watchers."

"You have to keep in mind that these men in public office control vast wealth," Rantor added, "Having, as they do, the legal right to dip into the pockets of the working masses – using force, if necessary, to exact their pound of flesh. And remember that famous epigram about power corrupting, and absolute power corrupting absolutely - which is one of the surest lessons of history. And as someone or other remarked, those who ignore the lessons of history are doomed to have to learn them all over again - re-invent the wheel, so to speak. We are given access to information about the corrupt and exploitative regimes of other times and places - Hitler, Stalin – but not about those in our own country, historically and on up to the present."

"Jacko would agree with you there," said Glennie. "He is always saying how highly controlled information is in this country, about history, government, current events – and medicine too, he says, especially as regards the causes and treatment of degenerative illness - despite appearances to the contrary."

"Yes," agreed Torvald, "An excellent example being our main interest, Rantor's and mine - the economic system here, and its carefully concealed deeply negative effects on the prosperity and well-being of the working people here. Economics, like the law, has been rendered formidably complex – or, better said, certain simple truths about money and economics have been overlaid with a baffling - and deadly dull - smokescreen of complexity.

"It was in the last decade of the 17th century that the Scotsman William Paterson sold the then financially hard-pressed King of England on this whole fiat currency/central banking scheme, telling him that it would be like free money for the Crown – which essentially it is, for the state – instant revenues, a virtually unlimited line of credit, for which the people are left to pick up the tab – the bill ingeniously coming to them a bit later in time, in the form of inflation – that sly *de facto* wage cut – but the connection is not an obvious one, to those ignorant of such matters – and the people, generation after generation, being carefully kept ignorant of such matters, never catch on."

Here Rantor picked up the ball, saying, "With their central banks, such as the Fed in this country, government and the banks working together create 'money,' as much as they want - out of nothing! - by merely starting up the printing presses, or, even easier, by simply making book-keeping entries on the public ledgers. '*Voila!* – you got money, Uncle Sam! Lotsa money!' Today, of course, this money-creation can be done electronically, and the greater part of the money supply is actually merely electronic book-keeping entry, having no physical existence even as worthless paper 'dollars' or the worthless silver-clad metal slugs that now pass for coin."

"Yes," Torvald continued, "And on top of that original 'nothing-money-out-of-thin-air' created when government debt is monetized, the private banks create more 'nothing money', expanding the money supply again by manyfold, when they loan more 'nothing money' to private borrowers – the exact amount of the expansion – or contraction - of the money-supply being under the control of the Fed, which has several means at its disposal for causing either inflationary expansion or recessionary contraction of the money supply - powers you probably have heard about in your banking classes - setting the reserve ratio for the private banks and the discount rate for loans the Fed makes to the private banks, and, as mentioned, simply buying or not buying government securities on the open market."

"Well, all rightie then," I interjected rather testily. "OK. Government and the central bank can together create substanceless fiat money, is what you are saying. Money out of nothing." I really wanted just to be allowed to go home and go to bed. None of this had anything at all to do with my making a living, and frankly I saw no reason for me to bother my brain about it. "Let's take that fact. Government and banks working together can create money out of nothing."

"Do!" Rantor qualified fervently. "*Do* create *the entire money supply* out of thin air, as paper dollars, metal slugs that just look like silver, or electronically as book-keeping entries."

"All right, all right. Admittedly, it sounds bad. But is it? Why should they not do so? Where's the downside? As long as the system works – as long as the monetary unit is kept sufficiently scarce, by fiat and practice, why is there any problem with this 'funny money' as you call it? I mean – don't virtually all the countries of the civilized world – this civilized world, I mean, of course – employ some variant of this general system? Are you telling me that they're all wrong, and you two are right? Is that what I am to believe, then?"

"Stranger things have happened, Ifford," Torvald opined in his usual mild tones, with a very small smile and a glance down at his latte, as though sharing a private joke with it. "In fact, the system does work, and work very well – for the big banking/big business/big government power bloc – for the flesh-and-blood people holding the reins of power – but their gain is the people's loss. And there lies the rub."

"Yes, agreed Rantor, his tail twitching and his eyes incandescent with that now familiar feverish amber light; "But just consider this, Ifford – the entire money supply is created as debt, and is interest-bearing – right? Or have we mentioned that yet? But anyway, it is; and yet - when is the money created to pay that interest?"

"Rantor is correct here," Torvald said. "There is indeed a permanent short-fall of the medium of exchange that is purely a built-in feature of this monetary system. So a sort of 'music chairs' effect of forced loan-default is built into this system, with too many people chasing too few FRNs, because the money to pay the interest on the debt-money is never created – which is a nice perc for the bankers who get to take possession of collateral put up on loans which they, the banks, made with monies *they* created out of nothing as book-keeping entries at the time of making the loans. The banks, you see, need to keep only 10% or so of their monies on hand as 'reserves.' The rest can be loaned out at interest, pyramided – each new loan forming – all but the required reserve portion – the basis for further loans of imaginary 'money.' "

"The fractional reserve expansion process."

"Exactly, Ifford. That dignified name for it making it sound respectable and inevitable – neither of which it is. And it in no wise benefits the people. However, I believe that the gravest objection to today's unbacked paper and electronic money is that its use inevitably creates inflation and recession/depression, thereby resulting in a continuous, on-going transfer of wealth – broadly speaking, from the have-nots to the haves. More precisely, *from* those whose wealth – and the value of whose labor – is denominated in the fiat currency, *to* those whose wealth is denominated in tangibles such as land and precious metals and infrastructure – factories, and so on. From, in Marxian terms, Labor to Capital."

"Yes," agreed his chum, "And it all hinges on what is used as money."

"That's right," Torvald continued. "Behind a wall of apparently impenetrable complexity lie certain very simple economic facts and cause/effect results of this set-up. And these simple facts and consequences were of course well understood, certainly, by the international bankers who from this country's birth worked long and hard, and across several generations, to install this European system of central banks here in this country. The country's founders were for the most part educated and worldly men who understood the downsides of this system from the point of view of the people - and fought it. Jefferson spoke and wrote at length against central banks, as did James Madison and most of the other founding fathers, as they are called. President Andrew Jackson worked mightily to rid the country of the second central bank that the banksters managed to install in the new country."

"And Daniel Webster said that of all the ways devised for tricking the laboring classes out of their earnings, none is so clever or effective as the paper money con," Rantor agreed, chiming in as if it were some vaudeville act the two had rehearsed. "And President Garfield said that 'whoever controls the volume of money in any country is the absolute master of commerce and industry.' "

"Yes - echoing Mayer Amschel Rothschild – the founder of the Rotschild banking dynasty, who so famously said – or boasted - 'Give me control of a nation's currency and I care not who makes the laws.' "

"And," Rantor continued, "There is John Maynard Keynes – the 'pre-purchase' Keynes, as I put it - who – before becoming a 'brain-for-hire' establishment intellectual – correctly said that by means of inflation, government can surreptitiously and continuously appropriate – confiscate was, I think, the word he used – significant amounts of wealth from the people – with none being the wiser. He later totally reversed his stance – many suspecting, of course, that his palm was well-greased to bring about that result – becoming a leading advocate and apologist for the same system of institutionalized trickery, as practiced by the Fed, with its FRN - which he had formerly decried. In fact, and as you probably know from your studies, a theoretical stream of current economic thought bears the name of Keynesian Economics."

"You see, Ifford," his pal continued, "The just-quoted objections or criticisms or whatever you want to call them are NOT true of sound money – money that has intrinsic worth, that is, such as gold or silver. But these statements ARE true of the 'money' this country has today – the fiat currency ('fiat' meaning by government decree, if we haven't already mentioned that) of electronic or paper 'money' issued by a central bank – essentially nothing more than a cartel of private bankers – which enjoys a government-protected monopoly on the issuance of the nation's currency, or medium of exchange."

"Yes!" agreed the lizard in that emphatic way of his. "The *surreptitious transfer of wealth* referred to by Webster and Keynes is *built into* this economic system."

"That's right. This transfer of wealth would not occur – would not be possible – with the kind of economic system the founders of this country wanted and initially created, or attempted to create – an economy with no central bank of issue, in which the money is money of substance, of intrinsic worth – such as the gold and silver coin specified in the Constitution."

"Of course," Rantor qualified, "There would still be the problem of fractional reserve banking ..."

"Well, I know about that, of course," said I, "From my coursework at the Bismark school ... but never have I heard fractional reserve banking referred to as a problem – as anything, in fact, but SOP."

"Well, let's just have a quick review of money – what it is, how it originated," suggested Torvald. "First, of course, is the fact that money originated with the people, with the customary practices of the people in the marketplace – not, as today, as something dictated, inflicted by law, by fiat, upon the people willy-nilly, by the edict of an over-arching governmental bureaucracy which rules arbitrarily and, in actual effect, pretty much non-negotiably, in the fashion of a monarch.

"So - originally, of course, trade was carried on by barter. And the precious metals, over time, became the money – the universal barter medium, and the store and measure of value - of choice, not out of any superstitious reverence for them, as insinuated by that famous phrase of Keynes' – the 'barbaric metal,' he called gold, suggesting that its use originated, and persists, in some sort of caveman-like magical thinking or fascination with bright and glittery things *per se* – rather then – as is the case - because the precious metals are ideally suited for use as money, being both sufficiently scarce and sufficiently in demand that they – gold and silver - have value in small quantities, and being portable, divisible, and durable, both physically and as regards their value across decades and centuries.

"So, anyway, the use in the marketplace of paper as opposed to coin money has a rather interesting history. Have you been told about it in any of your classes?"

"Not that I recall."

"Well, the use of paper money originated long ago, as IOUs, or pay-on-demand notes; and the first 'bankers' - indeed, the first fractional-reserve bankers - were the goldsmiths, who were the only ones, way back then, who had safes and security systems. So the goldsmiths doubled as bankers; people stored their gold and silver with them, and were of course given receipts for their precious metals. Over time, people got into the convenient habit of using these receipts, or notes, in the marketplace in lieu of the metal itself. Thus was born paper money. Although its use arose first, I believe, in China, where the first printing presses were developed. Anyway, over time, the goldsmiths realized that, because the people never all came in at once to withdraw their 'deposits,' the goldsmiths could loan out at interest some of the precious metals stored in their safes, with no one being the wiser. The goldsmiths kept some gold in reserve to meet the customary level of withdrawals, and quietly loaned out the rest – OPM, other people's money - at interest. And that is how 'fractional reserve banking' developed."

"Well? So? It seems to work well enough. It has become an established practice..."

"Yes, it is an established practice; and it might seem a harmless enough practice ... but - setting aside, for now, the issue of the deception involved - the non-disclosure to the depositors of what is being done with money that they think is safe in the bank - and setting aside also the matter of whether it is fair to the depositors that they are getting none of the interest being earned by their checking account deposits –

originally, the biggest problem with fractional reserve banking, when the currency was still backed by and could be exchanged for the real money, which was of course specie - precious metal of intrinsic worth - was that the banks, greedy to earn as much interest as they could, would loan out too much of their demand deposits – which conventional savings and checking accounts both are, of course - would sail too close to the wind, so to speak - and depositors would hear of it, perhaps from bank employees trying to alert their family and friends, and word would get around, and there would be a 'run on the bank,' and the bank could not satisfy all of its depositors' demands for their gold or silver – there being more notes, or IOUs, than gold or silver on hand in the bank's vaults, basically - and the bank would go bankrupt, and the depositors would be …"

" ,,, out of luck?" I ventured.

"Yes!" interjected Rantor, his voice gone boomingly *fortissimo*, and his moral outrage, in its vehemence, actually seeming to make the surrounding atmosphere shudder or flicker a bit. The thought occurred, as it had before, that I'd hate ever to get the fellow seriously mad at me personally. "And if you can believe it, the bankers would actually lean on their state legislators to *pass laws allowing the banks not to honor their own pay-on-demand notes*, their own IOUs. In other words – to enact legislation making it legal for banks to dishonor their own promises, their own obligations! And the state legislators, often enough, would do it! "

"Nice work if you can get it," said Glennie.

"Well, the bankers certainly thought – and think – so," agreed Torvald. "Of course, such obliging cooperation usually comes at a price. Corruption, thy name is government. Anyway, with fractional reserve banking as originally practiced, the money, the unit of account, did at least have value, value both intrinsic and stable. In other words, there was little or no inflation. However, the Fed, once in power, gradually changed the Federal Reserve Note from being *fractionally backed* by specie to being the kind of money they wanted all along – totally unbacked 'Monopoly money.' This removes all limits on the amount of funny money (and inflation) that can be created and thus is the instrument of choice for 'plucking the duck without making him squawk,' in the words of Paul Warburg, of the Warburg banking dynasty, who is often called the 'father' of our central bank, the Federal Reserve System – which the international bankers, working in collusion with disloyal or unknowledgeable people in this country's government, finally succeeded, in 1913, after about a century and a half of effort, in establishing here, as such banks had long been established in the nations of Europe."

"Yeah," said Rantor, "They finally got their 'funny money' scam up and running here in the United States. And the 'money,' the Federal Reserve Note, is indeed funny, having as mentioned no intrinsic value, being in fact monetized debt, and thus being, quite literally, *a claim on the value of the labor of future generations of Americans* – and having no stable value whatever in trade in the marketplace."

"Yes," agreed Torvald. "And the Fed should be called the 'Smoke and Mirrors System,' because it is as riddled with deception as - well, as an old wooden house in the tropics is with termites. The people were gradually dumbed down, weaned from using money of substance, and gotten accustomed to accepting, and using as their money, 'notes' that are not receipts for anything of substance, but are mere pieces of paper."

"That's right," Rantor chimed in. "Like the Federal Reserve System itself, the FRN is cleverly mis-nomered, not being a 'note' in the time-honored meaning of that word, because it is not a receipt or an IOU – is not redeemable from the issuer for anything of value whatsoever. *These* 'notes' are nothing but glorified pieces of paper; and the government and the Fed basically work together in producing them, in what amounts to nothing more, at bottom, and behind all the grand and mystifying language, behind the mystique, than a huge legalized counterfeiting operation."

"And the Federal Reserve System," Torvald continued, "Is not federal – perhaps you could call it an NGO or at best a quasi-GO. It straddles the line. But in actuality it is simply a cartel of private bankers to whom has been given, by 'our' government, a monopoly on the issuance of the nation's 'money' or credit."

"Yes," agreed his friend, "Under this system, all money is created as debt, is loaned into existence, and so all money *is* credit. The entire money supply is monetized debt, and is interest-bearing."

"And the suggestion of 'reserves' is comforting, but in fact there is no government or central bank 'reserve' of anything of value behind this currency. There are no reserves, in any meaningful sense of the word, the currency being unbacked by specie – how can one have 'reserves' of nothing ..."

"And," added Rantor, "It really is not a 'system' of banks, because all power and authority are concentrated in the Federal Reserve Board of New York. It was called a 'system' in order to create the impression of a diffusion of power, rather than what it in fact is – an enormous *concentration* of power."

"And as we have already mentioned, and as most people don't know," Torvald continued, "The 'money' so created - the entire money supply of the country – is, as we've mentioned, *borrowed* into existence, and is *interest-bearing*, every minute of its existence, until the loan that 'created' it is repaid – at which point that 'money' is extinguished - uncreated, so to speak - ceases to exist."

"Therefore," Rantor pronounced triumphantly, rather like a game show contestant who knows the right answer, "If the national debt *were* ever paid off, the country would have NO money!

"Come, now," I objected. "That I find rather hard to credit."

Well," said Rantor, "I happen to have right here in my notebook a very pertinent and corroborating quotation from no less then a former Federal Reserve officer - Robert Hemphill, who was the Credit Manager of the Atlanta, Georgia, branch of the Fed. I found it in an article online just this afternoon ..." and he withdrew from the breast pocket of his shirt a small notebook from which he read the following -

This is a staggering thought. We are completely dependent on the commercial banks. Someone has to borrow every dollar we have in circulation, cash, or credit. If the banks create ample synthetic money, we are prosperous; if not, we starve. We are absolutely without a permanent money system. When one gets a complete grasp of the picture, the tragic absurdity of our hopeless position is almost incredible, but there it is. It is the most important subject intelligent persons can investigate and reflect upon. It is so important that our present civilization may collapse unless it becomes widely understood and the defect remedied very soon.

"Yes," said Torvald, "I know it seems fantastic, but if the government stopped borrowing and fully paid up the national debt, the country would have no money in circulation at all – no circulating medium of exchange whatsoever! Which would of course bring about a huge depression that would throw the country into a crisis of unimaginable proportions. So all of this talk of trying to pay off the national debt is just more deception, more smoke and mirrors. But it gets more interesting – and puzzling. Because *the resultant huge national debt is totally unnecessary!* The founders wanted no 'funny money,' with which they had had previous disastrous experience – over-issue and thus inflation, of course, into valuelessness. Rather, they wanted a money of substance, of intrinsic value. They tried to insure a money or circulating medium of exchange consisting at least in part of gold or silver coin – the stipulation in the Constitution was that the states themselves were to use only gold or silver coin in payment of debt, thereby guaranteeing that gold and silver would circulate as money, along with warehouse receipts, and foreign coins – the people being free to use what they wanted in their private dealings and transactions."

"But the main point here," said Rantor, "Is that with an honest money supply of intrinsic value, there would be NO government debt created merely in order to have a money supply."

"Or," Torvald added, "If the government insisted upon having a money supply of no intrinsic value – which in itself is a very bad idea, whether the 'money' so is created is interest-bearing or not - government itself could create and issue the paper and electronic money *interest-free*, rather than *borrow* it into existence at interest from the Fed and from other purchasers of interest-bearing government bonds. The present system, as mentioned, monetizes debt. *All money – all circulating medium - is interest-bearing debt!"*

"But then, of course," mused Rantor, "None of the created money would ever be taken out of circulation, as it now is when the government bonds mature and their purchasers get their principle back plus interest ..."

"Yes, on the face of it, one would think that such a system would be even more inflationary than the present set-up," agreed Torvald, "Unless the money was extinguished, removed from existence and circulation, upon repayment of the loans extended by the government, as it is now when government re-pays its loans plus interest to purchasers of government bonds. But money created by direct government spending would not be extinguished ... unless some scheme were concocted to effect that ... but, earning all that money from interest, perhaps government would not have to create money for

64

its needs, but could 'live on the interest,' as the saying goes. I wonder if such a system has ever been contemplated – or tried."

"Interesting to think about, for sure – however, since it would leave the bankers out of the control-of-empires loop, I imagine it has the proverbial snowball's chance in hell … but anyway, Ifford, the bottom line is that giving *anyone* the power to create money out of nothing is a very bad idea," Rantor replied, "Since that power, in the hands of mortals, is as impossible not to abuse as it would be for a heroin addict not to use an unlimited free supply of heroin."

"Yes, to be sure," agreed Torvald. "But at least there would be no huge national debt if the Monopoly money were created out of nothing, debt-free, or as *private* debt, by the government, rather than being created out of nothing as *public* debt – borrowed into existence at interest, in the name of and at the expense of the people, as is presently the case. The interest payments on the present national debt are enormous, and a huge chunk of tax money each year goes just to servicing the debt."

"So - what, then, are you advocating? What is the main point, the meat and thrust, so to speak?" I pressed, sounding to my own ears a bit querulous. I was by this time, as the reader can perhaps imagine, certainly feeling querulous. I badly wanted to nudge these world-class explainers along, to get them to the main point, if there was one, so that we could wrap things up for the night and get Ifford to bed for his beauty sleep.

"We advocate, quite simply, what the founders of the country wanted, and what the country for almost a century had – money of substance – a permanent debt-free money supply, the amount of which in circulation *cannot* be so quickly and easily manipulated as can this 'imaginary' money of no substance," replied Torvald. "For it is simply by manipulating the amount of 'money' in circulation that the bankers who constitute the Fed's Open Market Committee achieve all the results so beneficial to themselves – to the bankers – and to government – and so disadvantageous to the people. The problem with this present system, as we have mentioned, is that it works poorly for the people, but wonderfully well for the big banking/big government partnership, and for their cronies in the 'good old boy' network – for, in a nutshell, the numerically tiny ruling financial elites - the plutocracy, the oligarchy, the hidden aristocracy of wealth. And their gain, is, quite precisely and dollar for dollar, so to speak, the people's loss."

If you think about it for a moment, Ifford," said his scaley pal, in a theatrically ironic voice, "The question does beg to be asked, in what way it could possibly serve the public interest, to craft and employ an inherently and, over the long run, hugely inflationary economic system in which every penny in circulation has no substance, no intrinsic value, no stable value in trade in marketplace, and is created out of nothing, as interest-bearing public debt, at the whim of an unelected cartel of private bankers operating in the guise of a government institution, behind closed doors, with no oversight or accountability whatsoever. The current 'money' has no fixed value, either by statute or in practice, in trade; and since it has a shifting and uncertain value, it obviously does not work well as either a store or a measure of value, or as a medium of exchange. I mean, can you imagine carpenters working with a measure of length that had a constantly shifting value – or grocers selling their produce using a measure of weight that constantly varied? And of what possible benefit to the public is the secrecy in which these powerful men operate - or this continuous inflation and loss of purchasing power of the monetary unit, or of this massive and ever-increasing national debt, which has grown into the trillions of dollars and is costing the public huge yearly amounts just to service?"

"Especially those questions beg to be asked," Torvald continued, "when one realizes that non-interest-bearing monetary units – 'dollars,' if you will – are available which possess NONE of these disadvantages – which work well as both a store and a measure of value, which create NO inflation and recession, as our current monetary unit does, and also create NO public debt merely by being in existence, and which have in fact been used as money for centuries by many societies. I am referring of course to the precious metals, such as the gold and/or silver coin still specified in Article I Section 10 of the Constitution ...where it says, no state shall use anything but gold and silver coined as tender for the payment of debt."

"In fact," Rantor added, "Far from being somehow outmoded 'barbaric metals,' they serve as well for money now as they have done over the centuries. Scarcity, or limited supply, is no issue – as is sometimes falsely claimed by adherents of fiat money - because the value of the gold or silver money on the free market automatically adjusts to the supply. If there is less, relative to goods and services, the relative value, in barter on the free market, is simply greater."

"And, of course, the massive public debt is, obviously, a big downside," replied Torvald. "But under the present system, without public debt, there would be NO money supply whatsoever. Bizarre and quixotic though it sounds, to pay off the national debt would be to extinguish the money supply - which would create a huge depression. Have any of your professors ever mentioned any of this to you, Ifford?"

"Actually, not that I recall." The chap was repeating himself.

"Perhaps you would at least agree,' prodded Rantor, "That these are significant features of the current system to neglect to mention in economics classes on money and banking – that it does smack of bias, of information control."

"Yes," agreed Torvald, "If there be benefits to this system, over that of the honest money of substance which the founders wanted – and which we advocate – then let these benefits be presented and explained – and let these seeming profound flaws, or problems, in the present system be openly discussed, and, if possible, explained away, or the use of this system in spite of these flaws be justified."

"Absolutely!" Rantor agreed. "Rationally, logically, empirically justified. And they don't do that because the system cannot be so justified and simply would not stand up to such open scrutiny. In your earlier comment about scarcity, you hit the nail right on the head, Ifford. Because the monetary unit is *not* kept 'sufficiently scarce,' as you put it, and therein lies the rub. Inflation. A major downside. But, actually, there are many downsides, many 'rubs,' for the people – as many, in fact, as there are upsides for the bankers, for government, and for the super-rich generally - the hidden aristocracy of the monied elite."

"Inflation is a hidden tax," said Torvald, "Brought about simply from the continuous creation of new FRNs, new 'pretend wealth,' Monopoly money, by the Fed and the government working together. And really – using one's common sense, who could have the power to create money, out of nothing – as do the government and the Federal Reserve, working together – and not misuse it?"

"That's right," Rantor concurred. "Now, about inflation – how and why it occurs under the present economic system, and its effects: inflation and recession are the direct and unavoidable consequences of any economic system which legally forces the exclusive use of an intrinsically worthless fiat currency the amount of which in circulation can easily and relatively quickly be manipulated – increased or decreased by any clique or group – such as, in the present instance, government and private bankers working together in a kind of partnership."

Absolutely correct," agreed Torvald. "This inflation/recession 'business cycle,' as it is called – making it sound respectable and inevitable, when in fact it is neither – arises from the fact that a whole lot of this intrinsically worthless 'money' can be very quickly released into the marketplace, as printed paper or electronic money."

And this is a problem, because …?" It seemed that this opera-length duet was their idea of being brief. Trustingly, I had neglected to define my terms for them. But I let it pass. My complaints at this point would only take more time and prolong the ordeal.

"At base, it is very simple, and it works like this," replied Torvald. "Money is a commodity that is bartered for goods in the marketplace, and like any commodity, it is subject to the law of supply and demand, which is simply and rather self-evidently, that when a desired commodity is in short supply in the marketplace, its value there, relative to those things for which it is bartered/exchanged, will rise; and conversely, when there is a lot of it available in the marketplace, its market value will fall. I am sure that you, as a banking/economics student, are aware of the law of supply and demand?"

"Of course."

"Indeed," the Nodic continued, "Throughout the history of fiat money of no intrinsic value, it has proven too tempting for government to over-issue the paper and electronic 'money' and over-issue it does, and thus, inevitably, as Rantor was getting to, the value of the paper money in the marketplace drops, relative to the values of the goods and services for whicn it is bartered, or exchanged."

"Just so," the lizard interjected feelingly. "Pretty self-evident – right? So simple a child could understand it? So - why is this not taught in the schools? Why do you, an econ major, not even know what causes inflation in the present system? Especially given that inflation is a problem of such magnitude, so worrisome, that the rate of it is constantly reported - actually, under-reported - in the media?"

"Right," agreed Torvald, "If – or rather when, newly-created paper or electronic money is released into the economy – which happens

68

continuously, as government spends - but even more so, for instance, when the government decides to fund a war – and this money creation is on-going as I said, to fund all of these socialistic entitlement schemes, and foreign aid – so anyway, this newly created 'money' when it is spent, *inevitably dilutes the purchasing power in the market of the monetary unit.* For an extreme example – and something that could, and well may, happen here - just remember the huge hyper-inflation in Germany in the 1920s."

"We are simply talking the law of supply and demand," said Rantor. "Flood the market with oranges, and the price of oranges will drop. Flood the labor market with ditch-diggers, and the wages of ditch-diggers will drop. Flood the market with Cocker Spaniels, and the price of Cocker Spaniels will drop. Flood the market with dollars – or what are called dollars, these days - Federal Reserve Notes, FRNs - and the value of dollars – FRNs – the monetary unit – will drop, relative to the goods and services for which it is bartered."

"So – there is some inflation. A certain amount of inflation is inevitable, isn't it? The Fed is always struggling to keep it low. So - there is inflation; prices rise. So what? Workers get cost-of-living increases, don't they?"

"Actually, as I think Rantor mentioned a couple of minutes ago, inflation is *not* inevitable, though the elites are very happy to have us believe that it is, and that one of the noble tasks of the Fed is to tame and subdue the great beast Inflation. Inflation *is* an inevitable consequence of *this* economic system, yes. But other, better – and inflation-free - economic systems exist – such as that so passionately favored by Jefferson and most of this country's founders - a free market economy with a monetary unit of intrinsic value, and with no central bank enjoying a monopoly on the issuance of a fiat currency. Fiat, by the way, means 'by law, by government decree' – this is money because government tells us it is. For the system to work as the planners – and beneficiaries – want it to work, people *must* use the fiat currency."

"And as to your question, Ifford," said the lizard, "Concerning to what is wrong with 'a little inflation' … for one thing, that 'small' on-going devaluation of the purchasing power of the monetary unit by continuous infusions into the market place of more and more and more of it is on-going, and cumulative. Over the long run the 'bite' is substantial. Witness the well over 90% decline in the purchasing power of the monetary unit, and the accompanying decline in the standard of living, in this country since the creation of the Fed over a hundred years ago."

"The 'cost-of-living' pay increases," Torvald continued, "That are supposed to take care of the problem – as if the continuous inflation were the only problem with this system, and as if there were no better system around, and we must simply hobble along with this one, with all its defects – these cost-of-living pay increases – or, for the millions on retirement incomes or the various entitlement programs, increases in benefits, increases in the slender monthly stipend – over the long run *never quite keep up* with the rate of inflation – no matter how much the statistics are doctored to disguise that fact, or at least reduce the apparent discrepancy."

"That's right," agreed Rantor. "Particularly for those on fixed incomes, or working at the low end of the pay scale, this continuous ongoing inflation of the money supply results, over time, in a fatal – a hard-hitting - shortfall – a significant decline in their purchasing power, in the actual wealth they have at their disposal."

"In other words," explained Torvald, "Every inflation, for the working stiff, is a *de facto* pay cut - to varying degrees, of course, depending on the degree to which their pay is or is not increased to compensate for the monetary unit's loss of purchasing power. And it is in large part *this very dynamic* of the central banks and their fiat currencies that makes them such effective instruments of covert plunder. Wars, for instance, those immensely expensive - and for some, lucrative - undertakings, are largely paid for by the *invisible tax* of inflation."

"In fact," Rantor said, "The prolonged world wars of the last century would simply not have been possible – would not have been tolerated by the people – if they had been funded by direct taxation rather than by the hidden tax of inflation."

"True," agreed his pal. "Over 50% of the cost of WWI, for instance, was paid by the unwitting public by means of inflating the money, by releasing millions in new 'money' into the economy, in order to pay the costs of the war, thus reducing the purchasing power of the dollar, causing real prices to rise and real wages to fall."

"And also," Rantor continued, "After every inflationary expansion – for instance, and most famously, the expansion of the money supply in this country in the 1920s - not coincidentally, just a few short years after the Federal Reserve System was created and endowed with just such inflationary powers - after the inflationary expansion there comes the 'correction', which is experienced as a recession or depression, as the market adjusts to the fact, basically, that the apparent flood of new 'money' into the economy was not really what its influx into the circulating money supply signaled the market that it was - an influx of new capital, actual new wealth, available for capital investments and improvements – such as opening new businesses or production plants, and improving and extending the infrastructures of old ones."

"In fact," Torvald elaborated, "That influx of 'dollars' is an influx of not real but of *faux* wealth – of counterfeit wealth, if you will - of paper and electronic 'money' that has no more real substance, no more real value, to it than Monopoly money. In fact, the printing press and electronic book-keeping entry 'money' represents, constitutes, no real wealth and yet gives the market a false signal – a false signal of increased actual wealth in the economy."

"You are talking about the business cycle, right?"

"Yes, Ifford," agreed Torvald. "Yet another dignifying phrase. That same mysteriously recurring 'business cycle' that so many learned brows have been furrowed and heads have been scratched over, and concerning which so many dense, convoluted scholarly papers and articles have been published in scholarly journals, attempting to account for or explain it. As history can prove, if one but consults its record, in economies which have sound money of intrinsic worth, and no central banks or fiat currencies, these mysterious boom/bust 'business cycles' simply do not occur and recur in the endless, troublesome pattern that is a standard feature of our current economic system. Period."

"But this is hardly," observed Rantor, with that withering, intensely felt sarcasm of his, "What those who are profiting so richly from the present system want eager young minds to be dwelling upon – lest all their good times, their pork and free lunches, for which the working public foot the bill – grind – heaven forbid - to a halt."

"Yes," said Torvald. "Imagine the wrath of the working stiff ..."

"If," Rantor finished his pal's dangling sentence, "It could somehow be gotten into said working stiff's admittedly rather thick skull - the extent of the surreptitious plunder to which he and his forebears have been - and are being - subjected."

Frankly, student of banking and economics though I am, I was having a hard time following this avalanche, this verbal torrent. Perhaps it was due to a lack of motivation, combined with the lateness of the hour. I am always at my intellectual best in the morning. Certainly, the version of things economic put forth by these two exotics was not the take on it all promulgated in my classes at the Otto von Bismark School. Perhaps these street-economists, these self-educated amateurs, were onto something, perhaps not. But I rather thought not, though I could not quite put my finger on their errors. At bottom, I just found it hard to believe that what they were saying could be true – could have been true, for so many decades and even centuries - and not have been discovered and made more widely known. These chaps seemed to be saying that modern banking was in essence one big government - sanctioned confidence game. How that could be so, and not have long ago been detected and remedied, was what I could just not swallow. It flew in the face of common sense.

"So tell me again - *Qui bono?* Aren't we all impacted by this inflation? You speak of plunder ... once again, who is the plunderer here, and who the plunderee, in what you – contrary to what all my professors have told and are telling me - regard as a zero sum game – who wins and who looses?"

"Basically, Ifford," Torvald retorted. "Very broadly - *those whose wealth is denominated in the fiat currency* – in this country, the FRN - end up the loosers. And realize that wages are by law, by fiat, denominated in the Monopoly money. The value of people's labor must by law be denominated in the 'funny money' that, like a balloon with a pinhole leak, is constantly, and invisibly, loosing its value. As the FRN looses value due to the constant increase in the amount of it in circulation, so do all workers experience a *de facto* pay cut, coming to them as a decline in their purchasing power. And, in general, the poorer you are - as we have been touching upon - the more impacted you are, and the more you end up a looser in this deal ... because if you are poor, you can't sustain this on-going haemorrhage, you can't loose too much real income and purchasing power, before you begin to find it extremely difficult to keep your little ship afloat, to make ends meet; and also, you are earning on the low end of the pay scale, where there is the biggest short-fall between the rise in the cost of living, and the cost-of-living increases in your rate of pay."

"Yes! Soak the working stiff, and especially the poorest among them, is what it ends up being all about, when all the returns are in, unfortunately," Rantor piped almost shrilly, causing me to wince. His remarkable voice at times seemed in his excitement to rise, when he gets worked up in these impromptu collaborative dissertations of theirs, and though the fellow was sitting right next to me, his mouth but inches from my ear, he belted out this remark like an operatic mezzo-soprano, or a demagogue addressing a multitude. "And furthermore, the poorer you are, the more it is the case that *your only wealth is your labor* - and the value of everyone's labor is denominated by fiat in the fiat currency. People have no choice."

"But this bleeding away of value," continued Torvald, "This hidden tax of inflation, is not uniformly experienced by everyone. The first spenders of the newly created FRNs get to spend the new money before it has entered the money supply and caused a general decline in the purchasing power of the FRN. The government is very often in this first spender position. And their fat-cat pals whose businesses land so many lucrative government contracts are also high on the feeding chain. And in general, as I believe we have mentioned, those whose wealth is denominated in tangibles, such as factories, real estate, and precious metals, for example - and who know how to avoid the bite of the income tax, as most of the middle class, of course, do not - come out ahead. The whole system in operation is sufficiently complex, and these truths about it sufficiently kept from being generally known, that these consequences are not apparent – not understood."

"However," Rantor added, "If this information were taught in the schools, it could be readily understood by anyone who can learn to read and write, or read music, or do basic algebra and geometry. It is, in its fundamentals, not all that complex."

"Very true," agreed his friend. "Basically, a great *created complexity* hides an underlying simplicity. And, interestingly enough, a similar situation – a created smokescreen of complexity overlaying a fundamentally much simpler reality – prevails in the area of law, and to quite an extent in medicine, as well, as it pertains to the causality and treatment of degenerative illness. Smokescreens of complexity and disinformation which hide simpler truths – truths affording much less potential for profit for the hidden aristocracy of wealth and power."

"Yeah," Rantor said. "The hidden aristocracy of the super-rich - the bankers, the great trans-national corporations - love the present set-up because of its financial privileging of themselves."

"After all," Torvald observed, "They are the very ones who, bit by bit, molded the country's present medical, economic, and legal systems into the cash-cows that they are for them today – systems which have been tweaked, massaged, into mechanisms which invisibly transfer wealth *to* themselves *from* the working classes, both the proletariat and the bourgeoisie, to use the Marxian terms."

"Though the proletariat and the bourgeoisie are led to believe that one another are the problem," said Rantor.

"Yes,"agreed Torvald. "That is the actual use, or function, to which the two party system has been put – has devolved. Divide and conquer."

"That's right," said the lizard. "And governments love the set-up, because they can spend, spend, spend, without having to ask for the money from the tax-paying public, as they would have to do with an honest economic system and monetary unit - if the country were using a monetary unit of substance - of precious metal, basically. The public does foot the bill, of course, and they vaguely sense that something is rotten; but they really don't catch on to how large a bill they are footing, primarily because it comes to them in hidden ways – such as the hidden tax of inflation, and the interest on the national debt, and the inevitable higher rate of bankruptcy and loan default under this system."

"But," his chum added, "Because there is so large a smoke-screen of complex disinformation promulgated as economic science, and because there is a time lag, between the cause – the creation of the fiat 'money' - and the effects – such as inflation and recession - and as none of the insiders ever points out this basic situation, this cause-and-effect nexus, to the new generations of econ students, or to the public – so the public, generation after generation, remain in the dark as to why their standard of living just keeps on slipping."

"And of course," said Rantor, "The media and government, being also on the take, have no reason to rock the boat – by, for instance, pointing out how much in fact the standard of living in this country is declining. Mum's the word. Better that the people be led to amuse themselves with sitcoms and the latest marriages and divorces of the movie stars."

"So it is deceptive," Torvald continued. "Con men never run about broadcasting what it is they are actually doing, and why. As we have been saying, the central banking and fiat currency arrangement is in fact *an institutionalized form of plunder* disguised as an honest, respectable, and fair - touted in fact as, in the mystifyingly complex modern word, the only feasible - economic system. And it is in so many ways a corrupt system, a veritable Pandora's box of effects and consequences damaging to the interests of the people generally, in a myriad of other ways beyond what we have discussed tonight. We have by no means detailed all its ill effects, from the point of view of the public. To do so would take a fat book."

"Boy, is that ever right," Rantor agreed. "Just think - the Fed's Open Market Committee has the power *to create inflation and recession or depression at will*, and by policy, so to speak - merely by expanding or contracting the money supply. Just having foreknowledge of which way the economy is planned to be shifted, towards inflation or recession, can be - is - worth a lot – and can be - is - used to reward 'team players' so to speak. So those who benefit – the bankers, government, and the captains of industry, you might say – are obviously motivated to keep the people – the working stiffs who are the ones being plundered – in the dark about how the whole set-up works. Otherwise, basic economics textbooks, and the media, would explain some of these downsides – for the people – of the system, as we are explaining them to you now."

At this point, Norse god and lizard seemed to be winding down, and hope stirred that I might finally be allowed to go home and get to bed. Torvald leaned back in his seat and glanced down at his watch, while his scaly pal breathed for a beat or two, rather steamily, tossed back a hefty gulp or two of his long-since cold latte, and then leaned back against his seat, letting his eyelids half-close and bringing to mind the appearance of his reptilian next-of-kin when sunning themselves on hot rocks as is their wont.

But something further seemed to occur to Torvald who, almost apologetically, and fairly oozing sincerity, launched one final onslaught against my beleaguered, my hunted, hounded, and cornered, *Welt Anschauung*.

"One more related matter, Ifford - about this business of the 'crazy right-wing paranoid conspiracy theorists' of whom we hear so much derisive and dismissive chatter in all the mainstream media ... that, you see, is a very clever attempt at 'damage control,' so to speak - an effort to *control and neutralize the opposition*. It actually is a very good example of the intellectually dishonest *argumentum ad hominem* debating ploy resorted to since time immemorial by debaters who know they have a weak argument based on the actual issues. Rather than loose the debate, they craftily try to *shift the subject and focus of the debate* from the actual substantive issues to the alleged faulty character and impoverished intellect of their debating opponent. Fairly obviously, such a ploy is only resorted to by those who realize that if they do stick to the substantive issues, they will probably loose the debate. This defamatory psy-op, as I believe it can very accurately be labeled, is a very clever one, exploiting as it does so shrewdly the nature of the beast - the average person's laziness, disinclination actually to think, and his fear of ostracism and ridicule."

And, here, finally, he paused, eye-balling me as if to gauge the impact of it all as he finished off his now cold coffee. The ordeal, it seemed was drawing to a close, for this round at least.

I don't know how the others felt as we said our farewells and went our separate ways, but I felt rather as though I were leaving the dentist's office after a particularly harrowing session. Rather used up and a bit numb, you know, but suffused with relief, and a general lifting of the spirit. And I was buttressed by a secret inner resolve that had quietly formed as I sat patiently weathering this latest prodigious outpouring - namely, a resolve indefinitely to postpone, delay, and re-reschedule any and all future proposed meetings in which my disbelief was to be further suspended, and mangled, until Rantor and Torvald should grow discouraged, take the hint, and finally resume wandering the deserted parks and alleyways of the metropolis in search of another hapless victim.

As I walked Glennie to her dorm, she analyzed me once again, so that I could truly say that I had been analyzed coming and going. I had been touching upon the subject of my spirited self-defense - for I had, after all, ventured a bleat or two of protest and objection, in the course of the long evening's onslaught; but instead of applauding my manly self-assertion, as I had faintly hoped she might, she merely analyzed it.

"You know, Iffy," she said thoughtfully, "I couldn't help wondering if what was really bothering you was just that Torvald is so good-looking in - you know - the humanoid way."

At times the girl has no tact. Absolutely no tact. But I let it pass.

CHAPTER 7: FEAR AND LOATHING ON THE WAY TO THE CONVENIENCE STORE; AND, A SURPRISE

Call it God, but row away from the rocks.

Hunter S. Thompson

After dropping Glennie off at her dorm, I remembered that I was nearly out of Grandma O'Houlihan's Krunchie-Krunchies, there having been bit a single one left in the cellophane package when last I looked. There was an all-night convenience store, The Friend of the Family by name, just a couple of blocks out of my way, and I decided to make the detour in case I felt in the mood to indulge as I read my mystery story in bed before calling it a day. This is an ancient habit of mine, and by now it seems I cannot get to sleep without reading a few pages before turning out the light. My only rule is that my reading material must be light - must not tax the mental faculties or be in any way improving.

It was pitch black out, except for the street and store lights, the night being a moonless one; the streets were deserted, and the air utterly still and extremely cold. Anxious to make my purchase and get home, I hurried along, hands in my pockets, shoulders scrunched up around my ears, and eyes to the ground as I picked my way along the icy, treacherous sidewalks. As I neared The Friend, as we called it, I saw a small crumpled paper bag lying there on the icy sidewalk before me. Curious, I picked it up. I was just about to look inside when I heard the sound of an approaching siren and saw, two or three blocks down the street, the blue flashing lights of the local *gendarmerie*.

Purely on impulse, I pocketed the bag, spun around, and marched smartly off, turning onto a darker side street at the corner. Perhaps the reader is made of sterner stuff than your narrator. Rantor, I am sure, would not have been so easily deterred from his mission. I, however, have from a lad been leery of the iron fist however it manifests, and have always quailed and tended to break out into a cold sweat when in proximity to anyone in a uniform. I find it particularly disturbing to be noticed by one of them. I think it's those pistols, stun guns, tazers, aerosol canisters of mace, and the billy clubs and handcuffs, mainly, that have that effect on me. Of course the facial expressions and body language of those chaps also seem vaguely ominous. And the uniforms.

And then the cars with the barriers between front and back seats. It is all thematically of a piece and speaks of coercion and incarceration, things inimical to the tender sensibilities of yours truly. Call me a craven coward if you will, but I have always disliked looming, stern-faced entities (particularly when they are packing deadly weapons), ditto the very thought of forced confinement in small enclosed places, and it is my firm policy to avoid anything even remotely connected with same whenever possible. And those menacing-looking vehicles *were* speeding in my direction.

I had hoped I had not been seen; and perhaps I had not been. Perhaps the police were patrolling other streets now, looking for whomever it was they were looking for. But no - they turned down the street I was on, flashing a very bright light onto the lawns and houses. Suppressing with difficulty the urge to run and cower behind the nearest lawn shrubbery, I trudged resolutely on, hoping to avoid being questioned, but they slowed and stopped beside me and called to me to come over to the car. I noticed that they had a large Alsatian dog with them in the back seat. The creature uttered a low growl as I approached the patrol car.

"Have you seen a reptoid around here? Big guy, wearing a black parka, maybe with a black ski mask over his face? Might have been in a hurry?" one of the officers asked.

"No, Sir Officer. I mean, Officer, Sir. I've seen no one."

"Aren't you a little young to be out at this time of night? Do your parents know where you are?

Perhaps I have neglected to mention that another of my burdens, as regards physical appearance, is that, like many hybrids, I look very young for my age. Ridiculously young for my age, actually.

"Just coming home after seeing my girlfriend is all, Sir. You see, Sir, I am actually older than I look."

"Are you off-planet?"

"Yes, Sir. An exchange student."

"Let's see your ID."

My heart galloping at an alarming rate, I attempted to appear calm and to keep the hand from shaking as I produced the requested documents, which I was required by law to carry with me at all times, just like back home. The officers looked them over and even ran a check on me. I leave it to the reader to imagine how I felt as we stood waiting for the results of the search. Had I forgotten to return any library books, or neglected to pay some tax or fee in connection with my schooling? Had my student visa expired, or had I misread some date or neglected to read some fine print? But evidently I had a clean record, for, after running the card and the results of the biometric scan of my irises, my ID card was returned to me and I was told I was free to go.

So shaken was I by the experience that it was not until I got safely home and in my bedroom with the door closed, that I remembered that I had not gotten my snack - and then remembered also about the paper bag I had picked up. It must still be in the pocket of my greatcoat. In my pajamas, I tiptoed out to the hall closet to check for it. I wasn't sure if Rantor was home yet or not; the light was off in his room, and I didn't want to wake him if he was sleeping. I was afraid he'd want to start talking to me about banking again. Probably nothing but a couple of candy wrappers and a receipt were in that bag, but I was curious. I retrieved the sack from the pocket of my coat, tiptoed stealthily back into my room, and gently shut the door.

Opening the crumpled brown paper bag and peering in, I was shocked to see what looked like money inside it. Rather a lot of money, actually. I shook it out onto the bed and beheld quite a pile of loot. I counted it twice - and found that by some strange twist of fate or my astrological chart, I was now the richer by only three dollars and a little change shy of $350. Baffled, too exhausted to know what to make of it all, still *sans* Krunchie-Krunchies despite the harrowing ordeal, I resolved to decide what to do with the money on the morrow when I would be fresher, and just shoved the swag under my mattress for safe-keeping. As luck would have it, when I lifted the mattress to stow my find, I discovered the remains of a forgotten bag of olive oil-fried potato chips, my favorite kind, dusted with sea salt and coarse black pepper, and so settled gratefully into bed with them and my book. *The Sickening Thickening Plot*, was the somewhat ridiculous title, but the reviews on the back cover had been ecstatic, and I was finding that it fully lived up to them.

"Miss Ida Mae Glatz"

CHAPTER 8: SQUINCH

Ah, my friend, this world is nothing but a vast attempt to catch
you with your trousers down ...

Louis-Ferdinand Celine,
Journey to the End of the Night

I have, I believe, not yet mentioned that we hybrids from Q'Oba'Aba'a
on missions to distant worlds are subject to periodic review by the
powers that be on the home planet, or their appointed minions. My
particular caseworker is a Mr. Squinchwell, a dry, desiccated-looking

chap who appears to have been placed on a high shelf somewhere long ago and forgotten. Squinch sports a small paunch like a four-month pregnancy carried high and a little Hitler-moustache gone salt-and-pepper gray, which somehow manages to come across as both sinister and pathetic. He wears drab, shiny black suits - or perhaps it is always the same suit - that always seems to look about due for another waxing and polishing - and peers suspiciously out at one, from behind eyeglasses of what must be the maximum potency, with hideously magnified aquarium eyes.

Since my mission is one of learning, Mr. Squinchwell is connected with the Board of Education. I'm not actually sure exactly what he's supposed to be finding out about me, or really even what I am or am not supposed to be doing or not doing, aside from keeping my grades up and not getting into any trouble with the local constabulary. Back home, the authorities like to keep things sort of vague. It does keep you on your toes. So, anyway, when I get a call from old Squinchwell asking if I could see my way clear to dropping in for a little visit at my earliest convenience, the cold fingers of dread always seem to entwine themselves immediately amongst the entrails, and an icy sweat to bead the brow.

Such a call came, as such calls so often do, at a bad moment, when I was on the rebound from one ordeal and painfully amassing the moral fiber for another. It was the very next morning, the Monday, just as I was leaving to make my way to that class in banking practice which I always find such heavy going, that the phone rang and I recognized the chilly, formal tones of Squinch's secretary, Miss Ida Mae Glatz, on the other end of the line.

Miss Glatz is fifty-something, rather torpedo-shaped, with a style of face and hair that she seems to have carried over from the days of her, or someone's, long-ago youth - the hair being dyed an inky black and piled into a sort of a stiff, immobile cone of curls, the puffy skin on the face looking very powdered and re-powdered, the cheeks rouged to a bright synthetic pink, the lips tinted a rather mordant mauve, and the eyebrow pencil, eyeliner, and lipstick applied with a firm heavy hand and a hard edge around all the perimeters. She sports a small dark mole, rather like one of those pasted-on beauty marks in vogue with the courtesans and court beauties of some long-ago era, positioned slightly off-center just above her upper lip. For some reason, I always find myself staring at it as at hypnotist's pendulum, whenever I am speaking with her - which probably does nothing to soften her heart towards me. Ida Mae Glatz and I have spoken many times, but I am always Mr. Furze to her - never Ifford.

"Mr. Ifford Furze, please." Although she knew that it was I, just as well as I knew that it was she. Miss Glatz always maintains the formalities.

Recognizing her voice at once, I felt the usual quick flash of heat in the center of the chest, and faint throbbing at the temples.

"Speaking."

"Mr. Furze, this is Miss Ida Mae Glatz, secretary to Mr. Pillsbury Squinchwell. Mr. Squinchwell was wondering if you could see your way clear to dropping in for a little visit this afternoon at about one or one-thirty."

"Do you have any idea what might be on the agenda?"

This occasioned a pointed pause of several heartbeats' duration. Never before had I had the temerity to ask such a question. Or any question, actually.

"Mr. Furze, Mr. Squinchwell does not usually, and did not in the present instance, say. I assume it is only routine, but I really don't know." Another pause. "Shall I tell him to expect you?"

"Yes, all right. Tell him one-thirty."

All morning, of course, I kept wondering why old Squinch wanted to see me. The chap makes me nervous. He has this way of seeming to imply, or seeming to be about to imply, that something is amiss in my affairs, that of all those whose progress he oversees, I am one of the least satisfactory, and that he has just received some particularly damning bit of intelligence that has put an end to his indecision and caused him to recommend in favor of 're-scheduling' - which is bureaucratic jargon for being yanked back to the home planet and put to work pulling weeds or sweeping floors - which is probably what poor Calvin is doing back on his home planet. If he has not been discontinued altogether.

On our world, there is much competition for the more prestigious and higher-paying jobs, and those who make the labor resource allocation decisions are able to set extremely high standards. The problem, from the point of view of one in my position, is that they never really spell out in detail what those standards are. Of course, you've got to work hard, and be a team-player, and dress right, and have the right opinions and values and so on. But we all know that they have standards beyond those, perhaps very esoteric and far-reaching things such as seemingly non-work related personality traits and sexual or leisure-time proclivities, which we would certainly assume at least the appearance of, if we knew what they were. That, I think, is why they don't tell us. They want to be able to identify the 'naturals.'

Well - after a bleak morning of trudging through the snow from class to class, feeling much impelled to fight or flight by the inner secretions, and thinking deeply of what life might be like living on coconuts and papayas and little fishes on some tropical beach without too many midges and gnats and sand flies somewhere well off the tourist circuit - one-thirty p.m. found me face to face with good old Squinchwell, he on one side of his nondescript, government-issue desk, and I on the other.

It is part of Squinchwell's tedious *modus operandi* to sort of ease into things with a bit of what he thinks of as friendly chit-chat.

"Well, Furze, good to see you again. You're looking well. How do you like the snow, eh? Keeping warm?"

"Oh, yes, Sir, thank you, Sir, I'm keeping warm enough, all things considered. The dorms are very well-heated. And I hope you are well?"

"Considering the number of miles on the odometer, not too bad, Furze. Ha ha! Of course, I couldn't keep up with a young fellow like yourself. What I wouldn't give to be twenty-five again. Youth is wasted on the young. Ha, ha, ha!"

I, having a mouth so dry I felt I might do some damage to it if I attempted to employ it, and drawing in any event a complete blank in the possible rejoinders department, merely goggled at him in what I hoped was a friendly and encouraging manner.

"Squinch"

"Well! Furze. As to that important matter of your academic standing, in general your grades are satisfactory - with one slight area of concern. In the mid-term report sent to this office last week by your professors, I noted with some concern that as of even date you are pulling only a C+ in your Fundamentals of Earthly Banking class. One reason I asked you to drop in today is to review with you the minimum standards you must meet in order to remain in this program. Realistically, we realize that we can't all be 4.0 whiz kids - although I do have some of those, of course, even in the hard sciences - but we don't expect that of our students in this program. *However*: we all should be able to score at least a B in every class that is pertinent to our major and intended vocation. In fact that, along with maintaining an over-all 3.5 GPA - is one of our minimum standards in the program. As perhaps you will recall. So: is there a problem with this banking class - the material too difficult, the professor mumbling, something like that? Do you need a tutor, do you think? Or is it just a matter of slacking off a bit, or feeling a bit under the weather when you took the mid-term? Ha?"

"Oh, the latter Sir. The very lattermost, that is to say. On the day of that mid-term, you see, I had a rather bad cold and a throbbing headache to boot. I had been unable to sleep well the night before. It was not a good day. The brain felt be-fogged. My brain, that is, of course. I can assure you that I should be able to bring that grade up at least to a B by the end of the term. I had not realized I had done as badly as that on the test - we have not gotten them back yet - but you can be sure I won't let that happen again. In fact, you can bank on it, Sir. Ha ha ha!"

My own nervous cackle sounded to my ear horribly like a pointed parody of my inquisitor's standard item - he always punctuated his remarks during these chats of ours with those little "ha ha's" and "ha ha ha's" - but it was actually only an involuntary expression of my extreme anxiety - fear and trembling seeming to be the only emotions of which I am fully capable. And in that department, I seem to excel. Glennie tells me I am a worry-wart. But it appears to me that I am only a realist.

"All rightie, then, Furze, glad to hear it. That's the 'can do' attitude we like to see in our students. Now - just a couple of additional matters I want to touch upon, and then I'll let you be on your way - I'm sure you've got a lot of studying to do, eh?"

"Yes, Sir, that I do, Sir."

"Well, Furze, I don't know if I've mentioned this to you or not - perhaps not - but it *is* explicitly stated in the printed rules, regulations, standards, and requirements that all of our students received at the commencement of their period of study, that one of our inflexible rules for you people on state scholarships to other worlds is that you must not concern yourselves with the political affairs of the host nation, or planet. It only makes sense, you know. We're guests, and we must tread softly. Don't want to get involved in anything sticky or risk offending anyone or jeopardizing any mutually advantageous arrangements. The greatest good for the greatest number. The individual is expendable, the good of the State is paramount, and the means justify the ends. Or is it the other way around? Anyway: I'm sure you've heard all this before, in your Politics of Ethics classes in secondary school. We all have. Just a word to the wise. Understood?"

"Of course, Sir."

"And one more thing, Furze. Your biological mother, I believe, resides on this planet, does she not?"

"I believe she does - or at least did, Sir. It has always been my understanding that she is - was - an Earthling. For all we know, of course, she's been moved to an underground pensioners' home on Mars ... or is dead by now. She must be pretty old."

"Yes. Well, Furze, I believe you are aware that our policy is that there be no contact whatsoever with biological parents. None whatsoever. It simply creates too many problems. Logic dictates that considerations of efficient utilization of energy be paramount. Concern about one's origins is essentially romantic daydreaming. Effective people, those who are making a contribution, don't have time for that sort of thing. One must live in the present. But I'm sure you remember all that from your Rational Attitudes and Orientations classes back on the home planet. Just - a little reminder, now and again - what?"

"Yes, Sir. I understand."

"As I'm sure you realize, being a young man of good sense, you are very fortunate to have been one of the relative few chosen for a professional track. So! I guess that about does it, Furze, I'll let you get back to the books, and I believe I've got another appointment in a very few minutes here, Miss Glatz keeps me booked up, makes sure I utilize *my* time efficiently, a real slave driver, in fact, so! - I'll be seeing you again in a few weeks, I imagine, Furze, just to make sure all is going well and that you have no major problems or complaints. We aim to please. So! Good-bye, then, Furze. Good seeing you again, and keep up the hard work."

"Thank you, Sir. Good-bye, Sir."

CHAPTER 9: MOM AND ME

'My country right or wrong' is a thing no patriot would ever think
of saying except in a desperate case. It is like saying, 'My
mother, drunk or sober.'

G.K. Chesterton

"Hello?"

"Hello, Mother."

"Ifford? Is that you, Iffy? It's good to hear from y-you. Lemmie turn
down the TV here ... I've been hoping that you'd call. How a-are
you?"

"Well, Mother, only passable right at the moment, I'm afraid. Squinch
called me in for an interview today. In fact, I've only just left his
office."

"Wh-where are you calling from? Your r-r-rooms? Your cell phone?"

"No - I don't have a cell phone - remember, Mother? I don't like them.
They make me feel hounded. No, I'm calling from a pay phone. To tell
you the truth, I'm afraid to use that phone in my digs anymore. I think
it might be bugged, or monitored, or something. Somehow, Squinch
seems to have gotten wind of the fact that you and I have been in
contact."

"I-is that what he s-said at your interview today?"

"No, Mother, Squinch's approach is more subtle. He doesn't come right
out and say things. What he did do is remind me that the rules strictly
and totally forbid any contact with one's biological parents. From that,
I'm afraid, it is impossible not to infer that somehow or other -
probably the phone - I don't know what else it *could* be - he knows, or
at least suspects, that we've been talking. I mean, I haven't told
anybody, not even Glennie, that I've located you and that we've been
in contact. I don't know what to do."

"Are y-you in any d-d-d-danger? I mean, what would they d-do to y-you?"

"For an infraction of this magnitude, I could be revoked."

"R-revoked?"

"You know - rescinded - yanked back to the home planet for keeps and demoted to something like third assistant to the Chief Cleaner of the Outer Mongolian Royal Kennels."

" What a-are y-y-y-y- .... going to d-do?"

"I just don't know, Mother. I'm going to have to give it some thought."

"Oh, d-dear. My only - my only known s-s-son ... oh, dearie me."

It sounded like she might start burbling here, and I had to extricate myself before that commenced. It can be very time-consuming. She has been through a lot and is not the most stable of persons. But she is my only know blood relative - and she means well. She has a heart of gold, my mother.

"Just don't mention a word about it to anyone without clearing it with me first. Have you told anyone that we've been in contact - or hinted or even joked about it?"

"Absolutely n-n-not, Iffy darling. Y-y-y you know I wouldn't d-d-do a thing that f-foolish."

"I didn't really think you had; I'm just trying to figure this out. I can't think why I'd be important enough to have my phone tapped. Unless it's routine, and all of our phones are monitored. But if that were the case, I don't know why Squinch would have waited until now to say something about it. But I've got to go. I can't really talk, out here on the street-corner. Anyway, these phones all are tapped, too, I've been told by my new roomie. I just wanted to let you know about this."

"You have a n-n-new roomie?"

"Yes. Quite a character. A reptoid."

89

"O-oh - I hate 'toids. How awful for you. I was f-forced - well, y-y-y-
y- ... know."

"Yes, I know. This one's unpleasant, but harmless, I think. Mother?"

"Y-y-y ... um-hmmm?"

"Have you been staying off the sauce?"

"Y-y-y- ... umhummm, I have. I really have. Just the t-t-teensiest nip,
now and then, to w-w-w-warm me up on these c-cold w-winter d-days,
y'you know. L-like I promised you, Iffy."

"Good, Mother. I'm proud of you. Keep it up. Best just stay off the
stuff altogether and stick to hot tea for your warm-ups. Well, I must
ring off ..."

" I ha-hate having you in trouble because of m-m-m-me, Ifford."

"It's not your fault. Remember, I tracked you down, not vice versa."
Well ... good-bye for now, Mother. Be good."

"Good-bye, Iffy dear. C-call soon. Take care of yourself. I l-love you."

"I will. You be careful, too. I love you too, Mumsie. Remember that.
'Bye for now."

CHAPTER 10: MOSTLY TRUTHFUL IFFORD

If I'd written all the truth I knew for the past ten years,
about 600 people - including me - would be rotting in
prison cells from Rio to Seattle today.

Hunter S. Thompson

All right. I omitted to relate the entire truth about my mother. Perhaps my brain is a little compartmentalized. After all, one changes one's behavior to suit the circumstances and the company - and one *persona* is not called the truth and the other a lie. Likewise, when I tell someone that I have never met my mother, it does not feel like a lie. It seems like absolutely the appropriate, the right, thing to say, to some people in certain circs. Surely the reader is enough the man or woman of the world to realize that expediency dictates some of these choices for one. In the best of all possible worlds, perhaps, this would not be the case, and old Diogenes would be so up to the rafters in honest men that he could take down the 'Help Wanted' sign, douse the lantern, and call off his dogs.

And besides, we've never actually met, my mother and I - we've just talked on the phone. We are, as it happens, living in the same city, and we could meet. I'm not entirely sure why we haven't. To be completely honest, I have thought about it, and I do have some ideas. For one thing, I might have been - irrationally, I know - hoping to preserve a little peace of mind by trying to hedge my bet and conforming to the letter, if not the spirit, of the rule forbidding contact with biological parents. Beyond that, though, I think my mother and I are a bit afraid to see one another, and to be seen, lest reality be a disappointment, and somehow change the feeling we have for one another.

I, for instance, am a hybrid and not exactly the archetype of male beauty by Earthly standards. Female hybrids, with their delicacy and smallness, are more sexy and attractive by Earth standards than are we small and delicate males. Could a male Pomeranian, or Chihuahua, ever look virile and manly to any, save - perhaps - a female Pomeranian or Chihuahua? And might not even she prefer - well, a Schnauzer, a German Shepherd, or, if she were absolutely honest, even a Rottweiler or a Pit Bull? I have few illusions in this department. Would my mother be able to accept how I look? Perhaps not. Perhaps, in spite of herself, she would even be repulsed - the oversized head, the fine thin hair, the albino-like paleness, the tiny nose and mouth and ears ... the truth is, I look like some short, early-adolescent incarnation of Andy Warhol, but with finer, thinner hair, Keene eyes, a pointy chin, and a pronouncedly ovoid shape to my head. I hate how I look.

And I don't know how my mother looks, either. I do have an (alleged) picture of her, but it was taken a long time ago, when she was young. She looks very pretty in that picture - and a bit like Yours Truly about the cheekbones; but I don't know what she looks like now. I do know that she's had a hard life, something that often ages a person. Sometimes, one's illusions are preferable to reality. One thing that she has told me, for instance, is that she's a bit overweight. To be honest, I don't really like the appearance of fat people. On the home planet, no one is fat. When I first saw fat people, in pictures, and here on Earth, I was simultaneously repulsed and fascinated. They are so - unhealthy-looking. Not all of them, of course. Forgive me if I sound politically incorrect here. But - what if my mother had down-played her condition, as people will do, and were one of those with an apron of fat hanging to her thighs, one for whom merely getting up out of a chair and walking to the front door to check if the mail has been delivered yet is a puffing, panting, red-faced major effort, a major accomplishment?

It's not as cold-blooded as it sounds. You see, I like the relationship that we have; and I like her - in the context of our telephone relationship. My mother is quite an understanding person, and I have gradually come to rely - almost to rely - upon our conversations - which once or twice have lasted for an hour or more. I am able - sometimes - to talk with her about how I really feel. She says the wrong thing less often than most people. This despite her problems, such that more than once she has slurred her words and been less than fully coherent when I called. She tends to drink too much. But she is a good soul nonetheless. And I am trying to help her with that problem.

It is because I do like her, and our conversations, that I don't want to rock the boat. In essence, I am trying to protect what we have. I believe I have previously mentioned the generally conservative nature of us hybrids. We proceed - usually - with caution. In seeking out my mother, I had been uncharacteristically reckless. That my act of recklessness would be laced and buttressed with prudent hesitation is only to be expected. Perhaps the behaviorists would simply call it a neurotic approach-avoidance conflict.

And now I, for whom decision is anathema, found myself faced with another decision. Did I dare to preserve the relationship with my mother? Was it even worth it? Did I even care? The worst part of the whole thing - aside from the anxiety, and sense of urgency, that I felt - was that I hadn't a soul, not anyone, to talk it over with.

Unless, that is, I decided to run the risk of taking a confidante ...

CHAPTER 11: IN WHICH RANTOR LEARNS THAT THE DUDES ON THE HOME PLANET PLAY HARDBALL

Idealism is the noble toga that political gentlemen
drape over their will to power.

Aldous Huxley

Before the four of us had parted Sunday night at The Ragged Edge -
and although less than 24 hours had passed, this now seemed very long
ago, belonging, as it were, to a relatively untroubled past for which I
found myself yearning with a surprisingly intense nostalgia - but,
anyway, upon parting, we had agreed to meet again Friday evening,
once more at a coffee house, for the willing suspension of my disbelief
- my secret resolve having been formed, as I have already mentioned,
to beg off at the last minute with a sick headache or some such excuse.

But now I was of a mind to go through with the meeting as planned. In
fact, I was seeing Rantor and Torvald in a new light, in view of this
afternoon's events. They seemed generally anti-establishment types,
and I now, willy-nilly, had a problem with the establishment. Of
course, they appeared to object to the infra-structure here on the blue
planet, and my problem was with the power barons back home. But my
intuition told me that theirs was probably a sort of generalized
antipathy towards all who would trammel the masses in any way,
shape, or form; and the ruling elite back home went in for trammeling
on a much larger scale, and more professionally, so to speak, than they
seemed to here on this rock. That, in fact, had been one reason I had
been unable to take much interest in the dynamic duo's cause. They
were objecting to a status quo which I rather envied. To me, they had
seemed a bit spoiled, and somewhat naive. The young will always find
something to rebel against - that sort of thing. But today's events had,
as they say, put everything in a different light; and thus it was that after
dinner I struck up a conversation with my new roommate, the object of
which was, in the argot of the streets, to feel him out.

"I say, Rantor," I began, "Which planet do you hail from?"

"Squank," he replied. "Have you heard of it?"

94

"Oh, yes," said I. "The Squankese have reputations for being great - lovers of liberty."

This was putting it with consummate tact, I thought. Actually, they are considered short-tempered and violent. The reason I had been so alarmed when I first beheld Rantor looming in the passageway outside my rooms was that I had immediately pegged him as a Squankese reptoid. Back home, these reptoids from the red planet Squank figure prominently in many stories for young children, usually in the role of villain or miscreant, or as sort of wandering, unpredictable Samurai-type warriors, with paranoid personalities, short fuses, and chips on the shoulder strongly reminiscent of the gun fighters of the Old West in the legends of this country. I had always shuddered and averted the gaze when passing one on the narrow footpaths of the campus. Actually, there are very few of them treading those footpaths, as they tend naturally to be drawn more to the active life than to scholarship and introspection. Also, their tails, about which they are, by the way, very vain, make sitting in chairs problematic.

"Do you have," I asked, "Some sort of overseer or caseworker from Squank with whom you meet periodically for a review of your grades and general situation here on *Terra* - a sort of warden-cum-counselor?"

"No way!" he responded energetically. "Why? Do you?"

"Yes, a disagreeable chap by the name of Squinchwell, who manages by the skillful use of innuendo and veiled threat to keep me feeling that only by the barest of margins am I squeaking by."

"What do you mean - squeaking by?"

"Well, you know, if you're not working out, in their opinion, you can be revoked. At any time. They don't have to give a reason. Just 'in the interests of a more efficient deployment of personnel.' "

"You're saying that whether you stay here or go back to your planet is not up to you?"

"That's right. Of course, I could *get* them to send me back by letting my GPA drop below 3.5, or screwing up in some other way. But nobody wants to go back. It's much better here."

"Did you choose to come here in the first place?"

"The decision was not mine to make. It's kind of like being in the military service here, from what I understand. They might ask for your top three preferences, but what you get might be something totally different. The call is theirs."

"Were you able to choose what you would be studying?"

"No. That was assigned too, on the basis of the State's needs and my performance on a bunch of tests. My own theory is that I was selected for the banking track because of my stoical capacity to endure mental torture."

"The official, cleaned-up, for-public-consumption version of economics - and history - is both bewildering and excruciatingly dull, I agree," Rantor said. "It's meant to be. But the truth is fascinating, Ifford. But, anyway - once you're out of school, is it kind of like being discharged from the Army, and you have more freedom of choice when you're out of school and on your own?"

"Alas - no. Unless you're one of those very rare and gifted individuals whose talents make you indispensable to the ruling elite. But actually, most of those are put under at least some form or degree of mind-control, trauma-based, you know, in the most extreme form, or so rumor has it - some of these things are rather hush-hush, you understand, even on Q'Oba'Aba'A - the highly talented being commodities too valuable not to control to the maximum degree possible."

"Is this the way it is just for hybrids - or for everyone?"

"For everyone. The individual is considered to be the property of the State. Though we hybrids are, of course, near the bottom of the status ladder, actually having, in fact, an inferior legal status. Ours is a stratified society."

"And people just put up with that?"

"It's all most of us have ever known. And besides - what could we possibly do about it? Trouble-makers just get their memories erased, or are given surgical or chemical therapy. Or sometimes, in the euphemistic expression, they 'get selected for a special mission' and are never heard from again. It's all supposedly in the best interests of the State. What's good for the State is good for the individual. We are

96

told from the cradle that one finds one's freedom in the service of the state. It's all very mystical, actually. They manage to make it sound sort of beautiful. I, myself, have never been quite convinced, but I always felt that the problem was with me and not the system."

"By the blood of Zeus and Hera, Ifford! It sounds nightmarish. On Squank, government could never get away with one tenth of that. The people would have their livers for dinner. Don't you hate it?"

"I have always just accepted it - or tried to. It's just the way things have always been. Everything not compulsory is prohibited - that sort of thing. But a new situation has arisen. For the first time, I am having problems with this set-up."

"How so? What's happened?"

"Squinch called me in for an interview today. He reminded me that I am strictly forbidden to involve myself in *Terran* politics. And that I am very lucky to have been selected for a professional track."

"But you haven't been doing anything political, have you?"

"Unless you count talking over coffee with you and that Greek god of yours. It made me wonder if either of you has acquired any sort of reputation or notoriety for your political views - or activities."

"I dunno. Not me, I would think ... but Torvald - perhaps. We had certainly better bring this up when we get together again on Friday."

"That's what I thought." And I let it go at that. I wanted to give myself a few more days to think over the business about my mother. No need to rush into things.

Rantor and I continued to chat for a while, and I began to warm to the fellow a bit. He was impulsive and emotional, certainly, and seemed to exist at all times within a sort of personal envelope or miasma of turbulent energy; he obviously lacked tact and self-awareness - was, in a word, a stranger to suavity, subtlety, and in general all the arts of concealment and deception. But this was not necessarily a bad thing. In fact, his lack of the statesman's art and underlying mental set had its positive side - I did not need to wonder about what was really going on in his inner being or resounding in the subtle mental recesses; I could just ask him, and he would tell me. In fact, he would probably tell me even if I didn't ask. He was not the type to conceive and conceal elaborate plots and stratagems.

Torvald seemed not to be quite such an open book. Few entities are, of course. It was one of the things that made Rantor like a breath of fresh air, or a splash of cold water in the face, not to mention gale-force winds and torrents. But at this point I hardly knew Torvald, and would be forced to rely on first impressions, in deciding whether or not it was safe to confide in him re this mother thing. I did ask Rantor where and when he and Torvald had met, and learned that they had been in a political history class together last spring semester. It seems that Torvald and the professor of this class had crossed swords almost daily, and, according to Rantor, the professor had usually ended up the one with egg on his face, the one who could think of no suitable rebuttal and was left hemming and hawing and appearing not to be up on the material.

In fact, if Rantor is to be believed, and as just discussed I don't think he has it in him to fabricate, the man of learning had undergone a sort of progressive decline as the quarter had wound on, acquiring an apparently permanent furrow to the brow, becoming increasingly nervous and unsure of himself in general aspect, and sometimes positively wincing, or flinching, when Torvald raised his hand to speak. He finally simply would not call on Torvald, ever; but Torvald handled that by just going ahead and talking anyway. Torvald even brought books in to buttress his points, and read aloud from them in class - books, needless to say, which were not on the professor's class reading list. The scuttlebutt was that the poor professor, who was relatively young, and untenured, even took up smoking again. I gathered from Rantor's approving summation of the contest that Torvald showed no mercy, regarding the fellow in particular, and his professional cohort in general, as little more than a sort of pollution in the groves of academe, a sad parody, or mockery, of what real men of learning should be about, in effect being well-paid to be intellectually dishonest, mere sleazy disseminators of propaganda packaged and sold as truth and gaining credibility and respectability by being put out under the University label. I take it that is how he regards almost all of the teaching staff, at least those in the economics, political science, and history departments. I will have to get his reading on Professor Forthwith.

It seems that Rantor had been deeply impressed with Torvald's style as well as content and the two had been fast friends ever since that class, with the reptile playing Plato to the other's Socrates and both parties enjoying the whole thing immensely. Rantor spoke of it all in tones that fairly oscillated with reverence and esteem, maintaining that had it not been for Torvald he would still be numbered among the brainwashed masses and would not even know how to draw out the truth from where it lurked, mauled and battered but still recognizable, to one in the know, behind the propaganda put forth as news in the daily media.

I sat there mulling all this over for a minute or two, as Rantor loomed opposite me, the tip of his tail twitching like a hyperactive pendulum, sipping his cup of coffee and eyeing me with keen interest while trying to appear not to be doing so, as though I were a wild creature that might not take the morsel with which his trap was baited if he, concealed near-by behind some foliage, breathed or blinked. He seemed to be attempting to assess how I was reacting to this influx of data, and was apparently waiting for me to speak, hoping that I would clue him in.

Deciding, after much sipping of the steaming beverage and mulling over of all aspects of the present situation, that no harm could come from presenting a few of my own views to this candid fellow for dissection - although I was still not sure why it seemed to be of such moment to him whether or not I interested myself in his ideas - I broke the silence that had settled over us.

CHAPTER 12: IN WHICH A GLIMPSE OF THE GRAND DESIGN IS WASTED UPON OUR HERO

The authentic interpreter of Machiavelli is
the whole of later history.

Lord Acton

"Rantor," I began, "You have heard a little of what the relationship is like between the individual and the state back on the old home planet. Considerably grimmer than that which prevails here on *Terra* – or at least, here in this country. Frankly, one problem I have had with your position is that you and Torvald seem to be objecting to what appears from my perspective to be, withal, a pretty balmy state of affairs. In fact, I would like nothing better than to be able to remain here. Although I do not think that would be allowed, so I have no great hopes. Anyway, I guess what I'm getting at is, is it really all that bad - as regards the prevailing systems of government and economics, here in your country? Where's the beef? Are you proceeding from the position that if it's government, it must be bad? Is it anarchy you favor?"

His tail now lashing like that of a cat before the mouse-hole, the great lizard leaned his scaly elbows upon the table, his massive torso angled eagerly towards me.

"Ifford," he began, seeming to choose his words carefully, "The problem is not government per se, or big business per se, or the church, per se. The problem is concentrations of power, any concentration of power. That is the awareness that is behind the founding fathers' Separation of Powers doctrine. A study of history shows that concentrations of power are inherently dangerous to the liberty and the earnings, the property, of the people – the masses. History clearly teaches us this, with many examples. Concentrations of power tend to come under the control – through bribery, through the use of force – of powerful individuals or groups who use these concentrations of power to force or to trick the people into handing over the fruits of their labors."

He paused as if waiting for me to say something, but when I remained silent, he continued. "I can understand how you feel in the light of what you've just told me about how things are where you come from. It

100

really sounds grim. In the Orwellian sense of the word. But, basically, things here are not all they're cracked up to be. The situation is simply less overt - more subtle. It's also in transition, and the direction it's moving in is one of a progressive aggrandizement and consolidation of the power of the state. There's a quotation I'd like to read to you, from the introduction of a book that Torvald lent me. Just wait one minute while I get it."

The lizardly creature dashed off to his room, and the sounds of vigorous rummaging emanated from within. I shuddered a bit, imagining what his room must look like. Rantor is not the most orderly of creatures and has this most amazing capacity for maintaining an inner poise and mental balance amidst physical surroundings of the utmost chaos. One problem that was emerging between us was the tendency of his casual housekeeping to creep out and infest the surrounding countryside. I require immaculate quarters if I am not to fall prey to an insidious unraveling of the inner being.

There was the sound of rustling papers as Rantor waded across his room to emerge in the doorway, a triumphant gleam glinting in the rusty orb and a small but thickish paperback book clutched in one great paw. A scrap or two of paper eddied in his wake as he surged towards me, and I suppressed an impulse to go over and pick up the debris and deposit it in the wastebasket.

"OK, here it is," he said, practically licking his lips in anticipation. "This is from an introduction by a guy named Max Learner to *The Prince and The Discourses*, by Machiavelli. You know Machiavelli, of course?"

"Frankly, the name does not ring a bell."

"Wow. Well, he's an important guy. The granddaddy of that Teutonic dude your school is named after - Otto Von Bismarck. You know the Florentine Plaza, on lower campus? - that area with all the benches and arbors and the vines and ivy twining around the reproductions of Italian Renaissance sculpture? It's right between the CFR Auditorium and the Tri-Lateral Stadium – just behind the Rothschild Arena, overlooking the lake - quite a nice little area, really, where couples like to go and make out on summer evenings. Well, it was actually named after this guy - Niccolo Machiavelli. He was from Florence, you see - Florentine. Among all those statues, there's a bust of him - the only portrait bust in the place.

"Anyway here's that quote from Max Lerner. I call him Lax Learner, because for all his education - and his slippery ways with words - he seems not to have actually learned all that much: '... the masses who are coerced in a dictatorship have to be wooed and duped in a democracy.' Did you get that? 'Duped in a democracy' - right? That's what I mean about the situation here being essentially not that different from what you've got on your planet - just at a different stage of realization and being accomplished – for now - by more subtle means. And right above that Learner says, '... leaders in every field seek power ruthlessly and hold on to it tenaciously.'

"He just says it right there for any and everybody who's paying attention," continued the lizard, "And can think a little bit on their own about what that means, and apply it to their own world, and see if it fits. You see, there are many fictions that are subtly maintained in the mainstream media, and in scholarly works such as these as well - and one of them is that, sure, there are these power-hungry dudes, who do really awful things - but they're always 'outside, over there, back then.' Or an occasional bad apple here in our own midst, who in most cases doesn't get very far before he's caught and punished. So it's OK to present the writings of Machiavelli, and even to generalize about leaders' tendencies to 'seek power ruthlessly,' so long as this information is not used in any analysis or exposé of the existing power structure right here in River City. You see what I mean?"

So earnest; so eager. A strange bird, my new roomie. Clearly a zealot. I sat looking, I hoped, politely interested, but the brain was churning, I can tell you. Are zealots to be trusted? Aren't they all, at bottom and at best, loose cannons?

"I think you will find, Ifford, that when you examine the general impression you have in your own mind from the major media, and other reading material and information - such as movies - readily available in this culture - concerning what the government of this country is like, you get a picture of over-all rectitude and concern for the welfare of humankind.

"Isn't that right, Ifford? I mean, isn't it? Don't you think that the government here is concerned about the rights and welfare of the people?" He so wanted me to say something.

"Well - yes. I mean - aren't they - for the most part? If they weren't, wouldn't they get booted out of office at the next election?"

He grimaced slightly, as though an invisible someone had just stuck him with a pin in some tender portion of his anatomy. After a brief pause, and a sigh, he again assumed the podium.

"I don't mean to be offensive, Ifford, I really don't. But what makes it difficult is that you are so ... steeped in the lore. Up to the eyeballs. It's hard to know where to begin. For one thing, with computerized voting machines, vote fixing is ridiculously easy – and actually, from what I have read, more or less routine. I could show you all sorts of scholarly articles on that - none of them published in the major news 'zines or mentioned on the nightly 'news' of course. But for now, let's go back to that quote from Learner about having to accomplish in a democracy by trickery what a more overtly totalitarian government accomplishes more directly by coercion and terror.

"So," he continued, "This country is highly touted as being a democracy – as having a government of, by, and for the people. Flags are waved on the 4th of July, et cetera. But keeping our knowledge of history in mind, we recall that however populist, and idealistic, its beginnings, a more totalitarian regime - a government over, rather than of, the many, and by and for the few – a plutocracy, or oligarchy - is what virtually every government, no matter how idealistically conceived, ends up being. Being shaped into, I should say, by those who want to put government's might and infrastructure to work for themselves rather than for the general public good. Cooptation, subversion of government. The record of history reveals it to be, as I say, an old story. And it's really all about wealth, money ... broadly speaking, about diverting to themselves, the power elite and their cronies, as much as possible of the profits of production, such capture of wealth being achieved by a mix of force and deception.

"Sun Tzu, was right when he said that all war is deception, and typically – historically - we see what amounts to a war, a conflict, going on over whose interests the powerful tool of government will serve. Even if subversion is achieved cataclysmically, as overthrow, by violent usurpation of the governmental powers from within or without, there will be elements of deception involved; and at the far end of the deception spectrum, we can see that usurpation can come from within, surreptitiously, very gradually, a step at a time over several generations, so that the people become bit by bit used to less and less freedom - the 'been down so long, it seems like up to me' effect. Gradually, each generation would live under a more coercive, less free kind of government. Gradually, the people would cease even to know what true

103

freedom is, or would be like. The teachings and writings of the founders would not be taught, would be forgotten – would become, in their actual content, unknown."

"And you are saying, I take it, that that is what is happening – has happened - here in this country?"

"Yes. As an example in the here and now, I recently came across a comment, in some newspaper article, I think it was, by a homeless man that he 'believed in the Constitution,' and that it is the duty of government to 'take care of' its citizens. He was referring, of course, to socialism and all such ostensibly benevolent wealth transfer schemes, and actually implying that such programs were somehow created or provided for by the Constitution! - thus revealing his deep ignorance of what that document actually is, says, and attempts to do. Because in fact, as you might know, to any such enlargement of the scope and powers of government the founders of this country, the writers of the Constitution to which he referred, were deeply opposed."

"And why might that be?"

"Because they knew their history, and thus they knew that big government is, as history conclusively proves, *never* populist government. And that a collectivist/socialist *in loco parentis* type government is, inevitably and unavoidably, big government with a capital 'B.' But anyway, speaking in general of the gradual transformation over time of a government into its diametric opposite - the changes made, to the extent that they are even acknowledged, discussed, would be presented either as *forced and unavoidable* - such as all these new 'anti-terrorist' laws that contain clauses applying, in the small print, so to speak, their draconian absolutist provisions to native-born alleged 'enemy combatants' - that term being so vaguely defined as to be freely applicable to any dissident whom the government might wish to put out of circulation, to neutralize – or, these changes can be *hyped as great new things* that will be of immense benefit to the people - the down-trodden masses - such as this cashless society they are trying to put in – or such as central banks and fiat currencies, or socialism, and forced wealth-transfer schemes generally.

"You get the idea? There's more than one way to skin a cat, is what I'm saying - to attain one's objectives. One can use force or the threat of force ... or one can resort to deception, as con men, on the small scale or the big one, have always done. Or one can use a combination of deception, gradualism, and force - or the threat, subtle or not so subtle, of force - which, in the usurpation of a government from within, is usually the case. The ideas are not new, nor is history empty of examples of them in action. But people here are carefully, methodically brainwashed into believing that their saintly heads of state and captains of industry, banking, and the media, are Boy Scouts who have no such ambitions and are above such low tricks - a view that a study of the record of history, up to and including the present, would instantly cast into doubt, of course."

It had dawned on me somewhere during the foregoing lengthy monologue that I was once again being finessed into employing the gray matter. I had even brought it upon myself this time. True, it was within the Monday to Friday time frame; but I might have neglected to mention that usually I only exercise my brain in pursuit of a grade - or a shekel, so to speak. This present effort seemed like a squandering of the resources. An unnecessary expenditure of energy. I just could not see the point of doing this sort of thing voluntarily. To me, it's rather like digging ditches in one's spare time for the sheer joy of it. But given that I had started the ball rolling this time, and that I had my own agenda, which involved currying favor with the reptile, staying on the fellow's good side, I felt compelled to proceed. And a thought had occurred to me.

"Yes," I interjected, "But this is beginning to sound to me like conspiracy theory talk, Rantor. No one group or faction has that much power here. That's the whole point of the separation of powers, and democracy, and voting and so on. Not to mention the two-party system. What you're talking about would require a concerted effort by a very powerful group, which would probably have to conceal that it even was a group, or existed as a group, and yet which would have to cohere as a group over several generations, beyond the lifetimes of its founders – frankly, it just sounds too improbable. Undo-able. And surely, though admittedly there be minor scandals and occasional bad apples in the barrel, these men in government would not betray their own people. Frankly, I just can't credit it. It won't wash, in my book."

"You're thinking, Ifford, and that's good." Rantor actually managed to say that without making me feel patronized. I will confess that I even felt a little proud. It was the first time the saurian had ever praised me. "But, if you will recall from past discussions, our example of organized crime - the Mafia – it does prove that organized crime on a large scale can exist and persist over many decades, and generations. If covert joint

105

criminal enterprises can exist in the private sphere, logic would certainly suggest that they can exist in the public sphere – especially because common sense suggests that organized crime could hardly exist and prosper over the decades without some degree of tolerance or collusion by those exercising the police and legal powers. And frankly, and as per the old saying that every man has his price, I am sorry to say that history is also replete with examples of men in key positions of power in government betraying their compatriots, their countrymen, for their own private gain and advancement. If you have any interest at all in that subject as it applies to this country, you might look into the books of Antony Sutton – such titles as *Wall Street and the Bolshevik Revolution, Wall Street and FDR, Wall Street and the Rise of Hitler*, and *The Best Enemy Money Can Buy*.

"So, keeping in mind this concept of organized crime ... and keeping also in mind the old joke that the petty criminal gets clapped in the hoosegow for his petty offenses, while the criminal on the grand scale gets invited to the White House for dinner ... if you go back in this country's history to the late 19th Century," he continued, "You will find, in the Congressional Record and in the newspapers and the writings of some of the less corrupt public figures, a great deal of concern and discussion over the growing concentration of power into the hands of a few – especially what was called in those days 'Wall Street' or 'the Money Trust.'

"What had happened basically was that the big banking houses of Europe had already achieved a tremendous concentration of capital, power, and control, in both the Old and the New Worlds, so to speak. And as the new century progressed, they used their power systematically and methodically to silence those voices attempting to alert the people here to the threat that these immensely powerful banking houses constituted to their prosperity here in this country, which at that time, still relatively free of the parasitic banking powers and their central banks of issue, was the envy of the peoples of the world, because of the success of its industry and the prosperity of its people, still operating, doing business, to a fairly large extent with a free market economic system and without a central bank of issue. But the Money Trust worked cleverly in collusion with highly placed men in banking and government in this country to, finally, after decades of effort, get their 'consummation devoutly to be desired,' their central bank here on American soil.

"This happened when the Federal Reserve Act was passed by Congress, after decades of concerted effort on the part of the Money Trust, in 1913. Much chicanery was involved in this process, as is detailed very interestingly in that book you saw me reading, *The Creature from Jekyll Island*. The author has a lot to say about the great banking house of Rothschild, and the reach – and consequences for us all – of its immense influence. He tells about the secret meeting on Jekyll Island off the Georgia coast between bankers and those in government here to draft and get passed the Federal Reserve Act; he tells how the Money Trust cleverly postured, for the media, that they hated and abhorred the very idea of a central bank of issue - realizing that most people, having no real understanding of the matter, would take the easy lazy way out and conclude that if this proposed banking legislation was so hated by the Money Trust, then it must be a good thing for the little guy, for the people.

"And that book mentions in some detail how the money men, in concert with elements within government and the large trans-national corporations, in most of which the banking houses are themselves owners of large amounts of stock – how these powerful few proceeded rapidly to complete their capture, by bribe and purchase, of the major centers of power in the country, and thus were able to see to it that those few who knew about them and what they were doing - and refused to be silenced with money - would no longer be able to get the word out to the people. They knew how important it is to control the information delivery apparatus, and they and their tools, both witting and unwitting, have been using their control of it for many decades now to convince the people that their government is still the same one created for them by the country's founders. And, to the unthinking superficial observer, it can appear to be still the same. But in fact the government today is NOT being operated according to the plan set down by the founding fathers in the Constitution. Not at all. If, that is, the Constitution was actually legally and lawfully created at the Philadelphia Convention. There are some who argue that proper lawful procedure was not followed. One school of thought among the many revisionist scholars who have sprung up in recent years. This is something, actually, that I am dying to learn more about."

That last remark casting doubt on the very legitimacy of the Constitution I had to ignore as being, one, incomprehensible and, two, just too *outré* to be given much consideration. But I did have a cogent objection to his line of reasoning, and to his apparent contention that the Constitution had over time devolved - had craftily been reduced, or

107

downgraded, so to speak - into being, in actual practice, little more than a set of optional guidelines rather than the rigid, and rigidly enforced, inflexible foundational law that the country's founders intended it to be – law that can be changed only by the people's will – and not, certainly at the whim of any government fuctionary, nor gradually and bit by bit, as legal usage and customs change, as is the case, historically, in the Anglo-Saxon tradition, with the so-called common law, the *lex non scripta*. The fellow was addressing me as if I were a mere schoolboy still in knee-pants, when I had, in fact, taken a class, and just last quarter – a required class, of course – in Constitutional law.

"Well then, answer me this if you will, my scaly friend. Just a couple of days ago there was an article in the newspaper, on the front page, all about whether or not some new little law, I forget which one, is or is not Constitutional. It wasn't anything major - just some little thing. That looks to me like someone up there is really watching the situation to make sure that government plays by the rules - you know - dots the 'i's and crosses the 't's."

"Beautiful point, Ifford! I'm glad you brought it up. That is one of their clever strategies - we do not deny that these are very smart men we're talking about here. They didn't get where they are by being stupid. The idea is precisely to make much of these fussy little points about unimportant aspects of public law and policy, in order to create in the public mind the very idea that you have just put forth."

"Yes, but how can I know that you are right? It sounds like a convoluted way of making something simple and straightforward into something sinister and complex."

"It is at such times as these that we must turn to the facts, Ifford, and draw our conclusions from them. I have got a copy of the Constitution in my room. I can show you where it says that no state shall make anything but gold or silver coin a tender in payment of debts. Article 1, Section 10, I think it is. This means that use of the fiat currency - those Federal Reserve Notes you've got in your wallet – by the several states is un-Constitutional. But where do you see that mentioned in any of the mainstream media, or in any textbook in use in any major school at any level?

"And all of this giving of legal precedence to international treaties over the Constitution is un-Constitutional. I can show you the section that says so, in plain language. They're giving the country away, man! In joining this super-sovereign world state, this country is handing over the keys to the castle! Control over its monies, its military, its vast territory, its immensely valuable infrastructure - and control over all of its citizens. And yet, as regards something as monumentally important as that, involving a total loss of legal sovereignty, and of course of the Constitution itself – have you ever heard about that on the nightly news, or from any of your professors in any of your classes?

"The income tax - that's un-Constitutional, for several reasons, which perhaps we'll have time to go into this coming Friday at The Denouement. Basically, the Constitution permits only two types of taxation, a head tax or an excise tax."

"The Denouement? "

"Yes, didn't I tell you? We're meeting there instead of at The Ragged Edge again. Torvald likes the music there better, and thinks you will too. They play more classical music, and ambient and electronic – and not quite so loud. Anyway, basically, the Constitution allows only excise taxes - on items for resale, that is, you know - and poll or head taxes - as when, say, the government, needing to wage and finance a defensive war, bills the states for so much per state citizen. But have you ever seen that issue raised in any of the MSM – the mainstream media? Or for that matter, in that class in Constitutional Law that you just took? And it pretty much goes without saying that the founders of the country did not believe in empire building, wars of aggression, pre-emptive strikes, that sort of thing – like this so-called 'war' in Iraq.

"And the Federal Reserve System itself - it's unconstitutional too, according to a Supreme Court Decision of 1935 which holds that Congress cannot delegate its constitutionally mandated powers and responsibilities – as for instance, to coin money - the founders never gave government the right to CREATE money - to a cartel of private bankers wearing the cloak of a government organization. But try to write a letter pointing that out to the editor of any major newspaper or new magazine, and see if it gets published - what should be headline news, the subject of a front page article, if the media, the so-called Fourth Estate, were really such zealous guardians of the rights of the people as guaranteed, supposedly, in the Constitution.

"Really, Ifford - there are so many unconstitutional institutions and practices and purported 'laws' out there today, perpetrated by this government that calls itself 'constitutional,' that one could write a book

109

just on that. It is not constitutional for government to require of the people a license or permit before they travel, called a driver's license, or before they work - called an SSN. It is not constitutional for the government to intrude on the people's privacy in any way - by regulating them in their everyday lives, or by taxing them on their labor, or their private property, such as their homes. In fact, it is not constitutional for the federal government to create law and exercise the police powers within the several states! It is a usurpation of the lawful powers, under original jurisdiction, of the several states – of the states' exercise of the police powers which is stipulated in the Constitution to be, outside of the District of Columbia and the Territories, the sole prerogative and within the legal domain of the state governments. It was supposed to be strictly hands off for the federal government, as regards law enforcement in the states. And this is not theory, understand, but a matter of history that is not disputed – just hardly ever discussed – buried long and deep under a blanket of silence."

The lizard paused here, perhaps to catch his breath, and to give me a chance to speak. But as I, feeling rather overwhelmed by the verbal deluge, remained silent, he surged on.

"These are very major issues, Ifford - vastly more important, I'd wager, to the welfare of the people and their nation than that little bitty whatever it was you read about in the paper last week. These larger, foundational issues are carefully not mentioned. Especially banking and money issues are not mentioned, at least none that reveal facts damaging to the current power structure. In fact, we're talking about the cornerstones of this edifice the power elite have erected - this secret, *sub rosa*, not-for-public-consumption set of rules, policies, and administrative procedures by which this country is really run - these major and blatant violations of the contract between the people and their government - the very purpose of which contract is to *prevent* such usurpations, to *limit* the powers of government. These facts of modern government functioning and practice – subversive of and diametrically opposed to the Constitution and the intent of the founders – these aspects of the current government which I have been telling you about, you will never see written about in the print media or discussed on the radio or TV - or in the halls of academe, from kindergarten on up. Or adjudicated in the courts according to a strict, and honest, interpretation of the Constitution, of original jurisdiction. I can guarantee you that. And, very interestingly, there are those revisionist legal researchers who claim that this curious fact is explained by their theory – or discovery, as they see it - that in fact a parallel, extra-

110

Constitutional jurisdiction has been created, and has long been functioning, and that all of the so-called 'U.S.citizens' are under it now – brought into it by receiving BPOs from the *de facto* government – which is not the *de jure*, original government of the founders. Another thing, by the way, that I am dying to learn more about. Sounds super-interesting."

I was in over my head again. He paused again, as if to give the other party a chance to interject an intelligent comment or question, but the other party - unfortunate I - could think of nothing and was reduced to toying with the coffee spoon, wearing the while what I hoped was an expression indicative of sober consideration of the verbal torrent - which I thought, if it could only somehow be harnessed, might provide a cheap source of energy.

Finally, to break the silence, I asked, "BPOs? What in heaven's name are BPOs?"

And Rantor, of course, was only too glad to tell me. Like the relentless force of nature he was or so closely resembled, he again subjected me to a verbal torrent, carrying me, bobbing willy-nilly on its surface, once more rapidly along, to some secret inner sanctum of knowledge, known, it seemed, only to himself and Torvald.

"Benefits, privileges, and opportunities, Ifford. Like licenses and permits, and unemployment insurance and other forms of welfare. The idea is that when people apply for and accept these things from the government, they are legally considered to have – though they don't know this of course – *voluntarily* entered into a separate, extra- or non-Constitutional jurisdiction, where a whole different set of laws operates. It is an interesting theory, one that would account for the blatant unconstitutionality of the government as it is now constituted - and one, as I say, that I want to learn more about."

"Isn't there a book about it? Can't you just read about it?"

"I don't think so. Maybe something privately published – or available online. The research is quite recent, from what I gather - and on-going. Work in progress and breaking news, you might say. Most of it, from what I've been able to piece together, being conducted by fundamentalist Christians of the most intense variety. But you don't have to embrace their religious beliefs in order to consider their historical, political, and legal researches. But anyway, when you scratch the surface, Ifford, just barely scratch the surface of this Disney version presented by the mainstream media, major incongruities well up like blood from a wound, and you notice overwhelmingly that the sound and the picture, the rhetoric and the reality, don't, do not, match.

"Look at the way the standard of living has been declining here in this country for the past several decades. If you think about it for a minute, you realize that, one, it is – though a subject conspicuously avoided by the MSM, the mainstream media - definitely newsworthy, and, two, that on the face of it, there is no reason that that should be happening. All the advances in technology in the last century and a half should have brought about steady and substantial increases in the standard of living of the workers who are employing the technology - not just for the owners of capital, but for labor as well, in any fair division of the spoils – of the profits of production, I mean.

"That's why we're always talking about the Federal Reserve System, by the way - The Fed is a device, a means whereby, a mechanism for carrying out an invisible, systematic, orderly, on-going plunder of Labor – of the workers. In fact, here is a short-hand definition of central banks that is totally accurate, although of course totally at variance with all the hype, and with what is taught in econ classes from the lowest levels on up - and here the lizard rolled his eyes heavenward and recited as if from memory – *Central banks are engines for the covert transfer of wealth, FROM labor, and all whose wealth, such as it is, is denominated in the intrinsically worthless fiat currency - FRNs, or Federal Reserve Notes here - TO capital - to those whose wealth is largely denominated in tangibles such as factories, land, infrastructure, and precious metals.*"

Hadn't he and his pal already covered this ground?

"By the way," he added, "I am by no means Marxist, but these terms - Labor, Capital - are useful, is why I employ them. And also it is relevant here to point out that for most of the working people, their labor is their chief – in many cases, and increasingly – their only – wealth … and that the value of labor, here in this country is and has long been denominated in FRNs. The workers have no choice in the matter."

"You're saying, then, that as the value of the FRN depreciates due to its over-issue, the standard of living is falling here in this country?" I asked.

"Yes. It is. It is readily apparent - especially to the struggling poor - that people are working more and longer hours for less real income. The gains in wages fought for, over a hundred years ago by the labor movement, are being quietly eroded. Not by accident, of course. It is the age-old struggle between Capital and Labor over the profits of production - and who shall get how much. When you look at the plight of workers in the Third World today, and hark back to the conditions in the sweat shops of the late 19th and early 20th Centuries, you see that Capital, historically, wants as much as it can get of the profits of production and doesn't give a tinker's damn about the sufferings of the workers. But here it is very important to mention that big government makes this rape of the worker possible – big government with its cronyism, its corporate welfare, its many - ultimately, pro-big business – tinkerings and interferences with the functioning of the free market.

"Of course you don't see this important fact - the decline in the standard of living - mentioned in the MSM. Exhaustion of resources has been alluded to as a future possibility, but is not yet a factor which could account for the present on-going decline in the general standard of living. And the rich aren't experiencing any mysterious, gradual reversal of their fortunes. Just the opposite is the case, in fact - I read recently that just 2% of the world population now owns over 50% of the world's wealth. The middle class is shrinking, and the poor are becoming poorer, and more numerous, such that, here in this country, an increasing number of those at the bottom of the wage scale, and even up into the middle class, although they work - increasingly, and out of necessity, the mother and father both, and each, often, at more than one full-time job - can't even afford the basic necessities of life, such as food, clothing, shelter, transportation, and medical care for themselves and their children. Witness the rise in homelessness, not just among alcoholics and drug users, but of families, and the working poor. Increasingly, people can't afford something so basic as shelter – a roof over their heads. I would imagine that, if this on-going impoverishment of the masses continues, the time could come when, as in India today, entire families here in this country live on the streets all their lives, are born there and die there, and that sleeping rooms are rented out in eight or twelve hour segments."

I didn't know what to say to this outpouring. For one thing, it was, again, so much information, delivered so rapidly, that it was hard to keep up with it all. Feeling quite overwhelmed, I shrugged the shoulders and raised the eyebrows in a sort of involuntary gesture, as if to say - well, I'm not sure what. Certainly not 'who cares,' which I think it might have looked like to Rantor, for a brief frown rumpled his visage, and he emitted what sounded like a very *sotto voce* growl - a fascinating sound which worked wonderfully to capture the wandering attention. Actually, he had me on the point of begging for mercy. Demands were being placed upon the mental apparatus which exceeded factory specifications; in a word, I felt frazzled, used up, and badly in need of a break.

But Rantor, himself deeply interested in what he was saying, seemed to have forgotten Ifford. He seemed to be developing new material as he spoke, and these new thoughts totally engrossed him. He wore the pleased and interested expression of one who has just spied what looks to be a ten dollar bill lying in his path.

"What gets me is that someone like this Lax Learner, whoever he is, can say some pretty straightforward things about Power, and its self-seeking agendas and ruthless methods, in an introduction to a book which was written about the time of the Renaissance and which brilliantly delineates Power's classic objectives and methods; but then he can end up with some mealy-mouthed and vague and faintly noble-sounding mush for the mushy-minded, sort of like putting it all together for those who cannot or will not exert themselves to do that for themselves - and that soft-minded bit of wishy-washy philosophizing, because it comes at the end, is what people walk away with. The general effect being more or less, that was then, this is now, I'm sure glad I didn't live back then, and things are all better now because we're living in a democracy, and I wonder what's on the tube.

"Listen to this, Ifford. Just listen to how Learner ends his introductory essay. Think both about what he actually says, and the vague impression, or sense of things, that he leaves you with."

 He picked up the little book and leafed through it until he found the passage he was seeking, which he then proceeded to read to me, editorializing freely throughout.

" *'Machiavelli sought to distinguish the realm of what ought to be and the realm of what is. He rejected the first for the second. But there is a third realm: the realm of what can be. It is in that realm that what one might call a humanist realism can lie. The measure of man is his ability to extend this sphere of the socially possible. We can start with our democratic values, and we can start also with Machiavelli's realism about tough-minded methods.'*

114

" Notice here, Ifford, that he seems to be suggesting, or implying, that a claimed, or alleged, idealistic, populist end justifies brutal, deceptive – Machiavellian - means. A favorite argument of the seizers of total power, of dictators, by the way. Though it's hard to figure out just what Lerner *is* trying to say here.

" '*To be realistic about methods in the politics of a democracy at home does not mean that you throw away all scruples, or accept the superior force of 'reason of the state,' or embrace the police state crushing of constitutional liberties.*' Then what exactly does it mean, Lerner?

" '*To be realistic about the massing of power abroad in the economic and ideological struggle for the support of men and women throughout the world does not mean that you abandon the struggle for peace and for a constitutional imperium that can grow into a world republic.*'

"Is he saying here that it is fine and dandy to amass power abroad, because we are doing so for a noble cause? If so, recall, Ifford, that big, powerful government is, historically, never, ever populist government.

" '*We may yet find that an effective pursuit of democratic values is possible within the scope of a strong social-welfare state and an unsentimental realism about human motives.*'

"Again, just exactly what is he saying here? Certainly he is implying that big government, and socialism, are not incompatible with populist government, which as I have said more than once, the record of history flatly and unequivocally refutes.

"I hope I'm not loosing you, Ifford ..." He had apparently finally registered the mutely pleading gaze, the glazed and fevered look, and the nervous tic in my left eyelid that sometimes manifests when I am, for one reason or another, feeling cornered, and at the end of my rope.

"Please hang in there," the reptile continued, rather imploringly. "I've gone on longer than I'd intended, but I just want to finish this thought. Let's just briefly analyze this concluding paragraph to what I thought was really a rather good and informative introduction to a work intensely relevant to the modern world - relevant in the sense that the men in power - here, today - are guided by principles and employ methods like these, like Machiavelli delineates in *The Prince* and *The Discourses*, I mean.

"So - in this last paragraph of Learner's, this - hopelessly vague as it is, when you really look at it, as to its actual meaning, what it is actually saying - this sermonette on socialism and the paternalistic state, and the New World Order and the end justifying the means - notice the approving references to 'a world republic' and 'a strong social welfare state' - all of the concrete fact and analysis of the earlier part of his essay is gone, along with most of the detached objectivity. The tone becomes preachy in a high-minded, pre-election speech-to-the-voters kind of way. You can almost hear the faint organ music in the background, and see the diffuse-focus, heart-warming family-togetherness scenes rolling by as in a TV commercial for one of the mega-corporations, or the subcutaneous ID-chip, or our public duty to 'rat on a rat' and report neighbors who might be harboring terrorists, or even just to be sympathetic to them. You feel a catch in your throat. Your emotions are being appealed to, albeit in a low-key, dignified, intellectual sort of way, and by one whose credentials are impeccable. But you don't really consciously realize it, and one reason is that you don't want to realize it.

"As by a work of art, we have been brought to a point of feeling, we hover on the brink of a little catharsis, and we want it. And these are among the better class of feelings, with which it is, you might say, morally ennobling to mingle - high-minded, hopeful feelings about the greater good of all mankind. We can all use a few of those. And it *is* helpful to be cued in by this obviously very intelligent and knowledgeable man, who has such dignity and writes so well, regarding what to think - this modern world is, after all, so confusing - not only what to think about Machiavelli but also about our own world, today. When you try to pin it down, Learner seem to be implying that what we have today by way of government is some sort of noble experiment in socialism and a new world order, a new global government that is trying to be born, one which might use Machiavellian methods, but only for the most noble of causes, one perhaps beset by grave difficulties - some of those forces 'outside/over there/back then' that we were talking about - but morally grounded, proceeding as an expression of the will of 'men and women throughout the world' - the masses - hey, that's us, folks! - and, well, not doing too badly, he seems to be suggesting.

"And this guy Learner, whoever he is, some professor somewhere whose field of expertise this is, is obviously far more learned in these matters than you or I; we're doing well just to have gotten through his introduction and between you and me, we may not even read the book, just leaf through it, since it is kind of boring, and not too relevant to the here and now, and since we pretty much know from this excellent introduction what it says, and what to think and say about it, when we're talking with - and trying to impress - our intellectual friends."

And here this biological heir of the dinosaurs stopped. It seemed that he was, at last, a spent force – had finally said every last thing he could, for now, dredge up to say on these many subjects and issues. Glancing down, I quickly surveyed the person and noticed that, externally at least, I had apparently survived the prolonged onslaught and was still intact. Furthermore, as I say, it appeared that the fellow had finished his impassioned monologue. I let out the breath in a long sigh and cautiously relaxed a bit, basking in the silence.

Goodness! I hadn't known that Rantor had it in him. To be honest, I had always regarded him as a sort of brute - perhaps lately as a more amiable brute, but still as being of that somewhat sub-mental type in which enthusiasm may abound but brains are in short supply. I now felt forced to revise my estimate and acknowledge that such was not the case. I hadn't been able to absorb all of that verbal effusion on the first go-round, but the overall effect was quite impressive, and I was glad I wasn't this Learner fellow and had never expressed any admiration for him in Rantor's presence.

Rantor, breathing heavily, and beaded with sweat about the brow and upper lip, downed a manly gulp of the caffeinated and impaled me with his gaze. His tail, during this passionate book-length outpouring, had wound itself all around the ladder-back of his chair. The effect was rather that of a python attempting to compress and squeeze the life out of an abacus preparatory to engulfing it, and I wondered if he was going to be able to disentangle himself. I hoped it would not be necessary to summon the fire department.

The saurian seemed to be tensely awaiting some response from Ifford, so I amassed the faculties and produced what I hoped was the desired item, or at least a near relation of same.

"It seems," said I, "That your ancestors were not merely idling away their time, during those untold eons spent lolling about soaking up the rays on various flat warm rocks in sundry remote corners of the Universe – not intending to cast any aspersions on your planet of origin, you understand. They were obviously engaged in mental exercises. That, my dear Rantor, was a most impressive performance, a

117

veritable *tour de force*, and I would like to be the first to offer - or is it proffer? - my sincere congratulations and encomiums. Bravo and well said."

"Well, thanks, but - what'd you think about it - content-wise, I mean? Did any of it make any sense to you?"

Content-wise?

"Rantor," I began haltingly, not knowing quite how to break it to him, "I fear you may find me an object lesson in frustration, a sort of a null set, a personal nemesis, and that you may be barking up the wrong tree and casting your pearls before swine. You see, I seem to lack the evaluative faculty. My personal theory is that I was simply born without one. Perhaps, as a mere blob of protoplasm – or perhaps even earlier in my career, somehow - I was genetically tinkered with, to produce this effect. Be that as it may, the nub, the essence, the main item, is that, for me, things neither resonate, nor fail to resonate. They just are. All ideas, to Ifford are just ideas. Equal members of a populous set. He has no favorites. He is incapable of choosing between or getting worked up about any of them."

"But, he - I mean, you - have certain things you believe to be true, don't you?"

"It is difficult to explain. My beliefs and I have this no-fault, hold-harmless, open marriage sort of relationship. It's very loose. I'm not always sure what they're up to and vice versa. I am a sort of cynic *sans* the bitterness. It seems that I am as near as you may ever again encounter to your polar opposite. You are all emotion, and passionate conviction. I am capable of neither. I merely exist, doing what I must and trying to keep out of harm's way. Detached - that's the word I was searching for. I am very, very detached."

"It sounds like - an affliction."

"Perhaps. Perhaps I am a sort of an *homme manque*. An entity *manqué*, I mean, of course. Perhaps it is all very sad. I really don't know. But now, at any rate, my secret is out. You know that I am a very tough nut to crack. Forewarned is forearmed." (I was hoping, of course, that the fellow would catch the unstated implications here to the effect that he was simply wasting his breath on me and should seek another victim.)

That eager look which animates his features when he has something he burns to impart was once again assembling itself on his scaly, rust-colored visage. Hastily, before he could launch himself yet again, I continued, "And now, my dear Saurian, I am off to bed. For it has indeed grown late, hasn't it, as we have chatted away the evening. Congratulations again on that most impressively improvised aria. When the juices get flowing, you are obviously capable of great things. Who knows to what heights you may not attain, God willing and the crick don't rise, as they say. Personally, I expect great things of you. Good night; may flights of angels sing thee to thy rest, and may the gods personally supervise thy slumbers."

And having thus, I hoped, dispensed the *bonhomie* in amounts more than ample to meet the requirements of the present exigency, I tottered off, with a sort of exhausted dignity, to the welcome privacy of the boudoir, planning to massage the brain while chanting a restorative mantra or two and then, perhaps, simply huddling in the fetal position while letting the mind wander without, absolutely without purpose, and to no drumbeat but its own. I was feeling somewhat ravaged, although I didn't hold it against the fellow, realizing that he could not help himself.

CHAPTER 13: FROM CONSTITUTIONAL REPUBLIC TO CORPORATE STATE AT BURGER BLISS

Communism is the tool by which Britain's international finance is knocking down national governments in the interest of world government, world police, and world currency.

From a speech by Nicholas Murry Butler, then president of Columbia University, at the Carnegie Endowment for International peace, Lord Cecil Luncheon at the Hotel Astor, November 19, 1937

This business with Squinchwell was naturally much on my mind during the days that followed, though not to the extent that might be expected. I have, you see, a certain capacity to distance myself from my distresses. I am not sure exactly how I do it; it seems to be a sort of a muffling process, which, though it does not work perfectly - the protective shield seems never to be up, for example, when I awaken in the middle of the night, or first thing in the morning, at which times raw fear can grip me most unpleasantly - is at least operative much of the time and provides welcome intervals of respite during those times, as now, when dread, nameless or otherwise, gnaws at the entrails.

A moment's reflection here leads me posit that it - dread, I mean - is always, to a greater or lesser extent, loitering in my vicinity, but perhaps it is only my present mood which makes me feel that way. One thing I know - the dreadless moments seem to come my way, particularly of late, with less frequency than the dreadful. I am reminded here, too, of that well-known maxim of Thoreau's that most men lead lives of quiet desperation. I have always wondered to what extent this is actually true – of humanish beings generally, I mean, of course. It seems that most entities have their pride and would not admit it, even if it were true. Not even to be able to be happy, even a little, seems a humiliation, an admission of defeat.

On Friday, Glennie and I had our usual agreement to meet for lunch at Burger Bliss after our classes, although I myself was wearying of all those greasy burgers and turgid chocolate malteds, compounded as they doubtless were more of synthetic chemicals and genetically altered ingredients than of any actual food, in the original and time-honored sense of the word, and even tiring of the naive music, excellent though the best of it undoubtedly is, and was thinking of suggesting to Glennie that we find another hang-out. I, for instance, am fond of Italian food. Though I cannot stand accordion music.

This entire '50s thing, at least as regards décor and food, was beginning to wear a bit thin for me, in fact, and I had, piece by piece, been getting rid of some of the more egregious items that festooned the living quarters. That very morning, for instance, I had, upon leaving the rooms for my first class, surreptitiously placed an authentic (purportedly, but I had always had my doubts) signed and framed portrait of Ricky Nelson and a somewhat battered but still working (most of the time - it seems to have a loose connection somewhere) lava lamp beside a trash can, where, I thought - who knows - some impoverished aficionado might discover them and gladly bear them homeward. He might even be able to figure out what's wrong with the lamp, if he is at all handy, or has any sort of background in electronics.

Though I had much of a personal nature that I was burning to discuss - Squinch, and the cash I had found on the street for starters - Glennie, as is usually the case, got the verbal jump on me, hardly waiting for me to sit down in the padded booth before launching into a detailed account of her latest informational find. I seem increasingly to be beset from every quarter by monologuists, raconteurs, and frustrated pedagogues. It has led me to wonder as to the exact nature of the particular karmic debt I am discharging. Did I, in some past life, bind innocent women and children hand and foot and then talk them to death, rambling on endlessly while turning a deaf ear to their shrieks of agony and pleas for mercy? Or had I merely been an extremely boring, long-winded, and long-lived lecturer on some exceedingly dry required subject at some humorless bureaucracy of higher hoop-jumping somewhere in the dusty back-waters of time and space? Whatever the case had been, I wished at times that there were a way I could just repent and have done with it - some kind of a lump-sum settlement. But then perhaps that was what this present incarnation was. A dreadful thought.

Glennie's enthusiasm this week derived not from a conversation with Jacko, but from a couple of tapes that it seems Rantor had let her borrow. I had not known that they were in any kind of contact outside of our meetings together, but I let it pass, not wanting to seem hyper-vigilant, possessive, unduly preoccupied with her doings, or anything along those lines. As previously touched upon, she has become, since taking that psych class, of an intensely analytical bent when it comes to

121

her old pal Ifford, and I had learned to tread rather carefully. Being analyzed all the time is fine at first, but it rather wears on one.

"I really want you to listen to this tape, Iffy," she said, waggling a cassette before me as I slid into the padded booth. "It's one of the best things I've come across in a long time. I even listened to it all the way through a second time."

"Just so long as it's not about the Federal Reserve System," I said. And I meant it, too.

"Don't worry, it's not," she said. "Or only a little bit. *Collectivism: Its True Agendas* does make passing mention of a central bank as being one of the planks of the Communist Manifesto or whatever its called - central banking and also a progressive income tax, and it's -"

"Refresh me here, if you don't mind. Collectivism, again, is ...?"

"You know - socialism, Communism, Marxism ... wealth transfer schemes under the direction of the government, and also government control of production, and prices, and so forth."

"Yes, of course. How could I forget. Rantor was just talking to me about all of that. At great length. The omniscient philanthropic modern state. From each according to his ability, to each according to his need. The greatest good for the greatest number. The wisest and most humane use of the means of production, as dictated and overseen by a paternalistic government. Profit-seeking as the source of all social ills. The Fabian Society and so on. Idealistic and populist, with all the stops pulled out. Right?"

"Yes ... except that this tape presents that movement less favorably - as being not quite so idealistic and populist as its promoters claim it to be, and as most of its adherents and boosters hope, or hoped, it would be."

"Hmmmm?" I badly wanted to bare the soul in re these personal matters that were troubling the mind and dampening the joyful spirit, but I knew she needed to get this off her chest first. Glennie is a great enthusiast. "Tell on, old chum ..."

"Well, first let me mention the other thing I wanted to tell you about. Have you heard of the C.A.F.R.?"

"Actually, not that I recall ... oh, yes ... it has to do with financial reporting, doesn't in - book-keeping, something like that? I recall something from that accounting class I had to take last year - remember the one I was always groaning to you about? That I just by the skin of my teeth managed to pull a 'B' in?"

"Yes - it stands for Comprehensive Annual Financial Report. There's this guy named Valdemar Hadrian who has a background in business and accounting, and he claims that most of the local governments here in the USA have undisclosed funds - invested undisclosed funds - in the millions, actually."

"By 'local governments,' you mean ...?"

"State, city, county - like that. He says this has been going on for years now, decades actually, and that a person can easily check it out, in his or her local area."

"I thought that all of these various governments were required to make some sort of annual disclosure of their financial condition, for the year past, and a projection of anticipated needs for the year to come. And that typically, of course, the projections for the year to come indicate that projected outgo exceeds projected income by a hefty amount and that thus more taxation will be needed or the sky will fall ... so, how can what this Hadrian fellow is saying possibly be true, Glennie?"

"Well, you're right about the annual reports. But Hadrian says that the governments only make public a *partial* account of their financial situation. What they release is true ... as far as it goes. They publish the part about next year's projected taxes not meeting next year's projected expenditures ... but they leave out the part of the CAFR that tells about all the public monies that they have invested - and the yearly incomes these investments are earning. Which in most cases is a lot, more than enough to meet public expenses for the coming fiscal year. Hadrian says that if the full truth were known, for the most part additional taxation would be for the most part unnecessary. And that this deception is sort of the local governments' on-going 'bilk the cash-cow public' operation that could be seen as analogous to the federal government's central banking 'bilk the cash cow public' operation."

"Why doesn't he alert the media, then? Public radio and TV, for instance? They'd go to town with this, wouldn't they?"

"Ifford. He did. He tried and tried. I keep telling you that public radio and public TV are *faux* alternative or free information sources - to help keep alive in people's minds the belief that they do have free, uncontrolled information delivery services here. Hadrian says that *all* the major media have access to this information, to the yearly CAFRs ... that they know all about it. But mum's the word. They're in on the deal."

"Interesting, Glennie, definitely interesting, and you will have to run it by Rantor and Torvald; perhaps you can teach them a thing or two. But you know, Yours Truly is feeling distinctly bombarded, of late, with information ..."

"Well, maybe some evening I could bring it over for us to listen to. Rantor and Torvald too, maybe. I'd make spaghetti, and we could have garlic bread, and red wine, and a salad ... it would be my treat ..."

Glennie is not much of a cook, but she does make tasty spaghetti marinara. And she knows my fondness for good food.

"That sounds nice, Glennie. I'd like that. But, you know, I have a bit of news of my own."

"I want to hear it, Iffy, of course I do ... but I have all this stuff on collectivism right on the tip of my tongue ... I'm afraid I might leave out something important if I don't tell you now. I was just listening to the tape last night. It is so fascinating, Ifford, really. There's this guy named Frederik Hayek ... have you ever heard of him, in any of your classes or anything?"

"The name does not ring a bell. If he is a critic of socialism, I would imagine that he is *persona non grata* here at the Otto von Bismarck School."

"His critiques of collectivism are so subtle, and thorough. But this tape only in passing mentions Hayek. I don't actually remember who the main sources were, but the analysis kind of stands logically. All you need to do is think about it. You know how collectivism, broadly speaking, is considered to be a wealth-transfer scheme to counter, or remedy, the tendency for the profits of production to accumulate in the hands of a few capitalists while most of the workers exist in some degree of poverty ..."

"Yes - the great white hope of the unwashed masses and all that. Well, it seems not to be working quite as well in that regard as expected, but still I'd hate to imagine the worlds without it."

"Well, Iffy, according to this tape Rantor lent me, collectivism is actually something that ultimately works not to the *detriment* but rather to the *benefit* of the big corporate and financial interests - what Marx called Capital - at the expense of the people - Labor, in Marxian terms - in many ways."

Rantor had just been saying something to that effect, as I recalled. He had said so much about so many issues, that it was hard to recall. But it just did not wash with me, and I told her so. "Tut tut! Come now! How could that be? That is nothing if not counter-intuitive, Glennie. We know that the big interests always howl and shriek like souls in hell at the mere mention of collectivism in any way, shape, or form ... and that the poor, and the idealistic and reform-minded intelligentsia, are always all for it. *Quod erat demonstrandum* - right? *Ipso facto* and all that? I am not convinced, Glennie, that Rantor is all that sound. A force of nature, yes, but I am not sure I would trust his advice on investing in the stock market. These enthusiastic types, you know ... leap in where angels fear to tread. Trigger-happy types. And then, he seems to be utterly under Torvald's spell, as you may have noticed ..."

"Well, just hear me out, Iffy. And just, you know, try to keep an open mind while I attempt to summarize the main points on the tape for you."

"That willing suspension of disbelief that Torvald was requisitioning?"

"Exactly. You see, this great sounding, high-minded idea of transferring government-confiscated wealth to the needy actually, sneakily, provides a rationale for doing a lot of things that in the long run benefit the financial elites, the power barons, and work against the interests of the masses, the workers. You yourself admitted that collectivism seems not to have lived up to its hype."

"All right. Got that. Nothing's perfect, of course - but, for the sake of argument and all that, just what are some of these negative consequences of collectivism, from the point of view of the toiling masses?"

"Well, first of all, collectivism provides a plausible rationale for BIG government - because if government is going to be the one confiscating and re-distributing all that wealth, it's going to get a lot bigger - right? Its functions have been significantly enlarged. A swollen bureaucracy. Enhanced police powers, to do the collecting from the reluctant. And of course, it legitimizes intrusions into the individual's privacy – privacy supposedly guaranteed by the Bill of Rights. A foot in the door, so to speak, in that regard. So what's wrong with that, you might ask? Well - just that *all* the evidence of history is conclusive that big government is *never, ever* populist government - just like Jefferson and all of them said back at the time of the formation of this country, when it rebelled against England. And not only does collectivism increase government's size - it also increases government's powers. For one thing, it necessitates increased police powers, to do the collecting by force from those individuals reluctant to go along with the program and, you know ..."

"Yield their substance, the fruits of their labors, willingly up to the State?" This indeed was just what - or a part of what - Rantor had been haranguing me about so recently.

"Right. And, collectivism attacks the very notion of private property – the foundational principle of personal freedom and private rights, by the way - by giving government the right by law to use its *monopoly on the legal right to the use of force* to confiscate private property. It provides a plausible, noble-sounding rationale for that confiscation. It also attacks the right of people to be private in their personal papers and doings - as long as they are not corporations - business entities, you know - because of course, even in a non- or pre-collectivist state, government does traditionally have the right and duty to regulate commerce in the public interest. And corporations do not have rights. Only people have rights. And under the original government put in place here after there Revolutionary War, government had no legal right to tax the earnings - the labor, essentially - of private citizens; actually it had no right to intrude into their lives in any way as long as they had not broken any laws by violating the rights of others."

"No harm, no foul ..."

"Yeah. So: collectivism attacks the concept and the reality of private property; it greatly extends government's powers over people in their private lives; it works to creates a large, powerful centralized government; and, it creates a whole new class of crimes."

Here, she pausing for a breather, and a lusty sip of her Chocolicious shake, I took the opportunity to get a word in. She can go on and on, when she gets worked up, you know. I was hoping she might be finished so I could tell her about Squich.

"That is on the debit side of the ledger, of course. We must look at the benefits as well, though, wouldn't you agree? But, as to this tape you listened to - does that about sum it up? Or is there more?"

"Oh, there's more. You see, collectivism both *neutralizes* the idealistic, reform-minded, watchdog intelligentsia, by convincing them that the wrongs of society are being righted, at least to some extent, and it assuages the ire of the lower classes, while using government's monopoly on the legal right to the use of force to extort property from the middle classes - or did I already say that? Anyway, it also has the effect of drawing the lower and middle classes - you know, the proletariat and the bourgeoisie? - into conflict and at each other's throats and *believing that one another is the enemy*, thus drawing interest and attention and blame for the economic ills of the masses, the lower and middle classes alike, away from the true authors of that economic distress – the true authors being, of course, the monopolistic banking and corporate interests at the very top of the financial pecking order. Which financial interests are also the true beneficiaries, in subtle and difficult-to-trace ways, of socialism and collectivism generally. Like I said before, history shows us that big government is invariably corrupt government – government of cronyism, political favors bought and sold, and corporate welfare. That sort of thing. The good old boy network."

She paused again to take a bite of her burger and another slurp of her shake, along with a chaser of ketchup-dipped fries. Glennie is a great eater but, like self, and hybrids generally, never seems to put on weight. On her, the slenderness looks very good. I think that is one of the reasons her - prototype, I guess you could say, or ancestor - was selected for cloning. I think I have mentioned Glennie's beautiful eyes - and her very pleasant personality, generally speaking - as long as you can steer her away from these youthful enthusiasms.

"Well, Glennie, I will have to give all this some thought. It certainly is thinking outside the box, I'll give it that. But ..."

"Oh, Iffy, I don't mean to hog the conversation [!] but just let me finish, OK? - before I forget this last part I wanted to tell you about ...

127

I'm almost done, honest ... according to the tape, the big money interests have long known that government is for rent or lease if not for sale, to the highest bidder, you know - and thus they favor big government. They're all for it. If they pay for the tool they want it to be the most powerful tool possible. Makes sense - right? You see, Iffy, the founding fathers here in this country knew this and the people would know it too, if they were being taught the truth in the schools. So collectivism, ingeniously, provides a *plausible rationale* - and creates a plausible ostensibly populist 'need') - for big government - to do all this collecting and redistributing of wealth."

"I think you said that already."

"Did I. I'm sorry if I'm repeating myself. But also, Iffy - fascism, just like Mussolini said, is nothing at bottom but *big money and big government in bed together*, with the former controlling the latter. Oh, and another really interesting thing the tape said is that it is incorrect to visualize the left on one end of the political spectrum and the right on the other end with 'democracy' in between. The founding fathers, by the way, aware of the dangers of big government, created this country as a democratic *republic* of carefully limited powers, rather than a democracy - the idea being to have elected representatives stand as judicious guardians of individual rights and freedoms - and to avoid mob rule - to prevent the majority from using their votes unwisely – such as, for instance, one numerically superior group voting themselves government money, or other abuses. Just as, for instance, in collectivism, where the numerically numerous poor clamor for various types of welfare, at the expense of the middle class. As I said, the proles and the bourgeoisie played against each other. Thesis/anti-thesis/synthesis – the Hegelian Dialectic."

Say what? Whatever it was, this Hegelian Dialectic, I didn't want to hear about it right now, having suffered long enough for one afternoon, and I craftily resorted to a diversionary tactic, guiding her into what I hoped would be a briefer exegesis. "So how does this tape say we would more accurately define and contrast the types of government, then?"

"It says that the more accurate set of governmental opposites or antitheses is not left and right but big versus small government. Fascism and collectivism - you know, socialism and communism - are not antithetical; just as in this country now, both putative 'left' and 'right' are big government. So to portray them as opposites is to set up a false dichotomy. It's misleading. The real dichotomy or set of opposites is big government versus small government. And like I said, historically, big government is *always* repressive and anti-populist, whatever its claims and PR blabber. AND - in the modern world, both so-called 'left' and 'right ' are just Joe Bleep and John Bleep - both are definitely big government, and as the legislative record shows, both keep furthering big government, and its fundamentally elitist, fascist, anti-populist programs, agendas, and legislation - the 'Republicrat' party, as they call it on the tape. And somehow, under both parties, for all of their claimed differences, the rich keep getting richer, and the poor, poorer ... are you OK, Iffy? You look sort of ... I don't know ... anguished, or something."

Well, dear Reader, I was. It was *deja vu* all over again for old Ifford. But I let it pass. "Oh, no - I'm fine. Just a touch of acid indigestion, or some such. I sometimes think we should occasionally try a different eatery."

"Yeah, maybe you're right. There's another burger place that Rantor says is lots better than Burger Bliss, and its prices are better too. And they use a healthier oil for the French fries. But anyway, to wrap it up - the Great Depression created a plausible need for government intervention by implementing collectivist 'solutions' to the extreme poverty of the Depression Era '30s. BUT - get this - the Great Depression itself was *engineered,* was brought about, by the newly created Federal Reserve System, which gives the private bankers who are the Fed the means to do precisely that, to inflate or contract the money supply at will. The Fed, like all central banks, has a monopoly on the issuance of credit and money, and hence total, or at least huge, very significant, control over the volume of 'money' in circulation. They used this control to inflate, or increase, the nation's money supply, during the 1920s. This was done, actually, in order to help Europe, and especially England, in the aftermath of World War I. The bankers wanted to raise prices here – which they did, by the simple expedient of inflating the currency – thus raising prices here, and lowering interest rates, causing investors here to buy English debt, thus moving gold from the United States to Europe.

"And, additionally," the old girl ploughed on, "The "emergency" of the Depression was used as an excuse - an 'emergency' tantamount to the emergency created by war, was the idea - to invoke broad governmental emergency powers and change the country from Constitutional Republic to its diametric opposite - a modern corporate mega-state. A guy who used to work for the Fed named Todd Wilkerson Toddly wrote a very good book on this subject called *Silent Coup, Bloodless Coup: From Constitutional Republic to Corporate State by Governmental Fiat*, according to this tape. I want to read it. And the men who had money - the big money men - made out like bandits, during the Depression, buying stocks, land, and newspapers for pennies on the dollar. So anyway - that about sums it up. Pretty interesting, don't you think? And Rantor says he has a lot of other tapes and CDs he can loan me. In fact I have one in my purse that I'm going to listen to this afternoon. You know about all the illegals that are pouring in from Mexico and burdening the schools and the social service infrastructures in the affected states?"

"Yes – one hears about it on the nightly news from time to time."

"Well, according to Jacko, the corporate elites could long ago have acted to ease the over-population problem in the developing nations by giving the people of these nations fairer wages in the corporate-owned factories and sweat shops and fairer prices for their natural resources. This would have – decades ago - raised their standard of living and automatically lowered the birthrates in those countries, because it's well known that when the standard of living in any country rises, the birth rate drops. But instead of doing the fair thing, the elites chose to go on bribing the various governments to allow them to go on economically raping the peoples of the Third World of the value of their labor and resources, thus assuring the present over-population problem, which they are choosing – as probably was the plan all along - to deal with by forcing the people of the United States and Europe – against their wishes and their best interests - to accept this influx of legal and illegal immigrants, thus forcing down wages and forcing up the cost of housing and in general stressing the infrastructure and particularly the social services infrastructure."

"Sounds like – if what you say is correct - the elites are running the world as one big plantation – their plantation."

"Exactly. The whole populist government thing is just for show. It's not for real."

"Well, Glennie," I replied, "This has been most fascinating. It does – at first glance, anyway - seem to cohere logically, and perhaps we - you and I - are being stripped of our illusions and finding out that the power elite are, here in what we have long considered to be a sort of political

Nirvana, operating under false pretenses and that the place is not all it's cracked up to be. That the sound and the picture do not match. What you say certainly does give one much to think about. Of course, it was a lot of information in one big chunk. Perhaps I could read that book you mentioned by that Toddly fellow. And listen to the tapes, of course, when I have the time. However, to move on ... I, too, have some news, and I am afraid that it is not any cheerier than yours."

CHAPTER 14: I TAKE GLENNIE INTO MY CONFIDENCE

During times of universal deceit,
telling the truth becomes a revolutionary act.

George Orwell

She urged me to tell all, which I proceeded to do. First, it was necessary for me to confess that I had been less than totally honest with her. Needing a confidante, I had decided to come clean, as the saying goes, with her on this matter of my mother. When she heard that I had tracked down my putative mother and had had several phone conversations with her, she got, in fairly rapid succession, an incredulous and then a somewhat resentful expression on her face. She actually came near to pouting, or sulking, something I had not, to the best of my memory, seen her do before. As I believe I have mentioned, Glennie has a very even disposition.

"Glennie," I said after a bit, "I'm sorry I kept it from you. It was not that I didn't trust you - honestly. It was more that I knew I was doing something that was against the rules and I didn't want my example to give you any ideas of doing some such thing with your - you know - mother, so to speak. I know how you feel about your mother, and I thought you might possibly be tempted. Also, I didn't want to make you an accomplice, a - what do you call it - an accessory after the fact, or whatever the exact legal phraseology is ..." I trailed off pleadingly. I did hate to see the old girl unhappy. And to have her unhappy with me.

Another lengthy pause, as with eyes downcast she swizzled her red and white plastic straw in her melting Chocolicious Shake, and then: "So what's your mother like?" Still a little stiff and displeased with old Ifford.

"Well, we haven't actually met, you understand. We've just talked on the phone. But she seems an intelligent person, and very practical, too, and very ... nice. A sympathetic listener. I guess she's had a pretty hard life. You see, she was extensively used as a breeder by the geneticists and planners back home, and I guess it really messed up her mind."

"Is she still being abducted?"

"Oh no. She's long past breeding age by now. They're not interested in her any more."

"Does she resent you for what happened?"

"She doesn't seem to. She says that she knows it wasn't my fault. Also, I guess I'm her only offspring that she's had any contact with or even knows about. Evidently all the forced procedures and - you know, man-handling she experienced turned her off to being touched and the whole ball of wax. She never married and never had any Earth children. She's quite alone now, from what she says."

"So, why did you choose now to tell me that you've been in contact with her, Iffy?"

Clever Glennie. I felt a flash of pride in the old girl.

"Well, Glennie ... I got a call from Ida Mae Glatz, last Monday morning it was, telling me that old Squinch wanted to see me. You know his roundabout way of talking - but it's always obvious what he's getting at. At this impromptu and unscheduled meeting he told me several things - one, unfortunately, is that I only drew a C+ in that mid-term in my banking class that I was moaning to you about last week. The one that I was afraid I hadn't done too well on. You know how I hate that class. But then he went on to say that we are forbidden to get mixed up in the politics here on *Gaia*, and that we must never under any circumstances have any contact whatsoever with our biological parents. And then this last one that just seemed a total *non sequitur*, something about how we've always got to obey all the laws on the host planet."

"Making it look like he must know about your contact with your mother ... I wonder how he found out," she mused.

"So do I. But what do you make of the reminder about the political taboo? And that bit about obeying all the laws?"

"I don't know. You're so un-political. Unless there's something else you're not telling me, Ifford ... all I can think of is - Rantor and Torvald. Although I can't imagine how Squinch could get word so quickly about your innocent -"

" And unwilling!"

133

"Yes, and unwilling involvement with their ideas ... or why it would matter to him at all. It's not like you're planning to over-throw the government or anything like that. I mean, you were just being polite, basically. It's obvious that Rantor kind of gets on your nerves, and that you're a lot less interested in their ideas and information than I am."

"Yes. Unless they are felons or belong to some cell intent on toppling the current regime or something, can there be that much harm in just a bit of talk over coffee? And are we really being watched that closely?"

"So, what are you going to do about it, Iffy? It's kind of worrying."

"Yes. I've racked my brains, but all I can think of to do is to take Rantor and Torvald into my confidence, and see what they have to say. There's no one else, really, that I can talk to about it."

We hybrids, you see, do not have the faculty of making friends easily. At least, I do not. Glennie really was about it in the friend department, unless you counted these new arrivals on the scene. And they were very dynamic and seemed brainy enough, and certainly conversant with the ways of coercive nation-states.

"Oh, but there's one more thing I almost forgot to tell you, Glennie. You're not going to believe this. After I dropped you off at your dorm last Sunday night, I swung by The Friend to pick up some snackables, and you'd never guess what happened ... I actually found a bag, just an ordinary brown paper bag, containing money! Quite a lot of money, actually - almost $350."

"What? You mean just lying on the ground? Or what?"

"Yes, like someone had dropped it - less than half a block from the store. But I didn't get a chance to look and see what was in the bag until I got home, because right when I noticed it and picked it up, these police cars came screaming down the street toward me with their lights and sirens going and I more or less panicked and stuffed the bag into my pocket and turned and walked away down a side street. You know how I am around storm troopers. And they actually did accost me, flashing their lights up and down the street I had turned onto, looking for someone, obviously, and even asked to see my ID. You can imagine how I felt. But they let me go ... and I was so shaken by it all that I didn't even remember about finding the bag until I got home. And then I found out that it contained all that money."

"Did they run a check on your ID?"

"Yes, in fact they did. First time that's ever happened to me. But it came up clean. I mean, naturally it did. I haven't even turned in a library book late, or gotten a ticket for jay-walking. Or spoken in class without raising my hand and waiting to be called on - or voiced - or even thought - any even faintly disparaging things about entities of color - or forgotten even once to floss my teeth ..."

"Well, Iffy ... since they did run a check on you ... I wonder if it got back to Squinch and that was what caused him to make his remark about always obeying all the laws here."

She had a point, and I told her so. It seemed rather dense of me, actually, not to have thought of that. I imagine our names are flagged with a request to report any encounters we may have with law enforcement to Squinch's office, or to some higher office which passes such information onto him who toils away in the trenches doing the actual grappling with the lesser minions.

Having pretty much talked ourselves out, Glennie and I sat there, more or less in brooding silence, while she finished off her food. The girl has a splendid appetite. Then, when I was thinking it about time to be shoving off, she looked at me with those great eyes of hers and asked one last question.

"Aren't you going to finish your Giganto-Burger, Iffy? Or your Chocolicious Supreme? If you're not going to finish them, or your fries, do you mind if I eat them?"

CHAPTER 15: AT THE DENOUEMENT

How dreadful knowledge of the truth can be
when there's no help in the truth.

Sophocles

Again that Friday evening it was snowing as we walked to the coffee house. All the locals were saying that so much snow was highly unusual. This time, Torvald had come to our rooms in the Warburg Hall - with no comment on the '50s decor of the place, only remarking on our excellent view of the George Herbert Walker Bush Quadrangle, and how beautiful it looked in the snow. My understanding was that he himself lived in a private room somewhere off campus, something the home planet does not allow us to do.

We three went over to pick up Glennie at her digs. As the four of us walked to The Denouement, Rantor and Glennie began cavorting like a couple of adolescent giraffes, heaving snowballs, chasing one another, splashing the stuff like water in one another's faces, and so on. Rantor revealed a new talent - the ability to write - crudely - in the snow using the tip of his tail as one might use the tip of a finger. It was a very light and dry snow, fresh-fallen, glittering in the streetlights, so dry that the snowballs exploded silently into powder upon impact, so that the two frolickers ended up with the powdery stuff all over them. Glennie looked very charming, the white snow dusting her dark coat and blonde hair, her face flushed, her large eyes very alive and merry. I thought that Rantor seemed to be good for her. I had never seen her play before. They looked funny together - Glennie so small and fair and slim, Rantor so large and dark and reptilian - beauty and the beast. Rantor complained that his tail got terribly cold in this weather; Glennie declared that she would knit him a tail-warmer, and asked if he would like it in red, white, and blue.

Privately, I doubted that she was capable of such a feat. Her roommate, who is one of those lucky hybrids who look absolutely human, only perhaps a little exotic, and who had been raised on this planet as a human, was teaching her how to knit, but Glennie seemed to lack the manual dexterity or the genetic underpinnings or something - the products of her endeavors so far had looked crude and mis-shapen, like a schoolchild's efforts. She also worked very slowly. She had brought

136

her knitting over to the rooms a couple of times, to work on while we watched a flic on the tube, and for all her determination and concentration, which were beyond reproach, the work had seemed scarcely to progress at all in an entire evening. If it ever got done, I thought, this would be a tail-warmer to write home to the old care-givers about; but it seemed to me unlikely that Rantor would be warming that remarkable extremity of his with anything knitted by Glennie, this winter at least.

Through this exuberant little snow-dance of theirs, Torvald and I strode along stolidly and for the most part unsmilingly, like a couple of bobbies on a beat, two entities grave of purpose and each weighted with a cargo of solemn thought, two tugboats plowing sturdily through the white stuff, pulling along with them wherever they went the intangible mental load. This new wrinkle in your narrator's life had indeed caused him to abandon his proscription against using the mental apparatus outside of the realms prescribed by academic necessity. However, such mental activity as occurred seemed little more than a spinning of the cerebral wheels on the slippery slopes of inevitable doom. But I did occasionally remember to remind myself of our - we hybrids, that is, of course - tendency always to see the darkest side of things and to expect the worst.

If walking through the silently falling snow, with the gaiety of the two playful ones as counterpoint to Torvald's and my own gravity, had had overtones of the dream, and somehow an almost medieval quality, like a painting by Rousseau, perhaps, then entering The Denouement, was like awakening to a Bruegelesque carnival of the crude and the frenetic - chattering voices, bright lights, and loud music - not unlike the atmosphere of rather hysterical gaiety that might have prevailed at the public hangings of by-gone days here on *Terra*.

As I was still a bit off my feed - dread gnawing at one can do that to an entity - and not up to anything sumptuous, I settled for the austerity of a strong Americano with a poignant curl of artfully carved lemon peel and a single stick of chocolate-dipped almond biscotti. Rantor had evidently told Torvald of our recent conversation, for we were scarcely seated at our table before he brought up the subject of my audience with Squinch.

Somehow, Torvald and I fell right into a rather strange sort of verbal *pas de deux* or volley. It seemed on my part at least partly to be a manifestation of the chameleon-like habit acquired in the care homes and schools of my youth, that habit of automatically shaping my thought and behavior into conformance with the mindset and expectations of those in charge - a bit, as I say, like assuming a protective coloration as a survival strategy or ploy. It also could have to do with that ego of mine, which at times seems to resemble an osmotic semi-permeable membrane rather than the sturdy all-purpose device it is supposed to be; at any rate, I have noticed myself often unconsciously aping the ego and style of whomever I am around. This personal amorphousness of your narrator's operating system manifests frequently in social situations, especially when he is under stress or feeling threatened - a sort of unconscious mirroring, perhaps, as I say, intended to placate or to curry favor. If the reader is wondering who the real Ifford Furze is, behind all the camouflage, floating boundaries, and nameless dread - well - I suppose that makes two of us. Discovering who one really is and what one really wants to do in life is not something one is exactly encouraged to do on Q'Oba'Aba'a, service to the state being what life there is all about. And it was indeed this very subject that opened our curious dialogue.

"Rantor tells me that they've apparently got you under some kind of surveillance, Ifford," was Torvald's opening volley.

"Several kinds, for all I know," I retorted. "He must have told you as well about the relationship between the individual and the State on the home planet - that it's heavily weighted in favor of the latter and so on, and that they believe - or so they tell all of us - that the only rational and workable way to structure a modern state is along these lines. Statism, I guess you call it. If not something worse."

"Yes. The political philosophy of the brain-for-hire court intellectual Hegel. And I guess Rantor put forward the idea to you that the much-vaunted freedom of the individual and sanctity of human life et cetera of this particular principality is little more than a bunch of PR hype. That in fact the country has since its inception done pretty much a 180 degree about-fact, but that the façade and rhetoric of populism are retained to disguise that fact. "

"Your burly alter ego did in fact harp again on that topic, claiming it to be fairly obvious to any astute observer that the sound and the picture no longer match. In fact, he went on to dwell at considerable length on the thesis that alleged democracies -"

"Democratic republics, of course you mean, if you are speaking of the original government of this country ..."

"Yes, yes, that democracies and/or democratic republics themselves can be, and usually do devolve into being, such in name only - are corrupted into false fronts behind which lurk the inevitable power- and money-mad aristocracy of wealth, whether recognized as such, as in the old days, or lurking behind a protective good-guy image and conspiracy of silence as of even date, if Rantor is to be believed ... that the elites in your average modern putative populist government, however styled, achieve with smoke, mirrors, and much artful manipulation of the minds of their subjects what is accomplished with more candor by sheer muscle, and the fear engendered by same, under a more overtly totalitarian regime. And so forth."

"Did he throw in that quotation from William James to the effect that people will believe any absurdity no matter how much logic and evidence contradict it, if it is repeated often enough, especially by respected sources?"

"Not William James, as I recall ... he might have mentioned Hitler's remark that big lies are actually better, because people just can't believe they could be lies ... although it could have been Glennie who quoted that one at me."

"Did he go into the whole thing about the so-called two-party system here being a sham, ditto the other alleged 'checks and balances' on the governmental powers - the impartial judiciary, the independent legislature, the vote - all in reality controlled, non-functioning, and mere window-dressing, at this point?"

"As I recall, he did not - but it would have fit right in. Perhaps you could say it was implicit. That the Constitution seems no longer - if it ever was – to be functioning as the Supreme Law of the land was touched upon. "

"Did he happen to mention jury nullification?"

Jury whatification? "I don't believe so."

"Well, that's another great idea of the founders - an additional mechanism for protecting the people from the rise of statism, fascism, totalitarianism - that has been studiously ignored and buried - tossed

139

on the rubbish heap, basically - by those who don't like having the scope of their powers in any way curtailed. The idea - and the law, as the founders created it - of jury nullification was that juries have the right - indeed, the duty - to decide in favor of a defendant, even against a law which they - the jury of the defendant's peers, that is, of course - think violates our pre-existing inalienable rights. A very good law actually. Yet another safeguard against despotism. But tossed, of course."

"We did not touch on that topic. There was not time to discuss everything. I mean, books could be written on these matters. As it was, we had quite a session. Practically as long as a Wagnerian opera, most of it a solo effort on the part of your burly sidekick. I was deeply impressed by the chap's powers of oratory, as I told him at the time."

"Well, just last night he and I were exploring a couple of other another interesting ideas having to do with the way the two political parties are used to divide, and thus effectively to neutralize, the masses. And the primary tool used to do this is collectivism – socialism. There were two main issues – first that the proletariat and the middle class are led to view one another as the adversary, the 'problem,' as it were, with the middle classes cast in the role of the 'haves' and the proletariat as the 'have-nots,' and government supposedly stepping in as some sort of beneficient, disinterested, omniscient referee with police powers who will correct the poverty of the proles by forcing the middle class to give up some of their property and redistributing that confiscated property to the neediest of the poor."

"But this model is false," Rantor carried on for him, "Because the truth is that it is *not* the middle class but rather the tiny aristocracy of the rich who are scooping up the wealth, to the detriment of *both* the ever more financially strapped proles and the vanishing middle class. The *true* dichotomy of interest – and of wealth – is between the wealthy elites of the corporate oligarchy and the masses, whether called middle class or proletariat."

"Right," agreed his pal. "Which home truth, of course, the corporate oligarchy do NOT want the exploited workers to connect with. The second idea about socialism which we were discussing has to do with the fact that the left and the right actually tend to be very similar in their information, their interests, and even their objectives – which on both sides of the political fence are fundamentally populist - differing largely, when one stops to reflect, only as regards the means –

140

primarily, the economic system - by which such populist objectives may best be achieved."

"One tends to think of the two parties as deeply and irreconcilably opposed, of course ..." said I.

"That is true, and it is the impression, I believe, that our social programmers want to maintain in the minds of the people. But after a good deal of reading and thought, Ifford, it dawned on me – on both of us, Rantor and me - that the masses, the people of both the left and right – the Republicans and Democrats of the present day – though they disagree on *means* – basically, that is, on the the issue of mandatory wealth-transfer schemes, socialism – but at bottom, the people of both parties have the same basic ideals and goals - in essence, of equity, of achieving a just government with just and fair institutions and practices."

"But," said Rantor, "*But* - the idea is inculcated and maintained in the public mind that the two parties are adversial opposites, and thus they are played against each other as a means of dividing and thus neutralizing the masses. Very roughly speaking, one could say that the lower and the middle classes – the proletariat and the bourgeoise, in Marxian terms – are cleverly led to believe that their interests *conflict*, are opposed, and that one another is the problem – and that collectivism, socialism, will 'fix' the problem. The proletariat and the bourgeoise are pitted against each other, with the Democratic Party touted as having the interests of the prole at heart, and the Republicans presented as the champions of the middle and upper classes. But the *real* dichotomy, and conflict of interest, is actually that between the *people*, both poor and middle and upper-middle classes, and the numerically tiny hidden *aristocracy of the super-rich*, the latter being the oppressor/ financial exploiter/puppet-master of both classes of workers.

"And furthermore," continued Torvald, "It seems pretty clear to us that IF the people of the Left - the Democrats - understood the hidden facts - the downside, the real consequences for the people of ALL income levels save only the tiny elite of the super-rich – if they understood, could grasp, the disadvantages for the people which are inescapably inherent in collectivism, and in the central banks and the income tax upon which collectivism depends - then the left, the Democrats would rethink it and cease supporting it – cease supporting government control of the economy, and forced wealth-transfer schemes – if they could be made to understand that collectivism is in actuality NOT beneficial either to the proletariat or the bourgeoise; that it is in fact ultimately beneficial only to the controlling aristocracy of the very rich and is not compatible with or productive of a free society, relying as this system does on the destruction of the concept and the reality of private property, on the forced confiscation of earned property, on an enlargement of the apparatus and powers of government. And that the statist system - essentially, and more precisely, the fascist system - which collectivism creates inevitably has the effect of destroying individual rights of all classes save the privileged elites, and of enhancing the power of the totalitarian monolithic state of, by, and for the inner circle of the super-rich and their croneys and lackeys."

"Hmmm. Rather a lot to think about there …"

"Well, just read the books of Antony Sutton to find documented proof that it has been all along the very wealthy who have backed and funded collectivism – Communism and socialism."

"Speaking of neutralizing the opposition," Rantor interjected, "I've been thinking lately of this matter of political correctness – particularly, the way racism has become such a big issue – and a big no-no. This tends to serves the interests of the international bankers very well, in that whenever the central banks are criticized, their foes and critics can be accused of racism – anti-Semitism. Certainly that tends to happen when populist researchers point to the fact that most of the great international banking houses are owned by Jews – such as the Rothschilds, and the Warburgs."

"Yes, Rantor, good point," praised Torvald, the two of them seeming as previously noted to have quite the mutual admiration society going. "And one final thought, which just now occurred to me, actually, as regards the created dichotomy between Left and Right … have you noticed how the two-party system comes to resemble a game, of football or basketball, with the fans wearing their team's regalia and shouting and chanting and jumping around, waving their signs and so on, at the political conventions?"

"Interesting comparison," Rantor said reflectively. "The whole scene also reminds me of student government in secondary school - throwing the kiddies an illusion of being in control, of some things, to some extent."

"Yes," agreed Torvald. "Also it is interesting to notice how the idealistic impulse that seems to exist in us all, but perhaps especially in the intelligentsia, is channeled into areas of concern and activity that pose no threat to the controlling elites – such as correcting the wrongs of racism and sexism."

"Yet again," agreed his pal, "Turning the attention – and resentment – of the people against other people rather than against the tiny elites who are in very real ways exploiting and harming all of the people regardless of race, color, or sexual orientation."

"Yes," said Torvald. "This is done in large part simply by publishing works - both fiction and non-fiction – dealing with sexism and racism and by not publishing or broadcasting information critical of the corporate oligarchy."

"Right," agreed Rantor. "You see a lot of courses offered at the University here on racism and sexism and women's studies, et cetera – but nothing exposing the real agendas and effects of collectivism or central banks and valueless fiat currencies."

"So anyway, Ifford," Torvald queried, "What was - is - your reaction to all of that – these ideas of ours today, as well as the lengthy discussion you had with Rantor?"

"Well ... you do realize that you and he are demolishing much of the internal scaffolding which underlay the Ifford we all know and love? That you are methodically snuffing out the illusions in which I found refuge, solace, and the strength to carry on?"

"Ah, yes... it is called growing up and entering the real world. A transition many, alas, never make ..."

"... Emerging from a sort of contest between the darkness of the false but comforting web of self-serving lies of the power elites, on the one hand ..."

"Which lies self-serving lies of course we all want to believe ..."

"Yes ... and on the other hand, what I suppose you chaps might call the harsh but ultimately to be preferred light of truth ..."

143

"Grim though the prospect might be, I think it is better to live in the real world. Safer, certainly - better than being suddenly blind-sided by that harsh reality. As the French say, if you do not 'do' politics, politics will 'do' you. The transition can be a difficult one, involving an agonizing paradigm-shift. The realities of the world - and the ways of power - are indeed considerably grimmer than we so desperately want to believe them to be."

"People do, I suppose, tend to cling to their comforting illusions."

"Yes. That is why it is at about this point, if not long before, that so many people to whom I have spoken resort to the Freudian defense mechanisms ..."

"And begin to entrench, you mean? To erect barricades, to employ the arsenal ..."

"Denial, rationalization, minimizing, and of course, attacking the messenger. Has it not occurred to you that I must be one of those crazy, right-wing conspiracy theorists you hear so much about?"

"The thought has occurred. More than once, in fact. I believe I might even have bandied that phrase about in one or more of my conversations with you and your scaly chum. Are you suggesting the above evasive action as an method of escape in case I decide that I am not up to the stiff straight shot of the 180 proof?"

"Well, it is the escape hatch most heavily employed by the media and therefore the means most favored by the masses for ..."

"Wriggling out from under ..."

"In order," Rantor, who had been so uncharacteristically silent, lustily interjected, "To be able to get back to feasting, untroubled by nagging doubts, on the meat of life - you know, the shopping trips to the mall, the football games, the sitcoms on the tube, et cetera. The circuses part of the bread and circuses with which they are so - cheaply bought off."

"And it is these same masses whose fate concerns you two?" I asked. "The very same who revile, snicker, and evade when you come bearing to them personally the bitter, but life- and freedom-preserving, brew?"

"Life is replete with irony, Ifford," said Torvald, with a half smile, half rueful grimace seemingly directed at the glossy, heavily lacquered knotty pine tabletop. "And in some causes, according to a fortune cookie fortune I once got - in some causes, it is noble even to fail."

I wondered if this was some sort of mantra or sustaining affirmation of his, he seeming possibly to be one of those chaps heavily dedicated to a cause involving the betterment of all sentient beings, or some such.

"Perhaps, for those who aspire to nobility. Which I do not. And furthermore, how much irony can the mind of one entity endure? Do you not feel yourself, at times, cracking under the strain?"

"Not to worry about my personal anguish, Ifford. We Nordics, you know, are basically of sanguine disposition."

"Even when sharing a lifeboat, filled to the gunwales and shipping water, with a bunch of - of cowardly mental midgets and high IQ idiots who are being led down the garden path and loving it?" This fervent emoting of course emanating from the scaly one, who until now had been, relatively speaking, so uncharacteristically silent.

"Well, at least," said I, "You can draw a certain lean, wintery satisfaction from knowing that you are numbered among those very few who are made of stuff stern enough to withstand reality's full chill blast, undiluted and unmitigated, square in the face, and buttressed, personally, by no artificial soul-stiffening aids or prosthetic devices. But what I want to know is - what am I to do about my mother?"

This just sort of popped out. I had not been planning to bring it up.

"Your mother? Who said anything about your mother? I mean - do you have one?"

CHAPTER 16: REGARDING MY INCUBATION

If biological manipulation is indeed a slippery slope, then we
are already sliding down that slope now and may as well
enjoy the ride.

Gregory Stock, author of
Redesigning Humans: Our Inevitable Genetic Future

Glennie and Rantor had been following our exchange with close
attention, back-and-forthing very much like spectators at a tennis
match, and at this bombshell both goggled - though why Glennie, who
already knew about my mother and me, should goggle, I am not sure.
She is a sympathetic girl, and perhaps she did not want Rantor goggling
all on his lonesome. In addition to goggling, Rantor went so far as to
jump a bit where he sat, like an actor in a silent film, as though
receiving an unexpected sprinkling of cold water in the face. The
fellow seemed made for melodrama - I could see him typecast as the
heavy in gangster films, sort of an over-grown and less subtle James
Cagney.

"Allegedly I do have an actual, *bona fide* mother. A personal mother.
Of course one never knows what to believe. Perhaps I neglected to
mention the bit about my mother to Rantor." (Ifford is such a sly old
dog.) "Squinch had several things on the agenda when he called me in
for our little talk. One was the political stuff - I did mention that to your
side-kick - and a grade that I need to pull up a notch or two by the end
of the quarter - and the *caveat* about obeying all of the prescriptions
and proscriptions of the *lex loci* - and then the remarks about my
mother."

"Not meaning to harp on sensitive topics, Ifford ..."

"Quite all right ..."

"But I really didn't know you had one. A mother, that is to say. I mean,
didn't you begin as merely an anonymous egg, fertilized by an
anonymous sperm ..."

146

"And gestated in some sort of communal pre-natal arrangement, which played itself out in some sort of an aquarium on a ship somewhere in the vast reaches of outer space, overseen by some steely-eyed phalanx of soul-less scientists? Yes, that is essentially correct, as regards all but the anonymity of the egg in question."

"These labs in outer space operate in a legal no-man's land, so to speak, don't they - rather like ships in international waters?"

"So I have heard. I believe one can more or less write one's own laws in them. *Carte blanche*, to a great extent. And indeed I am, as you say, in a manner of speaking a mongrel child of the Universe, eclectically conceived, the figment of a marriage between hi-tec hardware and a chilly, anonymous, highly educated someone's professional ambition. Funded by a grant, and written up, in impenetrable scientific multi-syllabic code, in some obscure journal, to end up finally as another item on a list of publications on a number of resumes. But I know from whence my maternal genetic material sprang, or was siphoned. At least I am pretty sure I do. The ovum was donated by a full-blooded human who, to the best of my knowledge, traces her lineage all the way back to the original unicellular organisms spawned somehow in that hypothetical aboriginal primordial broth of this planet."

"I see. And how is it that the subject of your mother entered into your colloquy with this warden of yours?"

"It so happens that she resides here in this city. My mother, that is. Allegedly. Not the warden, who I believe commutes from the suburbs. I managed to track her down and we have been in communication. At least I have been told by the agency I contacted that she is in fact my real mother. They claim to do a sort of genetic matching, you know, the privacy of all parties supposedly being strictly protected."

"If any information, these days, is strictly protected ... save that involving the most odious doings of the ruling elites," Rantor interjected helpfully.

This remark of his actually did help – did make me realize that it was quite possible that the agency I had consulted could indeed have secret agreements to pass on - doubtless for a fee - to certain governments, such as those of the home planet, the identities of all who used their genetic matching services. I had given them a false name, but it struck me now - how stupid of me not to have thought of it before – that the agency had a sample of my genetic material, of course, and could easily have passed that on, with or without a name, to - well, say, to Squinch & Company.

"Rantor might be onto something there, Ifford," said Torvald.

"Yes, yes, of course. I see that now. Stupid of me not to have thought of that before I even consulted the matching service. Especially in light of the fact that this quest for one's roots, you understand, is strictly forbidden by the Gestapo back home. In fact, I think that in itself it might constitute a yankable offense. I could be suctioned from your midst over this. It was foolish of me. And I am in a quandary now re how to proceed. Actually, I was hoping that perhaps you two might be able to shed some light on the matter. And on the other matters touched upon by my overseer. And perhaps give me some suggestions as to my best course of action at this point, what with being in the soup to a certain extent with those who hold me in the palms of their iron fists, so to speak. It has been causing me quite a lot of worry, to be perfectly honest. I'm afraid I might at the very least be shipped back home and put on a non-professional track, doing data entry or janitorial or other physical labor, working in the food service industry or some such. Hybrids in those professions don't even get their own apartments. They live in some sort of dormitory arrangement, rather like the homes in which Glennie and I were raised. Hybrids, you see, have a lower status back on the home planet than the full-blooded and normally conceived, more human-like general population - though the latter, of course, while of higher status, do not enjoy a very free existence either, and must devote their lives to service to the state."

"I guess I'd be concerned, too, if I were in your shoes," said Rantor, actually sounding sympathetic.

"Of course," I prompted, after a moment of silence at the table, "In addition to this thing about my mother, I'm wondering if Squich et al are aware of my discussions with you two ... and of course why Glennie has received no summons to be interrogated, if in fact these harmless discussions of ours are perceived by them to be ... sinister ... or in any way problematic ...."

Torvald and Rantor again exchanged the meaningful glance. Or perhaps it was a flurry of meaningful glances. I don't recall, but it did seem to be something they did all the time together. Glennie, believe it or not, brought out from her purse a little mirror and looked at herself in it. Women, you know. And I, toying absently with the curlique of lemon peel from my Americano, wrapping and re-wrapping it around one of my fingers, gazed absently at her as the tip of her little pink tongue, that always reminds me of a cat's tongue, emerged to scrub gently but firmly at the whipped cream mustache that had been left on her upper lip by her mocha drink. Our small mouths do make drinking from a cup a bit of a challenge. We hybrids, of course, I mean. Straws work better for us.

Then Torvald cleared his throat and gave other signs of preparing to utter, at which all eyes swiveled in his direction and every breath was bated.

CHAPTER 17: *REQUIASCAT IN PACEM* FOR THE REPUBLIC?

That men do not learn much from
the lessons of history is the most important of all the
lessons of history.

Aldous Huxley

"To be honest, Ifford," said Torvald, after a thoughtful pause and the usual glance over at Rantor, "I am a bit out of my depth here. I am not really up to speed on state-of-the-art surveillance technologies, either in the open or the protected literature. I do know that intelligence agencies here have a method of divining the conversation in a room from the pattern of vibrations of the glass panes in the window. But that is old news by now. As I say, I am not up to speed on this subject. I suppose it is possible that your rooms, or all dorm rooms, for that matter, are routinely wired for bugs. And most phones are, I believe, at this point tapped and monitored by computer for key words or phrases. Lines on which those words or phrases occur are given more personal attention, of course. They are, as we know, using the alleged 'terrorist threat' as justification for ever-heavier surveillance - and the dismantling of any remaining civil liberties."

"*Requiascat in pacem* for the Republic," Rantor interjected gloomily. As it wasn't his Republic, he being merely a visitor on the planet, I wondered why it seemed to matter so much to him.

"After the conquest, the peace," Torvald added wryly. "Although perhaps a rather stern peace. In which the new rules are imposed by the conquerors."

"According to a tape I heard on KROK," Glennie interjected, putting her little mirror back into her purse, "The 'terrorist threat' in actuality is almost entirely fabricated - 'false flag operations'."

"Yes," agreed Torvald. Old wine in new bottles The same old methods having been in use since before poor old banished Machiavelli grovelingly tried to curry favor with his prince by putting them into his little 'how-to' manual."

Rantor picked up the ball at this point. "Perhaps your home planet routinely monitors your phones. And then there are these microchips they're so hot to embed under the skin on the backs of the hands or in the arms of everyone. Tagging us all like so many cattle. And in lieu of credit card, identification card, and, of course, cash. Have you been injected with one of these yet? What they don't tell us in their ads and PR is that these spychips can also be used to ID and track their wearers. And to deny entry to work, or stores or - pretty much anyplace - even access to our own apartments, our own funds at the bank, if we get blacklisted."

What these RFID chips had to do with my current problem eluded me. It appeared that Torvald and Rantor were, as was only to be expected, of course, amateurs, up on the theory more than the practice - that their knowledge of the cloak and dagger aspect of statecraft was spotty at best, such *lacunae* being, I have read, the hallmark of the self-educated. I felt another little twinge of fear. These two were to have been my aces in the hole. Much as I grumbled and groused about them, I realized that I had been rather counting on them coming up with some saving idea, plan of action, or bit of information to pull old Ifford's chestnuts out of the fire and save his bacon.

"Uh ... the subcutaneous microchips, you say?" I replied rather dispiritedly.

"Yes. You are of course aware of them?" queried Torvald.

"Oh, rather. I am continually getting offers in the mail of all sorts of free gifts and lavishly generous lines of credit if I will only go in and submit to the free and painless procedure."

"As are we all, I believe."

"Yes, so it seems - and there are so many ads for them on TV, glamorous girls in scanty bikinis on white sand beaches, showing us their smooth pretty arms *sans* scars or marks of injection and marveling at the convenience of it all and so on; but so far I have not gone in for it. I don't like medical procedures and avoid them when at all possible. And in fact, I am not sure, as an off-planet entity, if I could be chipped."

"Your status would be encoded in the chip. And, as I understand it, the chips can be reprogrammed - updated and modified - from a distance,

151

after insertion and without the subject's knowledge or consent. It's just a matter of time before chipping becomes mandatory for all entities. Of course, the more or less captive or dependent populations - welfare recipients, the incarcerated, and those in the military - are already required to be injected. For the rest of us, for now, they're pushing it heavily as a freeing convenience. To find lost children and pets, to provide a complete medical history in case of accident or illness ... they might perhaps use the drug problem or the terrorist threat as the excuse for making it obligatory and universal."

"The fraudulent drug problem," Rantor snorted. " In which the CIA and other big players find such a favorable ROI - return on investment."

"Well, getting back to my problems, you know ..." I feared that they were off and running yet again. In their enthusiasm for their subject, they seemed to forget that I had an actual problem here to deal with.

"Yes," Torvald went on, as if I had not spoken, in reply to Rantor's comment. "Simply making anything illegal immediately boosts its price by ten or twenty-fold. Which, of course, is why drugs are treated as a legal rather than a medical problem. The illegality not being a problem for those who operate above the law."

"And that is also why marijuana," Rantor went on indignantly, "Which is not even physically addictive - is in fact the least harmful known intoxicant - is kept illegal - to keep its price high and also to protect the markets for the more expensive - and addictive - drugs. If marijuana were legal, everyone would be growing it in their yards or under lights and the demand for heroin, the amphetamines, and cocaine in all their forms would drop drastically."

"But drugs are a problem ... a great social problem ..." I could not help interjecting, rather weakly – expecting, at this point, to be proven wrong again.

"Yes. Admittedly," replied Torvald. "But for the best way to deal with the problem, look at the Netherlands, in which all drug use is decriminalized, and their use treated as a medical/mental health problem. They have a much lower rate of drug use than this country - and are not burdening their people with the huge cost of legally processing and then incarcerating millions of drug dealers."

"And do not have the higher crime rate associated with the use of drugs made exorbitantly expensive by being made illegal," added Glennie, she doubtless having listened to a tape about it that she got from Jacko.

"But, you know," mused Torvald, "I can't help but wonder if there is a hidden agenda in creating a pretext to incarcerate so many. For one thing, I sometimes wonder if the old debtors' prisons might not be re-instituted – once the world government is in place – and, in some nations, such as this one, right now, as a foot in the door to wider use. The practice of imposing jail time for failure to pay child support could be a step in this direction. You know that already they are privatize the prisons here in this country... and then they are already using prisoners as labor in various prison industries ... labor so cheaply paid - a few cents an hour, pocket money for use in the prison stores and canteens for cigarettes and such - as to be virtual slave labor, as is the common practice in China ..."

"Yes," said Glennie. "China, which gives people prison sentences of years and years, just for things like criticizing the government – and then uses all these prisoners as slave labor in the production of their cheap goods ..."

"Quite. Using slave labor does give one a competitive edge in the market," said Torvald. "And yet not a peep about violation of 'human rights' is heard, from this country, or from the U.N. – and have you heard that China actually executes prisoners for their valuable organs?"

"Yes," she replied. "I saw something online about these roving execution vans they have there ... it is so – just so bad – and yet – what can one do? Of course, as a visitor here, there is nothing I could do, without getting into some real trouble ..."

"Speaking of which ..." I said, trying, without any great hope of success, to steer the discussion back to my problems.

"Speaking of information online, of which there is so much available – and concerning false-flag operations, which we were just talking about the other day," interjected Rantor, "Yesterday I found this great paper which documents that most terrorism, historically, is in fact state-sponsored."

"I'd like to get the website URL from you on that one," Glennie said. "And I found something interesting online too, just the other day. This

153

article said that the major drug companies could greatly reduce the production of cocaine and heroine by just cutting off the supply of pre-cursor chemicals to the coca leaf- and poppy-producing countries. But that what they do instead is make the necessary chemicals available - but at prices inflated several thousand per cent above the normal asking price."

"This is all very interesting," I interjected, doggedly. "But, I say, do you think that we cou ..."

"We know," Rantor surged on obliviously, "That powerful people in this country - people in and near the government – in the CIA, of course, but also right up to the White House - are largely responsible for the influx of drugs into this country. Of course this is partly because they themselves are making so much money off of the drugs - the high ROI in contraband, you know - that being one reason they keep the drugs illegal, to jack up the price - but it's also because they are using the drugs for political purposes - to weaken the country, destabilize the existing social order - to corrupt - and neutralize - Blacks, and youth generally, and to provide a plausible rationale for larger police forces and stricter laws, such as their various unconstitutional search-and-seizure laws, and gun-control laws – total citizen disarmament being one of their major goals, of course - and to provide another crisis, since they remain in power by manufacturing crises, one crisis after another to keep the people frightened, confused - emotionally stressed and exhausted - and willing to tolerate a strong, authoritarian government."

"Yes," Torvald concurred, "Social de-stabilization. And they know that people under stress regress, becoming more childlike and willing, if not actually eager, to have in place an authoritarian, paternalistic, *in loco parentis*/Big Brother type government."

"The formula for the carefully orchestrated fools' march into the police state," agreed Rantor. "Actually, they used drugs to defuse – neutralize - the youth social protest movement and the black power movement of the '60s. Sort of like throwing a watchdog a nice meaty bone to chew on. Or tossing a drunk a bottle of booze. Or giving a government a central bank and a fiat currency."

"In fact," added Torvald, "All of this loosening of moral standards and the illegal activity of all sorts makes a convenient smoke-screen or camouflage for their own misdeeds and loose living. Instead of standing out, the elites' own sexual peccadilloes, drug use, and criminal activities just blend in, seem less outrageous to the be-numbed

154

citizenry. A tree in a forest of trees rather than a tree in the middle of a prairie."

"And all of the crime itself has its uses, its purposes," said Rantor. "Crime that of course is inevitable when you criminalize something that so many millions use and are going to keep on using - like marijuana. I mean, every society uses intoxicants of some sort. Why criminalize use of the least harmful known intoxicant – marijuana? Probably because, for one thing, the increased crime provides a plausible justification for beefing up law enforcement - and for demanding gun control. It's well known, just by examining the record of history, that populist governments, such as the founders of this country originally tried to create, always *want* an armed populace - have nothing to fear from it – and it causes the crime rate actually to decrease - while throughout history, totalitarian regimes always fear an armed citizenry and try to institute gun control."

"And, as you pointed out, virtually every culture ever known has had some form of intoxicant. You can't successfully outlaw something that is and always has been in universal use, as the elite planners of course have got to know," said Torvald. "And of course, it is not a proper function of government to take on the Big Brotherly role of dictating peoples' morals and conduct in their private lives. It is interesting to consider that back in the '20s it was considered necessary to pass a Constitutional Amendment to outlaw alcohol – while today, government just proceeds as if it were its perfect right and even duty, to outlaw the use of various substances like marijuana, and in other ways to regulate people in their private lives – ostensibly 'for their own good.' "

"And of course they tax the legal relaxation and recreational drugs to the max," added Rantor. "Booze and cigarettes. Kind of interesting, when you think of it, that the two recreational drugs which are legal are highly addictive and destructive to health."

"Well ... this is of course all deeply interesting, " I persisted - the tenacity of a limpet, being, it appeared, required to deflect these chaps from their obsessive concerns. "But we seem, you know, rather to have wandered from this issue of my mother. And these other problems of mine. I am not sure if there is any way that I can stay in contact with her without them knowing about it. Should I just sever ties? Continuing a contact that they can monitor, especially after having been issued a warning, would certainly get me sent back home, and ruin my chances

155

for any sort of professional career. And then, these other marks against my record ..."

Glennie entered the conversation at this point. "Oh, Ifford, I was meaning to tell you ... in regard to Squinch's enigmatic comments about not running a-foul of the law, have you heard that there was a hold-up at The Friend of the Family late last Sunday night? That was where you had your run-in with the police, wasn't it? It's possible they could have thought you were involved as an accomplice or something."

Torvald and Rantor looked keenly interested at the introduction of this new topic. It was the first they had heard of my run-in with the law, and I proceeded to fill them in - omitting to mention the bag of money I had found on the sidewalk.

"As a matter of fact,' said Rantor, "I heard that they found the guy who they think did it. He actually went back and robbed the same store a few nights later, if you can believe that! And the news report I heard said that he swears he didn't have the money he got from the first hold-up. He says he must have dropped it when he was fleeing the scene of the crime. They say they are looking for a fellow seen near the store shortly after the hold-up. You didn't by any chance find any money, did you, Ifford?"

Egad! So that was where the money I found must have come from! Would that make me, then, in the eyes of the law, an accomplice? I saw Glennie looking at me quite pointedly. But she did not mention the found money, though of course that was what she was thinking about. It did seem possible that rather than go 'round and question or arrest me themselves, the local law enforcement might first approach the agency responsible for me as an off-planet entity, and request that they bring me in for questioning. But it also seemed quite possible that if I did go in, I'd be – shudder - detained, at least for questioning - by the local authorities. And what if my quarters were searched, and the bag of money found?

This new bit of information jangled my nerves horribly, and I felt practically in a panic. Actually, in my worry over Squinch's calls, I had totally forgotten about the money I had found. It must still be under my mattress. It wouldn't look good that I hadn't immediately handed it over - say to those officers who had questioned me that night - or if not at that time, then the next day, at the very latest. So distressing was all this that I actually, acting on the fight-or-flight impulse that overtakes us all when we feel like cornered animals, half-stood, making a rather convulsive effort to abscond I knew not where, but Glennie reached out and held me firmly - and comfortingly - by the hand, smiling at me encouragingly as she did so.

A silence ensued. A longish silence, actually. Finally, Torvald took pity on me and broke it. "I wish I could be more help to you with all of this. Of course, as you have not actually done anything wrong ..."

"Except contact my mother ..."

"Yes, except for that seemingly rather minor thing."

"It's just that there is no such thing as a minor thing, to the powers that be on the home planet."

"Still, it could be worth it at least to call - and talk it over with that fellow Squinch who seems to be in charge of you."

"But wouldn't they track the call?"

"Possibly. Well - I might as well go ahead and tell you one thing I have on my mind ..." - a quick glance over at Rantor - "Have you ever heard of 'jumping the tracks'?"

I drew a blank here, but Glennie seemed to be familiar with the phrase. "Doesn't it have to do with probable, or parallel, realities? Or with time travel?" she asked.

"That's right," replied Torvald.

There was a little pause. I expected Torvald to enlighten us further, but he went all inscrutable, for some reason, and just sat there as if unsure whether or not to divulge whatever it was he had on his mind.

"Well," I said a bit impatiently, "What about it?"

I had no idea what he might have up his sleeve; but if there was one thing I did know, and know full well, it was that I did not want to go in and turn myself over to Squinch and his henchmen.

CHAPTER 18: JUMPING THE TRACKS

All the best stories in the world are but one story in reality - the
story of escape. It is the only thing which interests us all
and at all times, how to escape.

Walter Bagehot

"Have you heard," Torvald began, "About the Philadelphia Experiment
- and Montauk?"

Rather as to be expected, Glennie had. "Weren't they the 'radar
invisibility/disappearing battleship/time-tunnel/time-travel' very secret
projects of this country's government? Montauk is an old navel base on
Long Island, isn't it - the one reputed to have been used for secret
government research and experimentation?"

"Yes," answered Torvald. "Of course, as we know, the science of how travel between worlds is accomplished by those in power is kept by them as a closely guarded secret – ostensibly for reasons of 'interplanetary security,' naturally, and lest the information fall into the hands of rogue nations, or worlds, and other 'terrorists' who might 'mis-use' it."

"That, of course," Rantor said, "is the real reason that we who travel inter-planetarily are always put into a state of suspended animation during the journey. We're told that it is a necessity, or an unavoidable side-effect, of the travel. But in actuality, it is to keep us from knowing how the voyage is actually accomplished."

"Yes," agreed Torvald. "However: the scuttlebutt is that there's actually a good deal of off-the-books research and experimentation being carried on – some of it right here at this university. It's àll very hush-hush, of course, any such study unless ordered and authorized by the World Government being considered seditious. But, given how many light-years separate the various habitable planets, it doesn't take a rocket scientist, so to speak, to figure that travel within a human lifespan over such vast distances must involve some sort of time travel. And it is rumored – and perhaps more than rumored – that some of the young stallions in the physics department are working on the problem in their off-hours, and that they are making progress - with the help, some say - of entities from worlds opposed to the Inter-Planetary Union and which are actively, if surreptitiously, working to undermine it."

"The doctors Strangelove and Faustus in unholy alliance with the most diabolical geniuses of the far-flung worlds?"

"Perhaps not quite as bad as all that, Ifford. Actually these fellows are, you might say, freedom fighters." This from the fellow who was always cheerfully cueing me in as to just how bad it actually all was, in every quarter. And now I was to believe that some sort of good guys/bad guys *Star Wars* scenario was actually taking place in real time, so to speak.

"But - some kind of a machine, you are talking about? A time machine, like in H.G. Wells – like in the movies?" I queried.

"Apparently, it does not necessarily involve the use of any sort of vehicle," Torvald corrected. "The reality is not quite so literal as that. As I understand it, it involves what are called wormholes, or time tunnels, and the generation of very powerful magnetic fields, which are the key to creating dimensional shifts - movement - travel, if you will - in and across dimensions - the ultimately illusory - that is to say the conceptually-based - dimensions of both time and space."

"Just a minute," I interjected. A thought had occurred. "Surely you're not questioning our existence – suggesting that we are mere figments, or some such?" I was in a somewhat emotional frame of mind, the reader will recall, and this matter of non-existence was much on my mind. I mean, if time and space were illusions, what were the personal implications?

"Don't take it personally, Ifford. On some level clearly we all exist, even if it is only as pure consciousness. One mustn't make the mistake of confusing the envelope with its content," said Torvald with a smile. "I'm not suggesting that you - we - do not exist. However, the implications of what I am saying are that we are other than we think we are. You know the old argument as to which precedes which, thought or matter - traditional religion generally arguing, by implication, at least, and if not actually employing this terminology, that matter arises out of thought, though Thought, perhaps, with a capital 'T'… with science, the currently ruling priesthood, being of the belief – also in the absence of any form of actual proof - that consciousness somehow arose out of matter, in the mythic 'long ago' if not 'far away - that assumption seeming more scientific, more rational - more emotionally satisfying - to the modern mind, rejecting as it does primitive animism, positing no divine superhuman figure or cadre, no supernatural creator with courtly retinue - no godly pantheon."

"But both theories sidestep, of course, the whole thorny issue of where the material, or the immaterial, worlds came from in the first place, and when, and why, and how," said Rantor

"True enough," Torvald agreed. "If it is even meaningful to speak of a 'first place.' Both theories ultimately do rest on faith. Much that is called 'science' is, or rests upon, mere speculation not capable of being either proven or disproven experimentally, and hence lying in actuality beyond the scope of science, and its foundation, the scientific method. But as to time travel theory, research, and experimentation - the implications of the directions which current time-travel research is taking are that there do exist multiple dimensions of time and space - more than a single manifest reality, in other words - and definitely suggest that our physical bodies - and context - are a function or aspect of our minds – or of Mind, if you will, rather than the other way around. If our location in time and space can be instantaneously changed - drastically changed - then our former conceptions of time and space – as literally, inexorably, 'true,' and binding, so to speak - must have been erroneous. The constant, through this change, seems to be consciousness."

"But then," I asked, "Why must we manipulate a physical variable - electromagnetic fields or whatever - in order to bring about this shift?"

"Good question again, Ifford." Torvald was heaping on the praise to such an extent that I found myself wondering if he were not buttering me up like a muffin with some end in mind, in the manner of the walrus and the carpenter and the little oysters. You cannot grow up on a planet such as the home planet without developing a somewhat hyper-vigilant and cynical turn of mind.

Torvald went on: "It might actually be true that one can alter one's time-space location by use of the mind alone. There are of course the tales of the spiritual adepts of India, being seen in two places at once and so on. But then, religions abound in miracles. However, to be able to achieve such feats consciously and at will is said by the Oriental adepts to require considerable discipline and training in areas of human achievement not even officially acknowledged to exist by the current scientific establishment. And, as the saying goes, there is more than one way to skin a cat. In the case of time/space travel, the cutting edge research of which I am speaking, or certain currents within it, are based upon the theory that the physical and mental/emotional do interface and mutually influence one another, even if - or perhaps it would be more accurate to say, *because* - one is the manifestation - a manifestation - of the other."

"All is one and all that?"

"Yes. This planetary culture has a special proclivity for, or perhaps you could say, obsession with, the physical. It has specialized in exploring reality via the avenues of the physical and the rational. Therefore, it is working on accessing this less material aspect of experience through or via a physical/rational doorway, or process - or manipulation. If physicality and consciousness are really only two aspects of the same thing – whatever, or whoever, that 'thing' is - then the distinction between them must be spurious - illusory - and the manipulation of one not only can but must affect or influence the other."

161

"OK," I said. "But, my fine feathered friend" - and here, for some reason, the Norse demigod perceptibly blushed, making me wonder fleetingly about his remote ancestry and if I had not inadvertently touched a nerve - "Enough with the theoretical underpinnings. Let's get to the issue of why you have introduced this motif into the conversation. What is it exactly that you have in mind?"

"Well," said Torvald, with actually a little embarrassed smile - I think the first self-deprecating mannerism I had yet seen him betray - "I have a little project in mind. And given that you are having some difficulties in this particular time/space locale, I thought you might be interested in becoming involved with a project, or endeavor, which would, so to speak, afford you the opportunity to travel - to, as they say, get away from it all."

"Hmmm," I replied. "Hmmmm ... I see ..." I mulled it over. Of course I liked the idea of getting away from it all. But after a moment I continued, voicing a suspicion that had crept in and pervaded the old stream of consciousness, "But tell me, old man - honestly, now - is this offer being made to me - a relative stranger, in more ways than one, after all - out of the simple goodness of your heart; or do you, too, perhaps require some assistance?"

"Well, to be, as you say, entirely honest, Ifford - it is possible that you could lend a helping hand."

CHAPTER 19: TORVALD'S MODEST PROPOSAL

But you think that it is time for me to have done with the world,
and so I would if I could get into a better before I was called
into the best, and not die here in a rage,
like a poisoned rat in a hole.

Jonathan Swift

Another of those pregnant pauses ensued - this one so drawn out that my mind started to wander, as it so often does, even at times when one would think that the here and now would have it waiting with bated breath for the next outrageous utterance or bizarre event. Glennie, too, seems to be quite the dreamer – this being, I suspect, one of the reasons her knitting projects can drift into incoherence – causing me to wonder if the tendency to wool-gather is not yet another aspect of our genetic heritage. On the other hand, it may be only a personal idiosyncrasy, having to do with how very taxing I find this thing called reality, even under the best of circumstances, to be. I am always fleeing to the realms of fantasy for a little bucking up. I find these brief interludes both soothing and alluring in the extreme - one reason why the fate of poor Calvin resonated so ominously. He, it seemed to me, had merely yielded to the same basic nature which I, with the help and at the behest of Squinch and those of his ilk, was struggling to resist, quell, overcome, evade, or batter into submission.

But, back to the present moment - which found me, for some unfathomable reason, imagining Torvald's eyebrows, upon which my eyes were absently fixed, to be little arching strips of bacon. They were the most curious eyebrows, sort of mottled - the palest tawny gold interlarded, as it were, with strips of a rich, glossy chestnut hue - and in my mind's eye, I was reaching out to gently pull the left one away, as you might peel a single strip of bacon away from the rest of the package, carefully lest you tear it. It was coming away quite nicely, when Rantor spoke, his voice sounding like an old pick-up truck engine with a faulty muffler running very rough just a few inches from my right ear and causing me to jump as though someone had crept up behind me and poked me in the ribs. That throaty quality of his voice I had come to identify with the reptoid's more thoughtful aspect of mind.

When he gets excited his voice ascends the scale, becoming almost piccolo-like.

"The space/time journey...?" Here the glances of the dynamic duo interlocked meaningfully for a highly charged second or two, as was their wont, while I briefly wondered - not for the first time but more intensely, and poignantly, than ever before - if the two were quite in their right minds. It sounded like Captain America and Buzz Lightyear discussing their plans for the upcoming three-day weekend.

"Yes."

"1913, I presume...?"

"Thereabouts."

"And when ...?"

"... Shall we leave present time ...?"

"... Leave present time behind, for a while...?"

"The sooner, the better, it seems to me."

"Might as well get it over with, you mean."

"I see no advantage in delay."

Glennie had been following this exchange closely, her turquoise eyes aglow with interest, a tiny smile playing about her tiny little pouting rosebud mouth. (Where was that racial *ennui* of hers when I needed it most?! She never looked with such interest at old Ifford, I can tell you that.) Now she spoke.

"If Ifford goes, I think I should go too." Most emphatically said. My supportress, after all? Said, however, without so much as a glance in my direction. The great orbs shone upon Torvald.

Who beamed back upon her, a smile of brilliant warmth in which she seemed to bask, like a sleek seal on a rock in the sunshine.

"Of course," he said simply.

"We'll all go," Rantor said - or huskily fluted, I should say. His voice had begun its ascent of the scale and his tail its spasmodic twitching, as he and Torvald had performed their duet. The impulsive reptoid, as easily set ablaze as a prairie grassland in August, seemed ready for blast-off at that very moment. "We should all go. We all may be needed." This last in tones of quiet heroism.

"I'm afraid," said I, very firmly - the only anchor, evidently, to reality on the entire planning committee, "That I could not possibly do any such thing, without knowing a little more about it. I mean - good God - do you really expect me to step trustingly into some sort of time machine or vibrational field or whatever and accept your assurances that we'll get there - wherever 'there' is - and back, safely, and in time for my classes and so on? I mean - what if Squinch should call?"

Torvald turned his smiling gaze upon me. "Wasn't that the very sort of thing you were hoping to avoid?"

"Well, yes ... but won't this just delay things? Isn't it a bit like taking a vacation because the rent's due and you haven't got it?"

"Maybe you don't need to come back, Ifford. Not ever." It was Glennie who said this. I looked at her in amazement.

"Just - walk away - from everything?"

"Yes. Why not?"

"But - what if we don't like it there?"

"Then you'll go somewhere else - that's what," said Rantor. "You'll have all of time to choose from - right, Torvald?"

"Yes. At least, that's what we think."

"What you think?" I mimicked, surprising myself, sounding positively ill-bred. But I was exercised; I mean - there are limits even to the vast courtesy and obliging social tact of old Ifford. "I'm sorry, but it's got to be just a bit more certain than that for me," I went on. "I can't throw away my whole future like this, as casually as though I were ordering dinner in a restaurant. I'm not built that way. We hybrids are deliberate. We think things over. We weigh, we consider, we evaluate. We are not impulsive. Most emphatically not. Absolutely not. It goes against the grain. And rightly so, in my opinion."

I had expressed myself rather well, I thought - so well, indeed, that none of those assembled seemed able to think of anything at all to say in response, and around our little table, a brooding silence once again reigned, broken only by a genteel slurping sound from stage left as Glennie, eying me inscrutably over the demitasse, imbibed the murky brew.

So, after a bit, I went on. "Besides - what about the technology ... the equipment ... you know, the means whereby? Is there some kind of a bus stop or train station for this sort of thing? I mean - do you buy a ticket - or what?"

Glennie started spluttering or coughing a bit, as though a trickle of the dark and bitter had coursed down the wrong hatch. The problem, I think, is that she had actually started to laugh, if you can imagine that, mid-swallow. She seemed to find the whole thing wonderfully entertaining. Sometimes I really do wonder about that girl.

"The technology is actually surprisingly simple, Ifford," said Torvald. "In fact - I've got an idea. Why don't we all go on over to the laboratory?"

"Now, you mean?" asked Rantor, the ovals of his chocolatey pupils fattening in surprise, and the places where his eyebrows would have been, had he had any, leaping upwards in unison a good inch or so.

"Why not?" answered Torvald easily. "I've got a key to the building, of course, and I often go over there to putter about at odd hours, as the spirit moves me. The janitors all know me."

"What laboratory is this?" I asked.

"The SpaceTime Research lab, of course," came the answer.

"And how does it happen that you are *persona grata* on those premises?" I queried.

"I'm a grad student in the program."

Oh. Funny that I'd never thought to wonder about Torvald's niche in the over-arching bureaucracy under the long shadow of which we all live our antlike lives.

"Oh, let's!" said Glennie. "I'd love to!" Turning to me: "What harm can it do, Iffy?"

"Well ..." I was, after all, by way of being a wanted entity... "How far is it?"

"It's over on lower campus - no more than a fifteen or twenty minute walk from here," answered the space age demigod. And I could see that in everyone's mind save my own it was, as they say, a done deal. What could I do, dear Reader - but acquiesce?

CHAPTER 20: TIME TO GO NOW

I confess, I do not believe in time.

Vladimir Nabokov

The hour was late, and the weather at that hour gave no quarter, being absolutely life-threatening to the unprepared. Crunching along over the rough, crusty snow and ice, I had no appetite at all for this adventure of ours. Where I longed to be was, curled up in my toasty little bed, listening to the rhythmic creaking of Humphrey's exercise wheel as he went for his nightly stationary gallop (I have clued the reader in re Humphrey, my pet hamster, have I not? Pets, of course, are strictly forbidden in the digs, but he was an indulgence I simply could not refuse myself, when I saw him staring up at me with his beady little eyes as I lingered before the pet store window on a splendid autumn afternoon late last September. A limited creature, I have found him to be, but he has his charms. It is soothing to contemplate his world of simple satisfactions.)

So, to be safely in my cozy little room, as I was saying, and sipping a cup of hot cocoa with a slowly melting marshmallow languidly afloat in it (we don't have marshmallows on the home planet, and I find them absolutely fascinating), and munching on one of Grandma O'Houlihan's Krunchie-Krunchies, was what old Ifford's heart was yearning for, as we trudged through the dark and bitter cold. Oh, and reading *The Spycatcher Who Came in from the Cold* - my current thriller, and a very good one it is. I don't know how these writer chaps do it.

The campus looked very retro - and so *faux* as to be almost not *faux*, if you know what I mean - actually, it looked very gothic at that hour, what with the large and soaring old brick and stone buildings complete with arches and pediments and gargoyles, and wings and courtyards and crenellations and imitation flying buttresses. The great buildings looked like archeological artifacts somehow magically not eroded and crumbling, ancient things in an English-garden setting, all mysteriously untouched by time. In the frigid air, the trees, too, seemed under a spell, their glistening black branches stripped bare of leaves, standing motionless as if frozen in place, like fossil trees coated in ice. The ground all around us, as far as eye could see, was covered by glittering snow and ice, and the entire somber scene was illumined by the light of a chilly little gibbous moon, far up in the sky, shining coldly on all the white stuff that lay about everywhere. The general attitude conveyed was one of utter indifference to human - if you know what I mean - suffering - an attitude that I personally find to be the Universe in general's most disturbing single attribute. If I had to pick just one, I mean.

But my co-adventurers seemed oblivious to the starkly beautiful execution-eve setting so chilling to your narrator's core being. I was, that is to say, in the grip of the sympathetic fallacy, with, in the present instance, all its heavy hints re the darker aspects either of the human (that is to say, humanesque) situation-cum-plight in general, or ours in particular - hints and intimations, as already alluded to, of short, brutish, and nasty mortality, and which positively dripped like gooey icing from all those poor frozen trees, those inscrutable stoics - not to mention the grass enduring who knows what agonies, for months and months at a time under their frigid blanket of snow - hints and intimations which caused Ifford to writhe inwardly and regret having ever been a gleam in the eye of some mad scientist intent on arrogating the godly functions and thus get written up in some prestigious scientific journal and advancing his career - hints which caused self to think upon all things ultimate and final with a painful immediacy, poignancy, and clarity - all this, I say, seemed not to so much as have penetrated the threshold of awareness of my blithe companions.

That is not to say that they chattered animatedly, a feat hardly possible at those glacial temperatures - but they marched along determinedly and cheerfully enough, exchanging an occasional comment in low tones which I, in my chilled, fatigued, and generally frazzled condition, and bringing up the rear as I was, did not even bother to attempt to make out.

Our destination was one of those above-referenced gothic numbers that litter the classier groves of academe on this planet - another arched and vaulted soaring edifice, and fine if you like that sort of thing, I suppose. Though one can hardly not be moved by that somber grandeur, my own tastes in earthly architecture have always run more to the English country cottage surrounded by rose bushes, with a vegetable and herb garden just off the kitchen door, a tortoise-shell cat sunning itself in the window and a little spotted terrier with a tail about two inches long and a glad smile on his goofy face bounding up to greet one at the gate.

We trooped up the steps; Torvald plied his key; and we stepped into the tropical warmth of central heating. Suddenly a thought occurred to me.

"Which floor of the building is this laboratory on?" I asked.

"The fourth," Torvald replied. "The elevator's right over here."

"If it's all the same to you," I answered, attempting an airy and off-hand tone, which even I had to admit clashed conspicuously with my martyred and lugubrious demeanor on the way over to the lab, "I'll just use the stairs - if you'll just direct them to me – I meant, of course, direct me to them - oh, no need - I see them - right at hand, naturally - right where you'd expect them to be, at building's entrance, of course, of course." I could have burbled on and on, it seemed, but here I firmly brought myself up, flashed what I hoped to be a winning or perhaps endearing smile at my companions, and turned, jauntily, to my task.

"See you at the top, then," called Torvald cheerily.

"Right-o," I said. I could hear Glennie talking as I ascended - doubtless explaining that I do not like, and when at all possible absolutely refuse to ride in, elevators. All except the large carpeted ones that have glass walls that you can see out of. Those I don't mind.

And if you are thinking that I am a bit quirky, all I can say is that you would be, too, if you had been gestated in a test tube and raised in what amounts to a glorified orphanage by salaried care-givers, a generous sprinkling of them cyborgian, on the home planet. I am not trying to wring anyone's heart here, but merely to mount a sort of self-defense or apologia in order perhaps to salvage a shred of dignity. Battered but unbowed, and all that sort of thing. One simply does what one must, and what one can, and gets by. And since I must not ride on elevators, I do not. Escalators, of course, are fine.

They were waiting for me at the top of the stairs, upon my predilection for which, surprisingly, not even Rantor remarked or probed, giving me the sense that I was being jollied along, handled with kid gloves, even by the saurian. We all followed Torvald down a corridor which turned right, and right again, and then left, and up a little half-flight of stairs to a tiny, low-ceilinged landing with but a single narrow door. The whole set-up reminded me not a little of Alice in the great hall. I was tempted to peek through the keyhole, but bringing up the rear, could not. Again the muted jangling of keys, and we were in.

CHAPTER 21: IN THE HALL OF THE MOUNTAIN KING

Desperation is the raw material of drastic change.

William S. Burroughs

Torvald switched on the lights, and we beheld a queer sort of garret. Even in my fatigued state, I noticed that it was actually a delightful spacious corner room, with walls of what appeared to be hewn stone, and with alcoves, and nooks, and slanted ceilings, and gabled windows on two sides looking down, as from a secret room in a tower, upon the trees, walkways, and snow-covered lawns below. The room itself looked strangely un-modern, almost medieval, and I glanced at Torvald with a somewhat grudging admiration. He was just too good, and it wasn't fair. Looks, brains, taste, sensibility, a living stipend or teaching assistantship - he had it all, apparently. I didn't doubt but that he had already published something. Granted, he was not an Earthling, but he was even better, in physical type - a sort of super or prototype Earthling. A kind of Platonic ideal blueprint from which the earthly version seemed, even in its highest physical manifestation, a distinct step down.

Glancing over at Glennie, I saw that she, of course, was enchanted. Her complexion was very pink and pretty from our walk in the sub-zero night, and she looked like a child who as a special treat has been unexpectedly whisked away to Santa's workshop. She began to wander about the room, looking at the titles of the books, examining the objects.

The room did not so much resemble the physicist's chamber as the alchemist's. At the risk of repeating myself, I will say that it looked uncannily to be right out of the Middle Ages, in the best sense of that phrase. Or perhaps I'm thinking of the Renaissance. For instance, there was a painting on the wall, a portrait, done in many translucent hues of red and in deep, rich, glossy umbers. The whole set-up really did look more Renaissance that Medieval, now that I think about it. At any rate, the painting portrayed a scholar at his desk. He looked as if he had been interrupted in his writing: pen in hand, manuscript before him, he peered up at you from over his half-glasses, not impatiently, but somewhat quizzically, with a smile, or the promise of a smile, hovering

171

about his lips, which were delicately wreathed in wispy white tendrils rendered with the obsessive Germanic scrupulosity of an Albrecht Durer. The interrupted scholar sat with his back to an open window, through which one saw a fairly typical Renaissance exercise in perspective - the winding road, the vista of hills, dotted by ever-smaller trees, culminating finally in distant crags, all done in the characteristically subdued and somewhat muddy palette of the Renaissance. But the subject of the portrait seemed so intriguing an individual, somehow, a veritable male Giaconda, that all the magic of the picture lay with him, and it was upon him that the eye lingered.

"Found that at a garage sale for $7.00," said Torvald, noticing my scrutiny of it.

"Where is the time travel equipment?" asked Glennie. "Or is it in another room?"

"Oh, it's in this room," answered Torvald. "I haven't any other room. I keep it in this closet over here. Actually, it's not my thesis project. Like my delvings into revisionist economics and history, it's extra-curricular. A bit *sub rosa*, in point of fact. So I don't leave it lying about in view."

He had been walking to the closet door as he spoke, and now he opened it and began hauling stuff out. I could not begin to tell you what any of it was - generators, regulators, inducers, transducers, reducers, de-fraggers, fans, coils, auricular extenders, hypothermicators, discombobulators, radiant energy intensifiers, ambient energy traps, magnetic thermal enhancers, hypothecators, transmogrifiers - I can't tell one from the other. It looked scientific and technical and at the same time old and patched-together from things picked up at various liquidations, salvage yards, flea markets, and government surplus outlets. Torvald, with Rantor's help, arranged everything in a kind of circle in an empty space at one end of the room. A couple of thick, heavy-looking, dully gleaming, long metallic rods, mounted like fluorescent lighting tubes in some sort of stainless steel housing and suspended opposite one another from chains hanging from big hooks in the high ceiling, swung like sluggish pendula out of phase. Humming something rather manically Baroque-sounding under his breath, Torvald, seemingly in his element, happily wired things together and plugged heavy cords into grounded outlets with the casual flair of the expert. A couple of thingummies started to hum, and here and there little lights went on, green, red, and white, some blinking, others shining steadily. It looked like some sort of android's nativity scene, poised and waiting for the focal figures to clump mechanically to stage center. The whole assembly process took less than ten minutes.

"There," said Torvald, straightening up and giving what was apparently one of the chief movers and shakers of the assemblage a couple of hollowly-resounding pats on its metal flank as he moved over to stand with the rest of us and survey the little grouping of components with a sort of paternal pride. "That's it."

I have to tell you honestly that it didn't look all that impressive to Yours Truly. Of course, I'm not your scientific type of fellow, so I had to remind myself that I very likely just didn't know enough to be properly impressed. But, glancing over at Rantor and Glennie, I perceived that their very dissimilar faces seemed to be registering the same species, more or less, of disappointed bafflement as I was myself undergoing. In fact, I noticed within, with a sort of muted horror, a distinct sensation of quietly escalating despair, and again I realized that I had actually, despite all my grumbling and protest, been counting on this device of Torvald's for my salvation. I mean - what else was there, in this narrow box of a far-flung universe into which the gods, for reasons of their own - I mean, we can only assume they had and have their bally reasons - had seen fit to insert me? Simultaneously, I realized, once again with a sort of *frisson* of horror, that I had actually been much more shaken to the core by all of this than I had let myself know, if you know what I mean. That miasma of detachment in which it is apparently my fate to live out my days keeps me appallingly ignorant of my profounder emotions, which can then come up on me when my force field is at its weakest, when my defenses, as I said, are absolutely in abeyance, and quietly deliver, all in an instant, the most foundation-shaking blows to the sense of *bien-etre.*

I began to think again of tropic isles - there are these ones, this archipelago, called, I think, the Marquesas ... I know about the satellite surveillance and passports and all that, but just setting that aspect of the problem aside for the moment, I began to wonder if there are still such things on this planet as tramp steamers. It had always sounded so peaceful, going somewhere distant and tropical on some slow, very shabbily romantic old tramp steamer with engines or pistons or something going ka-chunk-a-chunka-chunka in its bowels, tended by splendid specimens with fine physiques and grimy hands, and captained by some thoughtful, fatherly, quietly insightful Joseph

Conrad type who would beam at one occasionally in an avuncular sort of way but mostly just let one be.

I saw myself sun-bronzed, tropic-shirted and be-sandled, with hair dyed black - no, it would have to be auburn (or a wig, perchance ... but wouldn't a wig be uncomfortably hot and sweaty in the tropics, not to mention an insurmountable technical problem, unless one resorted to a chin strap or perhaps some sort of Velcro arrangement, when spear-fishing and hunting for giant turtles?) and perhaps a small, dapper mustache - I have always wanted to try a moustache - chatting easily with the engine room mechanics, romantic-looking fellows with good tans and well-muscled arms, quiet, salt-of-the-earth types wearing graying, oil-besmeared cotton tank tops. I saw myself wading in brilliant, clear turquoise waters, sucking on a very juicy, very ripe mango, the juice dripping from my chin and elbow into the warm south seas as I combed the water with a practiced eye for bright tropical fish, a hand-crafted spear held casually at the ready in my right hand, in a practiced manner learned from some sort of brotherly brown-skinned native with a big smile, perfect teeth, and a heart of gold.

"So - how does it work? Have you ever used it?" Glennie's voice brought me back to the pitiless present.

"Shall we take it for a spin?" asked Torvald, glancing over at her with a mischievous little smile. Adroitly, I noticed, side-stepping her question. Again I found myself aghast that they could treat all this so lightly. I mean - was the lot of them a few straws short of a haystack - or was I?

"I don't understand," I almost wailed, more than a bit querulously. "What 'it' are we referring to? I see no 'it'- merely a quaint grouping of electronic flotsam and jetsam, as perhaps might be stumbled upon at some government sale of geriatric outmoded equipment dating from the dawn of the machine age."

I wanted to, and I didn't, you see. It made me petulant. I felt that I was falling, or being pushed, more and more into the role of the whining child, the baby of the group, always complaining, always in need of reassurance and mollycoddling. Hardly the stance to assume if you're out to impress the girls, and I made a mental note to remember to display lavish amounts of stoicism and *sang-froid* in future - no matter how gut-wrenching and horrific that future might be. No matter. When the going, in future, got tough, the tough would just hitch up the trousers, square the shoulders, gird the old loins and just bloody well get going.

Even in the midst of it all, that part of me that just watches everything was whispering in my ear that my present almost palpable anguish - I mean, you could absolutely have shoveled the stuff - stemmed, no doubt, from what those pitiless psychologist types, constructing the most fiendish predicaments for their white rats in cages, set-ups involving levers and food and electrically charged grids on the floor and deep tanks of water with nail-carpeted islands (I kid you not), would have called a classic approach-avoidance conflict. How much I did, and did not, want to leave all this behind - and how much I feared, and yet hoped, that it was possible ... and, when it absolutely came right down to it, which it seemed to have, how much I feared launching myself - apparently even *sans* the slight protection, the reassuring presence, however fragile and useless it might actually be when arrayed against the tremendous g- and other forces of outer space and asteroids and solar winds and sub-freezing temperatures and vacuums and whatnot - of a cocoon of metal and shatter-proof glass and an impressively dense array of knobs and switches and dials and lights on the dash - utterly naked, it seemed it was to be - into the space-time continuum. Whatever - when you stop to think about it - that might be.

CHAPTER 22: PLAYING FOR TIME

The eternal silence of those infinite spaces frightens me.

Blaise Pascal

"I was only joking, Ifford," soothingly intoned the Norse god cum boy wonder, sounding to my ears for all the world as though he were addressing a mental patient, or perhaps a frightened Maltese Terrier.

It took me a minute to recall what it was he was referring to - what he had been just joking about, then it came back to me - that 'what ho, shall we take it for a spin' remark he had propositioned me with.

"Oh." I felt mollified, not to mention relieved. I considered, but rejected, the idea of taking issue with his patronizing tone. I did not really see how it could be done. I mean, the fellow really did seem to mean well. He wasn't *trying* to insult me. So I stuck to the matter at hand.

"You were not seriously proposing that we step through the portals of time right now, then. Not right this very instant."

"Of course not. There are some things we'd want to do, first, I should imagine."

"Set our affairs in order - that sort of thing, you mean?"

"You make it all sound so final, Ifford. If I really thought this was just a fancy way of ending it all, do you really think I'd have brought you up here, or even mentioned the whole thing in the first place?"

I considered this. The way I saw it, it pretty much all boiled down to how I felt about Torvald - how implicitly I trusted him, I suppose you could say. I mean, either I was willing to crawl trustingly into the palm of the fellow's hand, or I was not. But the matter ramified, if you know what I'm saying. I mean, beyond the issue of trust, in terms of what sort of a fellow he was, morally speaking, and what his hidden agendas, if any, might be and all that - the good faith issue, basically, I mean - there was additionally the question of how sound he was - how firmly grounded in nuts-and-bolts reality, how commonsensical a cove he was, if you get my drift. Was he capable of putting on two socks that matched most mornings, that sort of thing. Did he hear heavenly voices directing him as their chosen agent in certain undertakings of great moment and consequence. You can't always tell, I've found - just looking at a fellow.

Then again, there was this matter of risk-taking. There are those, I am told, not certifiably insane and claiming no heavenly guidance or high purpose, who are nevertheless drawn to life's dicier moments - the very situations most of us go to great lengths to avoid. Habitual flirters with disaster, tempters of fate. Chronic cliff-hangers. It gets their juices flowing, or some such. So legend has it. They have their own psychological profile, I believe, and the way they see it, there's nothing they'd rather do of a Sunday afternoon than risk life and limb in some terrifying and pointless brush with the infinite, some objectless endeavor that does nothing to alleviate the sufferings of sentient beings, which rights no wrongs, settles no old accounts, and doesn't even go towards paying the rent or getting the kitchen floor swept or that cavity in the left rear molar filled. I was weighing the plausibility of Torvald's being one of these, when Rantor interrupted my musings to express, with his usual resonant forcefulness, a proposal which resurrected all my anxieties and chilled me absolutely to the marrow.

"Look here, Torvald ... I don't see why we couldn't just - you know - try it out. Just like you said, a little spin. What would be the harm? I mean, you've used it yourself, haven't you?"

Torvald appeared to be mulling it over - but, I noticed, skirted that direct question re whether the roadster had as yet been test-driven.

"Well ... where, and when, exactly, did you have in mind?" he asked, with a questioning glance that took in all of us.

"Right now!" chimed in Glennie. "Just for a little while. I've always wanted to do this! How about 1957 in, I don't know, somewhere in Orange County?" She probably meant, but was abashed to go on the record as to saying, Hollywood and Vine.

To my mind, recoiling in horror though it was, had nevertheless risen all unbidden, clothed in the sumptuous colors of Gauguin, thoughts of Maui, or maybe Kona, at more or less the time Mark Twain had visited those isles and Robert Louis Stevenson was dying - of consumption, was it? – in Samoa ... and Gaugan of leprosy, in a little grass shack in the Tahitian outback. But Rantor, the monomaniac, wanted to make it Jekyll Island in 1913, and naturally his was the voice that prevailed, given that Torvald shared his passionate concerns; and, he being the owner of the conveyance in question, his would tend to be the deciding vote.

I myself had no desire whatever to eavesdrop on the planning sessions in which had been drawn up the blueprints of the Federal Reserve Banking System. As has been previously noted, I think about such things as little as is humanly - you know - possible. Sort of like avoiding purely superfluous trips to the dentist. One of those decisions easily made.

"In that case," I said with dignity, and in what I hoped was an off-hand manner that communicated all sorts of *sang-froid* and easiness of mind, "I think I'll just sit this one out, if it's all the same to you. Keep the lamps lit and the home fires burning and all that, don't you know."

"But Ifford," said Rantor, turning and impaling me like a butterfly on a pin with that intense burnt sienna gaze of his, an experience uncomfortably akin to being scooped up and borne aloft by the presiding deity of all electric circuitry. "We need you. We need your help. The thing's no go without you."

"Whatever do you mean? Until very recently, you've managed everything without me. I know I'm pretty hot stuff and all that; but surely I cannot have become indispensable to you in so short a time as this."

The great lizard gave a little sound, a new one, something between a growl, a whine, and a whimper, and turned the remarkable orbs imploringly upon Torvald in mute appeal.

Torvald paused a lengthy moment, obviously considering what to say and how to say it.

Finally, he spoke. "It's like this, Ifford. We need an imaginer."

I waited for him to say on, but, no. He either felt that all was as clear as a mountain stream, or was at a loss how to proceed.

"An imaginer?" I said, in tones of utter bafflement. I mean, what next? "You need an imaginer? Whatever do you mean, old man? What does imagining have to do with anything?"

CHAPTER 23: PROCRASTINATING ON THE SHORES
OF TIME

When one's in this world, surely the best thing one can do, isn't it, is to get out of it? Whether one's mad or not, frightened or not ...

Louis-Ferdinand Celine,
Journey to the End of the Night

"Well, Ifford ..."

"Call me Iffy, please. If we're about to go glissading, more or less hand in hand, I take it, on the slushy slopes of time, we'd better drop the formalities."

"Iffy. Suits you, actually."

"Yes. More or less seeming to give credence to the superstitious apprehension that the planners on the home planet know all and are at all times several jumps ahead of one." I decided that the time was right to touch upon a troubling thought which had occurred to me. "I mean, if we can travel through time, can't they - the slavering hounds of the dark forces, you know - and yank us back, even from the remotest age - say, of those horseshoe-like whatzits and - well, even earlier, when you think about it - even unto the eons during which, allegedly, we were all mere blobs of protoplasm, getting about by means of flagellae, or cilia, or some such, engulfing one another, even as today, and nibbling algae in the rich primordial broth?"

"Concerning that, we shall see, I guess. I sometimes think that they enjoy a somewhat inflated reputation."

"The uni-cellular organisms, you mean?"

"No - the planners. Squinch & company, and their ilk."

"In the omniscience department ?"

"Exactly. Intimidation by rumor and reputation."

"The mere mention of their name causing all and sundry to hasten to toe the line, wipe all seditious thoughts from the mental landscape, and engage exclusively in officially sanctioned musings?"

"Well put, Iffy. You have a way with words, and what might be called a - Baroque imagination." Laying on the flattery with a heavy hand. "Whatever made you decide to go in for a study of banking, of all things?"

"Well, as I've already laid out for Rantor, and I'm surprised he hasn't given you a full report, these decisions are made for one, back on the home planet. We are mere ciphers, units to be deployed for the greater good. What they call the greater good. The phrase could mean practically anything, when you stop to think about it. Rather too general, not to say poetical/mystical, for the uses to which they put it, has always been my private opinion."

"I'd have thought they'd have wanted to put you to writing advertising copy, at the very least. Or propaganda for the state."

"Too sensitive, in my opinion. The symptoms being doubtless well-known to them, they early divined that at bottom I am the type whose loyalty was - is – suspect – lacking the requisite fervor, you know - and has been, virtually from the time I was being dandled for the prescribed amount of time daily from some cybertronic care-giver's prosthetic knee. Or occasionally, from some purely mechanical dandling device. And as to the advertising copy, my own thoughts on the matter have been that they felt I needed reining in rather than encouraging."

"I see."

"Though I wore the mask, they sensed that my heart just wasn't in their little game. Even though it was the only game in town. Hence, I suppose the flight, personally speaking, into the inner realms."

"Doubtless. Speaking of which ..."

"Yes ...?"

"Well, you know Iffy, I mentioned your imaginative nature, just a moment ago ..."

"Yes ? And?"

"And, interestingly enough, imagination has a part to play in this venture of ours..."

This venture of whose ?

"I see ..." I waited for him to go on, and when he didn't, gave him a nudge. "The breath is bated, old man. Fill me in to the fullest extent humanly - I speak broadly here - possible in the time allotted."

"O.K." In tones, now, of firm resolve. He took the deep breath, and made the plunge. "It's like this. Or, we're pretty sure it is." Had he known how troubled I was by such casually tacked-on qualifiers, he would, I am sure, have purged them from his discourse. "As we were just discussing, there have been two conflicting schools of thought for, oh, since way back ..."

"... To the earliest infancy of humanish thought, if not beyond ..."

"Yes."

"Regarding ..."

"Regarding which came first - thought or matter. Presuming that it makes any sense at all to speak of a first cause, that is."

"The religionists and metaphysicians staking all on its having been the thought of a Great Thinker, or perhaps a Committee or Conclave thereof, and the materialists being equally convinced that it's the things rather than the thoughts that have been here ever since your great-aunt Maude had her coming-out party, as it were."

"Yes."

"I remember that late Victorian bloke, an *eminence grise* of some deep discipline or other, or perhaps he was one of those polymath types, who mused for the record that the Universe was beginning to look to him a lot more like a great thought and a lot less like a great machine ..."

"Absolutely on point, Iffy. It in a nutshell."

"And, the relevance of all this to that little ensemble of wire and metal and twinkling lights huddled in the alcove over there?"

"Well, interestingly enough, once we escape the force-field - in a manner of thinking - of the present collective time/space node - a sort of metropolis in the space-time void, you understand - a sort of magnetic scaffolding of thought, you know ..."

"Oh, quite. Clear as a limpid pool, and all that."

"Good ... a sort of self-cohering gestalt which is held in place by the collective belief-structure of all the beings on and about this planet - in this particular strand of probable reality, that is - well anyway, once we leave its influence, we become extremely fluid."

"Soupy? Watery? Bouillabaisse-like?"

"More cloud-like, I think. Kind of like a drizzle - a fine mist, you know. The point is, that it seems that what is needed in those circumstances is a powerful, emotionally-charged imagination to give shape and direction to the proceedings ...."

"Focus?"

"Exactly!"

"Can't this imaginer fellow just sit on the sidelines and do it?"

"It doesn't seem to work that way. Apparently, he has to be outside the field of influence of the present - or any - system of belief."

"To get a clear signal?"

"Get - and/or emit - yes - to be heard above the white noise. Or, you could think of it as the roar of a waterfall, or of cars on a freeway. All of these are just metaphors, you understand ..."

"Mmhumm. Well, look here - can't just anyone do it? Be the imaginer, I mean?"

"Theoretically, yes. But in practice, it appears that, like pretty much everything else, some are better at it than others."

Every time I though I saw a way out, he blocked it. An extremely dogged fellow, I was discovering, for all his pleasant ways and physical comeliness. Rather like a used car salesman.

"All right. As of even date I think I read you loud and clear. But, I'm wondering here, how it is that you happen to know all this? From perusing the research and so forth?" I was wondering if he was not just theorizing. He seemed the type.

"Yes. Of course, it isn't in the open literature. You have to be - resourceful. And persistent." That, he certainly was.

"And bold," interjected Rantor, in tones that struck me as being a bit puffed-up and self-congratulatory.

"Yes, a little verve and audacity at the right moment," agreed Torvald, with - perhaps it was just my imagination - an appreciative, *entre-nous* sort of smile that seemed aimed at his scaly sidekick. It made me wonder whose data-bases they had been hacking into.

"Well, the picture is emerging; but I still have to ask - why me? I'm sure you've got a perfectly fine imagination ... and then there's Rantor - plenty of thrust there, just bubbling over with the stuff, vastly more oomph per ounce than you're likely to find amongst the purely local talent ..."

"Trust me, Iffy..." - though as I saw the matter, it was precisely the issue of his trustworthiness that remained open to question - "We've researched the thing pretty thoroughly. You're right - Rantor is the one to supply the raw emotional power. But to provide a good, clear map of our destination, a lock or a fix, I think you're our man. You and Glennie, that is." He gave her another of those beaming smiles of his, which she as usual returned in kind, only a bit more doe-eyed - which the poor girl can hardly help, of course, it being in the genes. "But mainly you."

I had to pause for a bit - to more or less let all of this sink in. Turning the gaze inward, what emerged with clarity was a sort of vague troubled sense that went beyond my fears about the actual procedure - fraught with peril though that more or less had to be. I mean, the way I saw it, there was just no getting around it. I mean, what was to keep some party of pilgrims from getting hopelessly lost in that space-time void, or whatever it was - between nodes, or metropoli, or ganglia, you know? Absolutely lost in the incoherent wastelands. I mean, can there be less than nothing? And can one get deeper and deeper, I mean, irretrievably, into it? When you think about it, traveling in space and time both, it seems you automatically double your chances of getting utterly, hopelessly misplaced. But beyond that, something was bothering me - an *Angst*, don't you know - a kind of *caveat emptor*-ish sense of foreboding that suffused the tissues and pretty much imbued the entire inner landscape with ominous darkish tones. A morbidly Teutonic *Gotterdammerung* of the *joi d'vivre*. I couldn't quite put my finger on it. Probably it was not just one thing but the whole *Gestalt*. The entire venture seemed entirely too experimental for one of my temperament. But on the other hand, there was that problem with Squinch. Every time the phone rang these days, the pulse raced and the knees trembled. I can tell you, it's no way to live. I had even on occasion imagined myself to be, possibly, followed by shadowy figures in trench-coats.

The really tragic thing about it all was that I hate decisions. Positively abhor them. Only lately had I come to realize that one of the things I had actually appreciated about the set-up on the home planet was the way all my decisions were made for me. All fore-ordained. It removes a burden, don't you know. I can tell you, being thrust so suddenly into a situation such as the present one in which I had to make these momentous decisions, pretty much cold turkey, took its toll. I kept thinking about Calvin. I didn't want to end up like him - a broken entity. And wasn't it Nijinsky - that dancer-fellow, you know - who snapped like a twig and had to spend all the rest of his life sticking straws in his hair under close supervision in the loony bin? These things happen, especially to sensitive types like Yours Truly.

I came up for air to find all eyes upon me. The others had evidently been standing around me in a hushed and respectful silence. It seemed pretty obvious that I had to say something.

Inwardly, I girded the loins. Stiff upper lip. *Noblesse oblige* and all that. It was somewhat nobly, I thought, and still think - given how absolutely used up, and in need of Humphrey's undemanding companionship - and my spy novel, and a Grandma O'Houlihan's Krunchie-Krunchie or two - I was feeling at the moment - that I rose yet again to the challenge.

"Look," I extemporized. At least, I think that's the word I want. "I need some time to think all this over." I made a conscious effort to keep any

185

note of pleading out of my voice. After all, I wasn't pleading; I was telling them. This is the way it's going to be. Ifford has spoken. "It's late and I'm tired. Anyway, I categorically do not believe in making rash, impulsive decisions - it amounts to a standing policy - and certainly not on an important matter such as this. I mean, it's only common sense. I need to let all this resonate in the inner chambers for a day or two. So: let's just adjourn for the evening, and I can allow all this to percolate into the innermost cracks and fissures, give the local collective unconscious free rein in processing the data and in its wisdom shooting out its determination re the correct course of action. All of which should not, as I said, take longer than a day or two; and I give my word, that as soon as I know, you shall know. I will, as they say in banking circles, be getting back to you with my decision soon."

Everyone looked distinctly crestfallen at this juncture, so I felt compelled to offer a few words of hope - "Which, you absolutely have my word on it, I will do. Get back to you, I mean. The proposal has its attractions, for one in my position, and it does indeed interest me."

After a longish pause, Rantor chimed in at this juncture. "One thing, Iffy - have you checked your phone messages recently?"

I had to think a moment. Had I? I couldn't recall. All of those times sort of blend together in the memory. And then, I had been rather avoiding that instrument of late, just between you and me, the atmosphere in its vicinity seeming pervaded with a particularly menacing ambience since that last soul-jarring encounter with Squinch.

"Because, if you haven't, couldn't you check them from here? Aren't you able to dial a code and get your messages from another phone? And find out if Squinch or anyone has called?"

I was about to deny it - being able to check my messages from another phone - when Glennie piped up helpfully. I'd forgotten that she jolly well knows I can do that because I've done it from her digs before. And she's done it from mine.

"That's a good idea, Iffy," she said. "I know you're tired. Do you want me to do it for you?"

I was cornered, it seemed. It was a good idea, I supposed. "Right-o," I said, a trifle wearily. Inwardly sobbing, you know. "Good idea. Thanks, but I'll do it, Glennie. Couldn't risk your finding out about the other woman." Followed up by a wan little smile in her direction.

Glennie got a sort of surprised look on the map. I'll tell you, we hybrids have the rest of the known Universe beat when it comes to gullibility. We positively excel.

"You have a phone here in your office, Torvald, old man? Or should I use one of your wireless phones?" I myself had never invested in one of those cellular phones, having pretty much no one to call or be called by on one of them. And little of an uplifting nature seems to come to me via the telephone. I dreaded doing it - checking my messages. Absolutely didn't want to know, when it came right down to it. But I seemed, under the circumstances, to have no choice. I didn't want to look a craven coward to this lot. We hybrids do have our dignity, you know.

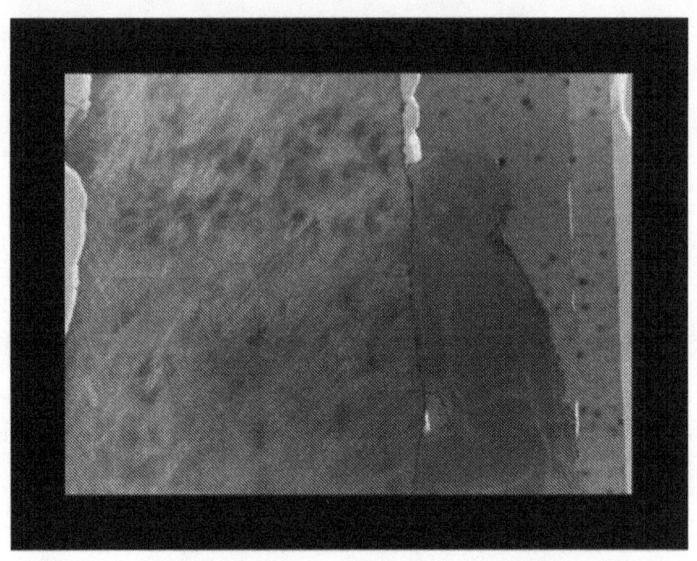

CHAPTER 24: HURRY UP, PLEASE, IT'S TIME

Not with a bang, but a whimper…

T.S. Eliot

Well - there were three messages. The first was from Ida Mae Glatz, saying in those haughty, glacial tones of hers that she couldn't understand why I hadn't been answering my phone (which more or less and to a large extent I hadn't been, had turned the ringer off, in fact) and that it was her policy to communicate directly, and that she knew my schedule of classes and had been calling at times when I should have been on the premises, and that Squinch required my presence yet again - at my 'earliest possible convenience.' Then there was another message from her, saying she couldn't understand why I hadn't responded to either the mailed notice (I hadn't been checking the mail, either) or her first message. Finally, there was a message from Squinch himself, saying that he couldn't understand, and did I realize - and so fourth.

When I put the phone down and turned to the others, it seemed that the truth was there for all to see. I imagine that the shoulders drooped, the face was both drawn and haggard, the eyes haunted, and the skin ashen. The works.

"Not good?" queried Torvald.

"Not good." I answered. "Glatz, Glatz, and Squinch, in that order."

"Well - what did they say?" asked Glennie.

"Just that they want to see me. Instanter."

There ensued another of those little silences in which we all brooded moodily over the news. At least, I brooded moodily. The others probably inwardly rejoiced. Then Rantor spoke.

"Well, this puts a new light on things, I guess. I mean, maybe we should just - you know - take off. What do you say, Iffy?"

"Oh, all rightie then. All right, all right, all right. But not tonight. I need to get a good night's sleep. I can't embark feeling like this."

Another hiatus, again broken by the reptile.

"I hate to bring this up, Ifford - but, yesterday, when you were off somewhere, there came a rap at the door."

Egad! I mean, what next?

"And?"

"It was the porter, saying that there were two gentlemen to see Mr. Furze."

"Two gentlemen? You're sure it wasn't one?" Somehow two seemed so much worse than one. When these official types come in pairs, watch out.

"He said two. Of course, I told him you weren't at home and that I didn't know where you were or when you'd be back; and then I went down later and asked if they'd left any message for you, and he said no, they hadn't."

189

"Why ever didn't you tell me about this before? I mean – did they look like door-to-door salesmen, perhaps?"

A sort of sheepish look came over him. I don't know if you've ever seen one of these reptoid types looking sheepish before. It's quite interesting. The eyelids scrunch up a bit with wrinkles and folds, and they get a very relaxed, almost inebriated smile - reminds you of the way those iguanas look when basking in the sun.

"I got to reading, you know, and it slipped my mind ... actually, they looked more - official - than door-to-door salesmen."

A pretty thin excuse. I didn't see how something of that magnitude could possibly slip any mind worthy of the name.

"But what I was getting at ..."

"I know, I know. Home no longer being the haven of safety it once was, we should not delay our experiment - or exodus. We should do it now."

I must have looked resigned and accepting - either that, or this speculative musing - I mean, clearly in the subjunctive conditional mode, or the next thing to it, what? - was expediently taken as a yes vote - because everyone immediately began to bustle about. Everybody except Glennie and self, who stood there numbly observing. At least, I felt pretty numb. What I'm getting at is that Torvald and Rantor exploded into activity as though the starting pistol had just been fired and the race was on. It looked like one of those old quiz shows from the '50s - you know, where Contestant A and Contestant B are strapped into roller skates, blindfolded, and pitted against one another to see who could coat the greater number of ping pong balls with aerosol shaving cream and stuff them down the fronts of one another's Santa Claus costumes or whatever, the prize being a freezer, car, or trip to Disneyland for the entire family. I couldn't tell you what they were actually doing - Rantor and Torvald, I mean, naturally - the entire venue being foreign to my jurisdiction, as I believe I've touched upon previously. Chemistry, physics, trigonometry, calculus, and so forth were all agonies for me. It has always been a mystery to me how I had passed them, having as I did so hazy a conception even of what they seemed to be about - the general topic, and all. I mean - why calculus? What does one do with it, and whatever for?

In Rantor's case, the activity seemed to consist mostly of opening drawers and cabinets, rummaging about within, and withdrawing things and stuffing them into his pockets - chocolate bars and trail mix, perhaps - that sort of thing. Torvald, on the other hand, was fiddling with the equipment - activating the thing, I supposed - pushing buttons, flicking switches, consulting his wristwatch, and scribbling hasty notations into a small notebook he pulled out of the breast pocket of his shirt. It seemed that hardly any time at all had passed before he turned and shone that brilliant smile of his at us full blast.

"Well - we're ready," he said.

To be perfectly honest, it was only my not wanting to look a craven coward in Glennie's eyes that kept me - just barely - from turning and bolting out the door. That, and wondering where I was going to spend the night if I could not safely return to my digs.

The whole thing seemed nightmarish. I couldn't believe I was going through with this truly hare-brained scheme of theirs. If you ever want to know how the condemned man feels while being led to the execution chamber - well, it's hard to convey, but maybe someday I'll try to put it into a poem or dirge or lament or something. Assuming that I survive. Anyway, I know how those poor blokes feel now, and I can tell you, whatever they may have done, they have my heartfelt sympathies.

But the image must be maintained. I swallowed - to me it sounded like an amplified recording of a pretty sizeable herbivore - maybe more than one - swallowing what had been a too large mouthful of grass and leaves and whatnot - possibly even including a few stray twigs and pebbles - and stepped forward. Who was it - some writer chappie, I think - who said that courage was grace under pressure? Well, it seemed a pretty tame description of what I was going through. Considerably understated. Positively clinical. Purged, you know, of that all-important feeling-state.

"All rightie, then. Lead on. I mean, what next? Where do we stand - position the *corpora*, I mean? Do we don any special gear? Attach any electrodes to the scalp? Stroke an amulet? Summon any dark forces? And - don't you want me to be doing something specific with the imagination?"
Torvald rummaged in a desk drawer and produced a slightly dog-eared three by five card with some words typed on it. He handed it to me. Even in my benumbed state, I recorded mentally that that detail alone

191

proved - positively proved - that this had been a set-up deal from the get-go. I mean, when you think of it, going back to square one, how ever did that lizard sidekick of the author of my current predicament ever get dropped by the stork on my particular doorstep? I ask you. It had all the appearance - I hated to use the word, but could in my fevered state think of no other - of a conspiracy. I guess I could have said 'covert joined planned action,' but that more dignified and tonier phrase did not at the time occur to me, what with the pulse thudding along at about 200 beats per minute and the general feeling overwhelming me, with all the (rumor has it) uncomfortable and compelling sensations of giving birth, or being given birth to, that I was poised on the brink of being shot out of a jerry-built backyard cannon straight into the arms of the Infinite, there to take immediate and non-negotiable possession of my eternal reward, whatever that might consist of. And given the apparent judgment and quality of mind of the devisor or devisors of this plane of existence, I did not feel much comforted re the probable ambience and gameplan of the hereafter. The deity or deities, as portrayed in most of the literature purporting to fill us in on their nature and motivations, come across to yours truly as distinctly unstable types - all over the map, if you know what I mean, and very impulsive and moody. They seem to like nothing so much as a good joke, and to have, taken collectively, a rather warped sense of humor. Also to be subject to violent mood swings and to be capable of just - I don't know - having it in for a particular entity for no very clear reason - or, in the alternative, for a rather bewilderingly multitudinous and shifting schedule of reasons. I know I make these somewhat critical remarks at the risk of setting one of them off, but it is my honest appraisal after much thought, and one from which there is - and this of course is my point in the present instance - precious little comfort to be drawn in moments such as the one I am, in my own rather painstaking and meticulous fashion, describing.

In a word, my unease intensified in a nanosecond to panic - and I do not engage in hyperbole, here, but merely state the facts, rather Hemingwayesque. I felt like a steer in a cattle-chute the wings of which had been cleverly concealed with brush. The only thing that kept me rooted to the spot, with what I imagine looked like a rather sickly grin plastered on my face, was the fact that I could conceive of no graceful way out. Ever the observers of form, decorum and *comme il faut*, we hybrids. I cursed my ancestry, my racial heritage, and my genetic endowment - but I stood firm. Or reasonably firm. The knees were feeling a bit aspic-like.

"Just take a seat over there ..." - pointing to four folding chairs he had placed in the otherwise ominously hollow center of the little group of gadgetry – "And read this list of words, associating freely. Just try to relax."

Here, I had to suppress a derisive snort of the most heart-felt variety. Relax? Try to relax?

"Just - let the mind wander, you mean - but on these themes?"

"Exactly. And Glennie, you read the list and do the same, relax - OK?"

She nodded - seemed a bit quelled, actually, now that push was actually coming to shove.

"Don't you think you'd ought to stay here?" I asked her in a quiet voice. "I mean, why should you volunteer? We'll do this trial run, and if all goes according to plan, we'll come back and pick you up for the real thing. Really, I don't see why we should each and every one of us fling ourselves heedlessly into the open maw of Fate. Just, you know, have a seat over there and provide a sort of beam on which we can fix to guide us home."

"No, Iffy. I'm coming along."

What was I to do? I could hardly plead with the old girl, much less order her to stay, as if she were some sort of pet spaniel. We walked over and sat where indicated, huddled closely together as if in an invisible elevator. I held out the list so that Glennie could see it, too. It was nothing to write home about. Very tame stuff.

"Jekyll Island," it said. "Georgia coast ... 1910 ... November ... Nelson W. Aldrich ... Paul Warburg ... Frank A. Vanderlip ... November, 1910 ... Benjamin Strong ... Jekyll Island, Georgia ... Paul Warburg ... Frank A. Vanderlip ... huge mansion, Jekyll Island ... Paul Warburg ... Abraham Piatt Andrew ... November, 1910 ... Henry P. Davison ... New Jersey railway station ... Paul Warburg ... Banking Reform Act ... snowy night, plush private railway car on very end of train ... destination, Georgia ... Georgia on my mind ... Charles D. Norton ... behind every great fortune, a great crime ... Paul Warburg ... Kuhn, Loeb, and Company ... J. P. Morgan, clandestine affiliate of ... Rothschild family ... too rich by half ... Jekyll Island, off the coast of

Georgia, in international waters ... November, 1910 ... Paul Warburg ... Rothschild dynasty ..."

"Turn it over," breathed Torvald into my ear. His breath smelled of chocolate and coffee.

I did so, and saw, Scotched-taped to the other side, a black and white photograph of an immensely large old brick building, with extensive covered porches and even a sort of cylindrical turret on one corner, projecting eccentrically above the building itself, with some sort of antenna atop its cone-shaped roof; and two widow's walks, or balconies, one a floor above the other and both protected by metal railings, everything looking as trim, tidy, and obsessively exact down to the last nail and shingle as a *naif* painting.

"Read the caption aloud, please, Glennie," murmured Torvald.

"Above is J.P. Morgan's private hunting club on Jekyll Island in Georgia where the Federal Reserve System was conceived in great secrecy," she intoned softly. "It is shown here shortly after its completion."

I was beginning to feel a little bored, and then a little relaxed, and then a little drowsy, when an intense, ecstatic sort of humming caught my attention - I had not noticed it before - like the buzzing of many bees, seemingly emanating from a spot between my eyebrows. The buzzing radiated as a vibration, very warm and relaxing to the various sinews and tissues as it spread in concentric rings from my forehead throughout my body and on into the space in which I stood, as I simultaneously began to perceive, at the very periphery of my vision, what put me instantly in mind of descriptions of those Northern lights which reputedly cavort in the heavens above the long, still Arctic winters on this planet ... these were pulsating, rising and falling, somehow in entrancing synchronicity with the buzzing of all those happy, friendly bees ...

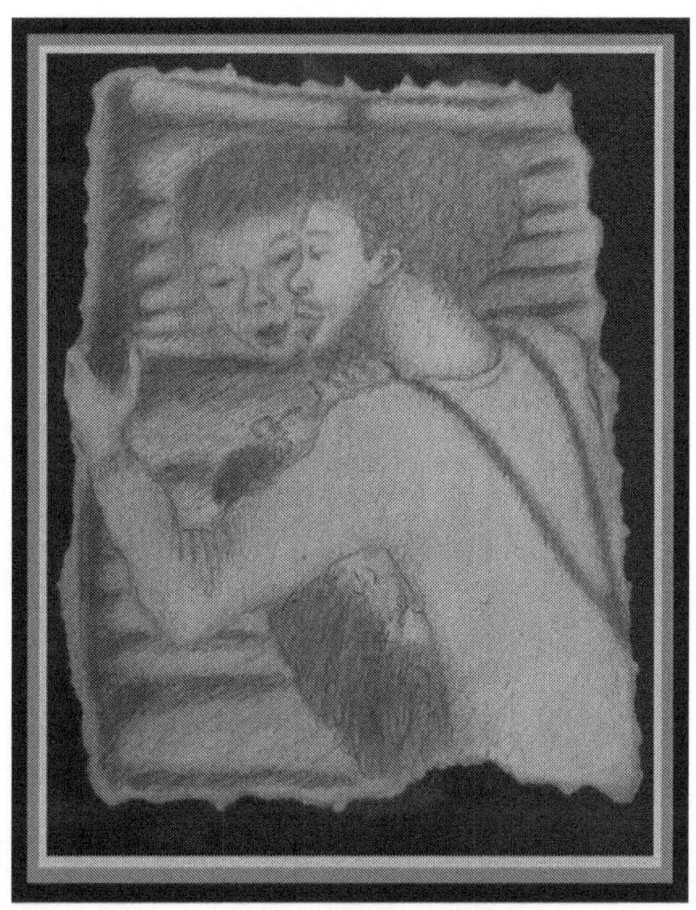

"Glenda and Gifford"

CHAPTER 25: STILL IN KANSAS

For a moment, nothing happened. Then, after a second or so,
nothing continued to happen.

Douglas Adams

I seemed to be hovering near the ceiling in what appeared to be some
sort of roomy walk-in closet. It was quite dark; but somehow, probably
by the cracks of light coming from the narrow spaces between the door

and its jamb, I could see. This closet - almost a small room, actually - was filled with drawers and shelves, holding what looked like sheets, pillowcases, and towels, as well as embroidered, lacy things like antimacassars and doilies, on the shelves. The inventory was extensive. These, however, formed but the backdrop; the action and focal point of interest were provided by a couple who appeared to be grappling steamily in the corner. I know this is going to sound very odd - it's deuced difficult to explain - but, in addition to observing, I seemed also to some extent to be experiencing what these two were feeling and thinking. However, there was a good deal more of the former than of the latter going on in the linen closet. A smallish female stood up against the rear bank of shelves, with this fellow in suspenders standing very close, looming over her and more or less surrounding her. Had it been I, I think those trapped and cornered feelings I get in elevators would have kicked in, especially as it was dark - the dark makes it much worse - but she didn't seem to mind it at all. In fact she was feeling wonderful. So was he. Extremely good. We all were.

Have you ever lain in a *chaise longue* in the warm spring sunshine, sipping a glass of champagne, maybe your second glass of the stuff, or perhaps one of those mimosas, made by adding fresh orange juice to the bubbly, in which fizzes a sugar cube with a dash of something dark carelessly splashed a la Jackson Pollock across a couple of its perfect little square sides, listening to the twittering of the birds, and being overtaken by deliciously warm and drowsy feelings in all the limbs and tissues? I haven't - never all at once, anyway - never with the champagne - but that's how these two were feeling - only better. It's the closest I can come to describing it. There were all sorts of warm and cozy sensations moving about inside. So much going on within, in fact, that it was a bit like a symphony orchestra - one of those tone poems of Debussy, perhaps.

The chap in the linen closet who was doing the looming murmured 'Glenda,' very breathily, and put a hand on one of her breasts. Sorry to be so graphic here, but that is what he did. Since it seems to have been an important, even central, part of the action, I don't see how I can omit it, and I hope the readership will understand and bear with me. She - the loomee, you might say - wore no bra. She certainly could have used one, as they were very full - her breasts, I mean - and soft and yet firm at the same time, if you can imagine that. Kind of like water balloons filled with warm water, but without that rubbery feeling and *sans* squeak. She murmured, 'Gifford - we mustn't,' in a sort of a breathy whisper, as he began to make a kneading motion, very slowly, with the hand on her breast, at the same time bending down and brushing her lips with his. She gave a little moan and made what seemed to me a distinctly half-hearted effort to turn her head to one side. He reached up with the other hand and gently held her chin with it. At this, she went kind of limp against him, sighed very deeply, and opened her lips slightly. He began to run his tongue very lightly here and there on her lips. I just can't describe how they - we - were feeling. It was pretty much off the scale. Better than Haagen-Dasz coffee ice cream with macadamia nuts and chocolate sauce, or chocolate mousse with slivered almonds, whipped cream and bits of freshly candied orange peel. Better than cream-cheese brownies. Better than waking up and remembering that you can sleep in today, and lying there, half-asleep, remembering the dream you were just immersed in. Better than a hot bath on a cold morning. Better than taking off a pair of shoes that have been hurting you all day. Better than TV.

Suddenly we were jerked out of all this by a voice that seemed to be coming from down a longish corridor.

"*Glenda*! Youah wanted in the kitchen! The gen'emuns is takin' theah tea in the librarah and it's ready to be carried in to them *raht naow* ! Glenda Louise?!"

Glenda and Gifford came out of the clinch and began feverishly smoothing and straightening the clothing and patting the hair - in her case quite an elaborate arrangement, twisted and pinned into some sort of a knot on the back of her head. I heard a sort of clomping sound that seemed - whoever or whatever it was that was doing the clomping - to be heading our way. I gazed in some fascination at Glenda's elaborate hairdo, trying to figure out how she did it, and how long it must take her to arrange it each morning. I didn't know women wore their hair that way anymore. But actually, Glenda's whole mode of dress and personal decor seemed antiquated; her skirts were down almost to the floor, and she was wearing some sort of extremely uncomfortable corset-type thing. I could tell, because I felt how it pinched her around the ribs and waist.

We heard the rapidly approaching clump-clump of very determined footsteps - made, from the sounds of them, by no lightweight. As it so often does, on this plane of existence, at any rate, push seemed to be coming to shove. The two lovers exchanged alarmed looks; she grabbed an armful of towels and shot out the door. And would you believe - this Gifford fellow reaches out and gives her a good pinch on the rear as she goes out, causing her to jump and give out with a little muffled yelp!

I, meanwhile, seemed to have floated through the wall and to be hovering near the ceiling in the corridor. I had never before hovered, not to my recollection, at any rate, and I rather liked it. A stout, middle-aged woman - like Glenda, the palest *cafe au lait* in color - I had not noticed the latter's exotic coloring in the dark linen closet - was right there, so close to the closet door that she could have touched it. Like Glenda, she wore what appeared to be an old-fashioned maid's uniform, the skirts of which practically dragged the floorboards, complete with a bibbed, white starched apron and some sort of perky, rather ridiculous little headpiece, perched on top like a bird, or like a tiny lace handkerchief that had been deposited there by the wind. Hardly chic, I'm saying, and more than a bit absurd to my eye but then - *chacun a son gout*, and all that. Totally *comme il faut* in their circles, for all I knew. Some of her graying hairs had come loose from the arrangement in back and framed her shiny pink cheeks in a kind of halo of wisps and tendrils. Glenda, emerging rather forcefully into the corridor due to the boost supplied by the pinch on her posterior, came within a hair of colliding with this lady.

"What you doin' in theah? Was that valet in theah with you, Missy? You done lost yoah hat. I'd watch that man if I was in youah shoes. These rich gen'emuns - and they gen'emuns gene'muns is the same - jes' plays with the likes of you an' then it be on to the nex' hussy. You doan' need to stand blockin' the doah like that. I'se not goin' to look in theah, if thas what's worryin' you. What you do is yoah business. But I'm tellin' you, mind what you do. Thas all. You know how Brookin's is. He woan' tolerate no goins on, not on these premises. An' I know yoah ma needs the money you earnin' heah. Now - you give me them towels, and I'll take 'em to the bafrooms, an' you-all run as fas' as you can on down to the kitchen."

Glenda, looking flustered, did as she was told, thrusting the armload of towels at the woman and legging it down the long corridor, still smoothing the apron and patting the hair-do as she went. The older woman stood looking long and hard at the linen closet door, as though seriously tempted to go back on her word to Glenda concerning having a peek inside. As she seemed a forceful personality, and this Gifford fellow impressed me as being of more or less equal wattage, I was pretty keenly interested in what would transpire between them, were she to do so.

198

Suddenly - with absolutely no transition - I was back sitting in the center of the pathetic little circle of electronic what-nots with my three companions. It was quite a come-down, I'll tell you. They were all staring at me with the most intently interested expressions on their faces, as though I had just come back from a pilgrimage to the oracle at Delphi and was going to tell them what could be done to save the year's harvest - or as if watching the closing moments of some crucially important football or basketball game, on the outcome of which rode some pretty heavy money.

"What happened?" asked Rantor.

"That's just what I was about to ask all of you. I mean - do mine eyes deceive me - or are we still in Kansas?"

PART TWO: ON THE LAM

The individual is handicapped by coming face-to-face with a
conspiracy so monstrous he cannot believe it exists.

J. Edgar Hoover

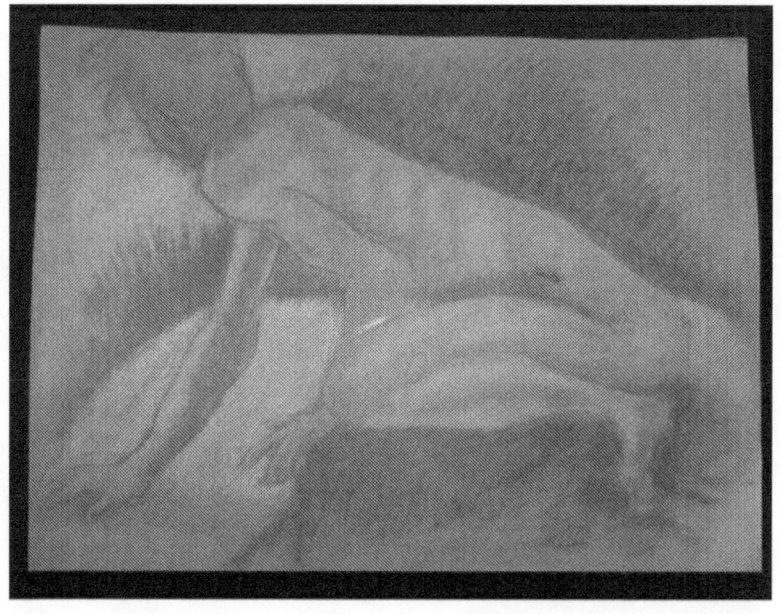

CHAPTER ONE: STURM, DRANG, AND I

I am sitting here, far away in Hungary.
I am often depressed.

Franz Schubert

Things are all quite different now, and I'm going to have to take a moment here to fill you in. The truth is that there was simply so much going on for a while there, that I was not able to keep up with the daily entries in this journal. And while I shall endeavor to maintain the light, insouciant tone of Part One, as I am thinking it now, that may not always be possible. So brace yourselves. Despite my best efforts to maintain the stiff upper lip and the positive outlook, the emotional ambiance may at times resemble that of Schubert's *Winterreise*, as considerable *Sturm und Drang* have infested the life of old Ifford, becoming almost a daily occurrence, or perhaps it would be more accurate to say, the element in which I live, as a fish lives in water.

I'm not sure if you're familiar with this piece - this *Winterreise* wheeze. (It translates into "winter's journey', by the way, for those not up on their Germanic languages.) I took a course on the Romantic Movement in Art and Music, a couple of quarters back, in order to

201

satisfy the distribution requirements, and the old bird who taught the course absolutely worshipped this Franz Schubert - the composer fellow, you know. Wrote the Unfinished Symphony, I believe. She said that Schubert was the absolute master of the art song, and played this *Winterreise* for us, to show us what she meant. Not just a section or two - the whole thing! The whole bloody song cycle, I think she called it, which lasts an entire hour - took up the entire class one day. I can tell you, I was never so glad to get out of a class. And remember, this is coming from one whose major is - or was - banking and economics! Absolutely the most depressing stuff I've ever listened to.

And it wasn't just me who was brought down by the experience. The whole class seemed to a man and woman positively suicidal, as they filed gloomily out of the lecture hall that day. My thought was that all those manic-depressive types you read about should keep a copy of this material on hand at all times and take a stiff dose whenever they detect themselves sliding over the edge into uncontrollable bliss, and staying up all night playing blackjack at the casinos or buying things on the internet with the credit cards of their nearest and dearest or composing or painting their ecstatic masterpieces, or flying on impulse to Kazakhstan to place heavy bets on the camel races, as I've heard is their wont when on the upswing.

But I am rambling. The problem I am rather avoiding is: how to tell you what's happened, while being gay and amusing. I'm not sure it can be done. You see, from just a lad, I've always hated it when people seek me out to unload a bunch of bad news on me, whether it be personal - the bunions, the boss or spouse or teen-age offspring, or whatever - or general, as exemplified by the obsessive concerns of my now erstwhile roommate, Rantor - and so it has been pretty much my policy not to do that to people. Rather, in general, I strive to uplift the spirits of those who stray within my orbit, to whatever small measure possible. I mean, I am absolutely without delusions of grandeur, I assure you. Mine is a humble effort - a strictly small-scale jollification operation.

Now, I don't know if you are a believer in the Satanic presence - you know, the dualist view of the cosmos, according to which we have the forces of Good and those of Evil arrayed against one another and duking it out, across the millenia, in some sort of godly, or ungodly - actually, when you think about it, it would have more or less by definition to be a sort of schizoid struggle - a quasi-sacred, quasi-profane cosmic slug-fest between God and an aspect of Himself, if I've got it right. The super-heroic subject matter of the comic book; the sort of thing Wagner might have written an opera about.

In general, yours truly looks askance at world-views such as these, finding them a bit too pat and ultimately unconvincing. The pathetic fallacy seems, at least distantly, to apply here. And then, such a view of things absolutely disregards - for all I know, may never even have heard of - the principle of Occam's Razor, which has always seemed to me to make a great deal of quiet good sense. But quiet good sense seems to count for very little in some circles; indeed, I believe some proponents of the theory go so far as to regard with fear and loathing the operations of the discursive intellect itself, feeling it - the rational intellect, you know - to be merely another venue by which pride and delusion may enter and gain a toe-hold within the soul. Faith, fear, and humility, in copious amounts and pretty much to the exclusion of all else, I take it, are the ticket and the only safe bet, the way they see it. And who am I, a mere hybrid gestated in an over-grown test-tube at the whim of some fellow with a high IQ, a big ego, and a government grant, to disagree?

In fact, now that I think about it, it comes back to me that I may very well not be, according to the script some of these dualists are working from, an ensouled being. Which rather makes one shudder. And I realize that to weigh in as a skeptic in this matter places me, in the eyes of the devout - to the extent that I am or may be ensouled - firmly, and horribly, in the Luciferian camp, they being of the fervent belief that all who do not subscribe to their system of thought, down to what I believe used to be called the last jot and tittle, belong to and serve, whether wittingly or otherwise, the Evil One, a/k/a the Great Deceiver. There being, in their view, no middle ground.

You can see the usefulness of Satan as a concept; though I personally tend to believe that it has been carried too far by many of its adherents. I mean, in all things be moderate, as one of those ancient Greek johnnies said. When confronted by such abominations as mosquitoes, slugs, and cabbage worms, and even sub-zero temperatures and icy sidewalks ... and Squinch, and Glatz ... well, I mean, it seems to verge on the blasphemous to suppose that God himself would have done that to us. Disrespectful, you know. And also - who can feel comfortable, living in a world the Creator and Ruler of which is such that He could sleep well after having personally unleashed such as these upon His own beloved offspring? On the other hand, are we then to believe that He, having created us, cares not a fig for us, and has done all this more

203

or less as an idle experiment - a way of whiling away Eternity? I can entirely sympathize with those who find it preferable to believe that a renegade sub-deity is responsible for all that is not copasetic, and that we, by properly aligning our beliefs and allegiances, can find, or fashion, some basis for a view that all's well, or can be - depending on how we play our cards - and some reason to believe that, as regards the eternal soul, at least, we are not to worry. If we are careful to observe all the prescriptions and proscriptions and humbly beg forgiveness and in some cases atone, then in the long run, all works out for the best, the Hand at the helm being, ultimately, and despite appearances being so often to the contrary, a beneficent One. Of course, in the other camp we have those who sneeringly refer to a supreme deity in any edition as being no more than a figment born of need and desire - the adult's imaginary companion.

Anyway - the reason I brought all this up in the first place is that it does sometimes appear as if an Unseen Hand of the most sinister possible variety is indeed lurking about and for some unfathomable reason trying to make things difficult for old Ifford. Such thoughts seem self-pitying - something which, as I believe I mentioned many pages back, we were warned by our caretakers to be always on our guard against. The phrase, 'ideas of reference,' doubtless the residue from some abnormal psychology class taken to fulfill the distribution requirements, also surfaces. I don't remember exactly what it means; but it seems possibly to apply here, and it can't be good. Few of the phrases one picks up in psychology classes have happy meanings. Taking all this into account, therefore, I try to keep the positive expectations in place and regard all intrusions of the negative as mere aberrations. But at times, you know, on life's rocky road, one feels almost forced to consider some of these other theories.

Specifically, it does sometimes look as if some malevolent being with a lot of time on its hands has taken note of my resolve to be a beacon of good cheer and out of sheer, impish perversity has set himself to make that an utter impossibility. If so, one wonders where these daemons get all their drive, energy, and singleness of purpose.

By way of example, just consider my present situation. Admittedly, I had my private reservations re the existing power structure on the home planet; but I was doing the right thing and not talking - I mean, scarcely even thinking - about them. Not questioning, just fitting in - all that sort of thing, as per the *lex non scripta*. If you doubt me, just go back and re-read the opening pages of this little narrative which you hold in your hands. It's all there in black and white. And as regards this azure planet, and those who hold power here, well, I pretty much worshipped them. Once again, I refer you to the first chapters of this epistle. As I have recorded, Glennie and I made practically a fetish of our adoration of all things earthly, which we felt had attained their greatest glory, their Golden Age, in American suburbia during the 1950's and early '60's. You just can't get much more uncritical than that. I mean: can you?

I did not ask to have Calvin crumble, forcing the return to store of the merchandise. I mean, I liked the fellow - what there was of him. He was the nearest thing to an invisible roommate I've ever personally encountered. And, what I'm driving at here is, that's the sort of roommate one wants, isn't it? What reason had I to ruffle the waters?

And, moving on, I certainly did not ask, and would have vetoed the plan had I been consulted, to have inserted in my midst any denizen of the planet Squank, being apprised as are we all of their reputation as hot-heads and trouble-makers. You know that I have come rather to like Rantor, or at least to appreciate certain of his qualities; but he is not my type. And, as you also know, my life has not been the same since his entry into it. And I fear, never will be again.

As I see it, my liability in this matter is limited to only two areas. I did contact my mother. That was my doing. I wish now that I had never done it; but I did, and I take responsibility for it. My other mistake was, as I have mentioned earlier, that I should have had the backbone to keep Rantor and all his theories and associates at arm's length. I did not like the way the whole thing smelled from what I believe is called here the get-go, and I should have had the strength of character to remain aloof. In fact, now that I think about it, I should have gone and complained about the incompatibility of self and lizard, the very next day after his arrival. But of course, they would have accused me of being racially prejudiced. And then, now that I think of it, I did forget all about that accursed bag of money I found on the sidewalk outside The Friend of the Family. Completely blanked it out, due to having so many other things on my mind. Which probably ended up more or less clinching the case against me, in the eyes of Squinch et al. Or would do so, if they knew about it. Which perhaps by now they do. So I suppose that makes three things.

Now that I think of it, I wonder what became of that money. I shall have to ask Glennie if she can locate it – still in its hiding place under my mattress, I hope – and get it to me. I could use it now.

Anyway, the reason I'm maundering on like this is that my life – never, at its best, all that much to write home about - has pretty much fallen apart. And I am not the sort of fellow for whom any sort of change comes easily. Let alone change of this cataclysmic magnitude.

The alarming fact is, that I am no longer living in my digs. I am no longer attending classes. I am no longer receiving my stipend. I have, as they say, gone underground. I am a wanted entity. And if I am found, I shudder to think what will be done with me.

CHAPTER TWO: NEW DIGS

Solitude is better than the society of evil persons.

Abu Bakr

The place where I am currently living – or should I say, am currently holed up? - is one that - who else? - Torvald and Rantor found for me, a small room in one of those big old places of which there are so many, in the area surrounding the University. I am told it was built around the turn of the Twentieth Century or before. It has three stories, plus a basement and attics, a large yard with guest cottage, and a garage and gardening shed. It must have been quite a place in its day; but now it has gone to seed. It is warren of dens inhabited by two or three of Rantor and Torvald's friends and acquaintances, as well as by a number of unaffiliated students who just happen to rent rooms here. To these, I am merely another foreign exchange student in need of a rented room within easy walking distance of the campus.

To some of Torvald and Rantor's associates, however, I seem to be of interest as perhaps having a knack for this thing they call 'remote viewing.' Evidently that's their term for what happened when our time-travel thing aborted and I ended up hovering in the corner of a linen closet as a sort of third wheel to a primal scene. It seems the group of them - not Gifford and Glenda, of course, but Torvald and Company - are engaged in some kind of historical researches in which they see a need and a place for talents such as they seem to think I possess.

And to think I'd always thought of it as daydreaming and been instructed by the old caregivers to consider it something to be overcome. I haven't met any of these researchers yet, the two or three of their group living here in the house being evidently not of the inner circle. The meeting is scheduled to happen soon, Torvald tells me.

I've been staying in this place for less than a week. As to how I've been spending my time - well, mostly it seems I have been lying on my bed, gazing out the window. You may think that sounds depressing, but actually, I rather like it. It's very restful and undemanding. I have one of the attic rooms - one of the smaller, and least expensive, rooms in the house - I think it must have been a servant's room, originally. Reminds me of an artist's garret. It's sort of cut off from the rest of the house - you reached it by its own little stairway that goes up from the third floor - and it is very quiet and peaceful. I have a partial view of the campus, and beyond that of a lake, or a part of it, that lies just east of the University.

It is still very cold and snowy, so cold that the lake has frozen - something that I am told has not happened for over seventy years. So, as I lie on my bed by the window, I can see people out on the ice - people skating, parents pushing prams or pulling their children on sleds and inner tubes. From here they look very tiny. I have my mystery novel - *The Coils of Fate*, it is now - not quite as good, so far, as *The Spy-Catcher Who Came in from the Cold*, or that last Peter Wimsy book, but perhaps it will get better - and I have a couple of books given me by Rantor and Torvald to more or less prepare the mind for some remote viewing project they have in mind. And then, I have Humphrey.

But I have concluded that hamsters are not very sociable. He's a little chap who has very much his own agenda and does not seem able to block in any time for Ifford. A very self-sufficient, impersonal little fellow. How he finds so much to do in a space little larger than the proverbial breadbox beats me; but when not sleeping - an activity which invariably occupies him all the daylight hours - he is as busy as any high-level executive, puttering about, moving things from here to there and there to here, shredding things, digging energetically in the cedar shavings, and whatnot. When all else fails, he makes a bee-line for the exercise wheel, seeming to have made some sort of deal with himself concerning how many hours per night he will put in on the thing to stay fit. A pleasant enough little creature - quiet, mannerly, and unobtrusive, as I have been alluding to, to a fault - but from my point of view, lacking in depth. Although I am new at this pet-owning business, we inmates never having been allowed to keep them in any of the facilities in which I was reared on the home planet, I am seeing the handwriting on the wall and wondering if that is not often the way it is with pets. You enter into the relationship with such high expectations of camaraderie and soul-to-soul communion, only to find their concerns to be relentlessly narrow. I mean, food and drink; in some cases, being scratched behind the ears, at the base of the tail, or on the tummy; and then, the exercise, of course, and sleep - and that seems to be where it begins, and where it ends, for them, you being in the loop only to the extent that you provide one or more of these essentials of life.

So as it turns out, Humphrey has been less a comfort and companion to me in my time of trouble than I might have hoped. But in a way, he has been all the company I have wanted, at least at this juncture in my affairs. When one stops to think about it, you know, one has to wonder if one's fellow beings, taken all in all, are not more of a curse than a blessing. I mean, they always seem to be impinging on one in ways that sooner or later reveal themselves to be part of the problem rather than part of the solution, recent events providing such an *embarasse du riches* in the way of corroboration of my point here that I think no more need be said. The facts speak, with a sort of soul-wrenching eloquence, for themselves.

And another thing - I have been living on this planet for over a year now, and I have yet to make a single friend from the genus *Homo sapiens*. Or the species, if that is what it is. I haven't felt shunned, exactly - but then, I haven't exactly been flocked to, have I? What I am wondering is - underneath all the *bonhomie* and the great, one might almost say ostentatious, display of non-prejudice here on this planet, does there not lurk a certain felt superiority - something that, put into words, might run along the lines of - oh, hybrids (or fill in the blank with the name of any other off-planet entity of your choosing) are all right, I suppose, in their place - I hear they make great accountants - but I don't see myself ever being friends with one. The gulf being too great, or whatever. Separate but equal, I'm sure the argument would run - or something like that.

Such attitudes, of course, cannot but wound the spirit of all proud off-planet entities such as your narrator, who long to belong, whose whole young lives have been spent, in off-duty hours, dreaming of fitting right in and being accepted as one of.

Actually, since a mere stripling hardly out of knee pants, I have wondered if it might not be my destiny to know and love an Earthling. In fact, I have almost felt it to be my destiny. Think of it as deep calling unto deep, if you will. I've been giving it a lot of thought, up here in the garret these past few days. I would not go so far as to say that I firmly believe it to be inevitable, already penciled into the Akashic Records and so forth. Let's just call it a sort of - well, feeling, I guess. A hunch. An intuition, you know.

It all goes back, I think, to a TV show I saw when I was no more than eight or nine years old. It was a series, actually, came on every Wednesday night at seven, and for all of us in the care home it was the highlight of the week. It dealt, as might be surmised from the foregoing, with a hybrid lad not unlike myself and an Earthling girl, a sort of a honey blonde who lived in a *Father Knows Best* sort of household and who had a deep and abiding interest in offworld entities. The other girls played with dolls or talked about boys, and she - she hung out in her room reading every book she could get her hands on about otherworlders.

So - the storyline goes - this girl was out strolling in a wood near her house after dinner one early evening - she was that kind of girl, you see, who took these long, thoughtful, solitary walks where she would commune with nature and so on - and suddenly she saw what looked like a very bright star in the sky which, as she watched, seemed to be getting closer and closer - to her! - where she stood aghast and rooted to the ground, in that copse of trees by the river that ran through her little hometown. As this light approached, she heard a sort of high humming noise, and then ...

CHAPTER 3: DEEP COVER

Politics, as the word is commonly understood, are
nothing but corruptions.

Jonathan Swift

I was interrupted in this reminiscence - which will have to be gone into
at a later time - by a rap on my door. Shave and a haircut, two bits.
Rantor's knock. Nevertheless, raps at the door these days tend to cause
the heart to surge about in the thorax rather like a mob in a theatre on
fire looking for the exit; but it was only Rantor, come to tell me that a
meeting was on for that evening between self and the blokes who are
doing the historical research.

"At The Classier Joint this time?" We had discussed changing our
meeting place to throw possible pursuers off the scent, and I, rather
liking the brew at this place, as well as its quieter atmosphere, had
suggested it, even though I knew that service there was a trifle sluggish,
the help, as the name suggests, reputedly slipping frequently into the
restroom or out into the alley to smoke their marijuana cigarettes.

"No," he replied. "We're going to meet them at The Silver Stud."

I thought perhaps I hadn't heard him correctly. "Did you say The Silver
Stud?"

"That's right. The Silver Stud. You know - the place at the confluence
of Cheney Drive and Bush Way, just up from that little park east of
campus?"

I knew all right. It was precisely because I knew that I was asking. This
bit of intelligence perplexed me. The Silver Stud, you see, is the
principal hangout of the black leather jacket crowd. These are the
current Bohemian set. Back home, they'd be gathered up and put into a
work camp for Attitude Adjustment and Opinion Restructuring, but
here they are allowed to loiter about the University District and other
haunts of their choosing, soliciting spare change. From what I have
gathered, they seem to be too disaffected and alienated to go to
University, or get a job. Seeing no options that appeal to them in the

modern corporate world (rather like myself, now that I think about it), they seem more or less to just - hang out together, experimenting, I take it, with other ways of having a go at this thing called life. Many of them are very young, little more than children, actually, apparently not having even finished high school, their disenchantment with the status quo seeming to have taken root in their infancy and flowered early.

They trudge the pavements dressed in what look rather like costumes, really - black leather jackets and boots with silver studs and chains and buckles, and tie dye, and ragged jeans, and then hair dyed either black or in various unusual colors, like maroon. And there's a fad among them of body-piercing. It looks quite painful and inconvenient and un-hygienic, but they have rings and other metallic ornaments inserted in places like their noses and eyebrows. And tattoos as well, many of them also unexpectedly placed, and some of them quite thematically shocking to the uninitiated.

One can give them the benefit of the doubt and surmise that some sort of statement is being made, but it would take an entire platoon of sociologists to puzzle out the meaning of it all. The most poignantly babyish faces gaze out at one from all the black upholstery, as, cigarette in one hand and leash of some rather weary looking canine in the other, they ask if you by any chance have some spare change to help them meet the dog food bill. To me it all seems a bit sad, but then maybe, being off-planet and a stranger in a strange land and so forth, I am just not in sync with the prevailing collective unconscious, by the lights of which the entire manifestation might be, if not exactly a sign that God's in His Heaven and all's right with the world, then at least not as *fin de siecle* as it strikes me as being.

But I forgot to mention the main reason for my objecting to that hang-out of theirs, The Silver Stud, as a meeting place, which is that the music this crowd listens to is exceedingly loud and unmusical, to my ear, sounding like - I find it difficult to describe, but sounding, say, like a jack-hammer attempting to slice its way through solid forged steel, backed up by a teaspoon being pureed in a blender by some very aggrieved or depressed chap who has to shout to be heard over the din, but the meaning of whose words still cannot be made out. So I think the reader can perhaps understand why I looked askance at the saurian who loomed in my tiny chamber, restlessly twiddling the tip of his tail and wearing a what's-bothering-this-poor-chump-now sort of a long-suffering look on his face. As I have mentioned before, much of the popular music on this planet grates horribly on my nerves, even when I am at my best.

"The Silver Stud?" I queried. "Why The Silver Stud, of all places?" My voice had risen to a rather hysterical pitch, and I strove to lower it. It occur to me to wonder if all the stress of recent events, what with my future being reduced to the equivalent of a heap of rubble, at least in part, it seemed, by the agency of this very lizard now looming over me in my tiny chamber, had not rendered me a trifle querulous.

"I mean, it's a longer walk, and the music there is sure to be distracting, and so loud we'll have to yell at one another to be heard over it - or resort to using sign language, or writing notes. And, ye gods - is it even clean? Mightn't we catch something?" (Many of this gothic crowd, as I believe they are called, look as if they go rather a long time between showers.)

The tail twitched irritably out of his hands as Rantor gave a rather theatrical sigh, and his great bulk appeared to settle a bit, like a pile of street sweepings in a time-lapse photo sequence.

"It's this way, Ifford. We don't want to meet at either of our usual - former - haunts. That's where they might be looking for us - for you - don't you see?"

"I know - throw them off the scent and all. We've discussed that. But - The Silver Stud?"

"Well - to be honest, I myself don't like the classical music they play at The Classier Joint. So … funereal. All those quartets and motets and octets. And septets, and quintets …"

"All right, all right." Good grief.

"Furthermore, it's so quiet there that we might well be overheard. We'd certainly stand out."

It was true that I had never seen a reptoid at The Joint, as it was called. It seemed that the lizard was to prevail yet again. It occurred to me to suggest that he ease up on all this motherly concern for Ifford, perhaps seek employment as a door-to-door salesman, or possibly as an enforcer for the mob, or the bouncer at a strip club. But I let it pass.

"It's hard to believe that self could possibly be worth all those man-hours of overtime pay."

"It's not just you, Iffy. You're just a part of the picture. Besides, you know, they spare no expense when tracking down the minor miscreants ... while the big players are, as the old saying goes, invited to the White House for dinner."

I saw his point, as regards self being merely a part of the picture - or maybe I didn't, but I found some consolation in it. I was used to being just part of the picture. I had always been nothing but, and to a certain extent, that was the way I liked it. It was just a different picture I was part of, these days. Nevertheless, another snag had occurred to me.

"But, won't we stand out like a sore thumb, at The Silver Stud? Without black leather jackets of a certain vintage, and huge heavy hobnailed boots, you know?"

"We've thought of that. I've brought you a disguise." And he gestured at the package he had brought in with him.

"A disguise? What am I to go as - Han Solo? R2D2? Baron Rothschild? Zbignev Brezizinsky? The Manchurian Candidate? Won't that just draw attention?"

A look appeared on the reptile's face, sort of a combination of mild disgust overlaid by an elaborate patience, that arose, apparently, from a determination to carry out the assignment, whatever it took, and jolly old Ifford along no matter how exasperatingly dense he persisted in being.

"I meant, naturally, clothing that will make you fit in at The Silver Stud."

"Oh. I see. Yes. But, fitting in with that set involves more than just clothing, doesn't it? When it comes to self-expression and making statements and all that, those kids leave no stone unturned. They grind the message on home. I mean, what about the tattoos, and the colored hair? And won't everything have to be sort of grimy? Clean clothes would be a dead give-away, wouldn't they?"

"Just relax, Ifford. We've thought of all that."

And he proceeded to pull out of his bag an assortment of old clothes, including: a shirt of the style I remember Errol Flynn wearing in those pirate movies, but tie-dyed in a sort of bull's eye pattern in gaudy colors, now much tattered and faded; and a vest, worn and fraying at the margins and missing all of its buttons but one, which dangled limply from a few threads, this vest being a patchwork of several shades of pink and celadon in different types of fabric in front, with beige satin in the back, and a strap made of the same beige satin and fastened with a tarnished silver buckle at a little above waist level, for adjusting the fit; and then a rather remarkable pair of pants that I think must have been gotten from some Army-Navy surplus store. These I rather liked; they were made of what appeared to be a very good-quality, closely-woven wool dyed a deep navy-blue, looking as if they would at least be warm, though perhaps rather scratchy to my sensitive hybrid skin. The sailor pants were bell-bottomed, and fastened in front by means of a rectangular flap with many button holes all around its perimeter that fastened onto these small, navy-blue buttons with a little anchor impressed in the middle of each, that were sewn neatly onto the front of the trousers themselves. It looked like buttoning yourself into this garment each morning was not for anyone with an attention deficit disorder and would require determination and persistent effort, not to mention fingers both nimble and strong. Finally, there were the regulation black leather boots, these being also, I believe, Army or Navy issue and what I think are called combat boots. They had those big bubbly front parts over the toes that made them look like boots in some old-fashioned cartoon strip.

I examined all of these items suspiciously. "They're not dirty," I observed.

"We washed them," he explained in a careful voice such as one might use when addressing a lunatic. "In hot soapy water. Except the woolen pants, which we had to have dry-cleaned. We knew you wouldn't want to wear them otherwise. But, see? - I've even brought you some dirt to smear into them." And he held out to me a little plastic lidded container that did, indeed contain some loose soil. They certainly had thought of everything.

"And this," he said, holding up a plastic bottle, "is for your hair."

"What do you mean - for my hair?"

"Just for the tips of it," he said. "The tips only. It's green dye. The kind that shampoos right out."

It seemed the next thing I'd be expected to submit to would be a session at the body-piercing and tattoo parlor. They appeared to think me mere putty in their hands. I knew a line had to be drawn, and I drew it.

"Absolutely not!" I said. I said it quietly but firmly. I had to let him know how things stood, and that it was hopeless to argue with one of so steely a resolve as that, when aroused, of Ifford Furze. I am one of those passive-seeming, mannerly types who give the impression of being eager to please and unable to resist whatever is suggested to them - as endlessly malleable as a sheet of origami paper, or a wad of chewing gum, in the right hands. True this may be, up to a point, but I do have my limits, as this reptile was about to discover.

"Look, Ifford," he reasoned. If that is the right word. Cajoled might be more like it. "It's just for the tips of your hair, which is really pretty good as it is - so pale and washed-out that it looks bleached already. But you see, we want to radically change your appearance. Don't get me wrong. Some things are fine as they are ..."

"I am gratified to hear it."

"The apparent absence, until you get up close, of eyelashes and eyebrows - that's great. Or we might darken them a little, which, since you can hardly see them, would be a snap. All that's needed is the right attire. Don't you see? - you'll be able to move about freely. It'll be to your advantage, actually. We also thought these decal-type tattoos might be a good idea."

"The ones they put in cereal boxes for the kiddies, you mean?"

"Well, like that. The same sort of thing. How do you know so many details about life on this planet, anyway? You continue to amaze me."

This I took as an attempt at flattery, and I did not respond, but instead bent my head to examine his offering. They were indeed wash-off decals - but instead of the brightly-colored images of The Masters of the Universe, the Olympians, and other such cartoon and comic book heroes - or anti-heroes - these, in the flat black and dingy red and blue of the tattoo, were of daggers dripping with blood, pentacles, skulls, golden calves, stiff, hawk-headed Egyptians in profile, heads of Baphomet, and other such icons - the waking hours of this sub-culture I was being asked to appear as one of being preoccupied pretty exclusively with thoughts of pagan religions, Thanatos and Eros, it seemed. *Fin de siecle* to the max, as they say, such that one wondered if they were following a script, or what.

"Well, I suppose the wash-off decals are acceptable, Rantor. And these clothes you've brought. But I draw the line at tinting my hair. Absolutely draw the line."

"Incognito"

CHAPTER 4: THE HONEY-BLONDE AND THE AIRDALE ...
AND GOVERNMENTS *DE FACTO* AND *DE JURE*

In reality the workings of your governing system are opaque
and covert, while hiding in the chattering spotlight
of an ostensible transparency, even though
the ultimate objective is clear.

Breyten Breytenbach

That evening found me crunching again through the snow and ice,
Rantor at my side, on our way to meet Torvald and his researcher-

friends at the coffee house. Glennie, of course, was also planning to attend. I kept stumbling on the uneven and slippery footing as I had a pretty hard time seeing, due to the fact that Rantor had convinced me that the wiser course was to conceal my hybrid eyes behind dark glasses. I also wore an old brown leather hat with a flamboyantly wide, undulating brim, and some chains and beads around my neck. The tips of my hair, now largely concealed by my hat, were - after all - a rather vivid shade of yellow-green, and altogether, I felt like some kind of walking neon sign, and ridiculous and conspicuous in the extreme; but Rantor kept telling me that I looked 'great' and that I would absolutely blend right in. His attire, though considerably less bizarre than my own, was also ragged, scruffy, and appeared to have been selected with the object in mind of making him look like an extra for one of those old Mad Max movies. He appeared to derive a rather childish pleasure from all of this dressing up and playing at counter-espionage, or cops and robbers, or whatever it was.

We got to The Silver Stud, ordered our coffee, and sat down. At first I didn't recognize Torvald and Glennie when they came in soon after our own arrival, for Torvald also wore different clothes and had either dyed his hair black on the ends, or wore a wig, and Glennie wore ragged blue jeans - her knees must have been very cold, I thought - and wire-frame granny glasses, and a rather ghastly black lipstick and nail polish. They were accompanied by what looked like two *Homo sapiens*, one male and one female, who were introduced to me as Riggs and Bevins.

Riggs - slightly the shorter of the two - was one of those fellows who is built along the lines of a dumpling. He had wispy brown hair, thinning on top, and a very broad, rather toad-like face. Bevins was a square-ish female who brought to mind some sturdy species of domestic animal bred for meat. She had short thick dark curly hair, prematurely laced with white at the temples, and was distinctly tank-like in build, although my impression was that the bulk in her case was more muscle than flab. She had the general aspect of one with whom I would not wish to tangle in a dark alley at night. Dressed in blue jeans belted at the waist, and what looked like a man's down vest, and hiking boots, she was of the type which – or would it be 'whom'? - it is impossible to imagine ever looking mussed or flustered. Altogether, she appeared to be from among the ranks of those very competent, well-organized, and motherly females who run doctors' and lawyers' offices, or households, for them. Riggs, on the other hand, appeared rumpled and shop-worn and bore every sign of being an absent-minded professor type who went about all day with his hair mussed and a smear of mustard on his upper lip, and who was forever asking if you happened to have seen his keys, specs, or checkbook lying about - one of those brainy coves who was perpetually pondering something or other and needing to be picked up after and reminded about things.

After the introductions, little time was wasted in chit-chat. At any rate, conversation was made a bit challenging by the noise level, which, as I had anticipated, was so high that one felt one practically needed to use a megaphone to be heard - or to cup the hands around the mouth and shout, as in a gale. Torvald opened the conversation by telling me that Riggs and Bevins were interested in the period of the 1930's.

"Oh?" said I. " Depression Era and all that? I thought the general focus of interest was 1913 and the passage of the Federal Reserve Act."

Bevins spoke. As foreshadowed by her appearance, her manner was brisk and business-like. "It turns out, Mr. Furze..."

"Please, call me Ifford."

"Ifford - well, it turns out, Ifford, as you probably know, that the Federal Reserve Board was very active with FDR during the Great Depression and the period preceding it. It was at their suggestion and prompting that he declared a state of national emergency. The idea was theirs. Apparently, their lawyers actually drafted the executive order by which he did it. Most of the ensuing legislation - you know, the legislation that nationalized agriculture, banking, business, and industry - basically, the dismantling of what was left of the Constitutional Republic and its replacement by the corporate state - was the result of their vision and planning ..."

I must have looked confused, or dazed, for she paused, wrinkled her brow in a quick little frown, and then said, "Is all of this information is new to you? Somehow I had the idea that you ..."

Before I could answer, Riggs, seeming to rouse himself with difficulty from some deep and pleasurable reverie, stuck in his oar. "Florence, my dear, that perhaps being the case, might it not be better to keep the lad's mind in its pristine state as regards these and related matters?"

The old girl nodded deferentially. "Of course, Ralphie."

220

Obedient as a spaniel, it seemed. I got the impression that she was quite devoted to her toad-like companion. And - 'Ralphie'? Well, it just goes to show that one never knows. One never, never, knows.

At any rate, Riggs turned to me, a sort of kindly avuncular smile stretching his broad face still wider, saying, by way of explanation, "Purity of the data, you understand. The less you know beforehand about what you might be viewing, the better." Though the reader will see, in the ensuing pages, just how quickly and completely they all of them forgot about this injunction of his.

"Oh, quite." It was fine by me. Saved me having to listen (or pretend to listen) to a bunch of stuff.

After a little pause, Torvald spoke up. "Well, as to remuneration, Ifford ..."

"Remuneration?"

"Yes. For your services, you know. Since you're not receiving a living stipend anymore. Riggs has kindly offered - *sub rosa*, of course - to keep you on retainer - he can't afford to pay much, but enough to keep your ship afloat, at least for the next couple of months."

"And possibly longer, depending on how the work goes," Riggs broke in. "We have so much that needs - exploring. Not just about the passage of the Federal Reserve Act - and the Great Depression and the changes that occurred during FDR's presidency, but also the Civil War, and the post-Civil War period ..." - the fellow was actually rubbing his hands together and beaming like a shopkeeper gazing at a fat till after a day's brisk business - "... That era, as you may or may not know, marked the initial giant leap in the government's transformation, from the limited and de-centralized form, created by the country's founders, into the large, powerful centralized state that all along had been the desire of the Hamiltonian Federalists - several of whom, of course, were the unofficial, so to speak, agents of the banking and business powers behind the British throne. In Lincoln, these power-seekers finally found their man and their opportunity ..."

The fellow appeared to be yet another of these unbridled enthusiasts to whom Fate seemed determined, of late, to surrender me.

221

"Why is it," I interjected, "If you don't mind my asking - just curious, you know, and all that - that you can't do your research in the conventional way, by going to the documents of the time and the works of other historians?"

"You see, Ifford," said Florence Bevins solemnly, "There is much that has been suppressed."

"And spun! As in 'spin,' you know," enthused Rantor. "And just not mentioned! Just not mentioned at all ..."

"The official version is not in all respects the true one, you mean?"

This was beginning to sound familiar. Same song, different dance hall.

"Exactly. Precisely," beamed Riggs. "In fact, the true story of the history and present state of this country's government today is so far from what is taught in the schools, and believed by the people, that most of them would - and, unfortunately, do, when exposed to it - reject it out-of-hand as absurd and impossible. It is most unfortunate that they do not even ..."

"Willingly suspend the disbelief?"

"Yes, Ifford, well said - they do not bother even to investigate - do a little reading, and a little thinking - before making up their minds."

As he lamented, I noticed a quite attractive youngish female Earthling wandering in, alone save for a large fuzzy dog on a leash, and seating herself at a nearby table right in my line of vision. What initially attracted my attention was her dress, a rather dramatic eye-catching number with a swirly skirt that reached to mid-calf and appeared to be made, in part at least, of some glittery material. I was to discover that the glitter came from small antique beads, in iridescent hues of rose, blue, and lavender, which she had painstakingly sewn, in various patterns and curlicues, onto the front of the dress - what I believe is called the bodice. The dress was of the scooped neck variety, made of a soft brown antique velvet, rather the rich color of mink - in fact, it appeared actually to be trimmed with some fur - it looked like mink - around the neck and the short sleeves, the puff of fur setting off to perfection her throat, bosom, and slim, lightly tanned arms. I thought that she must frequent a tanning salon, being careful not to over-do it. She seemed very young – no more than sixteen or seventeen, I thought

- and had a striking skin of a honey-gold color. Her hair was long, straight, and blonde, but that enchanting kind of blonde that is made of all different tawny shades of pale brown and gold and yellow. Her canine companion was of the breed which is called, I believe, an Airdale - one of those large, fuzzy, black and tan jobbies with long legs, terrier ears, and a tail docked to the length of about three or four inches. As the pooch sat beside her on the booth, she fussed over and patted it as if it were a child, or she a child and it her doll. I will candidly say that this young girl, or child - she seemed now one, now the other - in her glittering dress of soft velvet, was an absolute vision of earthly loveliness, and that my eyes and attention continually strayed to her.

"We think we have at least elements of the true story pretty well pieced together," Bevins was saying.

"A certain general picture emerges," Riggs agreed, "And a rather fascinating one it is - what might be called both a revisionist historical, and a sub-textual legal, reality, the former primarily from the records and accounts of the time, and the latter from the codes, the statutes, and the law dictionaries - and the Supreme Court case law, of course - once you know enough to understand the multi-layered 'code' in which these legal documents are written."

While he paused to sip his latte, Bevins carried on, as if the two were delivering some sort of practiced dialogue or routine, "Many key words and phrases have dual or multiple meanings - some of which - so at least the theory goes - are known only to the inner circle ..."

Yet another conspiracy, it seemed. Or a sub-plot of the main plot.

"The initiates, so to speak," continued Riggs, "The high priesthood, you might say, of what is called the law. And history. But in actual fact, the situation among the contemporary legal researchers is rather complex. There are what you might call schools of thought in what I suppose could be called the contemporary grass-roots legal research community. This is the work, you know, that we all do in our off-time. Not officially sanctioned, you understand. A sort of passionately pursued hobby of mine – ours – you might say. And there seem to be as many views, or theories, as there are researchers. It is at present a dynamic field, with individuals and small groups in various parts of the country, all working on their own time, doing their officially heretical – I suppose one could call it – research. Standing, as it does, in all its tangled variety, in opposition to, and casting doubt upon, the officially sanctioned dogma. Unorthodox."

"I've always regarded history as rather a settled matter. As regards the main points, history is history, isn't it?" I queried. "I mean, it's not theory – it's fact. And the law, likewise – there in black and white for all to see – is it not?"

"Well, with all due respect, Ifford, I would tend to call that view naïve," Riggs replied, smiling to soften the blow. "Concerning the law, as the martyr Algernon Sidney remarked shortly before he was hanged, the law was simple but hath been industriously rendered perplex. And history ... well, history is, after all, a story. In the battle for the minds of men, those in power often find it expedient to massage, to tweak, you might say, the facts. Just as, for instance, a picture of Lenin or Stalin might be touched up, and his biography and the record of his deeds expurgated of all that was unsavory, to make him look properly, convincingly, heroic. So with history in general. Truth, one could say, is a weapon to be, in a manner of speaking, creatively engineered, and strategically deployed, by those in power."

"Hmmmm. I see. Well – perhaps you could give me some examples, if you don't mind. The history books I have read, and courses I have taken, have been quite in accord, as to the basics, at least."

"There are examples enough to re-write what is called history – and much, of course, that is buried and forgotten and will simply never be known. The struggle for wealth and power is not a pretty thing, Ifford – being, as it is, governed, limited, by no rules of engagement. Anything goes. But anyway, to give you an example from an area I am currently studying, in my off hours ... and to leap to the extreme limits, then, of what some would call an extreme field of study and opinion - some researchers claim that the United States, the super-sovereign, so to speak, was not even properly - lawfully, legally - created by the Philadelphia Convention, and thus always has been and to this day still is *de facto* and not *de jure* - that is to say, does not even lawfully exist, as a nation, as a political as opposed to a commercial, entity ... that accepted parliamentary procedure was, inadvertently, not followed by the several states, you see ... "

"Interesting ..." mused Rantor, with that familiar gleam in his eye. This was new territory, it seemed, even to him. "Actually, this is the very subject - one of them - I've been dying to have a chance to ask you about. The present government certainly seems to be in full charge, whatever its antecedents, history, and actual legal status. You're questioning the legitimacy of its legal and historical foundations?"

"I myself need to do more research before I can commit to a position on this matter. But, yes, certain grass-roots researchers are questioning the official stories regarding the nation's actual legal status. I find their arguments, some of them, to be quite persuasive. Briefly, the line of reasoning is that, when the *Articles of Confederation* were rejected as the foundational document of the super-sovereign United States, the several states automatically assumed the basic legislative form of any body politic, that of the democracy. But it was as *republics* that they held the Philadelphia Convention in which they attempted to - but in fact did not - create a super-sovereign compact of states - the 'United States of America'and its foundational law, the Constitution."

"I thought that the Philadelphia Convention *did* recreate the super-sovereign," said Rantor. " 'We the people of the United States,' et cetera? That was its whole purpose, wasn't it?"

"Yes, that was its purpose; but whether it lawfully achieved that purpose is the matter in dispute. Basically, some revisionist historians claim that proper, lawful parliamentary procedure was, inadvertently, not followed, with the result that no super-sovereign – no lawful "United States of America' – and no foundational law for this compact of states - was in legal fact created. And that the Constitution never was and to this day is not 'admissible evidence of law.' The line of reasoning is that the states - in sending *representatives* to attend the Philadelphia Convention for the purpose of creating the super-sovereign, the United States – acted, first, as if they were political bodies, nation-states, when arguably they were, or might have been, still commercial entities - which is what the colonies had been all along, of course - and, that if they were in fact nation-states, after severing ties with King George, then they were democracies rather than republics. Because the default form, so to speak, of the nation state is the democracy, and they had never gone through the necessary procedure – necessary in the eyes of the law, the Law of Nations – of changing their legislative form to that of the democratic republic."

"Would you mind running through that again?" Rantor requested. Even he seemed to find it all about as clear as a brick wall.

225

"Well, initially all the colonies came into being as commercial entities, and ventures - commercial entities owned and operated by the government of Great Britain."

"Interestingly," his pal Bevins interjected, "A significant power behind the British throne was already by that time the privately owned Bank of England – owned by that inventor of central banking, the Scotsman William Paterson, who famously – and candidly – wrote, *"The bank hath benefit of interest on all moneys which it creates out of nothing."* The Bank of England was actually the first central bank with a monopoly on the issuance of a nation's circulating medium of exchange and the ability to plunder, in concert with government, the citizens through, among other methods, the ingenious hidden tax of inflation by the simple expedient of issuing more interest-bearing 'notes' than they had gold in their coffers with which to redeem them. But already by the time of the Battle of Waterloo, it was the Rothschild banking dynasty which had risen to the top of the heap."

"All true enough," agreed Riggs. "But at any rate - that the colonies were commercial entities is well-known and not in dispute. The question is – did that ever change? Examining the available papers and records, it appears that it did not. Even the *Articles of Confederation* did not properly create a super-sovereign compact of bodies politic, but rather, if anything, then of bodies commercial, you might say."

"But when they opted out of the British Empire, wrote the Declaration of Independence – didn't that automatically change?"

"Well, that is, or touches upon, the question. Certainly, they began to *act* like nation-states, and to regard themselves as such. They *wanted and intended to be* Republics, with chosen representatives making their law for them. And they began acting *as if* they all were (1.) nations, (2.) having representative forms of legislature and law-making - when in fact they, the several states, might still have been at that point, as I just mentioned, still private commercial enterprises. To the extent that they could be considered to have been legitimate nascent nation-states, they were democracies, which is, you might say, the default form of law-making, of any body-politic, until the people – who are the law-makers, in a democracy - go through the accepted procedure of selecting a different legislative form for their government."

"So," Bevins concluded, "Their law-making could only be legally, lawfully, done by a *popular vote* in each nation-state. Each state's legislative – law-making - power at that point in time residing in all legal voters, rather than in any chosen representatives."

"Exactly," agreed Riggs. "Therefore, the colonies needed first to create themselves as political entities, and then the legal voters of the newly created states, rather than representatives, needed - according to established law, the Law of Nations established by long usage, dating back to Athens and formally encoded in *Robert's Rules of Order* - to vote democratically, firstly, on creating and joining a compact of states, the super-sovereign United States of America, and secondly, on its foundational law – the Constitution – that very Constitution that was mistakenly supposed to have been created by the Philadelphia Convention."

"This is pretty complicated," Glennie said. "I think I get it. But …"

Rantor had a question. "But surely just by long acceptance and useage - by the people's tacit acceptance of this compact of states and its Constitution as legitimate – the United States of America and its Constitution would in fact be legally, lawfully considered valid?"

"Well, the question here is, can a commercial entity ever automatically, as it were, assume the status of nation? My understanding is that the answer to that question is 'no,' regardless of how long it has been functioning *de facto* in a governmental capacity. However … there are other revisionist researchers who *do* accept the Constitution as a valid legal document, and the United States of America as an existing legal entity. Perhaps what you suggest would be an element in their line of reasoning, if they were aware of this argument I have just presented … which not all of them are, to the best of my knowledge."

"But the most important point here," said Bevins, "Is that they, too – these other revisionist researchers - do not recognize the current government as *de jure*."

"That is correct," Riggs agreed. "Their claim is that, unbeknownst to nearly everybody, even the great preponderance of the functionaries of government, this lawful United States of America, though in their view it legally, lawfully exists, is NOT the entity that is actually running the country and holding the reins of power anymore."

"And they further claim," added Bevins, "That the original Constitution is NOT the foundational law of the entity that *is* exercising the

227

governmental powers. Obviously, the country is being run by an existing governing body – one in firm control of all its centers of power - but the claim of these other researchers is that this governing body's power is *de facto*, not *de jure* – that, though it is in power, it does not exercise its powers lawfully."

"And this is because …?" Glennie queried.

"First of all, because it is a commercial enterprise – a private commercial enterprise - and not a government at all," replied Riggs. "Both theories so view it."

"And," added Bevins, "Because allegedly the people are sovereign, and the people have not knowingly and intentionally authorized this state of affairs – government by the private corporate law of a private commercial entity …"

"Of a highly dubious and problem-fraught lineage, legally and historically speaking," Riggs added.

"In fact," continued Bevins, "if this research is correct, then the people have been deceived and don't even *know* that the 'government' that is running the country is NOT the same government created – or allegedly created - by the Constitution. They don't even have a clue. Actually, both theories, of course, claim that the people are clueless as to the fact that what you might call a rogue government is running the country as a business – as a highly lucrative commercial enterprise."

"So, are you saying," queried Rantor, "That the current 'government' is in fact *a private corporation* … and that its 'law,' then, is *private law, masquerading as public law…*?"

"Yes, exactly,"Riggs agreed, "As public *policy*, actually, to be precise."

And furthermore," continued Bevins, "That *all of our transactions with it are in commerce*, in what can be called a 'hover zone' jurisdiction …"

"Which is itself a legal fiction," Riggs carried on enthusiastically, "A mongrel admiralty/ maritime/equity jurisdiction over legal fictions, actually …"

"This mongrel jurisdiction hidden," continued the other half of the act, "'In plain view,' as it were, under the guise of 'one form of action' ... and that the people – one by one, individually and unwittingly - bring themselves into nexus with and obligation to this 'corporation' 'voluntarily' by – *in corporate capacity - contracting with it in commercial negotations.*"

They seemed rather to have jumped several pages ahead in the unfolding saga, causing the rest of us to goggle in varying degrees of wonderment. If that is actually a word. I shall have to look it up.

Riggs burbled a heartfelt, if rather moist and spluttery "YES!" - seeming in his enththusiasm to have choked a bit on his latte. "Yes! Rather amazing, isn't it?"

Here he coughed a bit, Bevins pounding on his back with the flat of her hand; then, having cleared his windpipe, he continued, "And to follow the rabbit to its hole is to understand that, behind all the subterfuge, legal jargon, and complexity, the power at the top of the commercial/governmental heap is 'the bank.' We have 'government of the banks, by the banks, for the banks' ... is to understand that 'the bank' is behind every single war this nation and its people have EVER been involved in, from the very, very beginning ... is to understand that 'the bank' IS 'the government,' here. Every single bit of what is marketed to us as government has nothing to do with any Republican Form, created by Law by the 'People at large' via any democratic Law-making process. We know that by simply looking at the 'funny money.' So, YES! EVERYTHING we see is nothing more than *a commercial shell marketed to us as 'government.'* The irony – and tragedy - is that it appears to have been this way from the beginning."

"But didn't the country's founders realize and attempt to correct this flaw?" asked Glennie.

"We're not sure, at this point – Florence and I, that is to say. The research is on-going. But if any of them did realize it, it would have been a touchy thing to make public. The country would have been thrown into upheval. Certainly, disclosure would have involved a loss of face, if not of power."

"What about lawyers, judges, congressmen, and so forth ...?"

"Well, you see – they have been exposed to the same 'information' as the rest of us – haven't they? From kindergarten on up through graduate school ... my understanding is that a select few – a very few – are in the know, as they say. It is rather like the intelligence agencies, which fragment knowledge - parcel out knowledge, on a 'need to know' basis."

So then," asked Rantor, "Would you say that all the reference to the Constitution and constitutional Law is – on the part of those who do realize the true state of affairs, I mean, of course - false front window dressing to keep alive the misconception held by virtually everyone that there is a legitimate Constitutional government in place?

"Yes. And the other side of that coin is that there are myriad clues as to the actual private, commercial, non-Constitutional nature of this 'government' in plain sight, in the style and content of legal documents, in the flags - certainly in Supreme Court case law – once you begin to understand, and to know what you're looking at. You must realize, of course, that even the well-educated are legal illiterates – as totally ignorant and illiterate, when it comes to the law, as the slaves were – in ancient Greece and Rome, and in the South here in this country - when it came to reading and writing. Knowledge indeed being power, why should these usurpers hand it out freely? It would be counter-productive, with respect to their goals and agendas."

"So you see, Ifford," interjected Torvald, bringing us back to our long-forgotten point of departure, "Given this complexity, and difference of opinion, and given all the secrecy and deception on the part of the *de facto* government, having someone listen in - as you did up in my lab the other night, to that scene in the closet on Jekyll Island - on key meetings and conversations and so forth, would be very interesting, and could possibly clear up, or shed some light upon, these disputed points."

"Indeed," smilingly agreed Riggs. "We are most eager to begin, and would like to start our work with you right away. Does that sound all right to you?"

"Fine. Yes, thank you. I'm not so sure I can deliver the goods, you understand, but I am willing to try, Sir." (It *was* rather nice, in my present circumstances, to be offered a living stipend.)

"Excellent. Would, say, three in the afternoon tomorrow be a convenient time for you to come by our office?"

"Oh, quite. I have nothing but time on my hands now, you know. Oceans and oceans of it."

He said fine, very good, marvelous, and so forth, and told me where on campus their offices were located. And then he attempted to turn the topic away from their arcane studies, perhaps – though certainly belatedly - in line with his earlier comments about 'preserving the purity of the data.'
"Now - I am quite interested in your planet of origin, you know - yours and this young lady's," he said, glancing at Glennie with one of his fatherly smiles. "I understand that you were raised entirely in group homes ..."

The subject turned out to be an ice-breaker, all except Bevins and possibly self becoming quite relaxed and chummy as Glennie and I - she in particular - spewed forth the reminiscences. She seemed particularly susceptible to Riggs' air of avuncular kindness, positively lapping it up or basking in it and becoming more expansive and confiding than I recalled ever seeing her before. These new acquaintances of ours kept bringing out new aspects of her personality.

After only a few minutes of that discussion, however, Rantor began to massage the tip of his tail in an agitated manner, to make paper airplanes of napkins, to doodle and fidget, and generally to exhibit all the now familiar signs that in his view enough time had been spent on chit-chat and that he had important things to say and ask that could no longer be kept from bursting forth. The fellow sometimes reminds one of that geyser - Old Faithful, I believe it's called - located in some park or other now, like so many other wilderness areas, totally off limits to the general populace - allegedly due to the fragility of their ecosystems – off limits to all save the elites, that is, whose private playgrounds they have become, according to Rantor - anyway, you know the geyser, I'm sure - the one that erupts on schedule every hour on the hour. Thus it came as no surprise to me when, as soon as there was the briefest lull in the conversation, the saurian broke in, obviously intent on steering the discourse into areas of greater interest to him personally. As I have mentioned before, this reptile, like reptiles generally, or so I am told, has little if any awareness of social forms, and, like a child, seems utterly incapable of regarding things from any perspective save his own. It makes one wonder what they are like in groups.

"Riggs and Bevins"

CHAPTER 5: A *SUB-ROSA* PARALLEL JURISDICTION ...

All those who seek to destroy the liberties of a democratic
nation ought to know that war is the surest and the shortest
means to accomplish it. This is the first axiom of the science.

Alexis de Tocqueville

What Rantor was burning to delve into in greater detail was the legal
system in this country – the real story, of course, staight from the
horse's mouth and such as cannot be gotten from official sources such
as the classes offered by this or any university.

Most beings and entities, you know, in my experience at least, when
they get the chance to steer the conversation in a certain direction, want
to discuss the latest football game or action-thriller movie they've seen,
or give the meaty details of some horrific surgery or health problem of
themselves or someone they know, or sink their teeth into some
particularly juicy bits of gossip about mutual friends or movie stars,
dalliances or divorces, eating disorders or rehab check-ins, or the heavy
drug use or compulsive and/or kinky sexual activities of heads of state,

or other illuminati – though not much is reported on the pecadillos of those highly placed in government and business, now that I think about it – but anyway, the stuff of the tabloids one sees tantalizingly displayed all about one when in the check-out line at the grocery store - but not Rantor. He's always champing at the bit to delve deeply into the heavy duty and industrial strength stuff such as might be found, undiluted and in fine print, on the pages of a journal written specifically for economists and business trend analysts of the upper echelon - such as, say, an in-depth analysis of the recent actions of the Fed to stimulate a stalled and turgid economy, or, conversely, to apply the brakes to the latest steamy inflationary rampage.

"Not to change the subject [!]," boomed the lizard in that rafter-shaking voice of his, "But I've been wanting to ask you a few questions about this business of *de facto* government versus *de jure* government. Just when I think I've got all the important pieces of the puzzle, I find out that there's more. Now you tell me – very interesting, by the way - that whatever their disagreements, it seems that most of the leading-edge populist researchers at least concur that whatever it is that's running the country, it's not who or what we all presume it to be."

A little light shone in Riggs' small eyes, as if someone somewhere had flicked a switch, and he leaned forward like a roly-poly runner at the starting line of an important race. The chap's earlier comments about preserving the purity of the data had given me reason to hope that we weren't going to go into all that – or any more of it, I should say - that I was to be spared, this time. I didn't like it. I didn't like it one little bit. It tended to confirm the horrid apprehension that had been forming, during the course of the evening, that I was in the presence of two enthusiasts. Three, counting Torvald - actually four, counting Bevins - in fact, like a wagon trail circled by a tribe of whooping Indians, I seemed to be hopelessly surrounded and out-numbered. Five of them to my puny one, actually, there were, when one included Glennie. As I suppose one must. But of the lot, I considered Rantor to be hands down the most pestilential, utterly unwilling and unable, as he had repeatedly proven himself to be, to staunch the verbal torrent - being, in addition to his other defects of character, and as previously noted, virtually helpless and a mere cork bobbing in a swift current, once the whole dread process was triggered.

"Ah, yes," Riggs intoned, "'*De facto*,' meaning of course, 'in fact,' and '*de jure*' meaning, 'in or by law.' Or did I already say that?"

233

He had. Or one of them had. These blokes repeat themselves.

That look of keen interest gleamed alarmingly in his little eyes, and a sense of impending doom settled over me like a cloud of gnats, along with that horrible trapped feeling. I gazed at his eyes. They were rather singular in their disproportionately small size. But as I examined them, it occurred to me that perhaps they are of normal size – the eyeballs themselves, you know - but dwarfed by all the surrounding flesh, rather like porcine eyes.

A feeling almost akin to panic welled in the bosom, and I might have stood and fled to the restroom for at the very least a lengthy breather, sitting quietly alone in one of the stalls and reading the graffiti, had I not been, like a sausage in a sandwich, more or less enclosed and hemmed in, right in the middle of the circular booth, with two or three of my companions on either side of me. And, who knows - once extricated, one could even just sneak right out into the night, and call from a payphone to give one's apologies and some excuse or other. But of course I didn't. To do so would so radically violate my conditioning, don't you know - would seem so utterly ill-bred. And then I had to keep in mind that I was looking to this motley crew for help in my current predicament.

"I don't know if I've got it right," Rantor was saying. "From what I gather at this point, the government as created by the country's founders had the right to create corporations, according to what Torvald has told me ..."

"Yes, that, at least according to several of the contemporary divergent and revisionist researchers and interpreters of the available data, is correct," agreed Riggs.

"And Congress - at least, that body known as and believed to be a lawful Congress - created some sort of corporation in the District of Columbia that somehow or other is running the country in some sort of extra-Constitutional parallel jurisdiction ...? I'm not at all straight on the details of it, you see ... but basically part of what I have heard is that the country is still to this day *being run under emergency and thus under martial law or rule ...*" He laid wondering emphasis on this last phrase.

"Well, there is a good deal of dispute, of course, on these matters, veiled in secrecy and encoded in complex legal language as they are.

Legal terms, you know, can have more than one meaning; and their meanings can change - or be changed - over time. If you are a lover of mazes, puzzles, and bewildering complexity generally, by all means go into law or economics. This complexity of course works to the benefit of the deceivers, the truth being hidden rather like the nut in the old nut and shell game. But, flabberghasting though the very idea is, there is a good deal of recent research and evidence suggesting that, unbeknownst to practically everyone, we do have a *de facto* parallel government running the country. And that it is, or grew out of, that private corporation brought into being on February 21, 1871, by Congress – itself a *de facto* Congress, many believe it to have been, and of course still to be, by the way. A private – not public - corporation brought into being by the District of Columbia Organic Act and given the Trademark name 'United States Government – or 'United States' as opposed to the 'United States of America', these designations most commonly being written in all capital letters. In accord with long-standing legal convention, names styled all in capital letters are used to reference the corporate entity and its franchisees or sub-agencies."

"Congress allegedly did this," said his sidekick Bevins, "Under its constitutional authority to pass any law within the ten square miles that is called the District of Columbia. It is claimed, by some of these independent researchers who have sprung up recently in various places around the country, that the private corporation so created is owned and operated by the federal government for the purpose of conducting the business of the government under martial law."

"Why under martial law? Surely the country was not still under martial law or rule in 1871? The Civil War was over by then, wasn't it?" Glennie asked. She is a pretty sharp cookie, actually, and had as usual been taking it all in most attentively.

"One would certainly think that, I agree," replied Riggs. "You do know, then, that President Lincoln, by General Orders No. 100, I think it was, declared martial law? This was, I believe, on April 24th, 1863, if memory serves me. When we get to the War Between the States, we enter an area of many theories, and much that was suppressed – has not been told."

"Actually, Ralphie," Bevins put in, "I came across a quotation today that made me think of you, that I knew you'd appreciate. It was from a General Meade – George Gordon Meade, I think it was, the victor of

Gettysburg – 'The truth will never be told, and I have a great contempt for History.' "

"Sadly, more literally true than most even of the more intelligent and better educated of the populace would believe," said Riggs. "Due to the many falsehoods upon which their minds have been nurtured. Indeed. Anyway - once in effect, and enforced by police and military action, this martial law authority gave, and still gives, the President, with or without Congress, the absolute powers of a dictator. And this 'conscription act,' which invoked the marital law state of affairs, according to some schools of thought remains in effect even now and is the foundation of the current Presidential Executive Orders authority, with which the acting president usurps the law-making powers which under the Constitution and the Separation of Powers Doctrine are the exclusive prerogative of Congress. So, as I said, this corporation of which we have been speaking was initially created by Congress, ostensibly to carry out the business of the government under martial law. And from there, the theory is that its scope and powers were expanded."

"It sounds almost too incredible to be believed," mused Torvald. "That this country could have been under some form of martial law or martial rule for over 150 years ... but of course, once the political animal has gained power - that heady elixir of absolute power concentrated into one controllable man and office - he is reluctant to give it up."

"True enough. History certainly does unequivocally teach us that much. Though most people seem happy to make the easy assumption that 'that was then, this is now' – that human nature, and the political animal, has somehow changed, become more saintly. Yes, this information is, taken all in all, quite a paradigm shift, isn't it? As I believe you know, the Civil War did mark a turning point, a great victory over the heirs of the Jeffersonian Anti-Federalists by the opposing camp - the political heirs of the Hamiltonian Federalists, that is to say, of course - the mercantilists: the champions of the British system of powerful central government, central banks, corporate welfare, cronyism, and political patronage - which they were by Lincoln's time, in that deceptive fashion of theirs, calling 'the American system.' Old wine in new bottles and all that, you know. The very 'good old boy' system the Revolutionary War was fought to expunge from the continent."

"Lincoln," Bevins commented, "Claimed the powers of a military dictator and, with Congress, seized the opportunity to alter the government - by fiat, and by force when necessary - into the powerful centralized state that those who use government as a tool in their quest for power and self-enrichment always seek to make of it."

"Yeah, Torvald and I have discussed some of this," said the lizard. "Lincoln was hardly the saintly populist hero he's hyped as being. For one thing, he refused to allow the South to secede, something that all of the founders and most Northerners as well as Southerners of the era regarded as incontestably one of the states' inalienable rights and freedoms."

"That is correct," agreed Riggs. "As indeed, it clearly was, legally. Lawfully. The war was not really fought over slavery - Lincoln himself was on the record as being a separatist - and not an abolitionist; and in any event, slavery was on the way out in all civilized nations, without wars being fought over the issue. But Lincoln did use the slavery issue to cloud his true agendas, to gain support, and to further his true objectives. It is generally agreed by his supporters and detractors alike that the man was brilliant, and a master politician. Fundamentally, he waged the war, in which so many died, to retain in the Union a valuable piece of real estate - the Southern states which wanted to secede - and to change the country into a centralized and powerful Union of weak subject-states. He - and his big banking and big business backers - did not like the careful, deliberate diffusion and limitation of power that was in fact the primary object of the 'States' Rights' government created by the founders. Lincoln's dictatorial acts are legion, and admitted even by his admirers and apologists, who like FDR's admirers and apologists, tend, oxymoronically, to present him as a 'good' dictator."

"But like virtually all dictators, in fact he did much that was not good ," said Rantor. " 'Power tends to corrupt, and absolute power corrupts absolutely... most 'great' men are bad men'..."

"Yes. Lord Acton knew whereof he spoke. In fact, Lincoln's abuses of the powers of his office were many. The list is a long one - the 'good' dictator launched an invasion of the South without consulting Congress, as required by the Constitution ... he imposed martial rule or law on both North and South, suspended *habeus corpus*, unconstitutionally blockaded the Southern ports ... he, um, threw thousands of Northerner dissidents and draft resistors in jail and kept them there for long periods without trial ... persecuted and even jailed or deported dissident Northern newspaper owners and Congressmen merely for exercising their rights of free speech ... most importantly, he refused to allow the South its right of peaceful secession, thus bringing about the deaths of hundreds of thousands in the bloodiest war the world had ever seen ... he routinely monitored and censored telegraph communications without warrants, and he nationalized the railroads, ordered Federal troops to interfere with elections in the North by intimidating Democratic voters ... um ... oh, yes, he confiscated private property, including firearms; he ordered or allowed his generals to pillage and destroy civilian life and property in the South, and his political heirs punitively taxed the South after the war and occupied their land militarily for over ten years after Appomattox ..."

"Quite a list," said Glennie. "No wonder the South was so bitter about it all ..."

"Yes; and in light of which, it is rather remarkable that Lincoln is popularly portrayed as a veritable saint ..." Bevins added.

"Just happened to see a book on the shelf while browsing in the Undergrad Library the other day," Torvald interjected, "An older book on the subject of the Civil War. Purporting to tell more of the true story, you know. In the forward, the author gave several interesting quotations from people at the time to the effect that the real story of the War Between the States will never be known. I checked it out, actually – not sure I'll find time to do more than browse in it. And I also checked out this other book, a more recent one, called *The Real Lincoln*. It seems to go into a lot of the stuff you're talking about."

I, of course, had all along been poised and ready to insert myself into any pause in the discussion in order to voice a plea for a termination of the proceedings, which as usual were dragging on endlessly, but I had not been swift enough to get a word in. However, throughout the ordeal I had found solace in frequent surreptitious glances, from behind my dark glasses, in the direction of that blonde girl in the beaded dress of beige velvet, who was, as the saying goes, so easy on the eyes. In her antique clothing, and with her glowing skin, she looked dressed and ready to play a part in some Elizabethan drama. And, perhaps it was only my imagination, but it did seem that her glance was straying rather frequently in my direction. Perhaps it was because she found my hybrid looks so strange. But then, I remembered, I was in disguise. Could it be that she actually admired my *dishabille*, the greenish tips of my hair? Or was I just imagining things, and was she looking at me no more often than at anyone or anything else?

"Yeah. Honest Abe was actually quite the anti-hero," Rantor was saying wryly. "But anyway, the 'train of abuses,' so to speak doesn't end with him, I guess - not if, in the aftermath of the War Between the States, essentially no less than a *sub rosa* parallel government, and jurisdiction, was created in DC, without the people having a clue ... and is it really true that all of the state, county, and city governments eventually came in as complicitors - as sub-agencies or franchisees of the parent corporation?"

"As we understand it at this point, yes - as instrumentalities. Of course, as you say, this was not Lincoln's doing, he having been assassinated. But he certainly set the tone and gave the example. Yes, the state governments were derelict in their duty of interposition against usurpations of the federal government under the Tenth Article of Amendment - but then marital law still prevailed, and the Constitution and all civil law were still suspended ... but of course the states could have objected to this very state of affairs, demanded an end to the 'emergency' and to marital law or rule ... but not only did the states not interpose - they actually entered into collusion with the usurpers."

"There was, however," Bevins added, "A rash of abrupt resignations of legislators in many states ... just as, in the 1930s, there was some quiet furor in the corridors of power, particularly in the Supreme Court, when FDR and his Congress to a large extent razed what remained of the *de jure*, constitutional government and put into place, without public discussion or vote, its virtual opposite, the infrastructure of the present semi-socialistic centralized corporate state. This whole long and gradual process carefully side-stepped, as should be obvious, the populist methods provided in the Constitution for changing the country's form of government."

"Yeah ... and Torvald also mentioned something about this corporation trickily adopting a constitution that is nearly identical to the original Constitution...?"

"Yes," replied Riggs, "In that act of 1871, Congress adopted as their own the original Constitution - except that they left out the 13th Amendment - the so-called 'lost' amendment, forbidding titles of nobility - and re-numbered the original 14th, 15th, and 16th Amendments as the 13th, 14th, and 15th. But most significantly, under this corporate government, corporate citizens – as all 'residents' or 'citizens' are presumed to be – have ONLY government-granted privileges – no 'inalienable rights' as per the founding fathers."

"Today you can find the corporate United States defined in 28 USC 3002, at 15, sections (A), (B), and (C)," interjected Bevins. "It makes very interesting reading."

"Centralizing absolute power to secure their empire," said Rantor.

"Not merely the land and its resources, and the wealth and power of government were captured," Riggs went on. "Also taken was that most valuable of all renewable resources - the labor force. So in short, the existing wealth and sources of wealth, you could say, of perhaps the richest nation in the history of the world were captured, in a silent coup, by legal sleight of hand. It really is a variant on what one would not be amiss in calling the oldest story ever told - the oldest political story, certainly - that of conquest, whether by collusion and deception, as in the post-Civil War doings we have been outlining, or by force or threat of force, as in the war itself."

"It makes me think of the *Wizard of Oz,* Glennie said. "Behind the curtain, running the show, pulling all the levers and pressing all the buttons. Only here, if what you are telling us is true, it's the big banks who are the little fat man behind the curtain."

"Indeed," Riggs answered. "Apt comparison."

"It's interesting to consider," Torvald remarked, "That in that general time period, Otto von Bismarck in Germany, and Lenin in Russia, also moved to create strong, centralized governments in their countries ... and Great Britain, of course, already had such a government in place."

"Yes, the modern, citizen-crushing super-states of, by, and for the hidden aristocracy of the super-rich. The top-of-the-heap boys. England, as we know," said Rantor, "Was the first nation to come under the control of the great European banking houses, back during the early 18th Century, with the creation of the first European central bank. The baited hook, for the financially desperate King, was, of course, as it is for all governments, unlimited funds for them, without having to increase taxes."

"Yes, the bill being paid by the people by the 'invisible tax' of inflation," concurred Riggs.

"One wonders," mused Torvald, "In how many other nations a similar covert conquest, by legal sleight of hand, has occurred, and a private corporate 'government' over corporate 'citizens' been installed ..."

"Indeed," agreed Riggs. "That certainly is the - or a - 64 trillion dollar question, isn't it?"

CHAPTER 6: AN IMPOSTER GOVERNMENT ...

'When I use a word,' Humpty Dumpty said, in rather a scornful tone, 'It means just what I choose it to mean – neither more nor less.'
'The question is,' said Alice, 'Whether you can make words mean so many different things.'
'The question is,' said Humpty Dumpty, 'Which is to be master – that's all.'

Lewis Carroll

I was by now only half following all of this, because that pretty blonde girl in the velvet dress with the glittering bodice had been glancing my way rather frequently. In fact, she was playing little games with me. Lest the reader think I am merely imagining things, I will give a couple of examples. Once, she picked up the dog's paw and waved it at me, as though the dog itself were waving; this was done - by the girl, not the dog, of course - with a smile both shy and impish. Once, she tapped or pointed to her chest, fingering the fabric of her gown in a gesture that signified I knew not what. Being clueless re the message she was (I assumed) trying to convey by means of this sign language, I, of course, had no idea how to signal back; I had no dog's paw to wave coyly back at her, and would have felt an absolute idiot sitting and tapping my own chest, and fingering the fabric of my shirt or vest; but, on mad impulse, and lest she feel that her interest did not interest me, I picked up the spiral of lemon peel that had lain on the foam of my *macciado*, and elaborately, as though I were a sword swallower, dangled it over the small O of my up-turned mouth, and then dropped it in and sat gazing intently at her over the rims of my dark glasses as I chewed and swallowed it. She gave a little laugh, blushed, and began lavishing attention upon her dog. The others at our table were so intent on Riggs' monologue that they paid my antics no heed.

"So the big bankers of Europe - the banksters - were involved in all of this - what could be called, I guess, the post-Civil War re-constitution of government?" asked Rantor.

"So it appears," Riggs answered. "According to one group of researchers, in latter half of the 19th Century, the corporate government began to generate debts via bonds and similar instruments, which came due in 1912; but they could not pay their debts. The several wealthy families that had bought up the bonds demanded payment - and ended up settling for no less than all of the corporate government assets and all of the assets of the Treasury of the United States of America."

"Hmmm. Sounds contrived. So, how did the country carry on, with no funds?"

"Well, modern history has been, in large part, one contrived crisis after another. Crises have proven so useful. With them you can justify using the essentially limitless emergency powers, and increasing government spending, and then you can terrify the public into accepting – even wanting, asking for – enlarged powers under a charismatic quasi-dictator – aka a 'strong leader.' But sometimes the emergency is not declared. As, if this information is indeed true, in the matter under discussion. Allegedly, the corporate government, in its orchestrated 'desperation,' went to these same wealthy banking families and asked to borrow. But the families refused, the corporate government having already demonstrated its inability to repay its debts. The families, of course, had forseen this – and the shrewd observer would of course suspect that, as you suggested, they, in collusion with key figures in power here in this country, contrived the whole scenario - and it was thus that the Federal Reserve System was created. Under this system, the government, working in cooperation with the Fed, creates paper or book-keeping-entry money out of nothing, and conducts its business by using fractionally backed, and finally by unbacked, notes, rather than money of substance – the arrangement being rationalized, in the topsy-turvy, cynical, self-serving view of the elites who engineered it, as a *benefit* to the bankrupt subject-citizens of a bankrupt nation."

"But being in actuality, of course, a benefit to those within the centralized government and to the bankers who engineered it - in all likelihood, who master-minded it … providing, as it does, virtually unlimited free money for Congress to spend - the offer, modern history tells us, that no government can refuse - and providing control of the wealth of empires for the bankers - and for the people, *de facto* slavery via the cleverly hidden taxation by inflation …" Bevins said, by way of summary.

"Precisely. This agreement was, you will note, between two private corporations. It did not involve the original jurisdiction government."

"So, where does the income tax come in?" asked Rantor "A lot of the guys I've been talking to say the income tax is unconstitutional."

243

"It would be – as would be the Fed itself - if the country were being run under original jurisdiction. It is true that the Constitution allows only two kinds of tax – a poll or head tax to be collected by the states based on population, or an excise tax, which of course is a business tax on items for resale. But these critics of the income tax err in supposing that the income tax has something to do with the original jurisdiction government they believe is running the country. In fact, the 16th Amendment amends the *corporate* constitution, and has nothing to do with any o.j. government. And as the Supreme Court has, so far as I can see, correctly found, the corporate government has a right to tax corporations."

"But - people aren't corporations ..." Glennie interjected.

"Well, true enough. But recall that under this system the people are, each and every one, assigned a *corporate identity*, and it is as surety for this corporate fiction - usually styled as their own name, but all in capitals rather than in upper and lower case - that they are taxed."

"So, tell me if I've got it straight," Rantor said. "By now, all acting 'governments,' state, county, and local, are in fact mere corporate subdivisions of the federal government? Of the corporate federal government?"

"Yes. Corporate franchisees, rather than the original political entities they are generally believed to be. If, of course, the research that we are delving into in some detail tonight is correct in its essential position that the present alleged state, county, and city governments are in fact *faux*, you might say - pretenders - mere agencies of the private - not public - District of Columbia corporation styled, in all caps, the UNITED STATES or the UNITED STATES OF AMERICA or UNITED STATES GOVERNMENT. Federalized 'states' and their agencies. And that 'federal government' itself is not even the same one that is defined in the original Constitution, but is also a private corporation, its private law masquerading as public law. I am not entirely certain, but to the best of my current state of knowledge, even those who deny the legal creation, by the Philadelphia Convention and their Constitution, of a *de jure* 'United States of America' do accept much or most of this research regarding the true nature of the current private corporate 'government' and the legal state of affairs in the country today ..."

"But of course," Bevins added, "The vast majority of the people, and most of those in government, and practicing law, are entirely unaware that there could or might be two parallel systems of government, and even two 'constitutions' - two of everything, so to speak."

"Every functional part of the original *de jure* system – whether it ever actually lawfully existed, or not - having a *de facto* corporate counterpart. It being a system of twins, of *doppelgangers* ..." mused Riggs, as if to himself.

"Isn't this fascinating, Iffy," Glennie marveled, turning finally to regard her forgotten chum.

"Yes. Ah, most interesting."

Privately, of course, I had been remembering Riggs' comment when we first got here about preserving the purity of the data and et cetera, and wondering what all this theoretical stuff had to do with my current plight, but being unable to break the chains of my training, found it difficult to bring myself to object, complain, or even to squirm meaningfully in my seat, clear my throat in a marked manner, or drum my fingers in an impatient staccato on the tabletop while directing steely gazes at my companions, in the manner of Rantor. No, old Ifford just sat politely sipping the brew and patiently enduring, as per his training back on the home planet. I had, however, formed the resolve to practice a few of the lizard's techniques when back in the privacy of my room, before a mirror.

"But I, uh, must confess," I went on, "That I have been left in the dust, to a degree, and am feeling somewhat baffled, it being, perhaps, a case of too much, too fast. It's as if the whole thing had ... oh, I don't know, streaked past me like a comet and left me standing benumbed on my street corner wondering who, when, what, where, and how. And why, and whether ... and then, I had rather been hoping we could wind things up soon, given the lateness of the hour and all ..."

As I made my confessions, I noticed that the velveteen girl had taken a notebook out of her back-pack and now sat writing in it, pausing frequently to gaze thoughtfully at me - or at least in what was indubitably my general direction.

"A false Christ will be seen on this earth ... he will have a counterpart for every word of God's truth, and an imitation for every work of the Spirit ..."

It was Bevins who broke in to utter this non-sequitur, speaking quietly but with feeling, almost chanting in an eerie sing-songy voice, as though reciting poetry, leading me to assume that the old girl was quoting something or someone. Her performance increased my discomfort with the entire set-up and pretty much confirmed my conviction that they were an assortment of certifiable and bona fide eccentrics, no two of which, I have found, are ever quite alike. She seemed to put a religious spin on all of it. I recalled Rantor saying that many of these researcher chappies were fervent fundamentalist Christian types. He'd also mentioned in one of his diatribes that the elites actually foster the belief that we are in the Biblical 'end times.' According to the lizard, it is prophesied in the Bible that in the end times the evil forces – being, in this take, of course, the evil New World Order - will triumph, but only briefly, after which the heavenly forces will prevail for a millennium or two, or even longer – it suiting the purposes of these globalist planners, he said, to have the many millions of Christians who oppose the N.W.O. believing they are living in the end times, because they will feel that the triumph of the evil ones is, as per Biblical prophecy, 'a done deal.' The record of history showing, he said, that people who think they will be defeated in a battle are in fact easier to defeat, such a belief having a dampening effect on the morale - the power of negative thinking, et cetera. Also, of course, if the good guys are prophesied to triumph in the long run, why worry about the short run. The reptile had gone on to say that one reason for the creation of the state of Israel – which according to him was part of the long-range globalist agenda, the masterplan, so to speak - was because that, too, would lead the Bible-thumpers to believe that these are indeed the Biblical end times. It seems to me that to convince believers that they are in the end times hardly requires such stratagems and machinations, as I recall reading somewhere that every generation of Christians since the first edition of the Bible came off the press has believed its times to be the end times.

But, getting back to Bevins, it seemed that another true believer and fervent proselytizer had wandered into my midst, this one better than half-way to being a religious fanatic, and once again I wondered, fleetingly but fervently - why me? How many lifetimes of crime against humanity or universal law was I currently working off, that my landscape was so thinkly peopled by these intense - and verbose - proselytizers?

The blonde girl had gotten up. She had torn a page from her notebook, and folded it once, and then again; now, she carried it up and handed it to one of the fellows who worked behind the counter. She seemed to be telling him something, and I saw her turn and gesture towards our table. It then occurred to me to wonder if she was an agent. So - Squinch's agent? ... perhaps the daughter of Ida Mae Glatz? A clone? A Nordic Blonde raised from a babe to do intelligence work? One of those CIA Project Monarch - or was it Project Blue Bird? - mind-controlled sex-slaves Glennie has told me about? Should I run? Should I alert the others? The nerves quivered a bit, but I really could not believe this of her. She was just so innocently beautiful, you see.

"But the original government still stands? - still legally exists?" Glennie was asking.

"Well, so the one theory goes," answered Riggs, simultaneously munching on his second or third chocolate chip cookie of the evening.. "The idea is, you see, that the whole corporate government modulation has been justified - rationalized - as being *voluntary* on the part of the people. In a nutshell, the changes are seen as having been rubber-stamped by the purported sovereigns - the people - as an 'experiment in democracy' into which they have voluntarily entered - and the original jurisdiction government has not been dissolved, but merely - one could say, set aside, vacated. Perhaps temporarily, perhaps permanently, the usurpers of course doing all in their power to ensure that it be the latter."

"And the people, as usual," added Bevins, "As clueless as babes."

"Yes, Florence," mumbled Riggs around a mouthful of cookie, "But, of course, we have to keep in mind that the 'information' which reaches them is highly controlled ... structured ... censored..."

CHAPTER 7: COLORABLE FICTIONS, *NOMMES DE GUERRE...*

Shallow ideas can be assimilated; ideas that require people to reorganize their picture of the world provoke hostility.

James Gleick, *Chaos*

"Voluntary?" queried Glennie. "If the people didn't even know what was happening, and all along have believed themselves to be under original jurisdiction, how could it be construed as 'voluntary' on their part to go along with this big, 180 degree change from original jurisdiction - a change they're completely in the dark about?"

"It sounds incredible, I agree. But, yes - voluntary. Or so presumed to be. They are actually, as I understand it at this point, *presumed* to have acquiesced by their silence, silence being *construed*, in courts of law, as *acquiescence*. It all sounds like some kind of Marx Brothers mistaken-identity farce, I agree, if not something rather more sinister - but the usurpers, planners, executors, masterminds - call them what you will - left - at least according to some researchers - they left the *de jure* 'original jurisdiction' infrastructure in place. It sits for the most part idle, vacant, and unused, like a genie in a bottle upon a dusty shelf, perhaps - but technically - as they, the, um, usurpers, view it, and in their legal system - the Republic yet lives."

"The lights are on, but nobody's home, in the Republic." Torvald suggested.

"Yes - at least according to some revisionist researchers. And in the meanwhile as they see it, the people are *voluntarily* participating in this other – venture, you might call it. An 'experiment in democracy' in the language of, if memory serves here, the Roosevelt Administration."

"And," added Bevins, "Those who believe that the o.j. government was lawfully created by the founders also believe that its jurisdiction can be invoked in court, if one knows how. And the pronouncements of the courts are read as some sort of code."

"Frankly," said I, "The image of the Delphic Oracle comes to mind – and divining the future from the intestines of a slaughtered chicken.

248

And so on. It all seems very hypothetical. Are you quite sure these chappies know what they're talking about? "

"It is true," Riggs admitted, "That I - we, Florence and I - have not personally examined the documents upon which these theories are founded – and, having no formal legal background, are in any event frankly not qualified to interpret them. 'The law was simple but hath been industriously rendered perplex,' you know. But we – and others - find these arguments both interesting and, on their face, plausible. And they do provide explanations for the known fact that the present government is not operating according to what it still claims – falsely claims – to be its own Supreme Law ..."

"And," continued Bevins, "They provide explanations and theories that are consistent with the observable, demonstrable fact that the present government has, to a very large extent, been turned into a tool of exploitation of the people rather than of service to them."

"It is easy to ridicule and dismiss these theories out of hand, I agree," said Riggs. "On their face they appear to be rather a far reach. But we are living in strange times, in which the populace is beyond a doubt being lied to by those in government and the media – is, from the cradle, being fed – and is largely believing – patently false information on many subjects ... and times in which, thanks in part to the internet, there is, easily available, abundant suppressed information re the unlawful, not to say criminal, doings of this country's government throughout at least the past century."

"Yeah," agreed Rantor, "And that book, *The Creature from Jekyll Island,* is a good place to find information on these subjects – like the engineered, and unnecessary, world wars, and the engineered Great Depression."

"One speculates, you see," Bevins explained, "That the usurpers realized – have realized all along - that what they have done, or participated in doing – the worst case scenario for them, the perpetrators – or as they could be called, co-conspirators - could be regarded as constructive treason – creating and maintaining an entire colorable – color of law - edifice of government that certainly does, on its face, appear to be an elaborate deception, and amounts to a virtual overthrow-by-trickery of the original government, or at least the original intentions, of both the country's founders and its people."

249

"Yes," her rotund pal agreed. "And there is also the related crime – and possible charge - of 'misprision of felony.' Fairly obviously, to us at least, the current government has no problem with deceiving the public, and does it all the time, and does it even by policy. Hence it is after all not such a far reach, perhaps, to regard the government as resting upon a bedrock, so to speak of deception by policy on a large – a grand, a monumental, a mind-boggling - scale."

"And to conjecture that, to save themselves, in the event of discovery -"

"Precisely. Exactly. To give themselves a legal leg to stand on, as it were -"

" - That the fiction is maintained – is officially maintained - that the participation of the people in this present system is not unwitting but *voluntary* - "

" Yes, when, in the present system," Riggs carried on, "The common man - or woman - is invited – or we would say '*induced,* by tendered offer - *to contract, in a corporate capacity,* with this federalized government, f*or the purposes of engaging in commercial activity* - which all of our dealings with the government do indeed seem to be legally regarded as being - commercial activity, that is. And the idea – the official position, you might say - is that the people have, each and every one, entered into these contractual agreements voluntarily. On its face, this theory is certainly plausible, and comports with available evidence."

"So, again, if you don't mind," asked Glennie, "What are some of these commercial activities that the people have 'agreed' to engage in, then, according to this theory - in the view of this *de facto* government set-up?"

"Virtually every contact with the *de facto* government is regarded as being in commerce, and many of these government contacts are regarded as being benefits, priviledges, or opportunities," Bevins answered. "Getting a driver's license - a permit to travel; registering a car; paying property tax; applying for an SSN - a work permit; applying for public assistence or other forms of welfare, receiving a traffic citation, using FRNs to 'discharge' debt ..."

"Indeed," agreed the other half of the sketch, the toad, as I privately called him. "Willy-nilly and whether we know it or not, it does appear that 'we're all in commerce now,' and thus, in our commercial/corporate identities, or capacities, we can legally be regulated, and required to perform, by government. Which is the whole object, point, and purpose, of course, of legally defining us as being in commerce. So that we can be regulated - and taxed - by the state - as we could not be in our capacity as flesh and blood men and women under original jurisdiction. So, as Florence has said, things like, um, receiving the 'benefit' of using Federal Reserve Notes - as bankrupts, which the corporate state and its agents and beneficiaries - which would be the people - are regarded as being - so, using FRNs to 'discharge' debt ... and receiving unemployment benefits, or merely being eligible to receive them ... and the privilege of being granted a driver's license ... and the opportunity for the low-income of receiving tuition grants to colleges ... and of course the various other welfare programs - these are all regarded as commercial activities. For instance, one signs up for a Social Security number - another 'benefit,' by the way. Merely having the number - which is actually a *permit to work within the system* - is considered a benefit. At the time one is issued a SSN and card, a *juristic person*, that is to say, an artificial entity or fiction of law - is created - which is referenced by the name of the real person, but styled slightly differently - JOHN JAMES DOE, quite often, or John J. Doe, rather than John James Doe. This juristic person is a *legal fiction*, and the living man or woman is the *surety* or *fiduciary* for the fiction. This juristic person operates, as to time and place, entirely in another legal fiction - a jurisdiction that is extra- or non-Constitutional rather than un-Constitutional ... the fictional time, being, I am told the date minus the A.D. written after it, and the fictional place being the 'hover zone,' that is regarded, legally, as being not *on* but *above* the land – essentially, or colorably, at least, an admiralty or maritime jurisdiction, or having at least many aspects of admiralty jurisdiction – most significantly, a venue that is not 'on the land' and the attachment of criminal penalty to civil cases."

"So devious," mused Rantor. "Kind of ingenious. You've got to hand it to these guys."

"True. However, it was created bit by bit, of course, over several generations. No one great genius imagined the entire complex structure in one fell swoop," Riggs pointed out. "It traces its roots to Europe, and particularly to England, where, for instance, the CITY OF LONDON is a sovereign legal entity, distinct from the city or City of London. Most people, naturally, assume the two to be one, just as they assume the CITY OF SAN FRANCISCO, CA, to be the same entity as San

251

Francisco, Calif. It is interesting to consider to what extent similar systems might have been set up in other nations – such as the nations of Europe. I know of no researchers who are working on that question."

"Perhaps it happened here – or happened here first – because the colonies started out being private for-profit business ventures, with the colonists being actually employees, or agents, of England," Bevins speculated. "Anyway, in this fictional 'hover zone,' we're talking about, John Doe, cluelessly using the corporate name of JOHN DOE and acting as surety for that legal fiction, is *presumed* voluntarily to have entered into a private contract with the private DC corporation and/or its franchises. It is private law masquerading as public law - as 'public policy' actually - for the presumed 'greater good' in times of 'emergency.' "

"Yes. Florence is, as I understand it, correct. The way the system is set up - and it is an ingenious arrangement - by certain *presumptions* which are made, regarding the identity and location of every one of us, and which we the people willy-nilly and out of our complete ignorance do not timely *rebut*, the *presumption* is created that we have *assented* to *waive* our Constitutional form of government and its protections against their absolute powers, and have chosen to contract - it is all done by contract - with their *de facto* federal corporation and its instrumentalities, the corporate states, cities, and counties - governed by its corporate legislation and administrative procedures and rules - its private law operating as 'public policy' - as interpreted and enforced by its, um, its absolute-power military/admiralty/maritime bankruptcy courts."

"So, what's this 'one form of action,' then?" asked Rantor.

"That is yet another piece of the puzzle – and device for concealment. Under the old system, inherited from the English common law, there were *separate courts* – separate *forms of action* - separate jurisdictions, basically of law and equity … law having to do with injuries done against the private rights of private men - flesh and blood people with rights and with legal standing - and equity being essentially the law governing legal fictions - contracts, juristic persons - business. Commerce."

"And then," supplied Bevins, "There was admiralty/maritime law…"

"Yes, the distinct admiralty/maritime law with its separate jurisdiction, governing things that occurred off the land, on the high seas – and, in these modern times of travel by plane, in the air. Admiralty/maritime law having, besides a venue 'off the land,' one important aspect, which the planners wished to incorporate into their 'one form of action,' namely, attaching a *criminal penalty* to a *contractual* infringement or offense in civil as opposed to criminal cases. Criminal penalty did not attach to contractual matters in the civil as opposed to criminal courts. But it was, many years ago, deemed necessary to create a separate jurisdiction to deal with such special problems, on the high seas, as a sailor endangering the lives - and property - of others by violating his contractual agreement to be obedient to his superior – obedient even at risk to his own life, in times of emergency - very much like the legal situation of a soldier in time of war. Just as a soldier can be court-martialed and given a criminal penalty – basically for violation of contract – if he refuses to carry out an order - so in the case of the sailor, say if he were ordered to do something dangerous to him personally but necessary to the safety of the ship and crew - and its valuable cargo, of course - something like, oh, let's say, going up in the rigging in a storm to furl the sails. In admiralty jurisdiction, sailors were required, under penalty of law, to fulfill their contracts and obey their masters, even at risk of life or limb, just as soldiers are required to do or face a criminal penalty - court martial, or even execution."

"Actually," said Torvald, "Isn't it true that the name of a person spelled all in capitals - the very designation that is employed by the *de facto* corporate government to refer to its citizens in their corporate capacity - was in times past, say as recently as the 19th Century, also known as a *nomme de guerre*, or war name, and was the style used for soldiers' names as well as sailors'?"

"I believe so," agreed Riggs, "Denoting, then as now, a particular jurisdiction and juristic person. It is also used, in general, to refer to corporations, corporate entities – artifical persons. Now: back to your question, Rantor, regarding the 'one form of action' ... for the uses and purposes of this present system of control-by-deception, it was desired to attach criminal penalty to civil matters – contract violation, primarily – and to obscure and confuse these distinctions between the law of real people and private rights, on the one hand, and the law of fictional entities and contracts, on the other ... and between the law of the land and the law of the sea. And so they came up with this fusion of the various courts and jurisdictions into 'one form of action.' "

"Yes," Bevins concurred. "But of course the reasons officially given for the change were not these."

"Naturally not. So the 'one form of action' fusion of the courts obscures the actual *jurisdiction* which people are under in court - and out of court - which was and is very helpful to the planners in this grand scheme which involved inducing the people to leave the protections and inalienable private rights of the old common law - or at least to be able to presume in court and in other official dealings with them that they had done so; and thus this clever scheme was concocted, in which the people are presumed *voluntarily* - by exercising their right to contract - to have entered this commercial corporate 'one form of action' hodge-podged jurisdiction," Riggs said.

"Yes. And the people, in their ignorance, not having timely rebutted that presumption, it is allowed to remain in place," Bevins added.

"Well, of course, Florence," replied Riggs, "We must keep in mind that the people are carefully kept as ignorant of the law as they are of economics."

"Then - for everything *de jure*, the usurpers indeed created a colorable fiction," Torvald mused, almost admiringly, while Glennie gazed at him, also rather admiringly, it seemed to me, and with a certain moist, spaniel-ish softness around the eyes that I never see in them when she regards old Ifford. I cleared my throat in a marked manner and stared in as marked a manner as possible at the girl in the velvet dress, hoping that Glennie might notice that she was not the only one with other fish to fry, but she seemed oblivious to yours truly, whom she had, after all, long regarded as merely a part of the woodwork.

"... a veritable bramble-thicket ..."

CHAPTER 8: ... AND, A STATE OF PERPETUAL EMERGENCY

A majority of the people of the United States have lived all of their lives under emergency rule. For 40 years or more [now 66 years or more], freedoms and governmental procedures guaranteed by the Constitution have, in varying degrees, been abridged by laws brought into force by states of national emergency. The problem of how a constitutional democracy reacts to great crises, however, far antedates the Great Depression. As a philosophical issue, its origins reach back to the Greek city-states and the Roman Republic. And, in the United States, actions taken by the Government in times of great crises have - from, at least, the Civil War - in important ways, shaped the present phenomenon of a permanent state of national emergency.

Senate Report 93-549

"Some of the guys I've talked to in the research community seem to think that if they avoid all these corporate-government entanglements, avoid taking any of these BPOs - benefits, privileges, and opportunities, like welfare and Social Security and licenses and permits and so on - that they will be allowed to go their way unmolested by the ..." for once the lizard was at a loss for the ready phrase.

"By the 'monster state?'" supplied Bevins, who as previously mentioned seemed highly censorious and rather unrelentingly intense about it all. Taking the moral high ground with a vengance, you might say.

"If you will," Torvald said. "It all does seem a bit monstrous. A monstrous deception, certainly. As Rantor said, these - would-be opters-out, you could perhaps call them, from the corporate-government scheme - seem to think that the existing power bloc are respecters of pieces of paper ... you know, the law. Despite all the evidence of history to the contrary. That they can just wave the right piece of paper in the, as they see it, foreign courts or at their uniformed enforcers, and they will be allowed to go their way unmolested. With a tip of the hat and a cheery 'Ave a noice dye, Guv'na.'"

"Rather like flashing a cross or crucifix or a rope of garlic at a vampire, thus causing it to snarl, wilt, and shrink obligingly into the woodwork, or melt into a black grease-spot on the floor?" I suggested. And then, rather pleadingly, "But, I say, don't you know, it is getting rather late, isn't it? Past my bedtime, I think ..."

"Yes, we shall have to wind this up very soon," Riggs agreed - or should I say, falsely promised. "And, an amusing and apt comparison, Ifford, that to the vampires. I am sure Florence would agree with you there. Well, as to that 'hold-harmless' theory of theirs, these would-be non-starters or abstainers or opters-out from the whole system ... I would be very happy to discover them to be correct on this point ... but, just *entre nous*, you know," he continued with a small smile, "I wouldn't bank on it. These suppositions of theirs do seem to me to be a trifle naïve. I would imagine the presumption that we are all 'U.S. citizens' and thus under the *de facto* government's jurisdiction would certainly be the operative one, if or when push ever does come to shove. And I hear of more adverse than positive outcomes for these researchers, administratively and in court. Of course, I am by no means up to speed on all of this. It is immensely complex, legally - deliberately so, of course. A veritable smokescreen of complexity. As Algernon Sidney, said back around 1700, 'The law was simple, but hath been industriously rendered perplex.' A veritable bramble-thicket, at present, designed to entangle the unwary ..."

"Well," said Torvald, "Their wistful optimism is understandable, given that the reality we are looking at is, after all, rather a cheerless one ..."

"Yes," agreed Rantor. "I've always liked that bit about most people taking their reality in small doses. Whoever it was that said it. T.S. Eliot? Anyway, even these researchers, so bold in their willingness to look grim reality in the face, seem to feel the need to limit their exposure."

"To take refuge and comfort in some - possibly illusory - out," added Torvald. "Who can blame them?"

"Well, one thing I don't understand." Glennie said, moving us on to plunge into the meaty depths of what, unfortunately, sounded like yet another aspect of it all, "Is this perpetual state of emergency. Someone came into the station once trying to tell Jacko about it, and trying to get him to play a tape about it, made by some veterinarian from Colorado, I think it was, who had done a lot of research on the whole thing, the guy said, and Jacko told him it was a bunch of nonsense. He wouldn't even let the guy finish talking. Just showed him the door."

"That makes me wonder even more if this Jacko might not be an agent of disinformation. They like to have their agents in positions of influence," mused Torvald thoughtfully.

"'Positions of influence'?" asked Glennie. "Hardly anybody listens to the public affairs programming on KROK. Remember, it's aired from 3 to 6 a.m. on the weekends. Everyone's asleep."

"Yes, well, some people tape it, don't they? And anyway, they - the power elite - want to monitor the politically active types such as those who volunteer to work on such shows. It's precisely the politically active minority that those in power are concerned about - those who are not being adequately controlled and contained - some would say duped" - here he glanced at Rantor with a quick smile - "by the mass media. Especially the radicals. Small in numbers now, maybe - but potentially damaging. Much of their information is sound, and their numbers are growing, and the elites know it."

"Anyone actually capable of original thought as opposed to the mere data intake and regurgitation which passes for thought in the rank and file - being of particular interest to the evil empire," Rantor put in. Or words to that effect.

My surreptitious surveillance of the velvet blonde had continued during all of this chatter; and I now saw that she had gone up to the counter once again and had come back bearing what looked like hot apple cider in a large, clear mug. She glanced at me and smiled as she sat down again at her table. While she had been gone, the dog had wolfed down what remained of the giant chocolate chip cookie she had purchased earlier, but his mistress seemed not to notice, or not to care, and sat stroking his head as she sipped her cider. He was quite large, very dignified, and sat fully as tall as she on the bench. Though his behavior gave no problem, still I wondered that the management allowed the beast on the premises.

"I believe it is true," said Riggs, "That special care and attention are lavished on the control of the intelligentsia - the academic and professional intelligentsia, the official intelligentsia, as it were, tending to be easier to control than those not officially recognized as such - those brighter individuals at loose in the population at large and not subject to the shaping and control exercised on the academics and professionals by the slanted information to which they are exposed in their schooling, and after that, by peer pressure, professional and financial leverage, and further disinformation in print - though of course for the most part not recognized as such – that, taken all together, pretty much tightly control the important academic and professional spheres such as economics, medicine, and law."

"Have the so-called intelligentsia boxed and wrapped up in brown paper with a string around it, is what it pretty much reduces to," snorted Rantor, in that lustily emphatic way of his that, at the higher revs, so to speak, seems to make the entire vicinity flicker a bit, rather like electric lights in a violent storm. "And then there's that mandatory 'continuing education' that they have to sign up for every so often or loose their 'privilege' of practicing their profession – right? But let's get back to the emergency. We're really being governed under emergency rule, then? From as far back as the Civil War, perhaps? That's what you were getting at, isn't it, when you said 'to the extent that we are being governed according to any written system of civil law at all?'"

"Yes. A state of national emergency, you see, evokes martial law - the rule of war - which is governed by the Doctrine or Rule of Necessity. But the Rule of Necessity is that *necessity knows no law.'* So military or martial law or rule is really no law at all. These principles are embodied in court rulings, and customs and maxims of law, that go back for centuries, by the way, back to the mother country."

"In fact," said Bevins, "Under the Doctrine of Necessity, deception of the populace - using the deceptive parallel jurisdictions, for example – might be construed as being not only permissible but appropriate - even 'necessary' - if it aids in 'preserving the public peace' - which is the primary duty of government under conditions of emergency."

"So martial rule - emergency rule – indeed removes virtually all limits on governmental power," mused Torvald.

"Yes," Riggs agreed. "Government under martial law becomes a *de facto* military dictatorship. The idea being that there is no time for the slower processes of the civil government under normal conditions. If you think about the conditions which would prevail in a *bona fide* emergency, you can see that there can be - and, in history, have been - circumstances in which martial rule would be - has been - necessary - the only alternative to utter and complete chaos, and perhaps to conquest."

"Invasion from without, insurrection or coup from within," supplied Bevins.

"And yet," Torvald marveled, "This very principle of law has been turned on its head and used to achieve what it was intended to prevent – regime change not by the will and knowing consent of the governed, but in the form of a bloodless coup from within, achieved, not by force, but by deception and trickery."

"Quite so," affirmed Riggs genially, as though we were discussing varieties of roses, or popular vacation getaways. He seemed not at all upset by the grave nature - and implications - of his material. It was a bit strange, actually. Torvald seemed rather to admire the cleverness of it all, and Riggs projected the general ambience of a Santa Claus sans the curly white beard and fur suit. Or a seal. Now that I think of if, except for the eyes, the fellow rather brought to mind a jolly fat seal in a zoo.

"Are you all right, Ifford?" asked Glennie.

I gave her a wan smile, what was probably a bleary-eyed and rather crooked little smile, such as might be seen on the sagging features of a stout-hearted three-something kept up far past his bedtime by thoughtless adults greedily intent on their own pleasures.

"Fine. I'm just fine."

"Good." Tragic tone and rather martyred air apparently not registering. "I was afraid you might by now be a little tired, and a little bored, and that all this might be a bit much for you."

"Well ... it is all a bit much for me, actually ... and I am ... a bit tired, is all, and rather wishing we could toddle on home soon ..."

And I smiled at her, rather too brightly, and rather foolishly, I'm afraid. I had hardly been listening to their palaver at all now, as I watched that lovely girl with the dog writing away again - at what? - her journal? Could she possibly be composing an ode to Ifford? After all, stranger things had happened to our hero of late. Perhaps it was my clothing that had caught her childish fancy. I resolved to frequent the second-hand shops on the morrow, in search of clothing and effects similar to those I now wore. They weren't, after all, so bad as they had at first seemed, if one didn't mind looking as if one were on one's way to a costume ball - or had come dangerously close to a total rupture of relations with what is commonly called reality.

"But the problem," Bevins was droning on, "Is that governments - and those who control them - once they have it, do not like to relinquish this absolute power that an emergency grants them."

"But surely the framers of the Constitution were aware of that tendency on the part of people in power, and wrote some safeguards against it into the Constitution?" said Glennie.

" 'Let us hear no more of the goodness of men, but rather bind them with the chains of the Constitution,' " intoned Riggs, rather theatrically. The way he said it made me think he was quoting someone. Probably one of the founders of the limited-government persuasion.

"Thomas Jefferson, of course," he appended. He spoke in a musing sort of voice, and it seemed for a moment as though he was going to fade out on us as I had noticed was his tendency at times, especially as the long evening wore on, rather like a radio signal from a station experiencing technical difficulties; but he seemed to pull himself back in focus and went on. "It is a rather remarkable omission. After all the elaborate safeguards and separations of powers so painstakingly written in to the Constitution. But then these fellows were amateurs, after all, in this business of creating an entire government from scratch ... bright, highly educated, and gifted amateurs, to be sure, but amateurs nonetheless."

"But, isn't a state of emergency automatically over after a year or something? Or can't it be over-ridden by Congress?" asked Glennie.

"Well, as I understand it," Riggs replied, "The presidents, each of them, just to be on the safe side, obligingly renew the 'emergency', on some pretext or another, annually or semi-annually. The 'war' on drugs, the 'war' on terror, the 'war' on crime, the threat of bio-terrorism, etc. etc. etc. But my understanding is that a state of emergency can only be terminated by declaration of the president, by declaration of a conquering nation, or by the people themselves reasserting proper civil government. Which some of them are trying to do, with their jural societies, as I understand."

"With, of course, much scrutiny, and spies and agents provocateur being sent into their midst." snorted Rantor. "The *de facto* rulers love to paint the patriot community as violent and dangerous."

"Mmm hummm," agreed Riggs. "How often throughout history we find it to be the case that the, um, the malefactors on the grand scale are guilty of precisely the crimes, and proclivities, of which they accuse and for which they persecute their raggle-taggle bands of populist resistors."

Bevins stuck her oar in here. "The reality is that the country is being run by public opinion. The limits on what government can and will do are set not by any rule of law or ideal or standard of what government ought and ought not to do or be, but merely by what public opinion will allow – by 'what the traffic will bear.' And the carefully cultivated ignorance of the people permits those in power to get away with such things as the persecution of whistle-blowers and dissidents - the persecution and, they hope, substantially the elimination, or at least the silencing, the neutralization, of those who would correct the wrongs being done, in the name of the people, by the government's elite controllers."

"Yes," Torvald agreed. "One can see that truth in operation in countries like China and Russia where long-established custom and convention dictating a social norm of subservience to authority have allowed the development of ruthless totalitarian regimes which essentially reign by terror. Where public opinion allows, government readily becomes more overtly controlling of the thoughts, speech, and actions of the people – as well as becoming more exploitative. And the more the people are exploited and controlled, the more dissatisfied they are, and the greater becomes the need for government to control them and to punish dissidence harshly, as an example and deterrant. Witness the brutal suppression of the Tiananmen Square student protests in 1989."

"That event," Bevins said, "Also demonstrates the general truth that once government has been permitted to grow so large and powerful, and so bullying of its citizenry, it is no easy matter to correct the situation. Many of the people in China supported the students but were afraid to come forward themselves. The Chinese today, many of them, long to have more freedom, and to live in less fear. But government has all the power – and the people, none.

"Indeed. And with these powers comes the power to define what 'truth' shall be, both by control of information sources and by stated or unstated policy – and by enforcement," added Riggs. " Witness the relatively recent phenomenon of the prosecution and incarceration of 'holocaust deniers,' whose only 'crime' is that of exercising their right to freedom of thought and speech. There is indeed a politics even of 'truth.' The United States has been a real thorn in the side of the statists because of its ingrained tradition of the freedom and rights of the individual. Their ideal, of course, is the Asian conformity and subservience to authority."

"And, Bevins added, "We see in the rise of what is called 'political correctness' how methodically opinion, social convention – and law – are being molded and restructured along statist lines. Increasingly, people in this country accept as an unstated given that government has the right to dictate to them all sorts of personal conduct and opinions. It is interesting to consider that only a hundred years or so ago, a Constitutional amendment was considered necessary for government to regulate by law people in their private habits - the recreational ingestion of intoxicants – Prohibition – something that public opinion now permits government to do with no Constitutional amendment, the people having come to accept this intrusion into their private lives and doings as government's 'perfect right.' "

"Dumbed down public opinion," was Rantor's gloomy contribution.

And it was at this juncture that I saw something which made the blood run cold and started the old heart a-pounding as though I were on my way to take an important exam in my theory of banking class. The door of the coffee shop had opened to admit, in addition to the usual icy blast of winter air and a few stray snowflakes that eddied in dreamily, three burly and fit-looking men, dressed in - egad! - blue uniforms, and wearing white helmets. These horrific creatures went to the counter and started talking to the fellows who take the orders and make the espresso.

"Don't look now, everyone, but it's the bloody Gestapo," I said.

Whereupon the chatter at our table ceased, and all eyes swiveled front and center.

CHAPTER 9: IN WHICH OUR HERO, BY THE BAREST THREAD, RETAINS HIS LIBERTY

After a shooting spree, they always want to take the guns away
from the people who didn't do it. I sure as hell wouldn't want to live
in a society where the only people allowed guns
are the police and the military.

William S. Burroughs

"Keep talking, everyone," advised Riggs, the usual placid smile on his face. Not only our table, but the entire place had grown eerily silent - except for the relentless blare of the music, of course. These U.N. police walk-throughs happen all the time, but no one really feels comfortable with them.

So - was my little blonde one-girl fan club indeed some sort of agent? Had she recognized me through my disguise, and somehow summoned these thugs - which she could have done on one of her trips to the front counter - and was it, then, all over for me but the inquisition and judgment? These – unlikely though they admittedly were - were the thoughts and fears coursing through me. My companions, after a moment, managed to keep some sort of conversation going, and to look fairly unconcerned. But I, of course, what with being a wanted entity and all, was in an indescribable panic to see the heat, as in some nightmare from which I could not awaken, heading so inexorably our way. My heart pounded most alarmingly in my chest, and I felt as though I had just downed about twenty straight shots of espresso, as in some contest to see who could drink the most the fastest, and had, on top of all the espresso - oh, say, just been handed an important exam in that boring trigonometry class that I had so despised, and had drawn a total and complete blank re the method of solution for every one of the five problems on it.

The U.N. police began to walk through the place, eyeing people suspiciously and every now and then stopping to ask someone to produce his or her papers. One of them kept muttering - to himself, I at first thought, adding to the air of nightmarish unreality the entire scene had for me, until I realized that he had some sort of communication device on his head. I could see what looked like a little microphone protruding stiffly from under his helmet just in front of his left ear.

These enforcers appeared to hail from Outer Mongolia, or some other Asiatic venue, and they clanked ominously as they walked, bearing as they did the full panoply of state-of-the-art clubs, weapons, zappers, numzers, restraining devices and God knows what else on and about their persons; and they of course wore, on their helmets and jacket-fronts, the sinister blue U.N. flag insignia with the bright golden perimeter. The air around them was charged with an almost palpable aura of menace, a force-field so powerful that it seemed to hover on the threshold of visibility - you almost felt that you could knead, like so much bread dough, the highly charged atmosphere that enveloped them, or swim through it as through turquoise water in a pool, or gather it up your arms and cram it like an oversized down comforter into a shopping bag. Their general demeanor and intense, focused energy, as they scanned the place with alert gazes, quite reminded one of a pack of large carnivores on the hunt on the African veldt. Perhaps it was only my imagination, but they seemed to take satisfaction in their power, and to bask in the intimidating impact they so clearly had on one and all.

"Well, to get back to the so-called emergency of the thirties," I marveled to hear Rantor saying, as he drummed the clawed fingers of one huge paw on the table top, which was an annoying nervous habit of his, "Didn't they do something like take an old war-time act - The Trading with the Enemy Act from World War I, I think - and somehow re-word it so it applied not just to enemy aliens but to American citizens as well?"

I could scarcely believe my ears. That the reptile could even remember what we had just been talking about - let alone put words together to form a question - with the minions of the absolute power of the world state bearing down on us ... from behind my dark glasses, I stared at the great creature in amazement. The only concession he made to the presence of the grim enforcers in our midst was to lower his voice slightly. But of course, and as occurred to me later, as a Squankese, he was not subject to the laws of this planet or - yet - those of the forming IPGA – the Inter-Planetary Governmental Alliance.

"Yes - that, among other things, is what they did." Riggs, too, spoke a little more quietly but otherwise seemed quite unconcerned. "This is not speculative, but is precisely what they did. A matter of historical record, though often mis-nomered. People speak of the 'War Powers Act,' but there is no 'War Powers Act' per se. Rather, there is the Trading with the Enemy Act; and its amendment - in the late '20s or early '30s, I believe - did indeed make the people themselves - in corporate capacity, that is, as juristic persons, US citizens or US persons - the enemy of the state - the corporate federal state. This was done, as an act of Congress, by deleting a clause excepting U.S. citizens from the Act's sweeping absolutist provisions."

"Incredible," murmured Torvald. "So naked. Gives new and deeper meaning to that famous remark by Major General Smedley Butler that 'war is a racket' Not only is it a racket, it provides a pretext for so many other rackets by 'the Bigs' as I call them – big government, big corporations, big banks ..."

"Smedly Butler ... I shall have to look him up," mused Riggs, as if to himself.

"The big banks seeming to be at the top of the heap," added Rantor. "Government, of, by, and for the big banking houses, when one follows the rabbit – or should I say rat - to its hole."

"The people *are* the government, in original jurisdiction," said Bevins.

"In their dream," scoffed the lizard contemptuously.

"But," she continued, "They, out of ignorance, didn't object to all the profound changes in government instituted, both gradually and bit by bit during peacetime, and more rapidly and sweepingly in wartime, and during the 'emergency' of the '30s. And so, increasingly, by their failure timely to object, the people became, not the sovereigns, but rather mere subject-citizens of a powerful, centralized Hegelian super-state."

"But of course, the people didn't know anything about this Trading with the Enemy Act revision, did they?" asked Glennie. "So already the media were in collusion, I guess you could conclude."

"Yes, the owners of the major media are part of the ruling plutocracy," agreed Riggs. "Without control of information, these huge changes in in the form of government could never have been achieved. So, yes, the people were silent because ignorant, both of specific acts and events and of their significance," agreed Riggs, "And, as during the emergency of the Civil War, so, using the plausible pretext of the 'emergency' of the Great Depression, great strides were taken - what amounted to a continuation of the re-structuring of government into, as

266

Florence says, a powerful, centralized corporate state. It was touted as an "experiment in democracy." The people, the alleged sovereigns, in their silence, were deemed to be in agreement with that 'experiment'."
"Emergencies are useful to those who seek to aggrandize the powers of government." Bevins said. "So useful that if they don't occur naturally, they are often contrived."

"Yes," said Riggs. "People in times of emergency regress – become more childlike – and are willing to accept strong paternalistic leaders and to give them greater powers - a fact of which modern power-seekers are well aware."

"Like any predator, or con artist," Bevins observed, "The planners carefully study the ways and habits of their prey or 'mark.' "

"According to what I've been reading in *The Creature from Jekyll Island*," Rantor said, "The Great Depression was essentially the result of the Fed's huge expansion of money and credit during the 1920s – something deliberately done to cause inflation in the United States, in order to cause prices in the States to rise, making British prices more competitive in the world market – arranging things so that the workers of the United States, willy-nilly, bailed out England. The Fed manipulated interest rates to cause U.S. investors to invest in British as opposed to American securities, thus, as was the intent, moving gold out of the United States and into England. Basically, by means of this gold transfer and the inflation which resulted from these manipulations by the Fed, the people unwittingly gave millions to England."

"In the process rescuing the big bankers who had invested heavily in British war bonds," added Riggs.

"Just try to imagine," mused Bevins, "The kind of prosperity the people could be enjoying right now, if they and their forebears had not had to foot the bill, either through taxes, or through the hidden tax of inflation, for all of these boondoggles – the Civil War, the world wars of the last century, and subsequent wars, the Great Depression, all of this ongoing corporate welfare and bribes to foreign governments under the guise of 'foreign aid'…"

As they spoke, my eyes, behind my dark glasses, continually darted to the uniformed men who were gradually working our way, still making apparently random checks amongst the customers in the coffee house. The apparent *blasé* indifference of my companions increased the air of unreality that pervaded the whole horrible scene and caused me once again and with renewed vigor to doubt their sanity. They were strange! Face it! The whole lot of them were terribly, terribly strange, and what in the name of the great god Mammon was I doing with them? Look - just look at what this association had gotten me so far. It hit me all of a sudden with great force that I hardly knew them - any of them - except Glennie. And Glennie was so much like me as almost to be me. My naive little alter ego. I was, quite literally, a stranger in a strange land - and had entrusted myself to strangers. Like a stray dog, I had allowed myself to be taken up by whomever would have me. What an absolute idiot I had been! I saw it all now, in a blinding flash of clarity. Squinch wasn't really all that bad, or the home planet, either, when you got right down to it - firm, yes - tough, yes - but at least they played a game with rules ... of a sort ... oh, if only I hadn't so irrevocably burned my bridges with them - my roots, after all ... my past and my future ...

"Yes - by Congressional amendment," Riggs was ploughing on in that bland and toneless voice of his. Evidently they were back onto this revision of the Trading with the Enemy Act. I wanted to throttle the fellow. He gave new and deeper meaning to the word, 'oblivious.' We shouldn't even have been talking about these things with the Gestapo a mere few feet away from us and lessening that distance as we spoke. I mean - what if they carried hidden microphones, for crying out loud?

But the fellow droned on, "The clause removed in and by the amendment was the one that *excepted American citizens* from the total powers the act gave the federal government over the dealings and transactions of the citizens of the country with whom the United States had been at war - the Germans. With the removal of that little clause, the American people - in corporate capacity, of course, but the presumption was and is that we are all in corporate capacity, all the time and in all our dealings with government - so, effectively, the people were turned into the enemy - quite literally, the enemy - of the *de facto* corporate government - and were deprived of legal standing, except by permission of the state - the American people were, that is to say, made legally unable - this is all according to the provisions of the Trading with the Enemy Act - unable to create or enter into contracts ... unable to turn to the courts for relief and redress of any grievance ... unable to carry on any sort of business - unable even to work, or to own property ... without the express permission of the state - the *de facto* corporation masquerading as the or a, legitimate state, of course I mean. "

"But it all happened so long ago! So what! I don't mean to be rude or anything, but, I mean, so bloody what?" I heard myself blurting out. I know it was the tension of the moment that had made me forget myself like that. Here I was, about to be arrested and carted off in manacles, and yet they maundered on. I had had it up to here with all of their blather.

"Well, for one thing, you see," Riggs replied, genially - or imperviously - ignoring my peevishly ill-tempered outburst, "The emergency, and this amended Trading with the Enemy Act - they are still with us to this day. The emergency is, according to my information, quietly renewed annually or bi-annually by the presiding President cum Commander-in-Chief of all the forces in the field; and that act we are discussing is still law. And this same amended Trading with the Enemies Act is a reason for the licenses and permits which are now required before anyone can drive a car or build on their own property or take a job - or even legally own a pet."

"And, looking at the larger picture, Ifford," Torvald added, "The issues are – does it matter, how we treat one another? Or is it 'anything goes'? Virtually all societies seem to agree that it does matter – else there would be no laws or rules of conduct – no 'crime and punishment,' so to speak."

"Yes," agreed Rantor in his *fortissimo* tones, "And - is it acceptable that there be double standards – different standards of conduct and judgment – a rule of law for the masses, and 'anything goes' for the elites? Because, on the one hand, the great majority of the peoples and governments, of this world, anyway, seem to agree that how we treat one another *does* matter, and most agree that there should be one standard by which all are judged. And yet – our topic, you might say – is that the practice deviates – prodigiously, egregiously – from the 'lip service' standards and codes of the advanced societies on this planet, with the elites literally getting away with theft and murder on a gargantuan scale, and the Joe Averages going to jail in greater and greater numbers for an ever-increasing schedule of 'crimes,' most of them minor compared to the deeds and doings of many of the elites - and, working harder and longer for less and less of the profits of production. In other words, government of, by, and for a numerically tiny elite who own well over 50% of the world's wealth – and still counting - and are ruling ever more harshly over the workers whom they are parasitizing ."

"All right," I said. "For the sake of argument, let's assume that what you all just said is true. But - the situation seems sort of hopeless, doesn't it? The elites always too clever and amoral, and the masses always too unclever and irresponsible, etc.? Wouldn't you agree that that is the picture which emerges? I mean – why bother? It's always going to be this way, isn't it?"

"Yes," replied Torvald. "It is always going to be a tug of war. The problem is that the situation is not static. It is evolving. And it is evolving into a world police/slave state along the lines of Orwell's *1984* that most people will find extremely unpleasant. Intolerably so."

"And," added Rantor, "By the time they finally *do* wake up and smell the coffee, it might be too late. The controls of the elites might be developed and in place to such an extent that revolt – change by any means – might be pretty much impossible – or at least, much more difficult and costly, in every respect."

"You see," continued Torvald, "There's kind of a race going on, between the elites and the resistance, with the resistance, or the dissidents, struggling to awaken the 'sleeping giant' – the masses – from their mind-controlled slumber, and the elites working as hard and fast as they can to to get their much desired New World Order, complete with universal citizen disarmament – gun control and state-of-the-art people-control systems, fully in place, up and operative."

"Agreed," Bevins responded. "Well said. So you see, Ifford – we think it *is* important and *does* matter. And that we the living, so to speak, have a responsibility, as to the kind of world we are leaving our children and their children."

"Mmm-hmmm," said Riggs. "Exactly. Precisely. Good question, by the way, Ifford. Very good question. So - back to the immediate topic under discussion – the amended Trading with the Enemy Act and related matters - the fact is that all of us are *presumed to be engaged in commerce* when we buy, sell, drive cars, work, and so forth. In commerce, because, the corporate government is a commercial entity; and because, under the old common law, commerce can be regulated - in the public interest - by government, while private people cannot. That was done even before the '30s, when the States began to require driver's licenses of all who operated 'motor vehicles.' "

"Yeah. That's one thing I do know about. The unstated presumption is that all the 'motor vehicles' are 'for hire' and 'in commerce,' agreed Rantor.

"And, umm, all the people were - are - considered to be insolvent ... corporate citizens of an insolvent corporate state ..." said Riggs in that musing, fading-out voice of his. "Um, the *fiat* money, the FRN - erroneously, or rather, deceptively, called the 'dollar' - having been changed into its diametric opposite, 'money' having been redefined as debt-bearing negotiable instruments – *faux* IOUs, basically, unredeemable for gold or silver and possessing no defined or definable value – meaning that there is no unit of account. FRNs are merely worthless slips of paper – Monopoly money. However, intrinsically worthless though they are, their use for the discharge of debts is considered yet another 'privilege' extended to all of us bankrupt US citizens.' "

The uniformed thugs, meanwhile, were drawing ever nearer. Rather bizarrely, the image popped into my mind of some cartoon character I must, in the by-gone days of my youth, have seen on the telly - a muscled bulldog type, with black ears like inverted exclamation marks dangling foolishly on either side of his beefy white face, clad in a too-tight suit and necktie, with an absurdly tiny porkpie hat atop his head, sweating bullets and nervously inserting a thick, stubby forefinger between his tight collar and fleshy neck, while grimacing apprehensively as some forbidding creature or other, a hulking street bully or cop, drew menacingly near. I think the ludicrousness of the image, and the black humor of the entire situation, caused me to titter nervously - or I should say, hysterically, as it must have sounded to my tablemates. At any rate, I heard some such sound issue strangely from my throat and saw my companions as one swivel their heads towards me with concerned expressions on their maps, such that I, in the midst of my terror, also felt a total and complete buffoon. There was a moment of silence as all seemed to be waiting to see if I was going continue on into a total rupture with reality and to require intervention - some restraining, subduing, soothing, or what-not. But after a few heartbeats, as I gave no further sign of slippage into any bizarre state of consciousness or conduct, the toad blandly resumed speaking.

"Umhmm ... and as I believe we have mentioned, and according to some researchers, the corporation has been declared bankrupt, and all of its corporate citizens along with it. And as such, we can be forced to perform for our creditors ... compelled performance ... and held to be

271

incompetents ... and all of 'our' " - the way he said the word, it had quotation marks around it - "... property was, and is, considered to be hypothecated to go towards paying off the debt, the alleged debt of the bankrupt corporate state, to the international bankers. Actually, the theory is that when we register any property, title is split. And that we are presumed to have voluntarily donated it - the controlling ownership of it - to the public trust ..."

By now the Gestapo were practically upon us. I had more than once made somewhat spasmodic, purely involuntary movements as if to stand and leave the table, or, Plan B, to slid under it, causing Glennie, who sat next to me on one side, to grab hold of my hand firmly with one of hers, and Rantor, sitting on the other side of me, to lean forward, placing his elbows on the table, thus blocking off that avenue of escape, unless I chose to attempt to clamber over him.

"What does "hypothecated" mean?" asked Glennie, with an encouraging little smile at me, while squeezing my hand in what was clearly meant to be a reassuring way. Good old, dear old Glennie. But I wished she would let go of me. It was literally nearly impossible for me to remain there, feeling, as I did, about to expire of fright. I hadn't known that one could be so afraid. And I believe it is possible to expire from fright. I am quite certain of it, in fact. I seem to remember something about mice doing it in some devilish experiment devised by those bloodless clipboard-carrying demons in white smocks in the various modern torture chambers called laboratories for what is called the advancement of science.

And they all sat there chatting about - about this monumentally complex, and convoluted, and hypothetical, and basically boring so-called history. For all I knew, they had made it all up or were totally wrong - as in, mistaken - about it all. I mean - how could they know all this stuff for certain sure? And what difference did it make, anyway? What's it all in aid of? On into eternity, if we can learn anything at all from the lessons of history, the masses will go their foolish way, grubbing for subsistence while being duped, exploited - anything to remain in the mental comfort zone as long and as fully as possible - allowing themselves to be played for fools by the clever amoral few at the top, who will go on deceiving and fleecing said masses to the utmost possible extent, while controlling or exterminating any competing factions who dare to aspire to that number one position at the top. That juggernaut hurtles onward through time-space with tremendous inertia. One or two, or even a few hundred, or a few thousand, sentient beings with law dictionaries, high ideals, and stars in their eyes are not going to deflect it from its course, not by the tiniest fraction of a degree. The most probable result of all their earnest do-gooder effort is that they shall land themselves - and/or their hapless casual acquaintances - into a good deal of hot water.

"It's right there in your *Black's Law Dictionary*," continued the inexorable lizard.

What was right there in my *Black's Law Dictionary*? What was it they had been talking about?

"Hypothecated," he continued smugly. "I looked it up just last night, as it happens. It means that the people get to hold the property and use it, but that at any time, its 'rightful owners' - those to whom it has been hypothecated - can take possession of it."

"Title has been split. None of the people in this country can fully own any property," said Bevins. "True title resides with the corporate State – and is liened, of course, by the bankers. The individual has use privileges - as long, that is, as he conforms to all the statutes and regulations governing the contract - and the use."

I heard this through a haze of blood pounding in my ears; but it sounded like stretching things a bit too far to me. "Come, now," I objected a trifle peevishly. I mean, I was about to be taken into custody. It makes a fellow feel peevish. "People here own cars, they own houses..."

"I know it looks that way, Ifford, but - if you really own something," she replied, "Under the English common law, and what was, or was intended to be, original jurisdiction in this country, you can't be taxed on it - unless, that is, you are engaged in commerce and own the thing for resale and can pass the tax on to a buyer, in which case the tax is called an excise tax. That is an old maxim and fundamental principle of law. It seems that the deeds people now have to their houses are called 'warranty deeds' and they are, in the legal phrase - what is it, Ralphie...?"

" 'Not cognizable at law.' Yes, it seems that the people do not own their houses, land - real property - lock, stock, and barrel, as the saying goes. The cognizable titles are held by the government, which is, of course, bankrupt to the international bankers. The people have only what is called an "equity interest" in their cars and houses - and it is not

273

the controlling interest. The taxes they pay - property taxes, yearly car registration fees - are actually use fees or taxes."

The slant-eyed Asiatic police were upon us now, and I closed my eyes and steeled myself for what I was sure was coming. It hadn't been a bad life, I thought. It had had its moments. Croissants and things. *I Love Lucy* re-runs, and watching Glennie struggle with her knitting. Listening to Humphrey squeaking his way energetically through the night. Grandma O'Houlihan's Krunchy Chocolate Morsels. Cream cheese brownies. Flannel sheets on a cold night. Soaking in hot bathes. Hazelnut lattes, of course, and Glennie with snow on her hair and eyelashes, swathed in that great, big navy-blue coat of hers and wrapped in that absurd red, white, and blue muffler, standing under a streetlight, with the snow drifting down all around as in a dream ... and perhaps I would find a sort of simple fulfillment in cleaning kennels - if in their mercy they elected to allow me live to clean their kennels. The laborer is worthy of his hire, and I would be, I would be indeed ever after unswervingly loyal to those who held this little blob of pink protoplasm I call home in the black velvet palm of their iron fist. If I were allowed to clean kennels. If I were not selected for a ... special assignment.

CHAPTER 10: WE'RE ALL IN COMMERCE NOW

Fraud and falsehood dread examination.
Truth invites it.

Samuel Johnson

But by some miracle, and as in a dream, the uniformed brutes walked past us - right past us. I could hardly believe my eyes and felt a great surge of relief, almost of exhilaration, like one feels walking out of the dentist's office, or upon learning that a test for which one is unprepared has been postponed - only much better. But of course, they would have to come back past us once more, as the place had only the one door.

"Apparently, it is all in commerce," said Bevins, who appeared noticeably to have relaxed a bit now that we seemed to have passed inspection - or at least the first sweep. "Your cars are all registered as commercial, for hire vehicles. Your real estate is classified as commercial. When you get a traffic ticket, it is commercial. Everything the corporate government does is in commerce and a matter of contract - equity. All the courts are equity courts. Or, aren't they actually admiralty courts, Ralphie?"

They were insane, the lot of them. Monomaniacs. Obsessives. What in the name of Pete was I doing, had I been thinking of, to have allowed my fate to have become so entwined with this bunch of certifiable loonies?

"To the best of my current understanding, yes. Colorable equity/ admiralty/maritime jurisdiction, with criminal penalty possible for civil, non-criminal offenses. The powers that be do not, of course, make the information readily available, or clearly explained."

"One must deduce? Do the Holmesian thing?" This, in a rather squeaky voice, was Yours Truly, trying, God only knew why, to appear comprehending. I felt a little ebullient, what with having been spared the guillotine this time around and all. Even though they were idiots, the lot of them, they were life - a part of life - and I loved life. Life was wonderful, likewise freedom, and precious - and mine - still mine.

"In a manner of speaking, yes, um, Ifford. When information is concealed, one must sometimes surmise, based upon the available evidence. Admiralty, you see, is equity with a criminal penalty - and their corporate courts do mete out criminal penalties for contract violation, which is a civil – not criminal - matter."

"So, again, why would they want to make all the courts admiralty jurisdiction courts?" I asked. "It seems unnecessarily elaborate."

"Well," answered Riggs, "It could be argued to be redundant, certainly. They have the permanent 'emergency' and consequent martial law or rule and military dictatorship left in place from the Civil War, and the amended Trading with the Enemy Act of the late '20s or early '30s, and then the parallel corporate jurisdiction under the District of Columbia, and the equity/admiralty/maritime jurisdiction – the fusion of the courts – and then the alleged 'emergency of the '30s. We are with these better than thrice done out of our alleged pre-existing in- or un-alienable rights. And then there are the many Presidential Executive Orders claiming absolute dictatorial powers for the President, pretty much on his say-so ... and the Anti-Terrorist legislation passed after the OKC bombing – another false flag operation, of course – and then the so ironically named Patriot Act rushed through Congress after the 9/11 false flag operation, and the subsequent Military Commissions Act giving government the right to hold suspected 'terrorists' - and American nationals suspected of being 'enemy combatants' - in custody, without being charged, without benefit of legal counsel, and incommunicado - permanently. Legally, I'd say we are trussed like ducks for the roasting – damned, God-damned, double God-damned, and gone to Hell in a handbasket ..."

"Ralph. Please don't blaspheme," Bevins remonstrated – but gently. And then, in reply to my question, "You see, Ifford - corporations are business entities. Remember that their courts deal only with corporate entities. Well, corporate entities are indeed highly regulate-able by government – and they have no rights. They have only the 'government'-granted 'privileges' as per their commercial contracts in an equity/admiralty jurisdiction. This would include, of course, your U.S. citizens - corporations all. In order to have more control over the people, they have, as I believe has been mentioned, been given corporate identities. DBAs. Corporations being, of course, legal fictions."

"DBAs?"

"Stands for "doing business as," Ifford," Torvald explained. The chap seemed to know everything.

"Actually," said Riggs, "As previously mentioned, the various jurisdictions - once separated, under the original common law, with separate courts - of law, of equity - also called chancery - and of admiralty/maritime - have been fused into what is called "one form of action." This allows a convenient muddying of the waters as to the nature of the jurisdiction in which one finds oneself in court and disguises the fact that we are all in an equity/ admiralty/maritime jurisdiction, when in court - for traffic infractions, income tax controversies, property tax disputes, and so on."

Gadzooks, I thought. All at once I felt exhausted, and I felt, all at once, that this absurd conversation had gone on long enough. Unconsciously, my eyes sought the blonde girl in the beaded dress - and didn't find her. She was gone, the dog was gone, the notebook, the backpack - everything. Only her half-empty cider cup remained on the table. I had been so preoccupied with the UN police that I had forgotten about her, and had not noticed her departure.

"Corporations, you see, do not - cannot - have rights. Only flesh and blood people have rights. But corporations do not. They are artificial 'persons,' business entities created by the state. They exist at the pleasure of the state. Whatever they have is allowed them, at the pleasure of the state ..." intoned Riggs in his going-into-a-trance voice.

I wondered if Bevins kept a 'round the clock watch on him. It seemed as though he might slip off into the dark waters one day when no one was watching and never be heard from again.

"Yeah," Rantor enthused. "They took the pre-existing and unalienable rights of the people spoken of in the Constitution and converted them - by fiat, as you say, and sneakily - into state-granted privileges which they then rented back to the poor idiots - in corporate capacity, of course, and who were - are - totally clueless about the whole ..."

"- switcheroo?" I volunteered - rather idiotically, as it sounded to my own ears. I still felt a bit giddy with relief. Not my usual self. I almost felt like dancing on the table.

"And the excuse – or an excuse - given for doing all this was the 'emergency,' you say?" queried Glennie. "And the pretext for the 'emergency' was...?"

"Well, in the case of the 'emergency' of the '30s, it was a rather thin "emergency," said Riggs. "But they certainly, like the plain girl from the family of modest means who marries a millionaire, made the most of what they had to work with. This emergency, you see, was declared by FDR - the president, you know, back in 1933. The pretext given by him for declaring a state of national emergency was the Great Depression. Actually, because his aim was to evoke the war powers, he used terms such a 'war on poverty.' The government still makes it a point to work that word in. War on drugs. War on poverty. The present 'War on Terror.' They like to bring the word 'war' into it, as they wish to appear legally justified in evoking the war powers."

"And an important point is that it was an engineered emergency, this depression," said Rantor.   "The direct - and predictable - result of deliberate Federal Reserve policy ... just a great big boom/bust cycle such as the Fed creates all the time, with its expansions and contractions of circulating medium - of credit..."

The Gestapo came back through just then, with a rather seedy, non-descript somebody in custody, a slight fellow in need of a shave, with thick-lensed glasses and thinning brown hair, whose hands were cuffed behind his back. Perhaps he had been the one they had been looking for in the first place; perhaps, it was simply that, as they say, his papers, in their random swoopings-down on this or that hapless espresso-sipper, were not in order - or he had neglected to bring them with him. He walked with his eyes downcast, looking at no one.

"The poor guy. I wonder what he's done," Glennie murmured sympathetically, after they had, to my inexpressible relief, again passed by our table.

"Quite possibly, nothing at all," said Torvald. " As discussed, with the new Anti-Terrorism Act, and the so-called Patriot Act, and the Enemy Combatants Act – actually called the Military Commissions Act, I think - and that whole raft of similar, blatantly totalitarian legislation, they can hold people indefinitely, for 'reasons of national and planetary security,' without any charge."

"Doesn't the UN get money from the taxpayers for each 'U.S. citizen' they have in their prisons? About $50,000.00 per prisoner per year, I heard."

"Yes," added Riggs. "The UN police actually have a monthly quota, I believe, just like traffic cops, that they are expected to meet. And I believe the arresting officers get a percentage of that $50,000."

"Bounty hunters," Bevins said with a frown. "And then the prisoners, of course, are, like in China, put to work as, essentially, slave labor for the large corporations who lease the prisons as business enterprises."

"Yes," Riggs took it from there, in that way they had of talking like a two-headed beast, "Like - as the record of history so clearly shows - any concentration of governmental power, the world government is actually immensely corrupt - is essentially looting its member-nations - whose clueless citizens have, without realizing it, *given up control of their own weapons, military, and police, as well as their monies and their taxing powers*. Incredible, when you think about it. And of course the fine print stipulates that the world government is a 'perpetual union' - in other words, opting out, once the full force and implications of what it actually is about and is doing to the member nations, is not a legal option."

"*Déjà vu* all over again - just like what happened to the South, in the War Between the States," said Rantor. "From voluntary to enforced perpetual union. Except that I think the European Union might never even have claimed to be voluntary. Just that part of the deal was not made known to the public."

"Or perhaps even to Parliament. Might have been the usual hundreds of pages of fine print, passed into law unread in its entirety by the MPs, or even by their support staff, as per usual," added Torvald.

"The words," said Bevins, "Of J. Edgar Hoover come to mind – 'The individual is handicapped by coming face-to-face with a conspiracy so monstrous he cannot believe it exists.' "

Which, as applied to Yours Truly, seemed to be pretty much on point. Not only could I not believe it existed; I was sick of hearing about it.

CHAPTER 11: A NOTE FROM THE HONEY BLONDE

The tone and tendency of liberalism ... is to attack the
institutions of the country under the name of reform and to
make war on the manners and customs (and freedoms)
of the people under the pretext of progress.

from a speech by Benjamin Disraeli

When I had earlier glanced over to her table, the girl with the dog had vanished. I sat now staring in a sort of benumbed stupor at her empty table, wishing rather groggily that they would wind this marathon conversation up, so that I could go home and go to bed, when, to my surprise, I saw the girl and her dog slip back into their former spot. She sat once again sipping her now cold cider and absently massaging the hound's ears.

That perked me up a bit. For one thing, it occurred to me that she might be a kindred spirit – that she, too, might be on the lam, or if not exactly on the lam, then for some other reason not eager to be interviewed by anyone from officialdom in any of its many guises and permutations. I wondered if she had slipped away as soon as the cops had come in, while they were talking to the counter help and their backs were turned - perhaps gone to the loo and stayed there for a good long while, until the heat had cleared out.

"Of course," Riggs was going on, "The Great Depression was a great opportunity for the wealthy, who acquired much property - land, newspapers, stocks - for pennies on the dollar. It furthered the consolidation of tangible wealth - and the news media - into the hands of the plutocracy."

"It's basically the same thing, of course, that happens in every 'bust' phase of the boom/bust cycle which is an inevitable result of the central bank and the government's continuous release into the marketplace of substanceless money," Torvald observed. "The small businesses and entrepreneurs go bust when the economy contracts and the big players who can ride it out buy the distressed properties at bargain prices."

"Exactly so," agreed Riggs. "One of the many ways in which this system benefits the very rich at the expense of the small businessman and entrepreneur."

"The purposeful unleveling of the playing field," was Rantor's sardonic editorial addendum.

"Excuse me," I said, standing up. "Sorry to trouble you, but I've got to get to the bathroom."

But this was a mere pretext; what I wanted to do was to go up and ask the fellow at the counter, the one she had given the piece of paper to, about that girl. I did so; and what he told me was that she was a friend of one of the fellows who ran the place, but that he couldn't tell me anything else about her, AND: he said that she had left something for me - a note. She had told him to give it to me as I left, so as not to draw the attention of the people I was with. But, since I was here now, well, this seemed even better - and he reached into his apron pocket, withdrew the folded piece of paper, and handed it to me. I asked him to make me a hot almond milk, telling him I had to go to the loo and would come back and pick it up. And then I legged it for the privacy of one of the bathroom cubicles, to see what she had written to me.

'where did you get that awesome antique vest?' her note began. It was printed, in a rather clumsy, childish hand, using no capital letters, even for the first person singular. But she did, at least, know how to spell – *'maybe it's a hundred years old! i'd love to see it close up, maybe sew some buttons on it – don't worry, i am very careful!!! i have some ivory buttons, very old, they are awesome, from fossilized ivory – and maybe do some beadwork on the front for you – like on my dress – for just the cost of the materials only – not much – it would look so cool if a few of the patches on your vest had beads on them, maybe just kind of in spirals, or around the edges or something – i'll be in here tomorrow night – see you then?'*

I sat for a minute or two in my cubicle, the black walls of which were adorned with the usual graffiti about love, sex, death, Marxism, and saving the planet, reading and re-reading the note, plumbing its depths, as it were. Had anyone ever written me a note before? I thought not. Save marginalia on papers and assignments, that sort of thing. Certainly no Earthling ... no green-eyed female Earthling with milk-white skin (where it was not honey-colored – I had noticed a tan line on her chest, and her un-tanned skin looked to be milky-white) - and hair that

281

brought to mind a field of ripe wheat glowing in the rich light cast by the sun in summer, just before it sets. So. Tomorrow night. She would be here tomorrow night to partake of the bitter brew with me, and to sew buttons and beads on my vest. Was she interested in me for myself alone, I wondered, or for my antique vest? Well, I would have to find out. Being loved for one's taste in clothing - even if it were not one's own actual taste in clothing - not yet, anyway - I mean, what changes could not be wrought by love? - might be better than not being loved at all.

As I slid back into my seat at the table with my mug of hot almond milk, I glanced up at the blond girl and gave her a little nod. Yes, yes, yes! - it was meant to say, and she seemed to understand.

"Then, you are saying, the whole depression of the '30s was orchestrated?" Glennie was asking.

"So it seems," Riggs replied. "We do not know to what extent events were planned far in advance, and to what extent made up as they went along - dealing in whatever way they could devise and could construct a plausible story-line for - with the problems they had created for themselves - and for the rest of us – in their efforts to buck up the English economy - and rescue their investments in English bonds."

"We do know," said Bevins, "That the goal of world empire was held consciously by the monied aristocracy since before the turn of the Twentieth Century, as they openly talk about it in their writings to one another."

"It seems so strange that I have never learned about any of this legal stuff," said Glennie wonderingly. "Not even at KROK. Not that I'm doubting you, you understand."

"Yes, well ... history as it is generally presented is more fable than fact, I'm sorry to say. However, there is an abundance of evidence, circumstantial and not so circumstantial that, as is said about God, had the Great Depression not occurred, they would have had to invent it. Now, of course, it was not constitutional to declare an emergency on the basis of a prolonged economic depression. The only legitimate causes for declaring an emergency were then and still are nothing less than insurrection or invasion - a *bona fide* and actual, literal emergency, in other words. War, essentially. Or a true exigency tantamount to war - an immanent threat to nation's survival."

"It really is so true," I took advantage of a brief lull in the gabfest to comment, "That bit about deception weaving a tangled web. All of this being an excellent illustration of the wisdom of that maxim. But - I say, you know - so sorry to break this up, but I simply must be getting home. Must. As in must, must, must, if you get my drift." I was about ready to scream from sheer *ennui*.

"Actually," said Torvald, "I think the place is closing soon anyway. And, interesting in the extreme though all of this is - has been -" with a respectful nod to Riggs and Bevins "- we all do need to get a little sleep before we have to get up and go to work or class or whatever in the morning."

 "I suppose so," conceded Rantor. "How about if we continue talking as we walk?"

CHAPTER 12: YET MORE MEANINGFUL DISCOURSE ON THE WALK HOME

A paranoid is someone who knows
a little of what's going on.

William S. Burroughs

It felt good, initially, to get out of the noisy and over-heated coffeehouse; but it was a clear and extremely cold night, with the stars twinkling wickedly above, looking themselves like hard little chunks of ice; I noticed that Rantor was careful to keep his tail tucked under his coat. No writing in the snow tonight.

"Now - where were we?" asked Riggs, as we crunched along through the darkness and cold.

"The military rule ... the parallel jurisdiction ... the complexity ..." prompted Glennie.

"The tangled web," I added.

"Yes," said Riggs. "They were constructing a puzzle, a maze, a labyrinth. It was their object to confound the truth, to disguise, bury, and scatter it so thoroughly that it could never be put together and understood. And that any who began to understand the puzzle and perceive the pattern could easily be dismissed as 'paranoids' who were just 'imagining things.' "

"And to create so complex a situation in law that they could perhaps get off on technicalities - before a sympathetic judge - and thus be saved from swinging for treason, if ever they were found out," said Torvald wryly. "At least, that is my theory. But actually, much of the truth is in plain sight, but just not perceived, not understood, for what it is – isn't that correct?"

"Yes," Riggs agreed. "Hidden in plain sight, as the saying goes. For those who understand what they're looking at. The law, medicine, economics, weaponry – have all become – or been rendered – so complex as to be arcane – and the people have thus been returned to a state rather like that of the so-called primitive cultures when they were discovered by the Europeans – a state of being very much out-gunned and thus, of course, at a great disadvantage in any conflict over property rights. Now - remember the corporate DISTRICT OF COLUMBIA we were talking about? And that all of the state and local governments came in as sub-corporations, instrumentalities - corporate counterparts, again, deceptively styled as STATE OF NEW YORK, STATE OF LOUISIANA, et cetera, and CITY OF and COUNTY OF and so forth? Not true bodies politic - states, counties, or cities under public law – but rather, private-law instrumentalities of the parent District of Columbia legislatively-created Federal corporation, legal fictions existing not on the land but only in that fictional hover-zone I mentioned earlier in our discussion? And that this network, this gigantic private corporation and its franchisees, is what is actually governing the country? Well, this corporate government, this commercial enterprise, has its own courts, with its own 'laws' - the codes and statutes – in actuality, private law functioning as public policy. Its courts are corporate courts. They are courts of, by, and for corporations. The actors in them - both the litigants, and the officers of the court - may only be corporations."

"So ... people brought into court are there in corporate character ... even for things like traffic tickets and so on ...?" asked Glennie.

"As sureties, I believe is the legal term, or fiduciaries - I am not a lawyer, you understand, but a historian - but as I understand it, as sureties or fiduciaries for those corporate fictions that bear their names but in a slightly different styling. It is in that character that the courts deal with them. That corporate identity is referenced by a man's or a woman's name being spelled all in capital letters - just as bold caps are used in STATE OF, CITY OF, and so forth. You will notice that people's names are everywhere spelled in bold caps - on driver's licenses, on bills, by the IRS, on their voter's registration cards. This is a usage long employed in law to reference a corporate entity. There are those researchers who think that the name all in caps is a *nom de guerre*, in the sense of not merely a pseudonym but a 'war name' - the literal translation of the French term. Whether the name all in caps indicates a corporate entity, or a war name – or both, which is quite possible,   given   that   soldiers   and   sailors   are   under   a military/admiralty/maritime jurisdiction and that is seems that we are being governed under an ungoing, perpetual 'emergency' and thus under martial rule by a military government – it is nonetheless true that the use of all capital letters in the writing of a name is not the style used in the common law to refer to a flesh-and-blood living person. And that

285

in the law, such details as changes in the spelling and in the use of upper and lower case are, by long custom and tradition, considered to be instances of misnomer, and as such, sufficient cause to dismiss a case. Historically, and properly, the law is and must be exact, and spelling, capitalization, and punctuation are all very significant. Therefore, it is reasonable to conclude that this shift to the use of all capital letters in the spelling of the names of people – or persons – the word 'person' can, as you might know, in legal use refer to a legal fiction, a corporate entity – is not without significance."

As he spoke, I trailed along with my shoulders hunched against the cold, my hands thrust deeply into my pockets, thinking about the girl who wanted to fix my vest. I was wondering what I would wear tomorrow evening. It could not be my usual garb. I'd have to go out and get something more in keeping with her tastes - something perhaps a bit raggedy - antique.

"So - not only are all of us assigned a corporate name," Riggs continued; "We are also assumed to live or 'reside' in a corporate location that, like the entity referenced by the corporate name, is a legal fiction. That location is referenced by the postal zip codes, and also by the postal abbreviations WA, OR, ID, CA, and so on. It is actually very clever, an ingenious system. You can think of this corporate location as a clear plastic sheet placed over the map of the United States. And the presumption prevails, when one is in court - whenever, in fact, one interfaces with this corporate government - that the corporation that bears your name - in capital letters - exists, not on the land, but in that legal fiction, that imaginary 'hover zone' above the land. You see, if they *forced* you to give up your unalienable rights and enter their corporate color-of-law private maritime/admiralty/equity military courts in which you have no protections, no rights, no guarantees - no laws, really - no Law - and to which you have no alternative - and no recourse - well, that would, arguably, be treason."

"Haven't they kind of forced everyone - really? Isn't that the actual reality?" asked Glennie.

"Well, of course, that is what we are seeing, and saying, tonight, as being the truth that underlies the sophistry, the artful word-play. But, they have given themselves a legal leg to stand on. There is the right to contract, isn't there? That is one of the fundamental rights guaranteed by the original Constitution – by the common law. According to the common law, a man can agree to contract away some of his rights,

286

can't he - as, for example, when he accepts a job and gives up some freedoms in exchange for being in a certain place at a certain time, doing work and getting paid for it. So, if he volunteers, or agrees - in their legal jargon or lingo, if he 'assents' - he cannot 'consent,' because the Supreme Court has decreed that you cannot *consent* to give up something *unalienable*, that is a contradiction in terms and in logic, so they try to avoid that contradiction by word play, by substituting the word 'assent.' So: if our hypothetical citizen under original jurisdiction assents, or contracts - everything that the corporate government does is by contract, it is all in commerce - to agree to their jurisdiction - well, he has that 'right' under the Constitution, in common law - doesn't he? So what they do is, they exploit his utter ignorance of the fact that there are two separate and distinct jurisdictions and use what are called the 'laws of presumption' against him."

Here he paused for a breather. He was, as I have mentioned, quite stout, and the walking seemed rather to tire him; so while he panted a bit, his alter ego Bevins carried on for him.

"Yes," she said, "Under certain conditions and in the face of certain behaviors, judges are allowed to form and be guided by certain *presumptions*. For instance, if a party to an action fails to bring up a certain issue, the judge may *presume* that the material facts pertaining thereto are against that party. As, for example, when King George remained silent and failed to respond to the colonists' grievances as set out in their petitions to him, the presumption then was that the King was silent because the facts of the situation were against him - that he was guilty as charged of violations of his contract with the colonies."

"So," Riggs went on, "Back to this present system which the usurpers have set up - they send a presentment to a corporate entity - your name spelled all in bold caps - residing in a corporate location - WA, or CA, or MO, zip-coded. The presentment might be, for instance, from the IRS, or a demand that you pay a property tax; or it might be something from the court regarding a traffic infraction - 'infraction,' by the way, is a military term, as is 'officer' - that you are alleged to have committed. If you accept that presentment - if you fail timely to *rebut the presumption* that you are surety or fiduciary for that corporate entity residing in that corporate location - then they can so *presume*. A 'person' by the way, as defined in their codes, is almost always a corporate entity, since, as I believe I already mentioned, their courts deal exclusively with corporate entities, that is their *personam* jurisdiction - and they can presume that you are voluntarily entering

287

their corporate jurisdiction - their military or quasi-military/admiralty court - in or as surety for your corporate identity, and voluntarily waiving all your lawfully guaranteed and pre-existing rights and protections."

"Think," Torvald mused, "As you commented earlier, Florence – just consider the immense wealth that has been surreptitiously appropriated, or transferred - and what this nation might be like if that wealth had been allowed to remain in the possession and control of those whose labor created it - the working masses. Think of the holdings that the previous, say, half-dozen generations of workers would have had to pass on to their children - think of all that real estate, that precious metal, the businesses and factories, the wealth - the capital - that would now be spread out in the hands of the people instead of concentrated into the hands of a tiny, hidden ruling aristocracy of wealth, who are not known for who and what they are merely because they realize that the success of their on-going scheme of legalized plunder required them to control the information reaching the public - the masses."

"Yes!" agreed Rantor, turning to address me as I tagged along in the rear of our little group. "Yes, yes, yes! That's what we've been trying to tell you, Ifford. ALL of the boondoggles have been paid for by the working people! Boiling down to just so many clever scams and plausible pretexts - to part the suckers from their bucks. Just trying to wrap one's mind around it boggles the imagination … the Civil War, WWI, WWII, the Great Depression, all the ensuing collectivist entitlement programs that would not have been necessary were the government and the mega-banks and other corporations not parasitizing the public and thus creating poverty and need … the foreign aid and corporate bail-outs and other corporate welfare, the Cold War, the Korean War, the Viet Nam War, the Iraq War … and on and on it continues. Try to imagine how many trillions we are talking about, and what life would be like today in this country – and elsewhere on the planet – if all that wealth had not been slipped away from the people, first and foremost by means of the iniquitous economic system, under the plausible pretexts of these various manufactured emergencies and the suggested solution of socialism with its regulation of commerce and its wealth transfer schemes."

We had, most happily, reached my digs. Gratefully I parted from my companions, Rantor, rather ostentatiously and, I felt, unnecessarily, insisting on walking me up to my little garret and glancing about behind the door and in the closet in order to ensure, or at least promote, my safety. As if he'd have been able to save me from the armed might of the *de facto* powers if they decided to descend upon me either on the walk home, or by lying in wait in my closet. I bade him good-night, threw off my rags - taking care to drape the admired vest - my ticket into the life, and perhaps - in the best-case scenario - the affections - of the velveteen girl - tenderly over the back of my only chair - and snuggled under the covers, too tired to read my thriller or savor a snack.

I whispered my usual good-night to little Humphrey, who was chugging away with his unfailing single-minded zeal in his rhythmically squeaking exercise wheel, and turned to gaze out the window, the sill of which was at a level with my bed. The moon, the stars, and the streetlights caused the snow and ice which lay upon cars, trees, bushes, walkways, roads - everything - to glitter enchantingly - to appear to be emitting from their own skins mutable little luminosities, *sui generis*. Marveling that cruelty carries beauty everywhere with it as its twin - or vice versa - I fell with profound relief into the other world - that of unknowingness.

CHAPTER 13: INTERLUDE

The central ton of every place ...

Delmore Schwartz

I awoke dreaming a troubled dream, that I had given away a dog - an Airdale, it was, just like the dog of the blonde girl at The Silver Stud the night before - a breed for which I have always had a positive feeling, perhaps because I find them attractive, and the ones I have seen seem so sensible. At any rate, this dog in my dream was sturdy, affectionate, loyal - my dog, and a good dog - but in my dream I had given him to my mother (why to her and not some other, I cannot imagine) to be put down - destroyed. In the dream, the thing had already been done, and the realization came to me too late that I had done a thing which had been neither good nor necessary. I could have given him away, found another home for him. I was talking to my mother, and she was telling me matter-of-factly that he - the dog - had not wanted to be killed - had known what was happening, and had resisted. But the thing had been done, and I awoke feeling a very painful double remorse, for the wrong done to my good dog, and for my own loss of him. This dream, and the poignant feelings of loss and wrong-doing which it occasioned in me, troubled me as I lay in my bath, languidly sponging water over my stomach, and as I dressed and prepared my breakfast of crepes stuffed with soft cheese and strawberry preserves, along with orange slices and some strong, milky coffee; but resolutely I dispelled its mood by opening my mystery story and losing myself in its diverting nonsense.

The day I spent languorously, luxuriously, alone in my room - drifting dreamily from one soothing, simple pastime to the other, only occasionally troubled as thoughts of my current plight, or guilty memories of my dream-crime, surfaced - gazing out the window, at that panorama, which I now regarded as my own, and which seemed an updated version of Breugel's (isn't it?) snow painting of the crows and hunters and dogs and winter-bare trees on the hill, and in the distance the tiny figures of ice skaters on the pond; or watching small Humphrey, dusted with cedar shavings and curled into a ball of orange fuzz flattened on one side against the glass wall of his home, twitching and murmuring in his animal dreams; or reading my mystery (which had gotten rather compelling) - these restorative pleasures being interspersed with soft-footed forays (when I hoped no one else was about) down to the communal kitchen for sweet, strong, milky tea and cinnamon toast, the latter made from a very excellent, chewy sourdough French bread.

Had it not been for the anxiety and uncertainty which suffused or underlay it all, I had to admit that I vastly preferred my present mode of existence to any of my former ones. Oh, I was following in the footsteps of that doughy aesthete and reprobate Calvin, I knew - yielding to fatal flaws in my make-up, taking the easy way out. Perhaps, from the very beginning of this whole business, that is what I had been doing - a sort of unconsciously willed suicide - a giving up of the ghost, a throwing in of the hand. Whatever the thing be called, I imagine that by now, dear Reader, you get my drift, and, however accounted for or explained, the fact remained that it had been done; irrevocable steps had, wittingly or unwittingly, been taken; and perhaps the rest of my life, however much remained, would be spent in rue, drinking the bitter dregs of that cup. Perhaps this time, now, was a mere interlude, a respite. Whatever - but the peace I felt - in which I positively swam - on this day was made the more pleasurable, was perfected, by the awareness that in the evening I was to meet that lovely girl and have buttons sewn on my vest by her own slender, milk-white hands. That was it, wasn't it? I hopped up from the bed and searched for the note in the pocket of my pantaloons - yes - old ivory buttons on vest was the ticket. But now that I thought of it, I remembered thinking last night on the way home after the marathon gabfest at The Silver Stud, that I should have other clothing to wear with the vest. Appropriate attire - a different costume for a different day. And wouldn't its acquisition entail a foray out into one or more of the seedy thrift shops that did brisk business in the University District? That meant I would need to sally forth from my lair at latest in the mid-afternoon, at the beginning of the dark's descent - before the end of the business day.

And actually, at about three in the afternoon, I felt ready to emerge from my den and mingle with - broadly speaking - my kind, in all its themes and variations, as it picked its way briskly or cautiously over the slippery surfaces of the commerce district. Surfeited on solitude, your hero now craved stimulation, and the proximity of others, it seemed. One can but obey the dictates of the spirit - so goes, at least, one theory - and so, donning the full regalia, including of course the vest, along with the wrap-around mirror glasses and the animal-skin hat with the ear-flaps and the wavery brim, I descended to the street.

It was one of those moody days overhung by that kind of vast, continuous, thick grayish-white cloud which looks to be stuffed like a down comforter with snowflakes, and in fact as I emerged from the faded old rooming house which I now called home and cast a weather eye heavenward, I noticed that what might be called an understated or perhaps restrained snowfall of pinhead-sized particles of white was currently in progress. Very *diminuendo* - like soft, widely spaced notes on a piano - these tiny flakes drifted down slowly, dreamily, with a kind of divine, stately tranquility. It all looked very ordained, if you know what I mean - deliberate, chosen - but by whom and to what end, I knew not. It seemed that there was a message, a significance, fairly longing to be communicated by the entire scene - if I but knew how to decipher it. Pregnant with a tantalizing, undiscoverable meaning, about sums it up, I guess. Life can be so maddening. It was absolutely quiet; there was no one else on the street; and this pageant, this silent show, seemed to have been staged just for me.

I had, of course, taken off the dark glasses, the better to absorb the nuances of the scene, and thus noticed, to my fascination, as I scanned the *mis-en-scene* slowly, from left to right, that a couple of snakes appeared to be copulating complicatedly amongst the fallen snow and dry brown leaves at the base of a large bare bush square on the corner of the rooming house, to my right as I stood on the front steps facing the snow-covered street. Never having seen snakes copulating, I felt drawn - ineluctably, is that the word? - to this little drama. In fine, I wanted to get a better look, it somehow not occurring to me that, one, what would snakes be doing in the city, and, two, reptiles, the feral ones at least, do not venture out at all in winter, but rather wait it out, in a state of suspended animation, in whatever crack, crevice, or fissure they call home. No, oblivious to the holes in my theory, and in a state of total concentration, rather like a sleep-walker, or as one mesmerized, I turned and stepped as quietly as I could over the crunchy, snow-covered lawn towards this, as I imagined, little scene of winter passion, my eyes glued in fascination to the slowly writhing mass of dark coils beneath the bare, frost-bitten branches of that chubby bush. Walking cautiously, as the hunter stalking his prey, placing each foot carefully, quietly down - not wanting to give the lovers notice of my presence - I approached the scene of the action - only to be startled, as I drew abreast of the corner of the house, by a dark lurking presence looming above all - towering above the snakes, the bush, and, most horribly of all, above Yours Truly. I can tell you, my heart gave a dreadful lurch, my insides were suffused with an instantaneous spasm of heat, and instinctively I cowered back, raising an arm over my brow to shield my head from a possible assault - before I peered up, to ascertain where and how this ominous looming presence terminated, at its northern-most perimeter - and beheld the scaly, prognathous visage of my erstwhile roommate and, it seemed, current self-appointed bodyguard - or tail, perhaps, in the lingo of those spy-thrillers amongst whose pages I occasionally sought forgetfulness.

CHAPTER 14: A DEVASTATING REVELATION

Stretches to embrace the very dear
With whom I would walk without him near...

Delmore Schwartz

"You!" I spat out with considerable - asperity, is I think the word I want. If not something more expletive-like. 'Venom' might be the better choice. I mean, the blighter dogged one's footsteps, positively hovered over one, making a mockery of one's pretensions to the status of discrete entity-hood. I mean: the soul absolutely wearied of it all, after a while.

"Yes," he rejoindered with one of his oily, ingratiating smiles which to my admittedly jaundiced eye partook of many of the tawdry qualities of its shirt-tail relation, the leer. Perhaps I was prejudiced, but to me it seemed that the fellow couldn't even smile right.

"And what, pray tell, might you be doing here, lurking in my environs?" I queried testily. It was all I could do not to pummel the fellow's huge chest like some tantrum-ish female in a Grade B 1940s movie.

"Not lurking, Ifford," the lout rumbled, in what he seemed to think were soothing tones. "Merely - standing, you know. On the point of rapping at the door, or perhaps throwing gravel at your window to attract your attention discretely ... just checking up on you, you know. Wondered how you were doing. Nothing sinister at all, so relax, Ifford."

"And how long had you been standing here, might I ask?"

"Oh - not long at all - just a couple of minutes."

"Why on the corner, here, rather than the front stoop? And why the delay? Why not just announce the presence like any normal visitor?"

294

"Well ... if you must know ... since you insist ... there is something I wanted to tell you. I was just ... taking a minute to think how to say it, you know."

At this I felt another violent lurch of the heart and hot flash amidships. Was my cover blown? Were the *gendarmerie* even now as we spoke closing in on me? Did I need to flee this place forthwith? Just when I was getting attached to it? Was it out into the cold, cruel world again for old Ifford?

But I wore the mask. We hybrids can do that sort of thing, when dignity requires.

"Well?" said I cooly. With consummate aplomb, actually, or so it seemed to me at the time. "Here I am in the flesh, and all, so - say on. Spill the beans. Unburden yourself, old friend. I'm all ears."

Rarely had I seen this dynamo, this firebrand, hesitate. And yet, verily, that was what seemed to be occurring in the instant matter. The fellow seemed positively bumpkin-ish - unable to decide where to look or what to do with his hands, the canine lips on the dog-like snout seeming almost to tremble, and the usually jaunty tail lashing slowly back and forth in a hesitant, pensive arc, sweeping a pattern in the snow that reminded me of the skirt of one of those snow angels which children make by lying in the white fluff and moving their arms and legs vigorously in and out and up and down. Taken all in all, he looked positively - abashed, is I think the word that covers it. Discomfited, you know. At a loss.

"Come, come!" I said briskly, although inwardly marveling somewhat at this new persona, this kinder, gentler reptoid, and musing along the lines of, will wonders never cease. "Out with it, man! I have - well - errands that must be run, things that need looking after. Come, let's walk over towards the Ave while we talk."

In case the Gestapo were closing in, it seemed prudent to vacate the premises - avoid the habitual haunts, become a moving target, and all that, you know. But beyond those practical considerations, it seemed as if a new Ifford - firmer, more decisive, more commanding - in short, a real take-charge sort of guy - was emerging from the husk of his former diffident self, or perhaps being shaped by the pressure of recent events. Some sink, you know, and some swim, and it seemed, by the gods, that Ifford was doing the latter. I felt a surge of can-do and general, all-around *bien-etre*, as I turned and strode up the street, not even looking back to see if the lizard was or was not in tow.

Well, he was, naturally; and we crunched along through the snow and ice in silence for several moments, he apparently struggling with some inner demon and self not wishing to loose face and dignity by importuning him childishly to reveal his secret, though of course I was pretty much on pins and needles to find out what it might be.

Finally, a look of what appeared to be resolve settled on his reptilian features, and he spoke.

"Ifford," he said, "It's like this. Glennie and I are, well ..."

Lengthy pause here. After several heartbeats, I decided to urge him on. "Are ... what? Collaborating on a cookbook? Embarking on a home-study course in Tiawanese? Crocheting woolen booties and mufflers for deserving refugees from war-torn planets and galaxies?"

"Ifford - we're ... an item. It seems." A - believe it or not - shy little smile and a flutter of lashless lids accompanied this disclosure. The expression on his face reminded me for all the world of the self-conscious and at the same time self-satisfied simpers worn by the dancing hippopotami with the pink tutus in Walt Disney's *Fantasia.*

"A *what?*" I didn't quite get his drift. "I'm afraid I don't quite follow you. Could you have another go at it? In plain English this time, avoiding the argot of the streets, with which I am only passingly familiar, I'm afraid."

"Well, I don't quite know how to say it, Ifford. We - we're - going together, I guess you could say."

At this, I got his meaning, and instantly felt indescribable sensations in my innards. The closest thing I can compare it with, to give you an idea of my state upon hearing those words and grasping their import, is to say that I felt as I have on occasion when in an elevator which from a dead standstill seems to have snapped all its suspension cables and be hurtling silently downward in its shaft at the rate of an object in freefall. A very sickish, hollow feeling in the pit of the stomach, coupled with senses of, one, impending doom and two, incipient panic. I fear my face must have registered something of what I was feeling, for, as if from very far, far away, and to the sound effect of a tinny ringing in my ears, I perceived a look of concern settle like a bird of prey coming to roost on the countenance of the scaly one.

"Oh," I responded, after a moment. Not very original, but for the life of me I couldn't think of anything else to say. The ringing in my ears had changed to a kind of cottony sensation as though the volume of everything had been turned 'way down and was coming to me through a long, hollow tube, and I wondered numbly - had this strange aural phenomenon just started, or had I just noticed it? Was my hearing going bad? Was this the beginning of the end? Had it started this way for Beethoven? Probably. All about me, everything seemed strange and eerie, and I felt totally alone, sealed off from all others by many invisible, transparent, intangible layers of something more hopelessly impenetrable than any material thing could ever be.

I mean - Glennie! My only real friend, my *doppel-ganger*, my soul-mate, my other self, my pal! In all of life, from the bizarre engineered conception and lonely institutional childhood we had in common, on up through time and space, turning the cosmos inside out and rummaging in all its corners, endless corridors, linty pockets, echoing hallways, and warped dimensions, there was no other - no one else with whom I had connection - any connection that felt like anything at all - that meant anything - that mattered. Glennie ...

"I'm sorry, Ifford," I heard Rantor saying in nice guy tones off stage left somewhere. "It wasn't planned; it ... just sort of happened ... the timing could have been better, I know ..."

The new, reformed Rantor, all sincere and heartfelt and possessing, *mirable dictu*, a heart and a conscience and, God bless him, an awareness of the feelings of others. Love must be working its magic on him, kneading and softening his rubbery lizardly little soul, bless him, bless his heart and bones and blood and - "And what, might I ask, is this 'it' that just sort of happened. Or is it too personal or - secretional, if you'll pardon my indelicacy - to be spoken of?"

"Ifford ... Glennie told me you two were just friends. Just good friends, like brother and sister, was what she said - those were her exact words. I had no idea ... she, I think, had no idea ..."

If he'd had no idea, then why all this hesitation when it came to breaking the news of it to me?

Suddenly the humiliating aspect of all this, this - wearing of one's heart - one's heart one didn't know one had - on one's sleeve - before one's - well, rival - struck me full force rather like - well, say, the shock wave from a large nuclear explosion - and I writhe in shame even now to recall that, in a few second's time, a horrid, dreadful, monumentally embarrassing blush rose in that plodding, inexorable way of all blushes from my neck upwards, covering my entire face and head with its bright pink color and its horrible heat.

I wanted in the worst way to turn and run, to flee this painful and embarrassing scene. But that would only make matters worse - would resolve nothing and only compound my humiliation. I pulled myself together, finally, and took refuge, like some miserable cornered rodent, pathetically but I suppose one could say gamely - the head bloody but unbowed - in sarcasm and irony, those old stand-bys of mine. And, of course, that universal favorite, the outright lie.

"Well," I said stiffly, with a sort of belated and bedraggled dignity, "Of course it's fine with me, just fine and dandy - I mean, we were - are - only friends, just as Glennie says, and will remain so, I'm sure, and I wish you both the best in your mutual ... endeavor; but I would have thought there would be this matter of, you know, genetic incompatibility, not to say outright clash or mutual exclusivity - you know, the round peg in the square hole, or vice versa, molecularly speaking, of course, or genetically, you know - and then there's the fact that she's practically small enough for you to wear around your neck as a feather boa - if she had feathers ... but, withal, I wish you both every happiness, every possible happiness, and …"

"Ifford …"

"If I looked a bit strained, just now, you know, it might have been due to a physiological component or aspect of the psychological condition or experience of grief - I meant to say, of relief - yes, relief - you see, I feared the worst, namely, that you were going to tell me that my whereabouts had become known to the authorities and that I must instantly re-locate. You know - well, perhaps you don't - what a home-body I am, at heart. I frequently blush when relieved, a sort of a genetic pre-disposition or quirk, I believe. You know my mottled ancestry. At any rate, please believe me when I say that I am very happy for you - and for Glennie, whom I care for as a sister ... a beloved sister, only that, as she said ..."

"Look here, Iffy . . ."

"Well! Here we are at the corner of 45th, where I must alas leave you, my business carrying me off this way, due west - go west, young man, go west, like the man said, you know, and I must and shall - so! Good-bye for now, and give my best and warmest wishes and congratulations to your beloved."

And making a hasty gesture of farewell, I turned and fled.

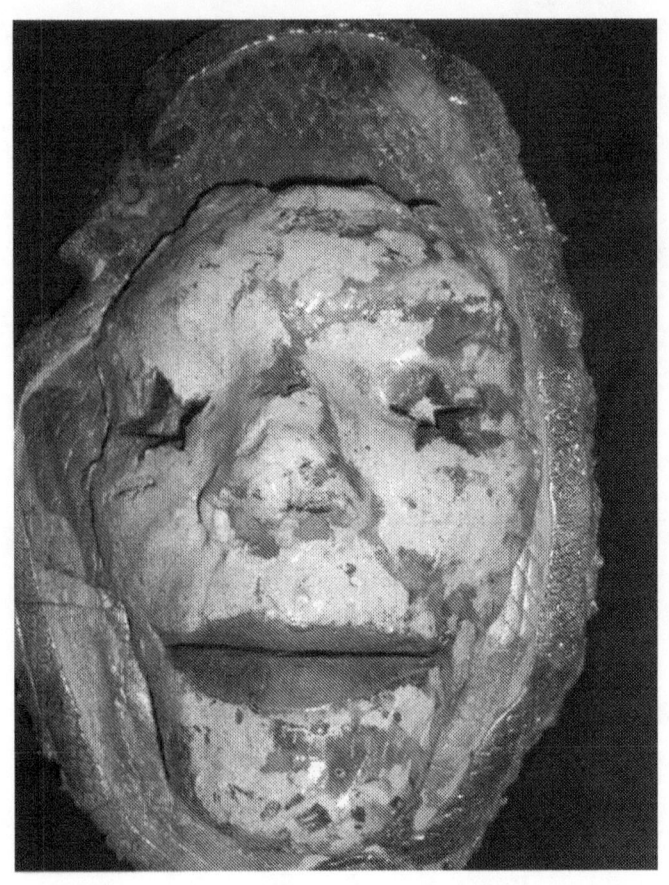

CHAPTER 15: IN WHICH I DO A LITTLE SHOPPING

A stupid clown of the spirit's motive ...

Delmore Schwartz

I felt, in addition to everything else, a complete ass as I scurried off westward like a defeated rabbit. And to think that, scarcely a half an hour ago, I had been feeling so masterful, so in control - such a man of the world. Where is it written that pride goeth before a fall? Whoever said it, Shakespeare or Dante or one of the Bronte sisters, or perhaps Sir Francis Bacon, or that hobnailed fellow who wrote *The Leviathan* - though I don't think it was any of the above - anyway, he or she was onto something, and I made a mental note to deal severely with any even faintly prideful feelings, if ever they were to dare to surface into my stream of consciousness or feeling state, either or both, again. I resolved to deal with them most severely - to absolutely and utterly stamp them out like a brushfire during the dry season in the high country.

And why, oh ye gods and little fishes, *why* had I gone on and on like that? My explanation of my blush, and of the pale and stricken look which I am sure preceded it, sounded absolutely fatuous even to my own ears - in addition to which, my general speech pattern had sounded even more absurdly antiquated than usual - stiff, formal and, in a word, totally unnatural in the extreme. The more ill-at-ease or distressed I become, the more stilted and pompous becomes my speech - the logic and rhetoric of my exposition, you might say. This has been the case ever since I stood approximately knee-high to a grasshopper - or would so have stood, had there been any grasshoppers on the home planet, which, to the best of my knowledge, there were not. At least I never saw any.

The reason for this - speech defect, I suppose you could call it - being, I believe, that I, having been a shy and frail lad, even for a hybrid, tended whenever possible to withdraw from the fevered fray with a book - thus acquiring these bookish patterns of speech.

So absorbed was I in my painful ruminations that I had entirely lost track of my actual purpose or original intent in leaving my cozy cocoon in the first place; but as I hastened along with no destination or object in mind but to get well away from that hulking lizard and his embarrassing, humiliating concern for me, I practically collided with one of those hinged wooden signs that had been carelessly set out almost in the middle of the sidewalk. "50% off all PRE-OWNED CLOTHING today!!!" was what it announced, and when I looked over to my right I beheld one of those very thrift shops in search of which I had - I now recalled - gone out.

In its display windows, old chipped mannequins with graceful hand gestures, and wearing shiny platinum or inky black pageboy wigs, slightly mussed and slightly askew, were modeling the faded, wrinkled, and pill-balled finery of a dozen years ago and leaning stiffly at subtly

301

grotesque angles, slightly off plumb, as though frozen as by the camera's shutter in the act of just beginning to fall, like so many bowling pins after a strike - their fall, if time ever unlocked and allowed them to fulfill their manifest destinies, to be cushioned, evidently, by the various cheap knick-knacks, kitchen utensils, ladies' handbags, and worn children's toys in which they had evidently been standing or wading ankle deep, when that fatal bowling ball, wielded no doubt by some bored or juvenile god to whom the whole thing had seemed a good idea at the time, had knocked them off their balance. Feeling a throb of compassion and fellow feeling for these hapless creatures, who hadn't even had the time to wipe those silly grins off their faces before the fatal blow had been struck and time had apparently clenched into some sort of protracted spasm, I turned and wandered on into the shabby little shop they called home.

Clad as I was, I blended right in - Glennie would have been proud of me, I thought with a kind of stifled sob - or at least, a feeling in the environs of the heart definitely worthy of a sob - and I received only the most cursory and uninterested glances from the other shoppers, most of whom looked like extras who had wandered in off some movie set. Ditto the plump, powdered, ringletted old ladies, who gave me only the briefest glance with their startlingly moist and mobile eyes - the only things in their entire pouchy, painted Dresden faces that looked alive as opposed to synthetic and mass-produced on some factory line during a water shortage - before resuming their animated conversations with their fellow volunteer shop-keepers of like vintage - this being, I noticed from various signs to this effect which were scattered here and there throughout the place, an enterprise the proceeds from which allegedly went to benefit the victims of genetic experimentation, cloning, and/or biochemical warfare experiments in various and sundry secret bases of some evil empire or other in an adjacent sector of the galaxy. People never seem to want to fight the resident evil, any mention of same being of course taboo, and instead engage in politically correct charitable endeavors for the victims of the home regime's political enemies. I mean, right here in their store these well-meaning ladies had a refugee from some pretty horrible goings-on, but I knew they'd only regard me as a mental case if I tried to clue them in about it all.

Listlessly, I surveyed the shabby racks and piles and stacks of old clothing, coffee cups, dog-eared paperback books, and fake silver candy holders. Pretty much *ab ovum*, yours truly has always been one of those stern, manly blokes who hates shopping, considering it, even

302

as a mere tot, except for proposed mergers with certain privileged items such as candy bars and comic books, a monumental bore and waste of my valuable time; furthermore, I was but recently bereaved, you might say, and still feeling the sting and tingle of the newest affront shipped my way by a malign deity or an indifferent, machine-like universe, some vast perpetual motion thingummy that just sorta happened - depending on one's metaphysical underpinnings - so it was with a feeling of mingled dread and weary, long-suffering resignation that I turned to the task at hand, planning just to get it over with quickly, grab more or less any old thing - and they were all old things, and what did anything matter, anymore, anyway - off the rack and then flee to some quiet dark alley where I could weep and mourn and gnash the teeth and tear and twist the greenish locks in private anguish amongst the garbage cans and dumpsters until the hour appointed for my tryst with the hippie girl, for whom - puppy-ishly sweet though I remembered her as being, even down, I imagined, to the milky breath and white little teeth - I had somehow lost all my erstwhile enthusiasm; but I mean - what, or who, else was there - my options having dwindled in a twinkling by 50% quantitatively, and considerably more qualitatively - there being no paramours like the tried and true, when it came right down to it, I now saw with a poignant clarity. Sort of like footwear. The new ones always rub and raise blisters - I speak figuratively, of course - and do not, in the long run, fill the bill. Had I appreciated Glennie properly, and conducted myself as the manly *preux chevalier* she probably was secretly longing for me to be, she would not have been hanging out there ripe for the taking, emotionally speaking, by any slithy tove of doubtful lineage who gyred and gimboled in the wabe - if you get my drift.

But, to return to the matter at hand, to wit, Ifford's maiden voyage in the new waters of shopping for pre-owned clothing - to my surprise, I found myself after a while rather enjoying the experience of rummaging amongst the old things in this shop. The old ladies were actually very kind, and some of the items were very well-made, brand-name things. The place itself was comfortable; it sort of enfolded one. I have always liked old things better than new ones - they are more interesting, somehow - definitely more approachable, if you know what I mean, more or less saying, 'go ahead - touch me, feel me, drop a bit of jam or dribble a bit of *cafe au lait* on me - it's OK with me and no great harm done, no fortunes lost.' The stakes are lower, the pretensions fewer, the fabrics softer and more pliable, more soothing to the touch. A homelier, friendlier experience, all around. And then I found myself speculating about the people who had worn these items,

303

wondering who had bought them new, and why they had given them away - with what feelings and under what circs the *res* had been tossed into the discard pile. And I did find some things that I quite liked, classy items I could never have afforded new. I browsed intently, quite loosing track of the time; and when I exited the shop I saw that the early twilight of winter was setting in.

Rather than try to scurry home and change there, I had decided to wear my recent purchases, stuffing the clothes I had been wearing into some sort of dappled brown flexible carry-all which one of the rouged old ladies had assured me was real lizard skin and a real bargain - from which fact - the bit about the lizard skin, I mean - whether true or not, I drew in light of recent events a certain grim satisfaction. The tote-bag did, I thought, look expensively made, and I felt almost aristocratic, and certainly quite - *Homo sapiens* - striding in my designer-label loose-fit stone-washed jeans, complete with ragged holes in the knees, down the street, the carry-all carelessly draped by its adjustable strap over one shoulder and a camouflage-patterned, tailored and fitted, genuine down vest underneath a very well made tweed sports jacket warming me against the chill wind.

"Riqi"

CHAPTER 16: ENTITY MEETS GIRL

Most of one's life is a prolonged effort
to prevent oneself thinking.

Aldous Huxley

In the thrift shop I had pretty much managed to forget about Rantor's recent revelation, but out on the cold street with a sharp wind blowing in my face and all the shoppers and students surging past me in twos and threes, chatting together in happy, easy intimacy, the sad tidings returned forcefully, descending into the old stream of conscious with a sickening thud, like - to resort to bowling ball imagery again - a worn-out bowling ball - if bowling balls do wear out - tossed into the mud of some tide-flats from a speeding car going over a low bridge on a gray and dismal day of incipient rain by a pair of gay lovers on their way to buy a newer, better bowling ball and then bowl the night merrily away, wrapped in the joy of one another's company. You know what I mean. It was like emerging out of sleep blissfully unaware and then remembering some terrible thing that either had just happened or was inexorably slated for that day.

Deciding that the feeling-state was in need of modulation, I made for the nearest espresso house, which fortunately lay less than a block away - caffeine having upon Yours Truly the effect of lightening the mood and elevating the spirits. I did not want to appear gloomy when I met with my new friend at The Silver Stud. For one thing, I wanted to be spared the weary work of either baring the soul or confabulating.

The place I headed for, called All That Jazz, had, in addition to annoying non-melodic jazz music, good espresso as well as an extensive array of world-class desserts and a few simple but excellent entrees; I had not supped and was feeling empty, if not hungry - the news of the recent coupling having dealt a death blow to my appetite for dinner. But when I do not eat, I am prone to headaches, and so I decided to take something light along with my *doppio*. What I really wanted was something sickeningly sweet - self tending to find solace in the sweet and gooey when the going gets tough - but feeling I needed something more substantial, I compromised by ordering an extremely good, lightly sweet soufflé that I remembered having relished here in happier, pre-saurian times, when out with Glennie after a virtual movie. It was flavored with Grand Marnier and the thinnest short spirals of candied orange peel, then blanketed with a velvety sauce of dark, rich chocolate and generously dusted with a very good almond praline - all items except the liquor being made on the premises according to recipes from the Old World, the secrets of which, I had been told upon making inquiry, had been jealously guarded since at least the days of the *ancien regime*. But I ate and drank listlessly, mourning in a distant sort of way the waste of this excellent repast, which normally I would have relished to the utmost - and thumbing through a recent edition of *Occult Galactian By-Ways and Their Exotic Life-Forms*, usually a favorite of mine, with near total indifference.

As I wended my way to The Silver Stud, I wondered - took myself to task, actually - re what I could have seen in the velveteen girl - I mean, seriously - and why, with my affairs already in a perilous tangle such that they were exhausting merely to attempt to catalogue, and utterly baffling when regarded with an eye to resolution or escape, I had encouraged her overtures - facilitated the innocent child's entry into this glutinous mess of pottage I called my life. She was a mere babe, in both senses of the word - that much was clear, and, judging from the way she had comported herself, not even particularly mature for her years.

But the coming evening in her company would, I thought, or argued, at least provide a distraction, and thus a temporary reprieve from naked confrontation with the anguish in which the soul currently percolated - and surely that was permissible, no matter how exacting the moral code under which one served. Merely a harmless *tete a tete* between consenting adults - or quasi-adults, if you will. What could be the harm in it? I mean, just how Calvinistic, actually, how absurdly retro, is the super-ego in the coils of which this little babbling, pissing *tabula rasa* - your author in his infancy - was enmeshed by those anonymous planners on the home planet - who for all anyone knows had been in petulant or vindictive moods or suffering from hangovers when they did it? I mean - really. There are limits. And furthermore - is the rule of accident absolute - or what?

Very well, then, I decided, adjudicating the inner controversy in favor of joinder under certain conditions, namely that self is sternly charged to keep ever in mind that dictum of Hippocrates which enjoins, first do no harm. Go ahead as planned - distract the fevered psyche and ease the taut nerves with an evening spent basking in the girl-child's lovely penumbra; use her to forestall the stark moment when the terrors and sorrows descend with the ferocity of a herd of hungry pterodactyls and rip the heart and soul into bleeding, palpitating shreds and absolutely have their way with one and there is no balm and no escape - but let her go, after this one time - take her kind offer of the ivory buttons, compensate her for them, buy her a cappucino and a chocolate chip cookie or a plateful of chocolate truffles or whatever is her heart's desire, and - bid her a final *adieu*. Do not further complicate your life, Ifford, and do not draw this pretty innocent into a relationship with a wanted entity reduced to living pretty much day-to-day in a kind of helpless, planless, nightmarish limbo.

Thus resolved, I squared the shoulders, threw back the head, and entered The Silver Stud with a firm and manly tread. Glimpsing the girl, minus her canine shadow this time - she was to tell me it was actually her sister's dog - in the back at what seemed to be her usual table, I waved, smiled, and, in a manner which I hoped might suggest how utterly old hat were trysts with members of the second sex to this particular man of the world, sauntered down the cramped, wavering aisle to join her. It seemed a very long way to attempt casually to saunter, in the manner of a man of the world, encumbered as I was by a rather bulky lizard-skin carry-all, with what felt like all eyes upon me, but I struggled to pull it off - I mean, what choice had I, or does one ever have, but to try to wear convincingly one's chosen persona, foolish and ill-chosen and totally inadequate though it may seem, when put to the test and offered up in the bright lights for public consumption. But I persevered, squeezing my narrow hips - my narrow everything, if the sad truth be told - between the closely placed tables and their leather and chrome-clad occupants, which were clumsily decoupaged - the tables, I mean, of course, not the occupants - with rather severe photos apparently snipped from 'zines catering to the bondage and discipline crowd.

For some reason I had not given too much thought to that aspect of the place heretofore, or to the question of why such an apparently sweet and tender young thing as the velveteen girl would select so apparently decadent a cave for her hang-out; but as I slid onto the dark wooden bench next to her, smiling, I hoped, warmly and yet confidently - with not too much the effect of the pleading Cocker Spaniel about the eyes, was what I had striven for, in my practice sessions before the mirror - my gaze slid across the wall beside her and noted the chains, riding crops, handcuffs, blindfolds, etc., which, artfully arranged and displayed, served in lieu of the more customary Monet and Matisse prints; and I noticed, now that I was closer to her, that she was pierced, multiply on both of her pink shell-like (really!) ears and once (as I thought I glimpsed between her half parted teeth) through - ouch! - the tongue. What, I wondered, as I beamed jovially at the beautiful girl - for she was very beautiful indeed - what bleeping ever, was old Ifford getting himself into now? And was this sweet young thing as innocent, as unblemished, as she seemed? And if so, then what was she doing here?

CHAPTER 17: NATIVE DANCER

The children who know how to think for themselves spoil the
harmony of the collective society that is coming, where
everyone would be interdependent.

John Dewey,
1899, educational philosopher,
proponent of modern public schools.

Our eyes met shyly, and we said 'Hi!' at the same time, causing us both
to laugh and look away in embarrassment. After what seemed a longish
- too longish - moment of silence, and not knowing what else to say to
break it, I essayed a compliment on her dress, another velveteen job,
this one with long fitted sleeves, looking to be about mid-calf length
like the other had been, and, like it, decorated with antique beads about
the bodice and cuffs; but today's dress was of a cool faded blue-green
color, rather than the soft brown of the previous evening.

"Oh thanks," she said, in response to my compliment on her dress, "It's
really nice, isn't it?"

"Yes, in a medieval sort of way. Makes you look sort of like a damsel.
Are you by any chance in distress?"

"I don't think so. Not right at the moment, anyway. I will be, if I ever
run out of velvet dresses, though. Like this one, which I got just last
week at the Universal Salvation Army on one of their half-price days. I
just love velvet, don't you? Real velvet, I mean - not that phony velour.
That's one reason I think that vest of yours is so cool - the one you
were wearing last night. You did remember to bring it along, didn't
you? Because I have the buttons – of fossilized ivory - and a needle and
a spool of thread, right here in my backpack."

Instead of a purse she pulled from its resting place on the booth beside
her a child's backpack, made in the likeness of a now rather threadbare
Winnie-the-Poo, complete with head, arms and legs, the body being
zippered and empty of stuffing so that it could be used to carry things.
She reached into the belly of the beast, so to speak, and withdrew a
small sewing kit housed in a dented metal box upon which were

painted in chipped, faded red and yellow letters a number of wildly enthusiastic endorsements of Grandma O'Houlihan's Krunchy Delights.

"Are you a fan, then?" I asked her - adding, when a confused frown took up residence on her lovely brow, and a baffled expression moved in to cloud her wide gray-green eyes, "Of Grandma O'Houlihan's goodies, I mean? I am. I just love her Tasty Morsels. And her Krunchy Morsels. Have you ever tried them?"

"Oh, they're my favorite, absolutely the best!" she exclaimed. "Those and the Krunchie-Krunchies. I could just live on them. But I haven't found one of these old canisters for them yet, in any of the thrifts. They're hard to find, you know."

"I suppose they would be. They stopped packaging them in those tins quite a while ago, didn't they?"

"Yes - before I was born," she said, a little sadly. "Now they just use cardboard boxes - or cellophane packages. But anyway, did you bring the vest? I want to see how these buttons look against that fabric."

"Oh, yes," I said. "Got it right here in this bag of mine ..." and I pulled out the item in question and handed it over to her. It looked pretty ratty to me, on its last legs for this karmic cycle, and ready for the retirement home, but she seemed to regard it as a going concern and definitely worthy of her ministrations. It was a patchwork job, with irregular blobs of velveteen in all differing soft shades of pink and pale green sewn together on the garment's front, the lining and back being made of a supple beigey-gray fabric, solid-colored and of a silky or satiny sheen.

"I thought so," she said, after scrutinizing it closely for a few seconds. "It's hand-made, and must be quite old. And it's in really good shape, considering. And ..." rummaging around in her little sewing kit and producing a couple of the ivory buttons, which she placed against the vest's front, "I think these will look really good on it - don't you?"

I had to admit that they did; their style was very simple - classic, you might say - just small roundish buttons, about a half-inch in diameter, with two neat little holes like empty eyes bored in the center for attachment to a garment, their only ornamentation being a concentric groove with smooth rounded edges incised near each button's circumference. The fossilized ivory of which they were made had taken on a warm off-white coloration, larded with streaks and lines of differing brownish hues, thus picking up the beige tone of the fabric used on the vest's back, inner lining, and edging. Now that I looked at it, it was a nice old thing, I realized, if you go in for that sort of thing. Which, I was thinking, I might; I just might. Someone had put a lot of work into it, once long ago.

"Yes," I agreed. "Very nice indeed. And it is, as you see, missing all of its buttons but one, and that one just hanging on by the skin of its teeth. Something needs to be done."

"Yeah, and that one remaining button is this ugly modern factory-made job - woven fake leather strips, wrapped around a metal form - and it's this ugly shiny black plastic - aren't these the kind of buttons they used to put on car coats, back in the '50s? - ugly to begin with, and it doesn't even go with the vest, and it obviously wasn't put on it by the vest's original maker."

That about summed it up. A veritable dissertation. "True," I agreed. Ifford the Agreeable. "These look much better - more in accord with the original intent or *esprit* of the thing, you might say. And, now that I look at them more closely - aren't those ivory buttons hand-carved?"

She looked at me admiringly. I kid you not, dear Reader; this meltingly beautiful girl, with these incredibly warm and soulful eyes, of this fabulous transparent gray-green color, like the eyes of a Norse goddess on a cloudy-bright day in the first blush of her youth - looked at old Ifford admiringly! That is to say, with admiration. She did. It was not my imagination. And then she said, softly, "That's really great, that you noticed that. A lot of people wouldn't."

Joy invaded the heart, of course - absolutely suffused the being - but thank God I didn't blush - or not much, anyway. A little roseate hue might have crept into the cheeks, is all.

"Oh, surely there are many others who could have pulled it off - that feat of observation I mean. Nothing to write home about." Then, feeling, or rather, realizing, that the comment had been asinine, and my tone so falsely modest as to be more boastful than otherwise, I hastily added, hoping to move on before she had time to think about it and began scaling down her evaluation accordingly, "Speaking of home, where do you hail from - this rock hurtling thru the void - or another?"

311

"Oh, this rock, this country - this city, actually. I've lived here all my life. Boring. What about you? You look like you could be from somewhere else."

"Oh yes - from a harsher world - if that be possible - far from here - on the other side of the galaxy. I doubt you would have heard of it. My mother, however, is an Earthling."

"And your father?"

"Well - it's a rather sad story. We're not sure, actually. The home planet goes in for genetic experimentation and eugenics and all that sort of thing in a big way, and it seems that I was concocted in a mixing bowl according to some Ph.D.'s bright idea, or to satisfy some planning board's whim, curiosity, quota - or whatever."

"How weird. So, your mother - what? - donated an egg, or something?"

"My mother's wishes in the matter were never at issue. That is to say, she was not consulted."

"What do you mean? Once she made the donation, she wasn't allowed to know what happened next?"

"Actually, her donation, as you call it, was not a voluntary one. She was abducted and the - ovum - more than one, I imagine - was taken without her knowledge or consent."

"Gee. How awful for her. Kind of like rape."

"Robo-rape, I guess you could call it. A very high-tech operation, as I understand."

"Then you must have half-brothers and sisters out there somewhere that you don't even know about. So it really happens ... I always thought all that abduction stuff you hear about on TV was just - you know, crazy. It just sounds like, you know, out of some science fiction movie. If it happened that way, then how do you even know who your mother is?"

"There are these agencies which - allegedly - help one track one's parents and offspring down - if one has been a victim - or - a result, you might say - of such - experimentation. Through the comparing by computer of samples of genetic material, positive identification can be made. Or such is the claim. One never really knows if they're telling the truth or just making it up. I choose to believe the former, and that I am not totally a stranger in a vast, possibly even infinite, and indifferent time-space continuum. But then, entities who long to know the unknowable - and/or to be soothed - will believe anything, it seems."

"I suppose so. I'd never quite thought about it like that, I guess. You say some awfully interesting things." And she smiled - shyly! - at me.

Again! A compliment! By the gods - so the inner monologue was marveling - I think I am making a favorable impression on this female. A first for old Ifford. It all goes to show that, just like the mathematician-johnnies say in *Popular Probabilities*, all theoretically possible events, no matter how infinitesimal their probability of occurrence, will at some point in space-time be actualized. That is to say, if I read them right, will occur.

Trying not to appear as astounded as I felt, I continued, aiming for something like a Rhett Butlerish casual suavity - "But enough about *moi*..." (Would old Rhett have said *moi*? I hardly thought so and it sounded just too too and not at all manly as I uttered it, making me wish I could snatch it back) "What about you - I assume your origins are more orthodox. Do your parents live near-by? Or - perhaps you are still living with them? And, do you realize - we don't even know each other's names, yet?"

"That's right, we don't. Well, everyone calls me Riqi."

"I'm Ifford ... Ifford - Calvin." (A small spontaneous lie, dear Reader, in the matter of the patronymic, in memoriam of my departed roommate - actually made with the idea in mind, vaguely, of protecting the poor girl from the knowledge that she was consorting with a fugitive from justice, in case that might be deemed a crime according to the *lex loci*.) "And you're just called Ricky?"

"Raquelle Angelina Nelson. But my brothers and sisters thought it was funny, sort of a joke, to call me Ricky Nelson. I never liked it that much - they were kind of making fun of me, because I like to sing, and mess around on the guitar, and because I was a tomboy, when I was a kid - but the nickname stuck. I spell it different though - R, i, q, i, Riqi - my little rebellion, I guess."

313

"Dictating some if not all of the terms of the agreement."

"Yeah," she agreed, laughing. "Having my say in the matter, I guess. It wasn't easy, with all those brothers and sisters - I'm one of 10, believe it or not. Counting all the half- and step-brothers and sisters."

"Gracious. A veritable tribe, or nation, resulting by the sound of it from several mergers or minglings of assets. Your parents and their various consorts must be lusty souls subscribing to the theory that there is strength in numbers."

"Whatever. They sure had a hard time taking care of all of us. Like, my sister and I were kind of adopted out when I was three, to our much older half-sister, which I still remember, my mom just saying, like, here's your new mother, and just leaving me with these people I didn't even know very well. Although I did get to visit my real parents a lot. Or, really, I think our older half-sister just got tired of having us around and dumped us on them as often as she could. But anyway - I don't actually think my parents went in for family planning. It - we - just sort of happened."

"Inspired improvisation ..."

"You make me laugh, Ifford. You have such - different - ways of saying things. Are you a graduate student at the University, or a teacher, or what?"

"A mere undergraduate." No need to fill her in on all the gory details at this point, such as that I am in point of fact an ex-undergraduate, pretty much an ex-everything, except fugitive, as of even date - especially no need to tell all if I am going to follow through and nip this relationship in the bud as planned. No need either to alarm or intrigue the dear child. What she doesn't know can't hurt her.

"So - who were those people you were with last night?" she queried. "They sure looked like an interesting group. Are they people you know from the university?"

"A pretty heterogeneous assemblage, but university types more or less. Radical political extremists, most of them, actually, or so some would say, attempting for some unfathomable reason to recruit me into their ranks. I might be doing some occasional work, sort of as an independent contractor, for one guy - the fat one that looks like a toad, if you remember him - but I am not really one of them."

"I think I'm sort of like you - non-political. It's all so confusing, and boring. I have these friends that are like that, too - like your friends. Really political. All these crazy theories. And, you know, who can prove anything?"

"How do you happen to be involved with these political friends?"

"Well, my boss, or manager - Silver? - I don't know if you know him - they're friends of his. So whenever we go out to eat, like after work, you know - well a lot of the time, we go out with them, or meet them at some restaurant ..."

"What sort of work is it that you do? - If you don't mind my asking, that is. I don't mean to be nosey, so just tell me that it's none of my business, if you want ..."

"No, that's OK. I'm a dancer."

"Oh? What sort of dance? Modern? Ballet? Ballroom? Belly? Break?"

"A little bit of everything, I guess. Whatever I feel like."

"Eclectic, eh? An artiste?"

"Not really. Actually, I dance at clubs. You know - like, The Silver Slipper?"

"Never heard of it, I'm afraid."

"Well, I'm kind of like a go-go dancer, if you know what that is."

"Oh." Good grief! I thought - Isn't that the same thing as being a stripper? Topless in a cage, or on stage, perhaps, looking a little foolish prancing suggestively around a gleaming pole, and don't leering men of all ages and social classes make improperly familiar remarks as they tuck fivers into the garter-belt and g-string, just in order to cop a quick feel of the smooth and silky? This - mere child? It did not compute. I struggled to make the paradigm shift.

"Are you - old enough for that sort of thing? You look like you couldn't be over the age of 16."

"Well, I am, actually, but just barely. But I do look old for my age - don't you think?"

No I did not, but I let it pass.

"Don't tell anyone," she went on confidingly, "But I have phony ID that says I'm 18. A lot of the girls do."

"But - aren't you - taking quite a risk? I mean - if you're found out, wouldn't you be fined, and sent to - I don't know - juvenile hall, or some boot camp for wayward girls, or some such place?"

"Ifford, you're kind of innocent, aren't you? I guess a lot of people at the University must be. Out of touch with the real world. That's what Silver is always saying. The cops are paid off, so the fake ID is just sort of a formality, really. There's no problem."

"Oh. I see." My head, as the reader might imagine, was as they say reeling. I felt all agog. This sweet child - a stripper? Was she then into prostitution? Was this Silver fellow actually, then, her pimp? My feelings were a melting pot of pity, curiosity, and fascinated horror, marinating in a sort of slimy sense of shame such as one feels for one's almost sadistic or voyeuristic curiosity when driving past an accident on the freeway. Another's life hangs palpitating in the balance, or is snuffed out in a moment of horror, providing cheap thrills and a topic of conversation for all who pass by to witness it.

I hardly knew what to say to the girl. "I suppose it pays pretty well," was all I could think of. Trying to strike the positive note, you know. I didn't want the aghastness to show through - didn't want to hurt the old girl's feelings. Ever the *preux chevalier*, through thick and thin - though I don't mind telling you, it was a struggle to keep the features composed, the tone light, and the manner off-hand.

Behind the bland and agreeable expression I strove to keep plastered on the map, my mind raced. Instead of a contaminating, underworld sort of influence in the girl's life, I now felt more like a knight - a potential savior - a wholesome, nourishing ingredient thrown into the stew - perhaps even, amongst the flotsam and jetsam of her young life, a piece of driftwood to which she could cling. A mixture of metaphors, but you get my drift. Surely - surely! - she could be doing better for herself than running in these circles of debauchery, routinely as a commercial enterprise exhibiting her body to lustful old men with beer bellies and a day's growth of beard in some sleazy establishment gaudy with blinking neon - GIRLS! GIRLS! GIRLS! Could she possibly enjoy such a life? - I asked myself. Wasn't it - a difficult, a demeaning thing to do - and depressingly sordid?

"Oh, yeah, the money is good," she said, agreeing, I realized with my own remark to that effect made, it seemed, a few light-years distant in time. "Real good. I make more than any of my brothers. My sister and I both do."

"I suppose it would pay well. I'm glad you're able to make good money; but isn't it sort of - hard work?"

"Well - what isn't?" she opined philosophically. "Waitressing, cashiering, babysitting - whatever I've done, it's all hard work. At least with my dancing I can make some decent money. And it is kind of - you know - creative. Yeah, my feet really get tired, I can tell you that. I think I'm even starting to get a bunion or something on one of my little toes. At my age. We have to wear these super high platform heels - you know - because they look sexy? It's really easy to twist your ankle. One of the girls fell down, right on the stage, just the other night. She started crying, right there in front of everyone. But all the guys cheered and threw dollars at her, and she felt better. A new girl. You have to learn how to walk in those things. Practice at home, in front of a mirror. And sometimes I get really cold, when the door keeps opening and closing, letting in all that cold air, and of course I can't put on a sweater or anything - just a kind of a feather stole that doesn't do anything to keep me warm. They really don't keep the place warm enough in winter. I keep telling Silver not to be such a cheapskate, to go ahead and turn up the heat. He makes enough money off the place, he can afford it. And then in the summer, of course, under all those lights, it can be really hot. I sweat, and it makes my make-up run. And it gets really boring. I mean, eight hours is just tooo long; I hardly ever work an eight hour shift. And I hate it, like when I have a sore throat, or a cold - all that smoke really gets to you. I don't smoke - do you?"

"No, I don't. Never saw the point in it."

"Me either. But, the good part is, since I make such good money, I don't have to work all that much. I just can show up at work anytime I want to. I don't have a schedule or anything."

"Doesn't - Silver - expect you to work a lot?"

"Oh, yeah, he wants me to, but I tell him he can't force me. See, he knows that I don't really need him. He lines up extra jobs for me, like bachelor parties and singing telegrams or sexygrams and stuff like that - private engagements - but I don't really need him, and he knows it. I mean, there are a lot of other clubs - and managers, as far as that goes. We're not going together, if that's what you think. He's just, like, a friend - but really we're not even really friends - it's more like a business arrangement - a friendly business arrangement."

"Does he manage your sister, too?"

"See, he and my older sister are, like, going together. Like, they're almost married. That's how I met him in the first place. He owns this place, you know - The Silver Stud - or I should say, he's a part owner. This, and The Silver Slipper, where I work. That's why I hang out here. He lets me have free stuff, all the free cocoa and herbal tea and cider and things to eat that I want. I don't drink coffee - do you? The caffeine's not good for you."

"Actually, I do indulge. One of the basic food groups, in my scheme of things. But to each his own, is my motto. Abstain freely, with my blessings. And speaking of which, shouldn't we go on up to the counter and order something? A little sustenance? I was going to say, my treat, but if your order is one of the percs you enjoy as the owner's virtual sister-in-law ..." (and asset, I thought of adding, but kept the thought to myself).

"Well, look, Ifford - I have a better idea. Why don't we go over to my apartment - it's not far from here, just a few blocks - and I can make us some hot chocolate - mine is lots better than what they make here, because I use better chocolate - and I have these really good hazelnut biscotti, dipped in dark chocolate, from an Italian store down at the public market - and I can sew on those buttons for you over there. It's a lot more comfy. We can put on some music, or a movie, and just - relax. Besides, I want to show you my place."

Well, this was an offer a being in my position could not refuse - I, as a wanted entity, or being - perhaps even a highly wanted being - following the prudent policy of keeping myself out of the public eye, whenever possible, and of never lingering too long in any one place. After all, the UN storm troopers could sweep through here at any moment, as they had done the night before. In addition to which, as previously noted, The Silver Stud broadcasts, relentlessly, the kind of hard-edged, high-volume, acrimonious music known as heavy metal, leavened now and then with rap, or some ghastly permutation thereof, and it was grating horribly on all the ganglia and requiring us to shout to be heard; so we picked up our marbles and went home - to hers, that is - and it was, as promised, a very cozy establishment indeed.

CHAPTER 18: *CHEZ* RIQI

The unadorned truth is that we do not need now, and will not
need later, much of the marginal labor - the very young, the
very old, the very uneducated,
and the very stupid.

Margaret Mead

As Riqi explained on the short walk over to her digs, she lived in an apartment in the upper story of an old house owned by her boss, Silver (Sylvester, as he was christened) O'Shea. In fact he and Riqi's sister, Honey (yes, Honey) lived in the larger downstairs unit. I wondered if the rent was another of the percs of Riqi's privileged position as sister of the boss's main (I hoped, only) squeeze, but it seemed too early in our acquaintance to ask such probing questions. Besides, I wasn't sure I wanted to know any more, just yet. I was still struggling to incorporate into the stodgy (apparently) old moral code the troubling details and possible implications of her employment, which this ingenuous child had already so glibly and casually divulged.

To get to Riqi's flat, one crunched a few blocks through the crusted snow and ice, turning to tread a dark and narrow cement walkway that led along one side of a large old white house - from within the ground level of which I heard a gruff bark or two from a canine which I supposed to be the over-sized terrier Riqi had had with her on the previous evening. Attached to the back of the large house was a sagging wooden stairway, with peeling paint and a pronounced list to starboard, which provided egress to Riqi's place – a separate flat, complete with a small covered porch, a kitchenette and a full bathroom, into which the upper three bedrooms of the house had been converted.

Her flat was, as she had promised, cozy. More than that, it was almost - inspired - a sort of a crystal palace in miniature. I began to realize, as I took it all in, that the girl was after all an artiste of sorts. The place was a veritable feast for the eyes - so charmingly, and originally, to my eye, had she decorated it. The reader will recall her penchant for beads and old fabrics - well, here in the place she called her own she had pulled out all the stops in those departments and pretty much gone hog wild, as the expression has it. I mean, there were beads, and old fabrics, and hand-woven fabrics, everywhere. There was simply no escaping them.

But it was successful - she absolutely carried it off. In fact, the effect was rather enchanting. The whole place - lampshades, bead curtains, doilies, antimacassars, bead-covered baskets, and what not - glittered richly with the deep, translucent colors of wine-red and indigo, of every shimmering shade of green and pink and yellow. And the effect of opulence was enhanced by the thick Oriental carpets - well-worn, but looking rich, old, and authentic - which were layered on the floors. The walls - several of which slanted inwards at about shoulder level, in the manner of attic rooms, adding to the cozy intimacy and informality, as well as the artistic atmosphere, of the place - were painted a soft, flat white, nicely setting off the glowing colors. There were a couple of thick black futon sofas - looking overstuffed, if there is such a thing in the world of the futon - strewn with an abundance of big, soft pillows which were covered with what looked like batiked and/or hand-woven fabrics in different patterns and designs. On the walls I noticed a couple of what I think are called dioramas - shallow boxes used to frame little enigmatic scenes which incorporated both found objects, such as children's small toys and action figures, and two-dimensional art - as well as several small, matted and framed compositions, mixed media, but done mostly in beads and fabric - abstract or non-figurative collages, you could call them, I suppose. They were very nice, I thought.

"Did you do these?" I asked her.

"Those things on the wall? Oh, yeah, I did. Do you like 'em?"

"Very much." And I did. I saw, in a word, that my new acquaintance had, if not sense, then sensibility, in full measure. Even, it seemed, that rare commodity - originality. So developed, so assured, in her sensibility, I mused - and still so young. Either that, or I was unfamiliar with the oeuvres and artists she was plagiarizing. But, whether derivative or otherwise, the decor of the place constituted indisputable evidence that the girl had the soul of a poet, in addition to the face and form of a goddess, and it made my heart bleed all the more for the sordid way in which she was forced, apparently, by the harsh economic realities of place and time, to earn her bread. Rantor came to mind - specifically, his assertions that the masses live out their lives in a condition of artificially induced poverty, the greater part of their earnings being siphoned off by that complex engine designed for that very purpose - that viper (if the lizard was to be believed) in our midst - the central bank. I wondered, for the first time seriously, if it were really true. I mean – was quasi-prostitution the only way that this young woman could earn a decent living, in the present economy?

"You're *en su casa*, as the *Mexicanos* say, so just make yourself at home. Put your coat anywhere, slip off your shoes if you want to, and just relax while I heat up the milk for the cocoa," she said. "The stereo and CDs are over there - see? - or you can put a DVD on to play, if you see one you like."

"Oh, I'll let you choose our entertainment," I replied. "As long as it's nothing too raucous, that is - if you don't mind my imposing that proviso. I hope my tastes don't seem too staid and conventional to you. In matters of taste and so on, we could be from different worlds in more ways than one, I suppose."

Actually, based on what I had heard so far of the girl's milieu, I had a hunch that we were indeed quite different, but naturally did not say so, we hybrids, as previously mentioned and whatever our failings in other departments, being by instinct and upbringing absolutely topped off and running over with tact and discretion. It practically amounts to a reflex - tap the little rubber-coated mallet on the right spot, and the tact just spills out, like nickels out of a lucky winner's slot machine.

The music Riqi put on was - just happened to be - one of my favorites - a favorite of a lot of people and beings and entities and life-forms, I know - that pellucid thing by Erik Satie, called *Trois Gymnopodies* or *Gnossien,* or something like that - played, it really sounded to me, on the gamelan, with variations, and quite nice it was. And though she didn't know the work or composer by name, it being to her merely the lead item on a set of CDs entitled *Music for Meditation* or some such - still, I felt it auspicious. Of course I was, although I did not realize it at the time, in that optimistic, not to say positively euphoric, state of mind in which one hopes for amour, and the soul-mate, and so on, and thus sees and greets with a glad cry positive augeries pretty much springing out at one from every nook, cranny, and happenstance.

Taking off my heavy combat boots as per her suggestion, I leaned back against some downy pillows on a thickly padded black futon, and I listened to her music, and I watched her ... Riqi ... Riqi ... Riqi ... I quite liked the sound of it - with her lovely child's face, grave in concentration over her homely task, and her slender figure, graceful as a ballerina's in her absurd bottle-green crushed velveteen dress, as she measured the cocoa into cups in her little ship's galley of a kitchen.

And if the reader suspects at this point in our narrative that our hero had pretty much lost all radar and radio contact with his recent resolve to nip this relationship in the bud - well, said reader would be pretty much right on the money.

CHAPTER 19: BUG JUICE

There will be in the next generation or so ... a pharmacological method of making people love their servitude and producing dictatorship without tears, so to speak. Producing a kind of painless concentration camp for entire societies so that people will in fact have their liberties taken away from them but will rather enjoy it, because they will be distracted from any desire to rebel - by propaganda, or brainwashing, or brainwashing enhanced by pharmacological methods. And this seems to be the final revolution.

Aldous Huxley, 1961,
at a U.S. State Department-sponsored conference at
the California Medical School in San Francisco

Riqi brought the libations in on a black tray, setting it down beside the futon on a low, Nipponese sort of table-like thing - which I realized, upon scrutinizing it more closely, was actually some sort of sturdy wooden crate of the sort formerly used to ship fruit, transformed, by a thick coating of shiny black lacquer-like paint and a small, neat tatami mat on its upper surface, into an end-table.

"Go ahead and start sipping your cocoa while it's still warm," she said, smiling. I liked the heartening way she smiled a lot, Ifford being a lad who needs lots of encouragement in matters of this sort. "I'm just going to get into something more comfortable. I'll be right back."

Something more comfortable. That sounded rather jolly. It took her longer than seemed necessary - but I guess that's the way it always is with females, regardless of which sector of the galaxy they and their forebears hail from, at least when viewed from the male perspective.

One thing I had already noticed about Riqi and pondered as I sipped the cocoa she had made - which as promised was very tasty - it was actually a mocha, I thought, with an added smoky bittersweet flavoring I could not quite identify, and I made a mental note to ask her about it; anyway, one thing I had noted approvingly - though hopefully might be the better word - was this way she had of making me feel very much the alpha male.

Which of course, as even the dimmest reader must by now have pieced together, I am not. In fact, here on this planet I think most of the locals just automatically assume that I have thrown in the towel altogether in this department and have renounced all claim to heterosexuality - that I appear this way - physically, I mean - in fulfillment of some misguided plan or aesthetic ideal - that I am striving to look sort of effete and wispy and insubstantial, like a clothed version of Pascal's thinking reed, with an out-sized ping-pong ball of a head stuck onto its tip at the whim of some wit with a couple of beers under his belt, with the idea of making it into a homunculus of sorts - that my agenda is to pass for a shorter, thinner, more delicately-featured, if less wasted and less exhausted-looking, twin of Andy Warhol. That, in short, my *outre* physical appearance is an effect I have striven for. When in fact nothing could be further from the truth, and I would mortgage my soul heavily in exchange for a pill, elixir, or home-study course that would transform me into a large, brooding, well-muscled male *Homo sapiens* of the most rampant, fire-breathing sort.

Actually, if the truth be known, I have always wanted to look like Marlon Brando in *A Streetcar Named Desire*. Laugh if you will, but it was for the unattainability of that goal that I used to cry myself to sleep at night, in my teens back in the dormitory, and, though buried deeply beneath other sorrows and pressing concerns, it remains today a frustrated ambition and source of ongoing *Schmertz* to the psyche. I mean, hypnotize me, suggest that I feel sad and ask why, and that would probably be one of the first things I would start blubbering about. These wounds stay with one.

325

My wistful ruminations were interrupted by the reappearance of the golden girl for whom, now, I yearned to appear virile and studly to the max - and if I did not look my part in the, I hoped, unfolding drama, she certainly carried hers off with such pizzaz and *eclat* that I could not help but goggle. Beneath an open robe of luxuriant baby-blue chenille - the fabric itself looking so soft and cuddly that one longed to reach out and press it to one's cheek and bosom and - sort of knead it softly, passing it wonderingly from one hand to the other, if you know what I mean - well, as I was saying, beneath this robe she had on what I think is called a teddy - the very first of its kind I had ever seen actually deployed in active duty, so to speak - of palest pink, a thin, luminous silk, with flat narrow shoulder straps of the same fine-woven fabric, such as you might see in a woman's undergarment from the *fin du siecle*, and sans ornamentation save a satin piping of a slightly brighter pink all around its margins, and a row of small, ivory-colored buttons that ran all the way down the garment's front - down, down, down, to ride above that breath-taking furred nexus of torso and long slim thighs that lay so tantalizingly just beneath the silk. The smooth skin on her thighs was finely-textured, a pale honey-brown to creamy white in color, with a thin sprinkling of barely perceptible short golden hairs which glimmered in the soft light. The total effect was such as almost to make one gasp and swoon.

As she plopped down beside me on the futon, I noticed that in one hand my Venus carried a cigarette lighter and a tiny, thin, bent-looking, hand-rolled cigarette, its ends twisted shut in what seemed an amateurish way.

"Do you mind if I light up?" she asked. "I'm in the mood to relax a little. You can join me or not - it's up to you. It is pretty good stuff."

"By all means, help yourself. But I don't smoke. I thought you told me you didn't, either."

"That was tobacco we were talking about. This is herb."

"Herb?"

"You know - *bhang*, bud," she replied, lighting the drooping little cigarette on one end, putting it to her lips, inhaling deeply - and then, it seemed, holding her breath. After about half a minute, she exhaled in a long, happy sigh and smiled at me, looking deeply - and I mean deeply - I physically felt a distinct jolt of energy from that direct gaze - into

326

my eyes. "Don't tell me you don't know what *bhang* is, Ifford. Gee - you really are innocent, aren't you?"

I detected an unfamiliar sweetish smell in the air. It definitely was not a regular tobacco cigarette that she was puffing away on.

"Bong?" I repeated - rather fatuously, to my own ear. It rang no bells.

"You know - mary jane - marijuana, silly. Have you really never tried it? You should - here," and she proffered the evil-looking little cigarette.

"Oh no - no, thanks, I mean. I mean, absolutely not, if it's all the same to you. *Nolle prosequi* being my policy in these matters."

What next, is what I was thinking to myself. What bloody next! First I learn that this, as I thought, child, keeps body and soul together by participating - starring, you might say - in what I can only call an on-going pornographic enterprise - and now I discover that she does drugs.

"I hope it doesn't bother you - that I blow a little weed, I mean. Just about everyone does these days, you know. I stay away from all the hard stuff. You don't need to worry about that, if that's what's bugging you."

"Oh - do I look - bugged? I'm not. Not at all. Or hardly. Well - perhaps a teensey bit. You would not believe the propaganda we were subjected to, back on the home planet, in re the use of recreational drugs. We were required to take classes, and view films, in what here would be called junior high and high school, in which drugs and their use - and users - were vividly portrayed as the very embodiment of evil and the very stuff used by Satan's road crew to pave the path to perdition. The effect lingers, I suppose. You know how impressionable one is in one's youth."

"Well, I've never even tried crack or regular cocaine or heroin or ice or meth, or crystal meth, or any of it, never shot up - though I admit I am curious, what they're like, you know. A lot of the other girls use them and I've heard they're pretty good. Heavenly, in fact. But I think it's better just not to mess with them at all. You've got to draw the line somewhere - don't you think? But marijuana's different - at least that's what I think - it's not habit-forming, you know - not physically,

327

anyway - and it's not refined - I mean, it's natural; and it really is spiritual."

At this a small, skeptical smile must have stolen across my features, for she hurried on, a trifle defensively, "Oh, I know it just sounds like an excuse, a junkie's excuse, but really, for me it is very spiritual. You know, the shamans of lots of the old cultures used it for spiritual purposes. If you would just try it, I think you'd see what I mean."

Actually, I was beginning to get the rather eerie feeling that I *was* trying it - or something - that I had walked smack dab through the looking glass, in fact. What I was feeling is hard to describe. But let me try. In general, and increasingly, everything was seeming both more vivid and more profound. Colors seemed more luminous; the music was more attention-grabbing, more beautiful, more . . . profound. I mean, profundity positively abounded; and it was a - a more profound profundity that the garden variety that had been my personal best heretofore. The music had a lot more to say, it now seemed to me, than I had noticed at first, and what it said moved me strangely. But so did everything, wherever I turned. The very space in the room was different, more - palpable. More - alive. The air seemed more like real stuff, is what I'm trying to say - something - some thing - that was between me and these other objects in the room with me.

And Riqi was - almost a little scary. Not that she was behaving oddly - just that - this is hard to convey - she was another person - so real. So - momentous. And here I was, very close to her ... and wanting to be closer ... something I both wanted and yet feared, with an equal intensity. And these feelings were not as pallid as my emotions usually were. Not such lap-dogs, such faded, two-dimensional cardboard cut-outs. They were - how can I say it - much larger and stronger. Definitely gorilla-like. But the real nub of the matter was perhaps this - that I was not the master of ceremonies, not running the show, as was my custom. That's what I am getting at - they were now running the show. These gorillas. My feelings, I mean. They were definitely in charge, and I was bobbing on their current - wrapped in their terrible embrace, you could say, without overstating the case one iota. And it felt both good - wonderful, actually, like a movie that was black and white suddenly becoming color, or like the difference between watching someone get a back massage and actually getting a back massage - and at the same time, frightening. Because they - these feelings of mine - were too big, and I could not control them. They just went where they wanted to, dragging me along with them – surging unpredictably about like some large animal, or herd of large animals - or like water, a big body of water, impelled by some mysterious internal energy of its own. And I, accustomed as I was to being the absolute petty dictator of this interior *menage*, was reduced to the role of spectator - and, as I say, and like it or not, rag-doll tagalong as they bounced off the walls of the world according to no discernable game plan or set of rules. The old caregivers had introduced us to a few Buddhistic-type concepts - detachment and so on - and I tried now to apply them to the present turbulence but with no great success. Deep breathing, become an observer of your own emotions, float above, stay detached, keep your sense of humor ... the advice came back to me but had always been difficult to apply even under the best of circumstances.

If I had to summarize, I would say that everything was intensified - packed more of a wallop. Which had, as they say, its upside - and its downside. And I was stuck - trapped - here, with, and within, this new, higher voltage state of affairs. I couldn't get back to my normal condition! At least, if there was a switch, I didn't know where.

When I kept the sensorium occupied, all was well - fabulous, actually - but when I started thinking, things got a little dicey, because the utter peril of my present situation - life-wise, I mean - the morass of quandaries in which I stood hip deep, and which extended to the horizon in every direction of the compass - loomed up at me, very large and very - you know, in my face. Above all, I was aware, with a rather terrible clarity, that I was flesh and blood - physically incarnate. That I - whoever I was - was - am - just this vulnerable soft little whatzit - thinking reed, or whatever - made by whom or what, with what end in mind, God (?) only knew. If it was reasonable to posit a beneficent creator. If that wasn't just some little - oh, I don't know - compensatory fantasy - just a sort of soothing, feel-good thought to cuddle up with when one needed bucking up. A prop, an anodyne, a placebo, a necessary fiction. What kept emerging with an uncomfortable clarity and distinctness, as a really palpable, undeniable - fact - was that I am flesh and that all flesh, sooner or later, is grass. And instead of being the usual distant realization, it was right there up close and personal and somehow it jangled my bells, got right in amongst me, and made me feel - well, I guess you could say, deeply anxious. Pretty much as if my number had been drawn, and the moment was at hand for old Ifford to be shunted off into the great beyond. I didn't like the feeling. In a word, I was afraid.

"Ifford? Are you all right? What are you thinking?" Glennie - I mean, Riqi - was asking me this, with a look of concern on her face. Oh, Glennie! - I thought, with, in rapid succession, potent gusts of love, longing, and then a horrible, indescribable, desolate sense of loss - of utter abandonment and bereft-ness.

"Oh, Ifford! I just realized something ... gee, I'm so sorry ..."

This utterance, and the look of concern on the face of my new companion - of this, I realized with a little frisson of alarm, this utter stranger - drew me in. She had said she was sorry. Things were a bit confused, but I was sure of that much. What was it, then, that she was sorry about? Did she know about my loss - about Glennie - and Rantor? How could she possibly know that, when I myself had only just learned of it?

"What?" I asked, the already hypothalamic eyes doubtless bulging out a bit more in alarm. "What are you sorry about?" Cagily, you know.

I was looking at the fascinating pattern of light and shadow as it lay across the smooth terrain of Riqi's face. The color of her skin in the light was a sort of impossibly rich, warm, vibrant Naples yellow (which is really a warm tannish beige rather than a yellow, self knowing about such things from a painting class taken to fulfill the distribution requirements); in the shadows, however, her face was the color of some - what? - some living mystery, it seemed - some bodiless entity that had chosen to incarnate as - umber, as shade - and that, as shadow, wanted to get my attention, to talk to me - something or someone with a sense of humor, definitely - some trickster. Some highly intelligent, interesting someone with a very subtle and assured and exuberant sense of humor, flitting over her features with mocking dexterity, sort of like the way Fred Astaire might have done if he'd been a shadow, or been playing at being one, on the planes and contours of the face of this demi-goddess in pale pink silk and robin's-egg blue chenille ...

"Ifford? Why are you staring at me like that? I'm afraid I did something, totally by accident, I swear, Ifford, that I should tell you about ..."

That - impish spirit - was not Riqi, but it certainly hovered in her environs, rather as if it was waiting for her to grow up a little so it could engage her in dialogue - or so it seemed to me, very forcefully, at the time. And it very much wanted to talk to me - or so, again, it seemed, from the lively, the sentient quality of that living breathing shadow that lay lightly aslant Riqi's cheek and chin as though the whole thing were some display, some signal - some private joke it was waiting for me to catch on to. Some - intelligence - that it - this entity with a highly evolved, or one might almost say sublime, sense of humor - wanted to share, to enjoy with me ... I wanted to get the joke, but it eluded me. I could not get its drift - but I was right on the verge of it - of understanding.

But she had said something to me quite a while back, it seemed, and was now, judging from that expectant look on her absolutely splendiferous shade-dappled face, a-waiting a reply from old Ifford. So I marshaled the faculties, swam to the surface, and vocalized.

"What?"

"I did something, Ifford. I accidentally put something in our - your - cocoa."

"What?"

"I put something in the cocoa. By accident."

"I know. What? As in, what did you put in the cocoa?"

But I knew, dear Reader. I knew, before she spoke, that it was some - mind-altering substance. Because the mind was quite definitely altered.

CHAPTER 20: TRIPPING

Politics is the art of preventing people from taking part
in affairs which properly concern them.

Paul Valery

"Please don't get mad, Ifford. I swear it was an accident. You see, I'm very near-sighted, and I should wear glasses - but I don't like how they make me look, kind of like a secretary, or a school-teacher, like I should be wearing sensible shoes and have my hair in a bun and all." (As if that girl could look anything but divine, no matter what she wore) "And, besides, they're a nuisance, and anyway I keep loosing them, or sitting on them and breaking them. I know what you're probably thinking now -" (she was wrong here, self being in the dark to the extent of having totally lost track even of what the 'they' and 'them' she kept coming back to actually referenced) "- that I could wear contacts, and it's true, and I even have some, but I've never been able to get used to how they feel - it's like I've got something in my

332

eyes that shouldn't be there - you know, the lenses feel really huge against my eyeballs, and hard and scratchy ..."

"OK. So ...?" I essayed a little smile in her direction, hoping to mitigate or counter-balance the churlish get-on-with-it impatience I detected in the tone of my curt utterance - but I was following her chain of logic only by dint of exercising to the utmost that iron will for which we hybrids - some lineages, anyway - are renowned among the *cognoscenti*. The plethora of beguiling stimuli which were bombarding the senses - a veritable meteor shower of fascinating objects, events, thoughts - made concentration on her current output both difficult and unrewarding. I wished the old girl would cut to the chase - either that, or say something interesting - so that I could re-immerse in this realm of the senses which was trotting out its stuff as never before. In a word, I wanted urgently to get back to being entertained by this new cartoon-world.

"What I thought I was doing - what I wanted to do - was, put a few drops of almond or vanilla extract in your mocha ..."

"Um hum. Got that. And ...?" This was like pulling teeth.

"Well, you see, there's this other little bottle up there, just like the almond extract bottle, and almost the same size and brownish color ..."

The plot thickens. Silence ensues. Girl gazes at one with furrowed brow. Say something, Ifford, old man. The girl seems to be waiting.

"Oh, really?" Really really rilly really rilly really rally really. Funny how when you keep repeating a word, it starts sounding foreign - strange. Arbitrary. A complicated grunt. We are all a bunch of grunters. Grunt, grunt, grunt ... To while away the time as she was working her way at her own speed to the meat and thrust of her tale, I picked up a small beaded basket that sat on the tatami mat which covered the black lacquered end table and examined its contents. It held - what else? - more beads - large ones, these - and shells, all kinds of tiny, tiny, intricate shells – delicate corkscrews and curlicues and cornucopias - and what looked like African trade beads - those thick, slightly curved tubes with a hole running through them, like stiff, swollen macaroni, variously patterned with bright flat colors, like lemon yellow, and indigo, and burnt sienna, and fire engine red, and Naples yellow ... hadn't I just been thinking about Naples yellow? - good old Naples yellow - having an encounter with the friendly fellow, it seemed, on

333

some sunny plain or other ... oh, I positively wanted to move to Naples, immigrate, I so liked the sound of the word, and the color of its yellow...

"Ifford, listen to me. What I'm trying to say is, that other little amber bottle has bud juice in it, and I think I might have put bud juice in your mocha instead of almond extract. By mistake."

Bud juice? Bud with a 'd' as in 'disaster?' Or 'distress?' Or 'dolour?' Never heard of the stuff. Or did she say 'bug juice?' Bug juice? Wouldn't that be kind of like 'eye of newt and toe of frog?' Perilously close, it seemed to me. Would just go down a little easier, is all. How would one go about making bug juice, anyway - with a mortar and pestle, or perhaps a food processor ...? Was this pretty girl a witch, then - a kind of a succubus or incubus - I never can remember which is which - witch is witch - of the spirit - and was I, the rube from another star system, having been enticed into the gingerbread cottage, now being bewitched? But bewitchers don't usually announce their agenda - apprise you of their progress - do they?

A dark thought occurred. Was this lissome *jeune fille* acting on her own behalf - or was she after all an agent of the Forces of Evil - Squinch, et al - and was this, this - psychedelic bug juice formula of hers, this Mickey Finn with a twist, merely her way of trussing me up - effectively rendering me *hors de combat* without laying a hand on me? Was she, in effect, boasting, or gloating - announcing the *fait accompli*? Were the jack-booted thugs even now wending their way hither, chuffing and chugging through the snow and ice all weighed down by their paramilitary paraphenalia, to collect the goods? At this vivid mental image, my insides felt bathed in molten mercury - I know that mercury is liquid at room temperature, but what it felt like was nevertheless very warm, if not actually molten, mercury - and I felt, *in toto*, rather as I imagine a mouse feels upon realizing that the pleasantly warm breeze which was ruffling the fur on the back of its little neck had actually been all along the breath of its arch-enemy, the cat.

I struggled to rise from the overstuffed futon, which seemed to hold me by a sort of suction, like a patentable non-liquid quicksand disguised as a comfortable piece of furniture. Will wonders never cease, I marveled inwardly, suppressing with difficulty an anguished moan. I mean, real men don't moan - do they? What will they come up with next, in the way of snares and pitfalls for the unwary, I grumbled peevishly to myself. Ifford, you are such a - such a whiner, I thought – or rather, realized - with a lucid, detached clarity devoid of judgment.

"Please don't go, Ifford." She laid a gentle, restraining hand lightly on my arm. She had such perfect, tapered fingers. "Please. I don't blame you if you're mad. I really, really am sorry, especially now that I know how you feel about m.j. I mean, from the way you dress and everything, I wouldn't have guessed - but, honest, it won't hurt you or anything. You might actually benefit from the spiritual experience ..." (shades of Glennie here, I thought, explaining me to myself and mapping out improving experiences for poor, bumbling Ifford, so in need of assistance from any quarter) "... and it'll wear off, I promise ..."

I mulled this over, the mulling seeming distinctly more laborious than usual - a bit like slogging uphill through knee-deep mud in rubber thongs, or hacking my way through Amazonian undergrowth with a paring knife. She seemed to be telling me, if I was reading her right, that the whole thing with the electric Kool-aid bug juice was some sort of ghastly error.

"Bug juice, did you say?" Striving, you know, to maintain a dignified, off-hand tone. Cosmopolitan man of the world meets bug juice. How would, say, Cary Grant, comport himself in the present somewhat anomalous circs, I wondered. But enough of this speculation. I yanked myself sternly back to the matter at hand. Furrowing the brow a bit with the effort of it all, I attended to the instant matter, namely, that I was in a social situation and the floor was mine. I had been, if I remembered rightly, and judging from the expectant, what-next look on my companion's face, mid-comment. Oh, yes. We had been discussing bug juice.

"Bug juice? I've never heard of it. It doesn't sound very healthy to me. More like something you'd put on a houseplant. What, if you don't mind my asking, is something like bug juice doing in the kitchen cupboard - among the comestibles?"

As I stood waiting, more or less poised for flight - or as poised for f. as anyone under the influence of some extremely psychotropic extract of bug can be - for the defense to present its - her - case, and explain away all the apparent contradictions and incriminating evidence, it slowly dawned on me that, one, I did not have my boots on, and thus was going nowhere in a hurry, especially as putting on and lacing up those formidable high, stiff boots seemed in my present state a feat requiring concentration and sustained effort in heroic measure, and, two, I seemed to be holding something in one hand - something about the size and heft of a largish bullet - not that I'd ever seen, let alone hefted, a bullet before.

Looking down, I saw that it was actually a sort of fat wiggling tube, apparently frozen by some mysterious force or paralytic agent in mid-wiggle. *Curare*, perhaps, judging from the free hand with which the pharmaceuticals seemed to be tossed about in this household. It took me a long moment - pretty much the polar opposite of a nanosecond - to place it - this object I held. A dark grub? One of those bugs she made the juice from? Fossilized, or roasted to a hard, rock-like crisp, perhaps? Or was it a thick piece licorice with spots of shiny white-out correction fluid applied in some sort of decorative pattern to its surface ... some sort of secret code, maybe? I struggled for a longish moment or two, awkwardly but determinedly, rather like a recumbent and very pregnant Holstein, with one too many beers sloshing about in stomach number one, struggling to get to her feet. None of these explanations really seemed to hit the nail on the head, to solve the mystery of this enigmatic little object that rested on my palm, patiently waiting for me to place it in the grand scheme of things. Oh, yes! - it all came back to me now - it was one of those African trade beads, from that little basket. It had something on it - letters, or some kind of symbol; looking at it more closely, I saw that what it had on it was little monkey faces, little round white eyes and smudged noses and wailing Edvard Munch mouths against a black - no, a very dark, dark green - ground, but wavery, distorted monkey faces - as if seen in a rippling mirror like they have in fun houses ... I couldn't tell if the monkeys were happy or sad, but they looked - worried, I thought ...

"No, Ifford. Bud juice. 'D' like in 'daddy.' It's this kind of concentrate of bud, this liquid concentrate - kind of an infusion, you know? If that's the word - that some friend of Honey's makes, and she - Honey, I mean - gave me some to try it - which I haven't yet. But she told me that it's very - well - psychedelic. But promise you'll never breathe a word about it to Silver, OK? He doesn't know that Honey occasionally smokes a little *bhang* to relax. He's so uptight about everything but *his* drug of choice, which is mostly vodka – and beer."

"Bud...?" What bearing have buds on monkeys? The girl was wandering. Oh, yes. We had been talking about that elixir of hers in the kitchen cupboard. The bug juice. So: she had after all said 'bud juice,' then. So. Bud. Unless it was the liquid essence of some fellow named

Bud, it was apparently something botanical that she was talking about. Buds, buds, buds. Buds are those little thingies that erupt on plants, in the springtime, aren't they? A plant extract, then? That sounded a little less alarming than the precious bodily fluids of denizens of the insect world.

"You know. Marijuana. Or, more like hashish. Very strong hashish."

"You - gave me a dollop of the juice of hashish buds in my cocoa? Is that what you're trying to tell me?"

"Something like it. Sort of a big dollop. I forgot it wasn't vanilla. Or almond extract. That's just what we call it. Sort of like a joke, you know? Bud juice? And actually the bottle kind of slipped and I poured in a bit more than I'd intended. But it was an accident, Ifford. And I'm sorry. Very, very sorry. I apologize. But it won't hurt you. It's all natural. And it will wear off. I promise. Please lean back and relax, Ifford."

"Oh. OK." And, feeling relieved to be able to postpone the tussle with the boots, I did so. Leaned back and relaxed, I mean. Whereupon that fat, cool piece of hardened macaroni that I held in my hand captured my attention again. "Look here, Glennie - I mean, Riqi - look at these little faces on this bead ..."

Those miserable little monkeys - what were they so concerned about, I wondered. Were they laboratory monkeys, and was their Dr. Mengele striding towards them, clipboard in hand, his white lab coat flapping about his knees and his fat peasant face wreathed in a smile of sadistic anticipation? Yes, those little simians looked distinctly more alarmed the longer I looked at them, and their being frightened - especially so very frightened - reminded me unpleasantly of all the things I had to be frightened about - of my Winstonish role in this sticky 1984ish waking nightmare into which I had blundered like a fly into a spider's web.

In short, I was feeling that old familiar gathering impending sense of doom, and a burgeoning need, really, and once again, to flee, to beat it, to make myself scarce, to vacate the premises - just on general principles, really - what with being a wanted entity - perhaps even a highly wanted entity - if for no other reason - when I felt something soft on my chin - under my chin.

337

Looking down, I saw that it seemed to be Riqi's hand. One of them. She lifted my chin gently, and turned my face towards hers. A bold lass, I thought. For all her diffident mannerisms, her 'sort of's' and 'you know's' and 'kind of's'... Our eyes met. Those sea-green eyes of hers. Another jolt passed through me, and I believe I oscillated a bit, like an aspic in a stiff breeze. And then she lowered her eyelids and sort of thrust her chin out and leaned forward and brushed her lips against mine, very lightly. It felt pretty good, and made me think that the monkeys might after all have been making mountains out of molehills. Monkeys do tend to be over-reactors, now that I thought about it - at least the lean, wiry, hyperactive sort of monkeys like these little fellows seemed to be.

"I'm so sorry, Ifford," she murmured, placing her cheek softly against mine, and putting her arms lightly around me - hesitantly, as though she half-expected me to rebuff her overture. "I hope you're not mad. Please tell me you're not mad at me. I wanted so much for you to like me - for us to be friends. And now I'm afraid I've ruined everything."

The whole experience was very disorienting, let me tell you, especially in my present, I suppose one could say, inebriated, four sheets to the wind condition, and I had the definite impression that I was fighting a loosing battle to stay in command of the situation. But on the other hand - did I need to stay in command of the situation? Squinch would doubtless have answered, yes, but I had after all cast the man and all he stood for boldly aside. A new Ifford was sailing in new waters - and, I mean - what was the harm in a - simple affectionate embrace among, or even better, between, friends? I mean - what are friends for? The girl certainly was friendly. And certainly I could not in all honesty say that it was unpleasant or in any way off-putting, sitting there in her gentle, tentative embrace - she did smell a bit milky, like a puppy, I remember noticing - and hearing her soft voice murmuring what I believe are called sweet nothings in my ear - something that no one had ever murmured in my ear before.

I mean, it distinctly seemed to me, as I struggled to interpret the augeries, that the girl was pretty much telling me that if I chose to press my suit, well, it was perfectly all right with her.

The puppy breath reminded me of that wolfhound that had been with her at The Silver Stud. Where was it now? But I decided the matter could wait.

338

CHAPTER 21: FALLING

I wonder what fool it was that first invented kissing.

Jonathan Swift

"Do you forgive me, Ifford? Do you forgive your naughty little girl? Tell me you do. Tell me you forgive naughty little me ... do you? Hmmm?"

All of this being delivered in a warm, breathy whisper right into my ear, very much *a la* Marilyn Monroe. I wondered if girls went to school to learn how to do these things, or if it pretty much came with the territory.

"Of course I do, Glennie. I mean Riqi," I murmured back. And indeed I did. In fact, I had pretty much forgotten what there was to forgive. That warm breath of hers against my ear made tingly feelings run across the skin on the back of my neck, and down my spine and - oh, just generally everywhere, to the best of my recollection. I had never felt anything quite like it, except in the closet that time with Glenda and

Gifford. Now, as then, it was wonderfully relaxing. I had the distinct impression that the purpose of life was finally standing up and declaring itself in language I could understand. Ambiguities and irresolution were dissolving like mist in sunshine, the whole process occurring pretty much at the speed of time-lapse photography.

"Yes, yes, yes," I affirmed jovially, generously. Removing all doubt, don't you know. Ifford the *preux chevalier* wanting to relieve the poor kid's mind. "Did anyone ever tell you that you smell milky - just like a puppy? Like a soft little puppy that's been lapping up hot chocolate ... that you're soft all over - at least, I'm assuming that it must be all over and everywhere ... this softness, I mean ... ubiquitous and all that ... just like a puppy is soft all over ... everywhere ..." God, what drivel I was talking, it seemed ...what absolute nonsense ...

"How do you know I'm soft ... everywhere?" And she punctuated this leading question by sticking the tip of her tongue right into my ear - very deftly, and very delicately. Sounds unsanitary, I know, but it felt wonderful, and I sat there just hoping that she'd do it again.

"Well ... I guess it's ... an assumption on my part, Glennie. Riqi. Just - judging from the look of you and all, don't you know..."

There was a pause here, during which we just sort of sat there, leaning against each other like a pair of windfall trees. After a moment she took one of my hands in hers and gently placed it on one of her breasts. She really did.

"Like - here?" she breathed. "Soft like this?"

It was soft. A soft and yet resilient little handful, with a most interesting heft and feel and a cheery, firm, rubbery something, a sort of intriguing be-all and end-all of some sort or other at its summit. I squeezed, gently. It yielded so nicely. So very nicely. I couldn't recall ever having felt anything quite like it. Except that once in the linen closet with Glenda and Gifford. I didn't really think about what I was doing, but just lifted up the other hand, to the twin hillock, and massaged it around a bit. Exerted a gentle exploratory pressure, you know.

"Mmmm," she murmured into my ear, with what seemed genuine pleasure - and with another moist little dart of her tongue against my ear, causing me to shiver in pleasure. "That feels nice, Ifford. So nice.

You have such nice hands - such long, slender, sensitive fingers ... you are an artist, you know. You do know that, don't you? Hmmm?"

I quite forgot my manners and left her question dangling in the warm humid air. Or rather, by way of answer I put my hand gently on her jaw, right about where it runs up to the plump juicy earlobe, and turned her head, and laid my slightly open lips on hers. And she - saucy wench! - stuck that little tongue-tip of hers right between my lips, causing all sorts of warm, cascading, sliding sensations in me - and causing me, rather to my own surprise, to meet her tongue with my own, right there on the threshold of my mouth, you might say - at my lips. Welcome to my castle. She was indeed - indeed - storming my castle. And all I wanted to do, with what I have heard referred to as every fiber of my being, was to aid and assist her in what seemed an entirely charitable undertaking. Or perhaps a mutually profitable joint venture. Certainly, a jolly good idea.

I will tell you candidly, dear Reader, that this was all unexplored territory for Yours Truly, self having, as outlined in the forgoing pages, led a life structured and sheltered in the extreme. My chaperones and then my programming, and what I had been led to believe to be my insuperable lukewarm genetic predisposition or fate, had combined to keep such experiences , such - opportunities, one might say - from me.

Perhaps it was the effect of the drug with which she had (I hoped inadvertently) dosed me - at any rate, I felt that I, despite my inherent disabilities, my disadvantaged childhood, and my under-privileged youth, was progressing with a marvelous rapidity in this new game of hers - that I possessed after all quite a natural talent for it, and that I had, in fact, finally found my calling in life - my *metier*, my niche, as it were. Do what you love and the money will follow - right? At last, at last I knew what I loved! My wanderings in the desert of indecision were over. Revelations of this nature were pretty much sweeping over me like waves over a windy beach at high tide. The general feeling-state and frame of mind could, had it or they been a painting, have been titled, I suppose, Tidal Wave of Euphoria. If not something even better. Inwardly, I was fairly shrieking 'Eureka-I-have-found-it!' It and her. The work and the love, by the gods, of my veritable life! She and I would carry on pretty much in this vein, on and on into the foreseeable future. No more nagging questions of what to do with my life. The way lay clear before me.

Her delightful little tongue, which seemed very sure of itself, as though it had been practicing this dance from the cradle, flitted playfully about on my lips and tongue as though playing some child's game, a kind of variant perhaps on hopscotch, while her hands began, the one to unbutton my shirt, and its mate to creep up underneath its hem. The touch of her fingers on my skin was such a relief - like something I had been needing, wishing for, without quite realizing it. I sighed deeply and pressed the tip of my tongue slowly, experimentally, luxuriantly, along the curve of her soft, yielding upper lip ... have I told you yet how full and soft her lips were, and of their natural dusky pink color and perfect Cupid's bow pout? ... this wondrous girl ... while my hand, one of them, moved slowly down, down her slender side, to her narrow waist and beyond, to stray then towards those ivory buttons which ran so coyly down the center of her innocent little girl's garment. She, rather than resisting, gave what sounded like a very happy little sigh and shifted her weight, arching her back and slightly thrusting her slim hips forward in a languorous, catlike movement while opening her golden knees just a little.

This was not the way I had been taught that good girls behaved; but there was no doubt whatever in my mind that I had been misled and misinformed - for here, under my hands, lay what I knew with a certainty to be the best girl that ever the Universe had, in all its endless eons and prodigal fruitfulness, thrown forth. My hand moved on down, down towards what seemed by way of being the softest, and certainly the most magnetic, of all her soft and mysterious places. I was overwhelmingly curious, desirous, to learn of it, of this place of legend, with all its plump smooth fissures - to learn as a blind man might, by feel.

Then without warning she tensed, put a staying hand on my wandering one, and sat bolt upright. Guiltily, and feeling more than a bit like a brutish molester of unwary girl-children, I hastened to withdraw the offending paw from her lap. Was I - diffident Ifford, the space-age Hamlet - cutting too quickly to the chase? Was her maidenly modesty belatedly sticking its head out of its foxhole to bleat a protest? An apology formed on my lips, but it remained unuttered. For as I raised my gaze from her lap upwards, her aspect, mien, countenance, attitude - or in the clinical and un-poetic language of our science-worshiping era, her body-language - told me that the problem was not one of outraged virtue. I saw that her fine features had arranged themselves like those of a mime or vaudevillian actor into an expression of concentrated attention to auditory cues, and her head was cocked in the age-old attitude of one who listens to, or for, small new sounds. Were she indeed treading the boards in the enactment of some Victorian melodrama, her next utterance would surely have been, 'Hark!' - which it in essence was.

"Listen!" she commanded. "Do you hear something?"

And indeed, dear Reader, I did; at first faint, but quickly growing louder - because nearer. It sounded chillingly like the heavy tramp tramp tramp of the black black boots of the Gestapo resolutely mounting those stairs leading up the back wall of the house to our little bower of bliss. Coming to get me, they were - and here sat I like a trapped animal. An inebriated, lust-besotted trapped animal, no less. Scorn would drip off Squinch like battery acid, would flash like laser beams from his piggy little eyes, burning holes deep into my cowering psyche. I would be maimed for life - whatever brief span of weeks, days, or hours the powers that be would see fit to grant me before tossing me into some black hole or other.

"Is there another way out of here?" I hissed urgently, cravenly, while resisting a sudden overwhelming need to relieve myself - fearing actually that I was, in spite of my desperately clenched sphincters, going to wet myself like an infant - my heart all the while hammering so hard and fast in my chest that I thought it must be causing my voice to shudder in time to its rapid thud-thud-thudding; foolishly, I glanced down at my chest, certain that my whole rib cage must be bulging ludicrously with each heartbeat like the thorax of some hapless cartoon character about to be torn limb from limb without benefit of anesthesia before being hurled into the Grand Canyon or off the Empire State Building by his snarling, hairy, muscle-bound nemesis.

Before Riqi could answer my piteous question, there came a sharp rap-rap-rapping at the door, whoever rapped using considerable unnecessary and excessive force and violence, in the opinion of Yours Truly, for the door fairly rattled on its hinges, and I feared the frosted glass windowpane mortared into its upper third would shatter and collapse to the floor like a sheet of ice struck with a rubber-sheathed mallet in some sort of classroom demonstration of the laws of physics. But then, that is ever the way of those overly enthusiastic brutes whose pleasure and prerogative it is gleefully to wield the police powers against the hapless citizenry. Gleeful, not to say orgasmic, overkill in the line of duty, you might say.

"Yes? Who is it?" called Riqi, in an undisturbed, even languid tone of voice at which I, in my state of near panic, could only marvel. The girl was either a superb actress, or genuinely unconcerned. But then, the Gestapo weren't after her; nor did the poor child know as yet that they were in hot pursuit of her paramour. For all she knew, I suppose it could have been a brawny, over-grown paperboy come to collect, or the iron-pumping Avon lady out trying to foist her wares off on the unwary in order to pay for another month of gym privileges or another week's supply of steroids. What I am getting at is that perhaps one (or more, for all I knew) of Riqi's circle frequently tramped up the steps like a herd of musk-oxen and routinely roughed up the door as if it had just stingingly insulted their entire matrilineal line of descent. Perhaps it was all *comme d'habitude* in her world. I was, after all, a stranger in a strange land. Faintly, roused by the total absence of alarm in my hostess's tone and manner, the hope stirred in your anti-hero's palpitating breast that he might, after all, not yet - not this go-round - be led off in manacles by horribly over-equipped, over-paid thugs to some state-of-the-art fate worse than death ingeniously contrived by the leading-edge high-IQ planners of the modern totalitarian universe-state.

"It's Silver, Angel. Who do ya think it is? The Pope? Open up, wench! You know you're not supposed to keep the door barred against me!"

The girl rolled her eyes heavenward and generally looked exceedingly exasperated - her whole manner expressing not so much alarm, or terror, as: here-we-go-again.

"Ifford," she whispered, bestowing a quick, reassuring kiss on my cheek, "I think if you don't mind you'd better just hide in the bedroom closet if it's all the same to you. If you wouldn't mind too much - Sweetums." (Sweetums!!! That was encouraging! This girl definitely had a knack for saying the right thing at the right time.)

"Silver is, you know, just this very, very *bossy* guy, who thinks he has the right to run my life just because he's practically married to my sister and is my employer and all. It'd just be easier all around if he didn't know you were here with me. It'd be better if I could bring you to dinner some evening first. He has such old-fashioned ideas about things. C'mon - we'd better hurry - in here."

The door trembled again beneath the fellow's fist; she grabbed my hand and half-led, half-dragged me - the girl was stronger than she looked - into her bedroom; and a small but cozy burrow it was, I noticed, with the commodious double (or perhaps even triple!) bed occupying most of the floor space, topped with an ivory-colored, cotton-covered down comforter and heaped at its head with what looked like a small truckload of fat down pillows in lacey off-white cotton cases. Although I was propelled through it at a pretty high velocity, I observed approvingly before I was whisked into the closet that the room's small size had the effect of making one feel enclosed and protected, with any tendency towards claustrophobia being relieved by two tall, narrow, old-fashioned, side-by-side windows which extended from about knee-height to well above one's head and which gave onto a beautiful dark expanse of snow-dusted park just across the street, behind which stretched the long curve of one of the hills of the city, laced and strewn as for some festive occasion with garlands and clusters of tiny, sleepily-twinkling yellowish lights. Riqi stuffed me rather unceremoniously into the large walk-in closet which opened off the wall opposite the windows, put a cautionary finger to her lips to enjoin me to silence, pulled the closet door shut, and, I presumed, left the bedroom.

I believe I have mentioned previously my tendency towards claustrophobia. Being thus afflicted, it was not really possible for me to remain in that pitch-black closet with the door pulled completely shut, half-smothered as I already felt by an extensive feminine wardrobe which pressed in on me seemingly from all sides - and which, as in a Disney cartoon, seemed, like some living, breathing thing, to sidle ever closer - to be moving stealthily in for the kill, as it were. In light of which, it was necessary for me to open the door a crack - which I did forthwith, and which enabled me to hear the lively conversation which ensued out in the living room of Riqi's flat.

CHAPTER 22: RIQI HANDLES THINGS

We shall not cease from exploration ...

T.S. Eliot

"What were you doing in there - my little angelic one? Why did it take you so long to answer the door, anyway? Is someone in there with you? And what's that I smell - beneath the incense, I mean of course - you haven't by any chance been blowing weed again, have you?"

This Silver - for I assumed it to be he who spoke - seemed to be one who believed in wasting little time in pleasantries or preliminaries. Generally I try to follow the old aphorism which enjoins against judging a book by its cover, but perhaps the new Ifford was a more decisive chap and altogether more the man of action. At any rate, I found myself heartily disliking this fellow upon whom I had yet to lay eyes and whom I, properly speaking, and except by reputation, you might say, did not even know. My impulse, which I had to check sternly, was to bound forth and tell him in no uncertain terms to watch himself when addressing a lady. What right had the brute to speak so roughly to gentle Riqi, a fair and blameless damsel if ever I saw one? In the dark of that closet, which smelled faintly of lavender and rose, I asked myself this rather rhetorical question with considerable intensity of feeling, more or less gnashing the teeth in what I have heard referred to as impotent rage, while the blood surged hotly in my veins and the temples throbbed. Indeed, this new Ifford was quite a fellow, I could not help observing to myself admiringly in sort of an inter-office memo, or what is more commonly referred to according to the conventions of literature and the theatre as an aside.

But now it was apparently, according to the rules of engagement, Riqi's turn to hold forth, and she showed herself to be fully capable of defending herself.

"Lay off, Silver! Just lay off! First of all, I am not yours! And second of all, the answer to all of the above is, none of your business. None of your effing business! What I do on my own time in my own private life is absolutely, and I hope this is the last time I have to tell you this, none ... of .... your ... business. Got that? You're my boss. Remember? Just

346

my boss. My employer, that is. And my business manager. Not my father. Not my keeper. Not my big brother. Not my probation officer.

"As it so happens, I am not entertaining a visitor this evening, but if I were it would be no concern of yours. No concern what ... so ... ever - of yours. And if I want to enjoy a little herb every now and then I'm going to and I'd like to see you or anyone else try and stop me! I happen to believe it's good for me, regardless of what you think - you and all that beer and vodka-and-seven you belt down in front of the tube every evening. Don't think I don't know about that. You're a holier-than-thou hypocrite - admit it! And beer is fattening, and all that Seven-Up is just sugar and chemicals, just empty calories, and the vodka's highly processed, and addicting, which *bhang* is not."

Here she paused for a second or two, and I thought her, having pretty well covered all the bases, to have retired, with perhaps a triumphal flounce of her petticoats, from the podium; but as it turned out I had, due to not yet knowing of her thorough and methodical nature when it came to these periodic hashings-out of differences with Silver, miscalculated: for in actuality, she was merely taking in a lungful or two of air preparatory to expostulating on one final matter.

"And - who is this - this guy - you've brought into my apartment at this late hour - into my place, for which I pay rent - without even asking me if it's OK or if I'm dressed to receive visitors - which as you see I'm not (though she had quickly donned the chenille robe before dragging me into the closet) - and it is late, in case you hadn't noticed. I mean, you could have used the telephone, instead of barging on up here unannounced at this hour."

The girl appeared, I noted with the awe and wonderment of all explorers and discoverers of new continents, to be multi-faceted, multi-talented, and, under provocation, like a mother grizzly apprised of the presence of an intruder in her domain, and definitely of the school which holds that the best defense is a good offense. I was deeply impressed by the vigor, skill, and audacity with which she pressed her case, and made a mental note never, if possible, to rub the girl the wrong way. Had I been this Silver fellow I would have crumbled like a cookie underfoot and lost no time backing out the door hat in hand while mumbling my sincerest apologies and assuring the girl that the bill for the damages could be sent to me and would promptly be taken care of in full.

But he, like she, seemed to be made of the sterner stuff. They appeared to be well-matched as combatants. Unfazed and undaunted, his head perhaps a bit bruised if not bloodied, but definitely, judging from his next bit if dialogue, unbowed, he continued on in attack mode. But what issued from his mouth stunned me to the max, causing the head to reel and the senses to swim. The knees, moreover, quivered like jelly, and, being overcome all at once with a distinct shortness of breath, and what with the general sort of quavering or swimming sensation in the old field of vision, and the ringing in the ears, I had to lean against the door-jam to steady myself.

"That's all very well and good and fine-sounding, Angel, but if you know what's good for you, you won't forget which side your bread is buttered on. You've got a pretty soft deal going and you know it. I treat you pretty damn good. That rent you pay is a fraction of what this place is worth in the rental market today, in case you haven't checked the going rates lately. You're not of legal age yet, and somebody with some common sense has got to look after you. So don't start going all high and mighty on me. It won't get you anywhere at all.

"As for this - guest - to whom, I might add, you've been so rude - he happens to be a friend of mine, who's here for good reason - an engineering student at the university, by name, Rantor ..."

Rantor!?! Surely mine ears deceived me! Or, surely if Rantor it was, then it was not - could not be - my Rantor- the one and only ... but the salutation which rumbled forth over the air waves was, alas, unmistakably delivered in the deep growling tones - aren't such low-octave vocal ranges always referred to as 'stentorian' by the literati? - in the excessively, annoyingly stentorian voice of my former room-mate, and it seemed, self-appointed nemesis.

Rantor? - here? Was I never, then, to be quit of this fellow? Was it his plan, then, to dog my heels even unto the portals of heaven or the bowels of Hades? Whichever came first? I mean - whose payroll was the fellow on, for Christ's bloody sake? I mean, pardon my French, but I felt positively hounded. Positively hounded and pursued, dear Reader, by this reptilian hound of hell, and it was all I could do to swallow the howl of anguish which arose in my throat. It was only by dint of my summoning the superb self-control and steely resolve for which we hybrids are renowned more or less throughout this galaxy that I was able to prevent myself from sliding slowly down the closet wall in a

348

gesture of defeat and submission to those higher powers which seemed determined to have their way with me in this matter of the lizard.

"How do you do, Mr. Rantor," I heard Riqi say in calmer tones. "I apologize for being rude, if I was - though it's actually my - my brother-in-law here who's the rude one, always treating me as if I were some - some possession of his, with no right to privacy or a life of my own. If I'm old enough to be supporting myself, then I'm old enough not to be bossed around by some guy who thinks he's my father or something. It seems to me that that should be obvious to anyone with a room temperature IQ - don't you think?"

"Well, uh, my, um, lack of experience in these matters pretty much leaves me without an opinion, I guess." (Egad! - Some semblance of tact, of discretion, - from Rantor? - the old boy had been holding out on me. Or, more likely, didn't consider me worth the effort. Whatever the explanation, it just went to show that truth really is stranger than fiction. And that one just never, never knows - does one?)

"I am sorry - I mean, I owe you an apology for having come up here so late," Rantor went on. "But I have a problem that - well, that Silver and I thought you might be able to help me with."

"Hmmmm?" Cooly. As in, this better be good. Putting the damper on the *bonhomie*.

"It's that a friend of mine is missing, you see, and we're kind of worried about him. You see, he's someone who's been under quite a lot of stress lately..."

Oh, if there be a God, just shut this reptile up, now, please. Just - stuff it, you stupid blundering lizard. What embarrassing facts was the idiot about to blurt out to this - I hoped, future helpmeet and life's companion of mine? I wasn't ready for her to know everything about me - not just yet. Her good opinion - certainly, her admiration, and her tender feelings - of and for me could not, I suspected, withstand full disclosure of all the facts just yet, in this fragile nascent stage of our perpetual union. Some things have to be led up to. And anyway, since I was such a changed man, or at any rate, being, and undergoing further metamorphosis at so rapid a rate, why perhaps some things would simply never have to be gone into at all. I feared that in order to shut the fellow up I might have to drop my cover and shoot out instanter into the fray, but fortunately, at this point, and before the reptile could go into the full account of why his missing friend was so sorrowful and stressed out, Riqi spoke.

"OK, well, I'm sorry to hear that about your friend - but - what's it got to do with me?"

"When Ifford - that's his name, Ifford - when he didn't turn up at his room, after he parted from me in a pretty agitated state this afternoon, and as it got later and later [lying in wait for me at my rooming house, for crying out loud!] I was worried about him and went out looking for him, at places where I though he might be, like the coffee houses in the U. District, and I made inquiry, you know, and they told me at The Stud that someone of his description had been seen leaving there with someone of your description ..."

"And," Silver put in, "Since they all know who you are, naturally, at the coffee house - my old lady's kid sister - and since Rantor and I know each other through mutual friends and discussion groups ..."

"Well - here we are," concluded Rantor. "We just wondered if you did see him at The Stud, you know - kind of a pale, thin guy with a large-ish head and big eyes - actually, when last seen he was wearing dark glasses, the wrap-around mirror kind, and a floppy hat, and combat boots - we were wondering if maybe he did come over here to your place with you - since it is pretty cold out there, and he's not at home, and I've already called around and asked at the other places he could be, like at his girlfriend's ..."

I wanted to throttle him, naturally. Now, at very least, I would have the job of explaining somehow that mention of a girlfriend to Riqi; I feared I would have to emerge from my closet, just to shut the fellow up before he did more damage - but before I took that fatal step, Riqi spoke up.

"Well, as a matter of fact, I did meet and talk with someone of that description at The Stud tonight. And it's true - we did leave together. But he didn't come home with me. I invited him up for a cup of cocoa, but he said he had somewhere else he had to be, and he only walked as far as the corner with me. So, I'm sorry, but I can't help you. I wouldn't worry about him all that much if I were you, though. He seemed in a pretty good mood when I was with him, and he said he was expected at a friend's house near-by where he planned, since it was already so late and, like you say, so cold out, just to crash for the night."

Bless you, my child. Bless you. As the reader might imagine, I was at this juncture more or less melting, like a cube of butter in a saucepan on the stove, with gratitude and relief. I had not relished the prospect of stepping forth to engage in repartee with the formidable lizard or the redoubtable Silver O'Shea. Especially when dealing with alpha male specimens such as comprised this duo, discretion had always seemed to me to be distinctly the better part of valor, just as the Bard had some one or other of his characters wisely observe so long ago. Some things seem to remain constant down the gleaming procession of light years and under the countless burning suns.

Well. I had to hand it to the girl - in addition to comeliness and an artistic temperament, she had aplomb. Loads of it. And she could think on her feet. Although young in years and seemingly to have been given the short end of the stick when it came to formal schooling, the girl appeared to possess that priceless and endlessly useful art, knack, or gift which Yours Truly despaired of ever acquiring - namely: street-smarts. And people-smarts. And the ability to think on her feet. Perhaps that makes three knacks.

"So," she continued, clearly intent on wrapping things up and putting them to bed for the evening, "Beyond that I'm afraid I can't help you in locating your friend. If I see him around, I'll be sure to tell him you're looking for him. So now, since it's late and everything, and since I do have to work tomorrow - don't I, Silver? - I'd ask you to stay and have a cup of cocoa to warm up, Mr. Rantor, but I'm sure your friend Mr. O'Shea can do all that for you at his place downstairs ..."

Well - what could the two visitors do? Their hostess had made it clear that their small bit of welcome had been all used up and that their account was now in the red. In all likelihood, her story left them not totally convinced. But what could they do about it? It seemed they had been finessed. Short of calling her bluff and forcibly invading the girl's sanctum and conducting a search of her premises, they were conspicuously short of options. And Silver seemed unwilling, when it came right down to it, to trespass so egregiously against propriety, and against this mere slip of a girl, whom he must have outweighed, judging by his deep baritone and general ambiance, by a good sixty or seventy pounds. Perhaps he was one of those who bluster and threaten but do not strike - whose bark is worse than his bite. Riqi, though incensed, had not seemed actually to fear the fellow.

351

In fact now that I thought about it, their verbal battle had had overtones suggestive of the whole thing's being a kind of sport or romp in which the two engaged frequently and with a sort of pleasure, not to say positive glee. Some friends get together for a cup of tea and a good bit of gossip, after all, and some for a nice invigorating session of thrust-and-parry to clear the head and get the blood circulating vigorously - some enduring marriages consisting, from what I have gathered, of little more than one episode after another of such lusty engagements. Perhaps Riqi and Silver felt a certain mutual attraction and worked it off in this manner. It was something to keep in mind, certainly - but for now I felt only relief as I heard the door close on the testosterone twins.

As the reader can well imagine, I was, upon emerging from the boudoir, loud in my praise of how Riqi had handled the threat, at how inspired had been her invention, and at how skillfully and loyally she had prevaricated on my behalf. And she - sweet, sweet girl that she was - never once asked me about this girlfriend that Rantor had made mention of.

As though it were the most natural thing in the world and indeed the established custom between us, we adjourned together to that large bed in the small cozy room and spent the night there together. I am sorry to have to draw the veil of modesty over what happened in that large bed as the evening wore on and one thing led to another, but I am just not one of those chappies who can tell all. Some things are personal in my book and that is that. Suffice it to say that Riqi went all out to make me feel welcome and that I took full advantage of her delightfully generous and loving spirit - as well as her - shall I say, expertise, in some areas. The girl was wise beyond her years in more ways than one, a fact upon the implications of which I expeditiously decided not to dwell. She was, after all, young, and had perhaps made unwise decisions, been led down some garden paths and drawn into imprudent *liasons* in the past - when she was much too young to have known better. But that was then and this was now. Right? And I reasoned that I was certain to have a salutary influence on the old girl's stance *vis a vis* entities - as in, all other entities - of the male persuasion - or so, at any rate, I reasoned then, in what could I suppose be called the rosy glow of passion fulfilled. But I am getting ahead of my story.

I might just say in passing that I began on that night to accumulate - or would *le mot juste* be 'adduce'? - evidence that we hybrids - some lineages, anyway - are not so totally lacking in passion and feeling as our institutional duennas would have us believe. The old self-confidence received a powerful shot in the arm that night, likewise the sense of general well-being and the theory that all is, after all, at least in some nooks, crannies, and intervals of the space-time continuum, right with the worlds, and I slept, finally, more soundly and sweetly than I had in months - nay, years - in the arms of the sweetest girl in the world. And although much has changed, since those golden hours, I still believe that, in some senses of the phrase, to be entirely true. The girl had - and has - the proverbial heart of gold - and many other absolutely lustrous and, as it were, honey-dipped, aspects to her being. And here, dear Reader, with many apologies, I shall have to draw the veil of proper modesty, as per the teachings of the old caregivers back on the home planet, who always averred that some private experiences are not suitable for general consumption.

CHAPTER 23: A PROPHETIC DREAM?

The subconscious has its automatic or hypnotic levels, but it
also contains the seeds of freedom: dreams.

Preston Nichols and Peter Moon

Though I slept like a god, nevertheless I awoke in the gray half-light of
early dawn like a mortal, with a start of anxiety, thinking for one awful
moment that I had overslept, that I had an early class, the dreaded
Fundamentals of Earthly Banking, and that I was going to be late for it.
Squinch leapt into the mind's eye so vivid and life-like - though that
word when applied to him seems a bit oxymoronic - but at any rate the
horrific vision was more awful and convincing than a 3-D version of
The Creature from the Black Lagoon - the part towards the end, you
know, where the thing finally emerges from the dark slime and stands
there hunched over and dripping, all absolutely inky dark and seeming
to exert a strong gravitational pull like one of those black holes to
which we are cautioned to give so wide a berth in our interstellar
travels, dark as the pit of hell except for those horrible, preternaturally
glowing eyes which glowered, of course, right at one as though he
knew and had been seeking one out down the corridors of time to settle
some ancient, perhaps ancestral, score, the whole phantasmagoric
interlude causing the old ticker to thud and skid wildly for a bit in the
thorax and sensations of heat and ice to dart like silverfish amidst the
old entrails. I writhed around a bit, half sitting up in an effort to
discover the time.

But the sitting up had been done only in the inner realm - one of those
false-awakening lucid dreams that I get on occasion, particularly when
oppressed by worry. With effort, I broke the bonds of sleep, opened my
eyes, and realized with immense relief where I was - though the feeling
that I had just missed being torn limb from limb by some pursuing
avenger or bounty hunter faded only gradually. Bit by bit, as I looked
about, and saw the frost-rimed branches of the trees in the park across
the street looking absolutely poetic in the early dawn, with a winter
mist suspended in utter stillness about them, my muscles relaxed as
though immersed in a hot-tub, and I stretched rather luxuriously and
turned my head to see Riqi sleeping peacefully beside me, a half-smile
on her lips and her lovely mottled blonde hair in a soft delightful

tangle, like the hair of some tawny mythic goddess napping on a cloud. I have mentioned - I know I must have - how lovely her skin was - honey-colored in places and sort of like milk in others, where the sun never reached, and with a slight translucence, and a few freckles across her cheeks and the bridge of her nose, like a faint spray flicked off the fingertips of a playful god, and this most beautiful, indescribable pale pinkish color on her lips, her cheeks, her perfect little nipples ... as I lay drinking her in, suddenly I thought with another start of Humphrey, for some reason. He could not be left alone too long, or he would run out of food and water. Although I had no desire at all to return, ever, to that little slant-roofed room wherein he toiled nightly on his creaking wheel, doomed like all his race, perhaps for some ancestral transgression against the dictates and general game-plan of the great Hamster in the sky, to run and run and run, he knew not why or whither.

Then it came to me - perhaps it was thinking of ultimate things that did it - I remembered that in the night I had had a dream, and that it had seemed, to my sleeping self, to be the solution to all my seemingly insoluble problems. I remember waking once briefly to a feeling almost akin to elation, only to settle immediately back into a sort of deep and rapturous slumber. The trouble was, I could not now quite recall the dream itself. It hovered tantalizingly on the threshold of memory. What had it even been about? I knew that if I could remember a bit of it, a scene or episode, a character or prop or the locale - some bit of the *mis en scene* - that the whole thing would probably come flooding back to me. What had it been? I made my mind blank and told myself I would remember. Nothing. I counted backwards from ten to one after telling myself that at zero I would remember the dream - but, no dice. I rolled over, back into the fetal position from which I had awakened, and relaxed all my muscles and let my mind go blank. Still nothing. Speak, memory, I commanded - the new Ifford, you know, who commands rather than implores - but still my mind remained a maddeningly inscrutable blank.

Then Riqi stirred, and in a sleepy voice asked, "What time is your appointment?"

"What appointment?" I asked, feeling a twinge of annoyance at being interrupted in this important task of recall - I mean, the solution to all my problems, don't you know.

"Mmmm," she murmured, not really awake. "You told me ... just before we went to sleep ... you have to meet someone ... this afternoon,

I think ... some guy who's doing some experiment, that you can help out ...? That guy who looks like a toad, I think ... he was going to pay you something ... so we could go out to dinner tonight, maybe ... at that Lebanese place I told you about ... that has the good baba ganooj and hummus ..." And then she seemed to drift back off into sleep.

A-ha! That did it. The old girl had triggered my memory, and the dream came flooding back to me. It had been about Riggs - about that time-travel or remote viewing experimentation of his, in which the reader will recall I had been enlisted due, it seems, to my imaginative gifts. Although I still felt that they were totally wrong on that score; but who was I, in my present state of need, to turn down an offer of gainful under-the-table employment. Yes! I had dreamed that I had kept the appointment, but that instead of going back to the '30s or to 1910 or '13 or whenever it was they were interested in, I had gone back to the '50s, and it had been great - just as great as Glennie and I had always thought it would be ... every bit as wonderful. The dream had been in black and white, just like all the old TV shows were - and I had been in some '50s-ish sort of house, with an upstairs and a downstairs and a porch and a lawn, sitting on a tree-lined street ... and I had a wife, or maybe it was a sister, who, quite frankly, was a sort of blend of Glennie and Riqi - to be honest she had seemed to be now one and now the other and then sometimes sort of six of one and half-dozen of the other. You know how dreams are.

This, I will admit, made me feel rather guilty - sort of disloyal to both of them, in a way - and as I remembered that dear girl in the dream - for I had loved her very much (and she had not been a sister), far more than as a hybrid I had imagined I could ever love anyone - I began to realize anew, and more poignantly than ever - sort of sickeningly , in fact - the downside of feelings - the pain of having them, I mean, and their frightening uncontrollability - and I realized in a flash - a rather paradoxically enjoyable little burst of insight incongruously surfacing in the midst of all that anguish - that they - feelings, I mean - are sort of like the cosmos itself, inscrutable and seemingly uncontrollable – but at times, absolutely topping, you know ... but anyway, the main thing I am trying to get across is that that damnable pain came back - and I writhed under it and wished it away with all the force of my being - and we hybrids do have our steely side, you know - but it was useless, and I felt again that horrible, almost unbearable pain of the loss of Glennie. My Glennie. I did not even know right then where she was, what she was doing, if she was all right ... and it made me feel for a moment sort of panicky, like I needed to run right out and make sure she was OK -

but anyway, the main thing right now, the gist, nub, or essence of this dream, the element most germane to my current seemingly unresolvable quandry, is, that I did not go back there, to the '50s I mean, just in my mind, as happened in that failed attempt up in Torvald's lab ... no, I - we - went back in the flesh - and we did not return! I remember quite clearly in the dream thinking - and saying to her, too - this is great, I love this, we are not going back - not ever ...

CHAPTER 24: THE MORNING AFTER

Reality is that which, when you stop believing in it,
doesn't go away.

Phillip K. Dick

I had covered a lot of ground emotionally since waking up just a few minutes ago, and I was feeling inwardly a bit tattered by it all. I lay there in bed, feeling both excited and keyed up and even euphoric and at the same time a bit drained - the way you can feel when you are tired but keep drinking coffee, trying to stay awake to cram for a test or write in one fell swoop a twelve page term paper assigned weeks ago and due the next morning. I have always likened that over-caffeinated sensation to what it must be like to have teams of tiny football players running and scrimmaging and passing and receiving and blocking and intercepting and tackling, and whatever else it is they do, in that rough and heedless way of theirs, all over one's nerves and ganglia in their little cleated football shoes.

In some novel by Henry James, I think it was, which I remember reading for some required lit. class - so much in life is required, isn't it, one way or another? - anyway, I remember one of his characters making a remark to the effect that there are two sorts of people in life - those who take things hard and those who take things easy - and when I read that I thought, exactly! or words to that effect, and knew I was one of those who take things hard and on the spot I made a resolve to try to take things easier. I even used affirmations to that effect - 'I take things easy now,' 'Every day in every way things are getting easier and easier for me now,' etc. I kept it up for a week or two after this minor epiphany, until I sort of forgot to keep on affirming and also started feeling sillier and sillier, and less and less convincing, talking to myself in those falsely cheery tones, saying things I did not really believe, and for which not a shred of evidence existed, and also, I just kept on taking things the same old way. Though it is possible that I didn't keep at it long enough to alter the ineffable determiners and parameters of what is called the real, something which the self-help books, which I confess having in my various fits of desperation from time to time consulted, stoutly affirm can be done - this re-shaping, that is to say, of what life, the Universe, and everything dishes out to one - but these books do caution that this new deal which one can allegedly wrangle out of the inscrutable infinite doesn't happen overnight.

You know, when I think about it, it just doesn't seem fair and never has, that I feel all the pain of life with ultra-intensity and spend much of my waking (and even dreaming!) life steeping in one or another of the many soupy permutations of dread, but that the intenser pleasures of life have been for the most part things I only hear about second-hand - rumors, as it were. Dim vistas, fabled lands, late-night TV shows. Except for last night, I reminded myself. Except for last night. Perhaps the worm is turning and a glorious new chapter just commencing, in the life of old Ifford C. I had, after all become quite a different entity of late, altogether more manly and decisive, and perhaps my fate even now, governed by those unwritten and only hazily perceived laws of the universe, was re-arranging itself accordingly.

And with that positive thought I yanked myself out of my gloomy musings, speaking to self kindly but sternly as the old caretakers always used to at the various nurturing institutes and reminding self that we hybrids are - or in my case, were - prone to self-pity and also to self-indulgent introspection and useless metaphysical musings and that we must just realize that and remember to distance ourselves from those futile pathways of thought as no good comes from them. I mean - the collective good is not advanced one iota by such things, and they are an inefficient use of time.

And furthermore - here, in my dream and hot off the press, I had just had offered to me - gratis - what seemed or could be considered a no strings attached gift from the gods - verily! - a way out of all my problems, a viable solution to all this *Schmertz* and *Angst* and *Sturm* and *Drang*. Yet here I had been lying limply like a boned and filleted luncheon entree musing sorrowfully about life.

Just then I heard what sounded like a rap on the door, and I stiffened and lay as alert as a wild beast, listening. Surely I had been mistaken. But no - I heard it again - a gentle but determined knock-knock-knocking out there on the kitchen door - its diffidence giving me cause to hope at least that it was not Silver and Rantor come back for round two. Due no doubt to the particularly keen auditory senses for which we hybrids are well-known virtually everywhere, I even heard the door rattling with a sort of vibrato effect in its casement, and the totally irrelevant thought flitted through my mind that this drafty and high-ceilinged old house must be expensive to heat in winter, and that perhaps that fact had materially contributed to Silver's surly attitude towards Riqi last night, since he seemed to be the one footing the heating and utility bills. Perhaps he was a different man altogether in the summer, if not absolutely full then at least partaking somewhat of *bonhomie*, geniality, and love of all mankind and perhaps even sentient beings generally (in which case, you know, there would be hope for Yours Truly).

"Riqi!" I hissed. I mean, I hated to rouse the old girl from her sweet slumbers into the bleak morning light of the real world, as it is called (one can always hope, erroneously) - but I myself, being only a guest in this house of (from some points of view) illicit love, and a wanted entity to boot, and furthermore not wearing a stitch of clothing - could hardly go out there and deal with this impending doom or wolf at the door, or whatever it was - could I?

CHAPTER 25: ANOTHER VISITOR

Like everybody who is not in love, he thought one chose
the person to be loved after endless deliberations and
on the basis of particular qualities or advantages.

Marcel Proust

"Riqi! Wake up, Sweetest! I think there's someone at the door!"

She seemed to be soundly sleeping and absolutely not to be hearing me,
so I gently shook her shoulder and whispered her name urgently a
couple more times, and at this she stirred and her eyelids fluttered, and
as if on cue, there came another episode of rapping at the door.
Whoever it was gave the impression of fully intending to wait out there,
rapping away every so often, for however long it took.

"The door. There's someone there. Do you think you'd ought to answer
it? Are you expecting anyone - or what?"

"Oh, I'd better get it, I guess," she murmured sleepily. "At least it's not
Silver - he never knocks as quietly as that." She got out of bed and put
on her robin's egg blue chenille wrapper, and some fuzzy soft gray
bunny slippers made of what looked like real rabbit fur, and went on
out.

Just to be on the safe side, I hopped out of bed and hurriedly began to
dress, wishing that I had fresh clothes - and some of my own clothes,
instead of these secondhand things with the holes in the knees. Then I
stepped into the closet, just feeling instinctively, like a hunted animal,
the need to take cover, to be prepared for the worst. I mean, what if it
were the U.N. Gestapo come to assist in my suctioning back to the
home planet? Surveillance these days is just so state-of-the-art, and of
course they don't let us know all their capabilities in these areas. Not
by a long shot. They keep us guessing. They could know exactly where
I was, could have known all along, with those satellites and cameras
and sensors of theirs and whatnot. And then to make matters worse, it
came back to me with a surge of what felt again like panic or one of its
near relations - I remembered Glennie telling me once between slurps
of shake and bites of Giganto-Burger that Jacko had told her that the
U.N. police usually come to pick up felons and dissidents from their

lairs and hide-outs and so on at just about this time, the early early morn, because people tend to be home then, and still asleep, and because it was deeply emotionally upsetting to their intended target and put him at a strong psychological disadvantage. And how! I thought feelingly. But now I was beginning to sound like Rantor and Torvald, wasn't I. But, I mean, could you blame me? At any rate, the long and the short of it was that I felt trapped. Trapped and doomed. Oh, how I hated life, positively hated it! Why was I ever artificially conceived and gestated? Why? There was no way out of this flat save that single door which was even now being rapped upon. None, at least, that I knew of.

Over the pounding of blood in my veins, my own ragged, shaking breath, and that unpleasant continuous high ringing sound, just like an emergency alarm bell, shrieking in my ears, I heard Riqi's voice: "Just a minute, please, I'm coming..." ... then a cautious "Who is it?" And then the sound of the door opening and some murmuring that I couldn't understand, because I was in the closet, and because the voices were so low - except that it did seem that both of the voices were female, which caused me to feel some relief, and abatement of the symptoms of acute distress. If it was only a female, one solitary female, well then probably it wouldn't be the Gestapo ... and it couldn't be Rantor and/or Silver. Perhaps it was - I don't know, some neighbor come to ask for a smidgen of bud-juice to enhance the jolt of the morning coffee, some friend returning a borrowed hookah ... some co-worker come to borrow a g-string, pasties, and a few ostrich feathers - but whoever it was, it was, blessedly, female; and women, and especially solitary and unaccompanied women, just generally, in my experience, seem less often to be the harbingers of doom - of totalitarian police-state doom, at any rate - than men, especially groups or gangs of men.

If my nurturers had really wanted to give me some good practical advice that would have been helpful to me in life, I thought bitterly, they would have counseled me to beware of gangs of men, especially gangs of men in suits or in uniforms, men in or from offices and who claim to represent truth and justice and law and order, to be from the government and here to help.

But really - under all this pressure I was doing that chameleon-like blending in again, was sounding again just like those - those conspiracy theorists who had gotten me into all this mess, and a conspiracy theorist is that which I was not, am not, have never been, and will never be. Politics is admittedly distasteful to me. It is dirty and ugly, and it is beneath me. That is how I have always felt, when it came right down to it. The thought of the '50s came to me again - a haven from all this. Back then no one had even heard of a conspiracy theorist and everyone believed in government. That was the world for me!

"Ifford?" in a sort of a whisper, you know. Riqi's voice, so I felt that it was safe to answer.

"Yes?"

"I think you'd better come on out. I think it's safe and all. It's someone who says she wants to see you."

"See me?"

"Yes. She says she just wants to talk a little bit with you, that it won't take long. Oh, she says to tell you that she brought you a clean change of clothes and that she fed and watered Humphrey for you."

"Who is it?" I asked - but I was pretty sure I knew the answer to that question, so I suppose my question was one of those time-buying rhetorical jobbies.

"She says that you'll know who she is. Her name is Glennie."

CHAPTER 26: TWO GIRLS

Life is the farce which everyone has to perform.

Arthur Rimbaud

At this announcement I had, as the reader might suppose, what are generally referred to as mixed feelings. Very mixed, and very many. I won't go into them all here as to do so would impede the flow of the narrative and, anyway, I imagine that said gentle reader can inventory them all pretty much as well as could I. Essentially, and as so often happens in life, I was of two, or at least two, minds. Part of me wanted to see the old girl - indeed, to rush gladly into her arms - and part of me didn't.

"Ifford?" That would be Riqi again. Still standing there, it seemed, her head poked around the bedroom door, with a sort of goggle-eyed questioning look on her divine countenance, as in - Hello-o? She seemed to be implying that the ball was in my court.

"Yes?"

"She's waiting to see you. She looks nice. Aren't you going to come on out and talk to her? I wouldn't feel right, telling her to go away."

"Just a minute. There's one thing I'm wondering about." Something had occurred to me. That questing hybrid intellect, you know, never off-duty for an instant.

"What's that?"

"Just one little matter that needs clearing up. How does the old girl know I'm here? Last night the word was put out that I am not now and have never been. On these premises, I mean. So, what gives? What brings her 'round here, sniffing at this door?"

"She explained that. She really does seem very nice, Ifford. And such beautiful eyes. But anyway, it seems that your large friend - the one with the tail, you know - well, he noticed your boots lying there on the floor by the futon. And your vest too, I guess. When he and Silver were here last night."

"He did? And he didn't say anything at the time?" This sounded so very out of character for that outstandingly impulsive and unstable force of nature as to strain the bounds of credulity. "I can hardly credit that ..."

"Well, she - Glennie - says that he knew you were here and he figured you were OK - safe and all - and he didn't want to embarrass me in front of Silver by drawing any attention to your boots - so he just didn't say anything. Are you coming out, or not? She must be wondering what's taking so long."

It seemed I had no choice.

"Well ... all right. But could you just ... bring me a comb? My hair must be a mess."

"You look fine, actually. I like your hair when it's sort of messed up like that. It looks so natural. But there's a brush right there on my nightstand, if you want to use it."

Which I did; and then, having absolutely used up all the delaying tactics that had occurred to me, I squared the shoulders, took a deep breath, thought a positive thought or two about how great everything was, had been, and would be, and, after running the brush through my hair and taking a quick glance at myself in the mirror, exited my sanctuary, moving a bit unsteadily, but under my own steam. We hybrids can, when called upon to do so, bite the bullet with the best of them.

"What-ho, Glennie. Fancy meeting you here." I had decided on that long, long trip from bedroom to the rest of the place - aside from the small bedroom and bath, and, as I say, that long, long hallway, it was all just one room, to wit, kitchen alcove, dining nook, and living room - I had decided that the best tone to take, all things considered, was the cavalier, man-of-the-world tone of the cosmopolite man-of-action to whom all of this was more or less just routine. Actually - although I am bored by those mindless and formulaic films, reducing as they do to little more than glamorous people, special effects, nifty tricks, and endless highly imaginative brutality - James Bond came to mind, as played by Sean Connery, who one has to admit is an absolute knock-out - when viewed, of course, from the feminine perspective - and the very archetype of the wordly, intellectual *Homo sapiens* alpha male.

I believe I raised an urbane, sophisticated, ironically questioning eyebrow as I what-hoed and then slouched casually in a chair by the dining table, rather as James Dean might have slouched. Dignity was important here, and I knew better than to sink into the futon, as I had learned last night that it was impossible either to sit in it, with one's knees and chin pretty much competing for the same airspace, or to free oneself from its marshmallow-like embrace, with anything approaching dignity. Not sure how Sean Connery or, for that matter, James Dean, or, say, Arnold Schwartzenegger, would have dealt with that futon, but I'll bet you anything that they, like I, would have side-stepped the entire thorny problem and opted for the chair. In, or upon, the rigid geometry of which, I attempted to lounge with an air of bored indifference, pretty much succeeding, I thought, in driving home the fact that it would take a good deal more to rattle Ifford's cage than being hunted like an animal on an alien planet by the highly equipped minions of Absolute Evil at the behest of a sawdust-filled bureaucratic functionary and then, for act two, abandoned - for an over-grown lizard! - by one's dearest - really one's only - friend in all the cold and indifferent known universe.

But when I saw her, all that faded into inconsequentiality. I mean to say, it dissolved into nothingness, like one's breath on a cold morning, only faster. I didn't have it in my heart to blame her, with that committed grudge-holding till-death-do-us-part keeper-of-the-flame sort of blame, you know, that provides the meat and drink of life for some of those who wander the various firmaments, and the glue that binds so many intense attachments of the perpetual union persuasion. For one thing, I just don't have the energy for that sort of thing - I sometimes think I must be anemic or something. Besides which, Glennie, after all, knew not what she did to the inner Ifford when she took up with that lizard - we two, she and I, having been platonic buddies and only platonic buddies from the get-go and on up to even date to the best of her knowledge and belief. She did not seem to have an inkling, number one, that I had feelings, except the nearly universal garden store variety dread, desperation, fear and loathing, nausea, sickness unto death, and so on that the philosophers always carry on about; and in the second place, she had no way of knowing that these non-existent feelings of mine had somehow bloomed - and now yearned - in her direction. No - my beautiful girl was blameless - my number one beautiful girl, I mean to say, though the same would hold for Riqi, too, I had no doubt.

Glennie looked as pretty as ever this morning, the cold having put roses in her cheeks and a sparkle in her turquoise eyes.

She began on a note of gentle reproach. "We were worried about you, Ifford - when you just more or less vanished without leaving any note or calling one of us." As she spoke, Glennie walked over from where she stood by the door and took a chair at the dining nook table where I casually slouched.

It was a chilly little nook - I had noticed the air growing perceptibly colder as I had moved nearer the table - this chilliness being due to the alcove's having been built along the lines of a sort of large bay window and thus having three walls - a long framed by two shorts, you know - on the exterior of the house - walls which were all window from above the height of a man to about mid-way to the floor. The old-fashioned bay window, which contributed so much to the chilliness of the area, gave this morning onto a view of the somber winter cityscape (if that's the word I want) - icicles hanging from the eaves of houses, snow-encrusted streets with tire tracks on them leaving icy ridges and crusted patterns, and the dark trees standing out against all that white and looking very cold with nothing at all clothing their bare branches, which seemed to extend heavenward in mute heartfelt supplication for a break in the weather.

The nook, then, was more or less refrigerated - a sort of enlarged hanging flying buttress of an alcove, thrust out, in this season, into the frigid air of winter. In summer it would be awfully hot, I imagined, especially with the sun on it. Rather a damned if you do/damned if you don't sort of a dining nook, it seemed.

Due to the chill air, and perhaps also to the uncertainty of her welcome, Glennie had not taken off her great full-length navy blue pea jacket of a coat, and in it, with that absurd patriotic red, white, and blue muffler of hers wrapped loosely around her neck and shoulders and dangling its excessive length down towards the floor, she once again brought to mind a child playing at dress-up. She was looking at me askance, as though it was now my turn to hold forth, and I remembered her opening sally.

"I'm sorry, Glennie. It just didn't occur to me to - well, that my absence would be noted. I've been gone less than 24 hours, after all." I strove here to keep the bitterness and self-pity out of my voice, to speak in a light and off-hand manner, as though I were just on my way out the door in my immaculate white sporting garb for a couple of rounds - if that's what they're called - or is it sets? - of tennis.

"Ifford! Really! How could we not notice, what with them possibly looking for you and all? In fact, that's one thing I came to tell you about. I got a call from Squinch's office. A call about you."

"You did? About me? What about me?" This intelligence caused the icy fingers of fear once again to trace their rapid course up and down my spine. I was overcome by an unreal this-can't-actually-be-happening-to-me sort of feeling, and almost a vertigo, or a falling sensation, as if it were a dream I was in and I had just fallen backwards off a cliff - a black, snow-dusted, jagged, perpendicular, wintery cliff somewhere very high and exposed in rugged snowy mountains - definitely above the timberline - and was falling down, down, down in super slow motion through open space. It was rather like being in a commercial for a rugged new 4-wheel-drive wagon or jeep and then due to some slip-up - ha ha - sliding off that precipice and into that immense white bowl of airy nothing.

All along I had been hoping, and about half the time had felt more or less convinced, that I was over-reacting - that I was being as they say paranoid - and that this misunderstanding with Squinch, and, one supposes, those higher up his chain of command at whose behest he drew breath and tweezed his nostrils and brushed his teeth and tongue and waxed and polished his suits and scratched his rump, might be easily resolved. I still found it hard to believe that I was really and truly in the soup and my life in a shambles - for nothing more than having a few entirely innocent phone conversations with an Earthling who might or might not be my mother, biologically speaking, but who was in any event nothing more than a harmless and lonely old, or at least older (sorry, Mother), woman, and for having, through no fault of my own, been assigned as a room-mate a forceful and persuasive obsessive-compulsive Squankese national - I mean, we all know what they're like, don't we? – hard to believe that I was really a hunted entity on the 'most wanted 'list, for these minor matters, and perhaps that matter of the found loot – which, God only knew at this point what had become of it, and whether it was still under my mattress, and if so, I wondered if I should try to draw Glennie aside and ask her to try to get it to me. High crimes and misdemeanors, these are not – though the found loot did perhaps complicate the picture.

But the point here is that I had in point of fact always all my life - Alec Guinness in *The Lavender Hill Mob* comes to mind - been so abjectly servile in thought and deed - well, certainly in deed, and most of the time in thought as well - that I felt I deserved if anything encomiums (I believe that is the word I am after here) and some kind of medal - Most Self-Effacing Citizen-Subject of the Year - from the home planet, rather than this - persecution.

"He - rather, Miss Glatz, you know," Glennie went on, "Just said that it had come to their attention that you had missed several entire days of classes - she emphasized the word 'entire' pretty heavily - and that they were - these are her exact words - concerned about you."

"Concerned? She actually had the nerve to say that? Can you picture either of them concerned about me - or anyone ? I ask you!"

"Well actually, no, I can't. Not easily, anyway. There's something just so, you know, Third Reich-ish about those two."

"They look like escapees from a wax museum, I've always thought."

"But anyway, she pumped me as to your whereabouts and health and so on and so forth and said that if I found out where you were, I had a duty to inform them at once - she said the 'at once' twice for emphasis - and that I should pass it along to you that it was important for you to check in with them."

"Check in?"

"Well, that was how she put it."

"How did she sound?"

"Like she always does - very formal and official."

"Haughty? Distant? Glacial? Like a rod of well-chilled steel had just been thrust up her nether orifice?"

"Yes - like she always does. But that's really not important, is it, Ifford? How she sounded? What's important is - what are you going to do next? Don't you have an appointment with Riggs this afternoon? Do you plan to keep it - or - well, what are your plans?"

"Actually, Glennie - it's funny you should ask that. Because the fact is, I have got one. A plan, I mean. A *bona fide* idea re a course of action that I think just might wrap this messy situation up and put it to bed once and for all. It came to me, actually, in a dream - just last night. It is enough almost to make one think that there is after all an Unseen Hand that guides our passage through this life."

"That's good to hear - about the plan, I mean. I've been worried about you, Iffie. We all have. So - tell me about your plan."

While we talked, Riqi had gone into the kitchen area, where she appeared to be making a pot of coffee. I didn't want to leave her out of this. In fact she figured into the plan - or would - if she wanted to. The more the merrier, was the way I saw it, at least as far as Glennie and Riqi were concerned. Once out of harm's way, we could sort out our feelings and inclinations and decide who would be what to whom.

"Riqi, can you hear from there? Over the sound of the water faucet and the coffee grinder and all? I don't mean to be leaving you out. I'd like you to hear this too." Might as well let Glennie know that I, too, had a pretty serious love interest these days.

"Oh, I can hear just fine, Ifford; and I'll be over in a minute or two, as soon as this coffee is ready. Do bagels sound good, too? How about you, Glennie? Hot *cafe au lait* and toasted bagels with jam and cream cheese all around?"

"That sounds wonderful. Riqi. Thank you. I haven't had any breakfast and I am sort of hungry. And cold."

"I'm awfully sorry, Glennie, about how cold it is, there by the table," said Riqi. Feel free to move on over and sit on the futon, why don't you. It's warmer there. That's where I always eat. There or in bed. Don't worry about the crumbs or anything. I never do."

These two women in my life certainly seemed chummy. It would have been a trifle more flattering to the old *amour propre*, perhaps, if they had shown just a little bit of jealousy, or at least reserve, towards one another; but this was not the time to make niggling requirements of that Unseen Hand. I was not in what is called a strong bargaining position. To make good my exit from this particular rather intense and humorless time-space node and my insertion into a more bucolic slot just generally far less interested in Ifford Furze was right now all I asked of life.

"Just leave out the bug juice this time, if you don't mind, Riqi - at least for me."

"Gotcha." And so saying, she glanced at me with a little smile. With what I hoped was not a mischievous little smile. Much as I worshipped at the shrine of this adolescent goddess, her idea of harmless fun and mine, did not, I was beginning to surmise, always coincide.

CHAPTER 27: IFFORD'S PLAN

Adversity has ever been that state in which a man most
easily becomes acquainted with himself.

Samuel Johnson

When the food and drink were prepared, with coffee steaming and
butter melting on the bagels, and we three, now warmed by a small
portable space heater which Riqi had brought out of a closet and placed
at our feet, were gathered 'round the repast, I got right down to
business, to the brass tacks, the nub and essence of the way out
suggested to me in my dream. (I was, I noticed, under the duress of my
imperiled situation, inclining at least sporadically to believe that some
sort of benign powers must, after all, exist and take a personal - and
possibly, even, if I played my cards right, a benign - interest in the
affairs and doings of old Ifford).

We busied ourselves for a minute or two with the food and drink. I
noticed that Riqi prepared a pretty good brew and even provided heated
milk for *au lait*. Riqi, I noticed, was drinking a hot almond milk rather
than coffee, and I recalled that she claimed not to go in for the
caffeinated. But the quickly assembled repast showed that the girl had
taste.

Glennie interrupted these musings of mine. "So, anyway, Ifford ... you
were going to tell us about your plan ..."

"Right. Absolutely. Well - in a nutshell, what I need to do, I think, is
have another go at this jumping the tracks business. That, as I see it, is
what my dream seemed to be telling me. This dream I just had this
morning – not an hour ago. I know it didn't work out that first time, in
Torvald's lab; but I am hoping that Riggs might know of others
engaged in such research - and perhaps a little further along in it."

"So - are you going to keep your appointment with him this afternoon,
then?" asked Glennie.

"Well - perhaps we should discuss that. Initially - that is to say last
night and even when I woke up this morning - that had been my plan.

372

But I've been thinking - especially since hearing about that latest sinister phone call from the embalmed ones - that perhaps my best bet might be just to lay low for today. Maybe you could ask Rantor if he or Torvald could arrange another meeting at a different coffee house for tonight - not quite such a long meeting, of course - so that I could sound them out on this matter. You know, as to whether they or perhaps a colleague of theirs might not have more state of the art equipment and all - if, that is, the technical capabilities actually exist to accomplish such a feat."

"Well ... I could ask Rantor to set up a meeting, or try to. He and I were going to meet for lunch ..."

So now it is Rantor with whom she is munching the Giganto-Burgers and slurping the Chocolicious? Love, oh love oh careless love. It stung a bit, I'll tell you; but I affected to be unmoved. We hybrids can wear the mask.

"But, Ifford, I've been thinking. Don't you think that perhaps you - we - might possibly have over-reacted; and that even now you could quite possibly negotiate and explain your way out of this mess. I mean, after all, what have you done wrong? Just contacted your mother by phone is all - right? You know how they are on the home planet ..."

"Very detail-oriented and procedurally driven and so forth ..."

"Yes. Maybe all they wanted was to nip your unapproved tendencies in the bud ... not, you know, throw the book at you. Wouldn't it make more sense for them to give you a warning before ... doing anything more drastic? I mean, they do already have a lot of money invested in your rearing and education. And, wouldn't it make sense for you to try to find out a bit more about what their intentions are before you do anything drastic? Burn your bridges and all?"

This did not sound like the girl who was so eager to take a joyride in Torvald's whatzit just a fortnight or less ago. But I let it pass.

"Yes, they are very hyper-vigilant, beyond a doubt. And they do have a procedure for everything. The lot of them must have been subjected to very stern, Germanic upbringings, toilet trained too early and too harshly as tots, et cetera. Perhaps, as you say, things, even at this juncture, are not as drastic as they seem to me. Perhaps I have over-reacted. But I've been thinking a lot lately, Glennie, with all this free time that I've had ... and the upshot of it is that I do not think I am temperamentally suited to this time/space node. I find it deeply uncongenial. And given how uncongenial I find it, I think it inevitable that sooner or later old Ifford would be thrown on the discard heap - gathered up and decanted into the appropriate receptacle for recycling or experimentation in the interests of the advancement of science or whatever. That it is only a matter of time before this Ifford-business would be viewed as a no-go operation and something to be tidied up and put to rest and the spot left vacant filled by a more suitable entity."

"Hmmm," mused the old girl, munching a mouthful of bagel, and rolling the eyes thoughtfully heavenward while she chewed and swallowed. "OK ... but ... where would you go, Ifford - in time and space, I mean?"

"Where would you suggest, Glennie?"

"Well - the late '40s or early '50s ... in, maybe, Orange County ... if it were I who was going, that is ..."

"My thoughts exactly. The Golden Age and the Sunshine State. The pre-smog, pre-housing boom City of the Angels. And - you" - spreading my arms wide in avuncular fashion - "you two - are cordially invited along for the ride. If at all possible, that is, of course. Most cordially invited."

"Um," Glennie equivocated around a mouthful of bagel, "How about if I ask Rantor to try and set up another meeting tonight and we can all talk it over. I'd like to hear what the others think about the whole situation as things stand now. And learn if there are any new developments. And you can ask them about this jumping the tracks idea of yours. I guess Ranto - Rantor, that is," she corrected herself, coloring a little, "Knows your landlord, Riqi - Silver, I think his name is? – and can get word to you two through him about a meeting tonight. OK?"

Ranto? They were now on a pet-name basis? Was she then Glennie-poo ... or Glennums ... or Glendelicious?

Well, no matter.

We agreed that it sounded like a plan and then she, after glancing at her watch, took a last slurp of her coffee, and, glancing at her wristwatch, stood up and walked toward the door, saying, "My, it's gotten late. I've got to run or I'm going to be late for my first class." Her hand on the doorknob, she turned to Riqi, saying, "I'm sorry to barge in on you like this, so early in the morning, and drink your excellent coffee and eat your good food and then just dash off without even getting to know you at all ... but we have this little problem, as you can probably tell ..."

Riqi said not to worry and she hoped Glennie could come back soon because she wanted to get to know Ifford's sister better. Somehow she seemed to have gotten the idea that Glennie and I were brother and sister. We certainly look enough alike to be siblings.

After Glennie left, Riqi did not press me to talk about my problems; nor did she ask me to leave, as I had feared she might, what with me being on the lam and all. She didn't even seem curious about what jumping the tracks was all about, or what I'd done to get the authorities interested in me. Perhaps this sort of intrigue and cops and robbers stuff was all *comme d'habitude* in her world. Whatever the reason, she seemed to have a sort of unfazed tranquility about her, almost a serene obliviousness to the external world - except perhaps when it came to Silver. Perhaps it was just that she had plans for the day, for now she was bustling about, getting ready, she said, for a modeling shoot she had scheduled for the morning. She told me as she got dressed that she did a bit of modeling on the side. After the shoot, she said, she was scheduled to pop out of a cake at some sort of office bachelor party, and then planned to come back home, probably in the late afternoon. And so, after giving me what could be called a full body hug, and nice lingering kiss, and a sweet parting smile, and blowing me a final kiss for good measure, she left, telling me to make myself at home, just not to answer the door or phone - something I hardly needed to be told.

CHAPTER 28: AN AMBIGUOUS NOTE

When one burns one's bridges, what a very nice fire it makes.

Dylan Thomas

You know, all this business of being a hunted entity really takes it out of a fellow. For instance, delicious though the repast laid out by Riqi had looked, I had not been able to do it justice. I had picked at my food like an anorexic and truth to tell had not really enjoyed it much. All that chewing and swallowing had just seemed such an effort. Furthermore, I found that I now had to exercise caution when it came to the caffeinated beverages - my beloved coffee. In my present uncertain conditions caffeine seemed at times to plunge me into that state of stark anxiety which lurked more or less continually, now, on the peripheries of my inner landscape and which I was usually just able to keep to a level *diminuendo* rather than *fortissimo*.

I don't know if the reader has ever been plunged into that state - surely he or she has - when sitting in a dentist's waiting room, or just before an important test in school - well, this present dose of the stuff was like that, only considerably more so. Under its stern tutelage I saw the world with such pitiless clarity for the harsh and uncharitable place it really, when you come right down to it, can be. I mean, whatever happens to one, the trees and the birds and the sky and the landscape just remain there, blandly, serenely, obliviously the same, don't they? No sympathetic smile, no helping hand extended. Push comes to shove in one's personal affairs and the entire manifest Universe remains unmoved. Seems, in fact, not even to notice. If it's a nice day, well, it continues on inexorably being a nice day - doesn't it? And likewise if it's what I have heard on this planet referred to as a shitty day.

One isn't taken into account, is what I am getting at, not even in one's hour of direst need. Unless, of course, one believes in signs and portents. But consideration of that subject would definitely exceed or surpass or outstrip, lie beyond, et cetera, the scope of the present work. Suffice it to say that I myself have always viewed the subject of these alleged or purported covert signals from the Almighty or one of His staff with a skeptical eye. I mean surely One all knowing and all powerful could at least manage a clear and unambiguous communication, if communication was in fact His intent and design - wouldn't you think, dear Reader? Or is God one of those who enjoys messing with one's mind? Hardly godly behavior, in my book, mere mortal though I may be.

Anyway - after the girls left, my plan had been to go back to bed for more sleep - a bit of forgetful oblivion and so on - but I found myself after the coffee (of which I had taken but a single cup) too keyed up for that plan and so ended up just pacing and fidgeting, sitting down and then getting up again, walking from bedroom to dining nook and back again to gaze out their windows - until I realized that I, what with being a fugitive and all, should probably avoid both the windows - from which I might be seen - and the pacing - which might make creaking noises detectable in Silver's domicile directly below. Perhaps, had I brought my current mystery novel, which had gotten quite juicy, I could have blocked reality out in that manner, but it, alas, was back in the garret room to which, if all went well - well being a relative term here - I might never return.

What I ended up doing, to pass the time, after easing the spirit by writing a bit in this journal, was something of which I strongly disapprove - namely, rummaging about Riqi's apartment looking at her personal things. Let me hasten to explain that I did not do this thoroughly or systematically, or even, when it comes down to it, by design. I simply had nothing at all to do and was too restless just to relax and so tiptoed about in my stocking feet gazing absently at this and that. Actually I was looking for something to read, a mystery novel ideally, or perhaps a popular magazine - something light and foolish to take my mind off my worries. I came across a pile of papers and just absently began pawing through them - actually Riqi seems to be a bit of a sketch artist and I found some of her little doodles to be quite good, amusing - little cartoon figures of mice and piglets and puppies and kittens and nude females, really rather charming and individual - when I came across what seemed to be a note taken from a telephone call or passed by hand - saying merely, *'will be at Stud - make contact tonight if possible.'* At least that is what I thought it said. It was scrawled in light pencil on a crumpled bit of paper - the back of a grocery store receipt, actually - and was a bit hard to make out. But I looked and looked and that was what it did indeed seem to say.

Well! I leave it to the reader to imagine the feelings that enveloped me at this juncture.

CHAPTER 29: TRUST

Where thieves and pimps run free,
and good men die like dogs ...

Hunter S. Thompson

When one is young, you know, one trusts. One merely, beautifully, trusts. Unless, of course, one has been born into one of those satanic families Glennie has told me about, which - she claims she has this on

379

good authority - practice child abuse including sexual abuse right from the get-go, thus producing those split personalities so useful - I have this from Glennie who got it from Jacko - in the intelligence industry - and the sports and entertainment industries, not to mention what she calls kiddie porn and prostitution - as slave-operatives.

The several 'personalities' are actually memory compartments, most of them with amnesia regarding the others and thinking self the only one at home. As I understand it, the various 'personalities' can be more or less constructed, under hypnosis, from the basic elements, tendencies, and themes of the individual personality, and then taught to come when called, so to speak, by a certain trigger or cue, and programmed to do this or deliver that - and the host personality, as it is called, hasn't got a clue save that he or she does experience 'missing time.'

Once 'created,' as it were, these split blokes are useful because they have enhanced abilities - memory, visual acuity, endurance, indifference to pain, etc. - all the sorts of traits that would be useful in an extreme emergency. The mind only splits, or dissociates, in this extreme fashion, Glennie said, under the direst of emergencies. Like being tortured in what a I remember Glennie calling 'ritual abuse.'

Those satanic groups are not just a bunch of misguided loonies, she told me; they are a bunch of misguided loonies - sociopaths, closet sadists, criminal elements, and so forth, yes - but: oftener than one might think, a bunch of misguided, or should one say tragically confused, loonies - what Lenin I think it was might call 'useful idiots' - under the control of some underworld syndicate, businessman, intelligence agency, or politician of the grand or petite mal variety but obviously of broadly liberal ethics. Glennie claimed that many of these highly placed individuals are actually into the child porn industry, drugs, kiddie prostitution, gun running - illegal contraband being the source of the highest ROI, or return on investment, in the jargon of economics. This whole satanic wheeze comes in very handy, Glennie says, not only for programming those under this trauma-based mind control, but for controlling the other operatives - the handlers, you might say, and the handlers' handlers - through a sort of 'this is what could happen to you or one you love if you get out of line' kind of control-by-terror. Also, she claims, the trauma – one might better say, the nightmare-ish horror - of witnessing torture bonds the on-lookers, making a more loyal and cohesive band of thugs.

This is what was passed on to me. I cannot vouch for its truth. At the time, I scoffed. But now, I am wondering. The world is a strange and not particularly a nice place, I am coming to realize, peopled by all sorts, some of them very rough trade indeed, and some of these, if Glennie, Jacko, and Rantor, et al are to be credited, holding some of the very highest seats of power, in business, the military, and government - though it is counter-intuitive to us average Joes because counter the beneficent and blameless image that is inculcated in all of us, by the schools and the various media, of those high personages who order, weave, manage, and direct the entire fabric of the social order.

When you think about it, Glennie's information makes a certain chilly sense. If indeed, as that Lord Acton fellow said, power tends to corrupt, and absolute power to corrupt absolutely - and, then, thinking, as the Shadow said on that old radio show they used to play for us kiddies as a before-bedtime treat, 'Who knows what evil lurks in the hearts and minds of men' - something along those lines, anyway - I mean, given what we know of humankind and its tendency to put self and its pleasures and dearest wishes before everything and everyone else ... I mean, these pillar-of-society types could just know when to and when not to, if you know what I mean, unlike the more impulsive and less modulated sort of miscreant - if you see what I am getting at. The mind quails at the thought, and yet ...

Yet, I know - because Rantor quoted it at me one day during one of his many rants, that the poet T.S. Eliot has written that "Humankind cannot bear very much reality; it takes its truth in small doses." I think that is how it went. At any rate, I can relate, for so, did I, dear Reader - take my reality unwillingly and in small doses; and so would I even now, if it were but possible for me yet, or still. I have, by the events of my entire life, and particularly those recounted in this journal, been ripped from the moorings of my comfortable illusions and dragged all unwilling into this, if not the real world, than I think perhaps a realer one, at any rate, than the one I formerly inhabited. Others, I know, can and will continue to evade contemplation of these possibilities by denying them stoutly and promptly forgetting all about them and immersing self in pleasanter - if largely fictional - worlds and realms, doings and beliefs. That I think is the method of choice of the masses. It seems that I am no longer able to do so, my companions, and experiences, of late having subjected illusion's fragile bubble to an all-out frontal assault.

And now it seems that perhaps even Riqi could be but a part of this initiation into what could I suppose be called the real world - a world most would rather shut out with their televisions and sports, and shopping trips and Disney cartoons, and their comforting notions that bad men in the highest of high places are aberrations and not the norm.

Which reminds me ... when I was but a lad and knee high to my cyborg nannies, I used to long to have been born into the United States in the early 19th Century and be able to be one of those mountain men. That, for a while, seemed the life. Talk about untrammeled, what? As I have grown older and wiser, I have come to realize that, as the poet says, freedom always travels with responsibility - kind of a good cop/bad cop duo, you know - so I am thinking that I would no longer opt for so stern a situation as that of the old mountain men, where extinction due to starvation, grizzlies, freezing, and/or hostile aborigines with an ax to grind was a distinct and ever-present possibility and one could not dial for assistance in an emergency. Still, though, it at times gives me a sort of peace to contemplate being one of those rugged characters, and enjoying miles and miles and miles of freedom ... and solitude.

Generally, trust seems to be the province of the young and uninitiated, is what I have, in my rambling way, been getting at here. Take self, for example - I used to be pretty damned trusting, for one reared by various cyborgs and paid attendants in various public institutions on a planet which believes the individual to be entirely and thoroughly subservient to the state and to find freedom and fulfillment in suppression of self and service to said state ... but anyway, despite all that, somehow I managed to be really quite trusting as a tot. I mean, the world - it was the only world I knew - seemed a good enough place - I had my favorite dandling devices, a favorite care-giver or two, be they cyborgian or fully flesh - they did keep changing the guard, it seemed, and one had to keep finding new favorites, and be careful not to get too attached to any of them - but there were my favorite corners, in the various rooms in which I was kept, where I crept to huddle and suck the thumb and stroked the bit of soft blanket that I thought of as a real live person and called Pooge; and then I had a few mates, you know, chums - other hybrids of my cohort raised along with me in the institutions and with whom I became pally. As I have mentioned, we hybrids generally are not emotionally intense; so perhaps these attachments were lukewarm compared to what real humans experience.

But I am getting away from my point again, which is trust, and, in general, the optimistic view, the sanguinary mindset. The remaining shreds of my capacity for which were being subjected of late to intense pressure from several quarters. I will not make a laundry list. The reader who has stuck with me knows all about it as well as I, for I have held nothing back on these pages. But - Riqi? Riqi? The one with the honey-colored skin and tresses who whispered sweet nothings in my ear just last night? *E tu, Brute* and all that jazz? The mind reeled, positively reeled, and I sank, feeling rather as if I might have to throw up, onto the conveniently near futon.

CHAPTER 30: UNCERTAINTY

The world is governed by very different personages from
what is imagined by those who are not
behind the scenes.

Benjamin Disraeli

I know, dear Reader - I know. Those few words on that slip of paper prove nothing. Surely if the Gestapo wished to add me to their collection and knew I would be at The Stud on a certain evening, they would, logically, merely show up and nab me, as we had seen done the other night. And yet, the enigmatic few words scrawled on a slip of paper struck a chill note in my already jangled inner realm, suffused as it was with fear and trembling, causing me to feel that, to be on the safe side, I had best be shoving off and cutting my moorings yet again, rather than wait for the return of Riqi, as had been my original intent, or wait for further intelligence from Glennie. The impulse to flee possessed me once again, and quite urgently.

I will confess that a counter-wind was blowing. I was tired of running, tired of being a wanted entity, of being on the lam, of quailing whenever I saw anyone in uniform, of waking in the night thinking I had heard the creak of a floorboard, the rustling of pant legs rubbing together as a stealthy someone approached on tiptoe while I lay slumbering between the sheets. Yes, the tendency here was to more or less give up. I admit that I felt overwhelmed. My will felt unequal to the task and I felt, in a word, ready to turn myself in, to let whatever it was that fate seemed to be wanting so badly to dish out to me just occur, and get it over with.

I came within an inch of phoning Squinch and telling him to send his thugs out and haul me in. It was what you might call one of those dark moments. But I rallied. Your hero pulled self together yet again and began working on a plan - another plan. Yet another plan ...

This note, of course, had no date. It could be months old. I had no proof that I was the one whom she - or whomever - was being told to try to meet. I sat thinking about it all. The thing that troubled me was, why would anyone be passing cryptic notes to a sweet young thing? If she was in fact merely and nothing but a sweet young thing. Then - at about

384

this point in my musings, I mean - a sort of awful thought occurred. It came back to me that Riqi had these rather strange scars on her back. I had noticed them in bed last night. One can feel them - sort of little whorls of very slightly raised skin - scar tissue. I had not asked her about them, not wanting to embarrass or seem to be criticizing or finding fault - that old eternal tact of the hybrid, you know. But what came back to me as I sat musing and pondering was another thing that Glennie had told me about these poor tortured souls who end up somehow in the clutches of these - programmers. It was that some of the 'programming' involves the use of cattle prods, electric cattle prods - which do sometimes leave small scars. She told me of one poor girl who, allegedly, had them all over her body, the part, that is, that's covered by a swimsuit. When this memory came back to me, the blood started pounding in the ears again. Not proof positive, of course - I mean this whole mind control stuff, from the more mainstream perspective, which until so recently had been my perspective, seems so fantastic - hardly believable. But the thing is, according to Glennie, there are reputable therapists and other mental health professionals who swear that there is something to these tales - that they have in their professional work encountered actual escapees from this nightmarish netherworld. They claim that they, too, were at first highly skeptical - but ended up believing in the veracity of some of these patients.

The thing was, in my present circs I was in a mood to trust no one, especially not so new an acquaintance as Riqi. When I thought about it, it seemed strange that she had found me at all sexually desirable. I mean, no one else has, or does. Of course, I was only too glad to believe the girl and fall into her arms, her bed ... her coils, designs ... then I had a cheering thought. Not immensely so - but somewhat. If, let us say, Riqi were under mind control and programming and so forth; and if I were merely a sort of assignment of hers - as in - go and reel this chappie in, there's a good doggie - well, even if that were true - for the sake of argument, let us say it is true - well, the sub- or splinter-personality whom I met and became entangled with - shall we say - that 'Riqi' is sincere. She really does mean all the nice things she said, about finding me attractive and preferring entities with pale coloration and willowy frame - which she did say, by the way. She said all of these things and more, dear Reader - and more.

I know not how long I sat on that sofa, that futon, actually, pondering what to do now. But slowly an idea, a plan, emerged. I no longer felt comfortable loitering here in Riqi's apartment. I decided that I would keep that appointment with the toad. But I would go in disguise.

Surely, here among all of Riqi's extensive wardrobe and showgirl paraphernalia, I, with my slender frame, could find something that would fit me; and I had noticed in my prowlings and pokings about among her things that she had several wigs. Suitably disguised, I would emerge from this little haven, and I would keep the appointment and then - well, throw self upon the mercy of Riggs and Bevins.

CHAPTER 31: MORE INCOGNITO

I believe there's someone out there watching us.
Unfortunately, it's the government.

Woody Allen

It was cold out but no longer quite so very cold. A melt seemed to be in progress, and the icy winter of the soul had eased into the cold and soggy winter of the soul. I took it as a good sign. Change. For the first time in weeks, not snow but a very light rain was falling, making the footing slushy and even more treacherous, and I trod carefully as I trudged the mushy, watery byways, for I wore unaccustomed footwear.

Riqi has quite an assortment of footwear, some with platforms and heels that seem absurdly, impossibly, high. These must be for her work. I can conceive of no other possible use for them, as I cannot imagine anyone voluntarily subjecting him or herself to such torture devices; and I of course had sensibly rejected these very highest heels, these Mt. Everests of footwear, as being beyond the realm of the possible for self - without the aid crutches or a walker, that is - I mean things were complicated enough as it was. Rather, I had chosen a pair of black boots made of real leather that reached practically to the knee - yes, we hybrids do have knees - and they did have heels, not really high ones, but still - they were a tad small, and the heels felt strange, and all the ice didn't help any. But the boots, being lined in fake fur, were the warmest as well as the largest footwear I had found in Riqi's closet. I had a long trudge ahead of me and wanted to keep warm.

The home planet - at least the parts I called home - was a distinctly warmer affair, temperature-wise, than what I had been undergoing here on Earth. At first I was enchanted by winter, which I had longed to experience as a child - and I still cannot deny the beauty of it all, all that whiteness everywhere, and the frost rimeing dark tree-branches and dry yellow grasses and so on, not to mention the wondrously white and solid lake - but it had gotten a bit old by now, and I cursed and muttered under my breath, as I made my slippery slidy way to the address on the scrap of paper that Riggs and Bevins had given me.

Naturally I felt apprehensive about being detected en route and hauled off to some slammer or other - but it seemed that my disguise was effective. In addition to the boots, I wore warm black tights, which kept needing hitching up due to the fact that I have no hips to speak of, and a curly black wig, and a brown tweed maxi-skirt of silk-lined wool, very warm it was, and a soft angora sweater of pale pink, and over it all, a wonderful sort of parka filled with goose down and with a fur-lined hood. The parka being sort of ice-greenish - just so you know how to imagine me as I made my way through the cold. Oh, yes - I was also wrapped about the neck and chin with a muffler also of pale pink angora that seemed to go with the sweater. And, as females seem never to venture forth without some sort of handbag, I slung a large black leather purse over my shoulder. In it I stuffed this journal, which I had gotten into the habit of keeping with me at all times. It made not a bad-looking outfit, actually. To be perfectly candid, I had always been a bit curious how it would feel to wear female clothing. They get to wear so much more varied and interesting clothing. To complete - and, so to speak, authenticate - my disguise, I had put on some make-up - pink pearlescent lipstick - it went with the sweater, - and rouge, eyebrow pencil, mascara - wanting to look the part. We hybrids tend to be thorough and consistent - whether that is genetic or inculcated by our planners, I do not know. For the record, I have absolutely no inclinations towards cross-dressing or anything like that, in case the reader is wondering. I am very normal in that regard. Either that, or I have yet to plumb the depths of my own depravity - or, I suppose it would be more politically correct to say, diversity. But it was sort of fun, I have to admit. Like dressing for a costume ball.

Anyway, I was most apprehensive and felt very exposed and vulnerable the whole way - especially leaving her apartment, as I dreaded meeting Silver. Though it was a walk of several blocks, perhaps a mile, I was, happily, un-accosted the entire way, except by street people begging for spare change and - once - an Earthling male who seemed to be attempting to flirt with me [!]. I of course gave him the brush-off - wordlessly, just acting very haughty and offended. No need to haul out the handbag and slug the fellow - just the frosty manner sufficed. Still, it did start me to thinking ... if what I really wanted was acceptance and - congress - with Earthlings of the *bona fide* and authentic sort, it seemed that my best hope might be to try to go it as a female ... but did I want acceptance into the club *that* badly? I thought not. Still, it did occur to me that it might be pleasant to at times saunter forth as a female. I have always thought girls have more fun. But what was I thinking of? At issue here was no less than my freedom, my ability, to do anything at all but wear manacles (of the physical or electronic sort) and/or have my entire memory erased and re-programmed, and/or be shuttled unceremoniously and, in perhaps more than one meaning of the phrase, off into the great beyond. In light of my present circs, this train of thought and speculation seemed absurdly frivolous.

The building in which R & B plied their trade - did whatever it was they did - was an ordinary sort of building - not on campus but just across the street from it - one of those boring, cheaply constructed modern things of concrete and glass. Very institutional. Naturally I used stairs rather than elevator, and I hesitated not an instant but entered their offices as might a mouse its hole - gratefully, you know. As the reader can see, I had already, mentally speaking, placed all my chips on that square on the gaming table's shabby green felt surface marked 'Salvation through time-travel facilitated gratis and out of the goodness of their hearts by Toad and Company.' I mean, was I desperate, or what? But at the time I tried not to think of it that way. I strove to be more upbeat, as per the counsel of the caregivers and programmers of my benighted youth.

CHAPTER 32: A PLEA FOR HELP

Laws are like cobwebs, which may catch small flies,
but let wasps and hornets break through.

Jonathan Swift

Inside, I was grateful to find only R & B - no secretaries. The duo looked at me questioningly when I entered, failing utterly to recognize me beneath the wig and make-up - which I will admit gave me a little charge, a feeling of gratification. I mean - I had at least succeeded in something, in this whole tawdry progression of ill-luck, bad companions, misjudgment, and ruined prospects. Not to mention ultimate disaster. But, rather dramatically ripping off my wig, I managed soon enough to make my identity known to them, and we adjourned into a private office - it must have been Riggs', for it was very untidy, as I believe I have mentioned his person also being, he by all the evidence being one of these thinker-types who are largely oblivious to the realm of the merely physical. Which, when I thought about it, was all to the good, as it was to his brain that I was entrusting my future, such as it was. My future in the cozy - relatively speaking - past, that is. Or such was the straw of hope to which I clung.

I cut immediately to the chase - my plight, the recent information from Glennie re the latest call from Glatz, my fears and suspicions re Riqi - in short, my, as I saw it, utter and total peril, were I to remain much longer in this hub of space-time, which had grown very hot for me, through - I still privately felt and feel - no fault of my own. I explained that I had thought and thought and could come up with only one solution to my problem, namely, flight by means of time-travel to a more congenial conjunction of the parameters of time and space, in which I would be *desconocido*. It would give me a sort of *tabula rasa* identity with which to begin again. A way of making lemonade from lemons.

I did mention Glennie – my concerns that she might be at risk here too, especially given that she had aided and abetted me, concealed my whereabouts – and Riqi - the mysterious note I had found in her flat, and the odd scars on her back – omitting, naturally, any explanation of how I had happened to have been fingering and gazing upon Riqi's back. As I had rather anticipated that it would, my information about the scars seemed to fire up the old girl's furnaces noticeably - Bevins, I mean, of course - for all sorts of expressions flitted across her map, and she fidgeted as though sitting on a gravel road in her cami-knickers.

Having told all, I sat there in mute appeal, looking, I hoped, innocent, vulnerable, winsome, and loveable, sort of like a wet black Cocker Spaniel puppy on the doorstep in a wind and rainstorm, begging with its big brown eyes to be let in.

Riggs broke the silence. "Well - that is all most interesting - and, as you say, it does seem a rather worrying situation, if all you tell us it true ... and of course I have no reason to doubt you, but rather, based upon Torvald's and Rantor's belief in and corroboration of your story, every reason to accept what you tell me. "

Here he paused a bit, as if in thought. I considered it better to say nothing and keep the ball in his court and his eye focused upon it. That is, I believe, a sales technique - I remember being instructed in it in my 'Techniques for Total Banking Success' class last year - and I was, indeed, trying to sell the pair of them on this plan of mine.

Riggs, after a moment, went on, peering at me keenly with those glittering little eyes of his, which were embedded in his fat cheeks rather like glazed currents pushed into a marshmallow and seeming in danger of - or in the process of - slowly sinking totally out of view, as though the fellow had been placed on a warming tray and had begun to soften and melt.

"But I am wondering, Ifford - what is it that you think Florence and I could do to help you? We do work in the area of remote viewing, as you know. But it seems that you are hoping to be not merely mentally but actually physically transported to another place and time. What makes you think we could help you with that? Or that anyone could, for that matter?"

"Well, Sir, it is that I do know that there are people working on that problem. We both know one who is" - discrete reference to Torvald, here, of course - "And I somehow got the idea from him and his burley pal that perhaps you, too, were, could we say, dabbling in those waters. If that rumor happened to be true, I thought it possible that you might be dabbling more successfully than he. Or to know someone else who is. As of even date, I mean, of course. Who knows what the future may hold. I do not mean to cast aspersions on our mutual friend's competency, brain-power, or ultimate success."

I paused here a moment - partly for effect, I suppose, and partly in sheer anguish. Or what passes for it in my species, If, that is, I could be said to have a species.

"You see, Sir - and you too, Ma'am - I don't know where else to turn. One cannot simply vanish into the woodwork in these days of high-tech surveillance. One cannot even walk the streets without being viewed by the cameras that are placed everywhere - and sometimes even spoken to, admonished, by them! – or automatically ticketed for jaywalking or littering. And don't those cameras scan the irises of all passers-by for the purposes of biometric ID, and flag those who are wanted for any offense or infraction, no matter how minor? And then the random searches, the RFID and iris-scans, on the streets, and in buses and subways, and along the freeways, seem to be increasing in frequency. And of course, because of all the terrorism they no longer even need a reason to apprehend you, and hold you incommunicado indefinitely. 'In the interests of national security,' is all they have to say. And aren't dissidents now regarded as insurgents, and their property confiscated? Glennie just told me that a few days ago – she got that from the Public Affairs Director at the radio station where she volunteers. And according to Rantor, the biometric ID system is being extended and integrated inter-planetarily and even inter-galactically. You know how they do these things, make these advances and implement these programs before they tell us, the public, that they are doing so – if they ever do tell us. And the subcutaneous RFID chips, which I understand will soon be mandatory, and can be used as tracking devices … as also, Glennie tells me, the RFID chips already embedded in virtually all our purchases, and certainly in our ID cards, can be used. I mean, when you think about it, it's a wonder I haven't been picked up already – as a suspected terrorist, since it seems to serve as a kind of a catch-all pretext for arrest."

Here I quit speaking, having realized that in my nervous and overwrought state I seemed to be going on and on at greater length than necessary – and, of course, was preaching to the choir. Perhaps I was afraid to yield the floor to the toad for fear of what he would say – for fear of being turned down. Turned down, and shown out. But what I *had* done was, get him off again on his favorite topic – namely, of course, his arcane researches.

"Well, Ifford," he intoned in that familiar lecturer's voice of his (seeming, as noted, to be shifting into pedagogic mode), "The terrorism is an interesting subject, of course. Most interesting. Being used, as it is, to justify all of these police-state measures of which you have just given a partial catalogue. Have Torvald and Rantor mentioned that, historically, most terrorism is actually state-sponsored?"

"State-sponsored?" I parroted rather stupidly. Actually, as soon as I spoke I dimly recalled having already heard something about state-sponsored terrorism from Rantor, Torvald, and Glennie at a previous session in one of the coffee-houses. But it looked like I was to hear about it again.

"You see, Ifford," the toad-like fellow continued, "The oil-wealthy Islamic nations of the Mid-East are not falling obediently into line when it comes to the matter of this global puppet government – the New World Order, you know – that the great banking and other corporate interests are so determined to install in power here on our planet. And, it has long been the case that nations which don't play ball with these top-of-the-heap powers get very bad press in the corporate media. Thus it hardly comes as a surprise to see the Islamic nations being so demonized, in the mass media and official government propaganda, as terrorists and potential nuclear warfare belligerents."

"But – they *are* terrorists – and belligerents ..."

"Depending on where you get your information from, Ifford," advised Riggs, while his sidekick nodded in emphatic agreement.

"One must always consider the source," Bevins explained. "And history is littered with false flag operations."

"False flag operations?"

"History, my boy, is indeed littered with false flag operations. Heinous acts attributed to one's enemy in order to justify initiating open hostilities against them. Case in point, right now, there is abundant information on the web, the internet, all of it from independent researchers – you can look it up for yourself - many of these writers and researchers being university professors and other professionals, by the way – claiming that 9/11 - the infamous attacks on the twin towers - were actually the work of elements very highly placed in this country's own government – as, in and near the White House – in order to justify

393

waging war on the nations which both have rich oil deposits and are opposed to usury – hence, of course, are opposed to central banks, fiat currencies, and that whole set-up. These countries are standing in the way of the completion of the New World Order of by and for the banks."

"Yes, but – is there any evidence at all to substantiate these claims of government involvement?"

"Oh, these independent researchers are not merely claiming. There is abundant evidence that the towers were all brought down by controlled demolition. And that our air defense were ordered to stand down."

"All said evidence being studiously ignored by the MSM, the main stream media," Bevins interjected, "And, of course, by the official alleged investigators and nominal investigations as well."

"Yes," Riggs continued, "The way the buildings fell in just a few seconds, at free-fall speed, in their own footprints, was just exactly as buildings fall in controlled demolition – at free-fall speed, into what was the path of *greatest* resistance – unless explosives were used to remove that resistance, as happens in controlled demolitions."

"You don't have to be a rocket scientist," Bevins added dryly.

"Yes," Riggs agreed, "It's not only simple Physics 101 science, the fundamental laws of physics, but just common sense ... the fact that huge steel girders were cast out hundreds of feet, with great force and at high speed, as would never happen in a simple collapse ... the fact that the concrete and other wreckage was pulverized, such as simply does not and cannot happen without explosives ... and the pools of molten metal found in the basements of the buildings, even weeks after the buildings collapsed, indicating, actually, the use of thermite or thermate to cut through the steel girders ... and the many reports, from by-standers, firemen, and building employees, of hearing explosions, even prior to the first building's being hit by the plane, and in *all* of the buildings just prior to and during their collapses ..."

I had concluded by now, of course, that it was happening again - another impromptu installment of my re-education. It was really rather remarkable that even at this tense moment Toad and Company could be doing this to me yet again.

"And," Bevins added, "The known fact that jet fuel – which is just kerosene, basically - does not ever – and certainly did not then – burn hot enough or long enough to cause the huge steel girders to melt and collapse, especially not in unison ... nor does the pancake theory, or the floor support-collapse theory, hold up. Even if that were possible, and had happened, it could not have happened at free-fall speed – and all three buildings collapsed at free-fall speed, each in its own footprint, just as buildings do in controlled demolition, when timed explosions collapse the floors in a sequence, the explosions carefully timed to remove each floor at the perfect time to permit the entire structure to fall in its own footprint, at free-fall speed and without damaging near-by structures."

"And then," Riggs carried on, "There is the highly suspicious fact that the government's cover-up – which they called an 'investigation' – did not even *attempt* to account for the collapse of Building 7, which was not even hit by a plane and which stood further away from the twin towers than other buildings which did not collapse ... and the fact that NO steel frame buildings have *ever, ever* collapsed due to impact or fire ... and yet on this day we are expected to believe that three of them did, three that were redundantly constructed to withstand far more in the way of structural stress than these were subjected to ..."

"All in all, a textbook example," Bevins continued, "Right in our own back yard, of a false flag operation – a shockingly heinous act attributed to a regime's enemies but actually carried out by the regime's own operatives in order to inflame the emotions of the populace and provide a plausible justification for initiating aggressive acts against said enemies – the 'enemies' often being regarded as such for no better reason than that they have valuable resources."

"I see – but, why have I never heard of any of these false-flag operations?" I asked. Though I was pretty sure I would be told that knowledge of such things, along with so much else, had been suppressed by the power elite.

"History abounds with other instances of false-flag operations," Riggs hastened to inform me. "But the elites don't exactly want the information broadcast about for public consumption. Don't want to get the public to thinking too much, or at all, along certain lines. The most famous is the Reichstag Fire in pre-WWII Germany. Even mainstream historians are now pretty much in accord that it was a false-flag operation, perpetrated by the Reich and falsely attributed to a patsy.

Hitler used it as a pretext to suspend virtually all civil liberties in Germany, just as Bush has done here using 9/11 as the pretext."

Another one by the Reich," said Bevins, "Was the 'Gleiwitz incident' of 1939, when Reinhard Heydrich – I think that was the man's name – fabricated evidence of a Polish attack on German forces, in order to get the German people outraged against Poland and provide a pretext for war against Poland."

"Yet another false flag operation, this one by Japan in the early 1930s, is called the Mukden incident." Riggs said. "Japanese officers fabricated a pretext for annexing Manchuria by blowing up a section of railway."

"And, another example, in the late '30s," Bevins volunteered, "Was when the Soviet Union created for themselves a *causus belli* against Finland, by shelling their own village of Mainila on the Finnish border, and forging casualties."

"Yes ... but what about here? I thought this government was different," I rather weakly objected. Clinging to my illusions to the bitter end, don't you know. Some things die hard.

"Well, Ifford," said Riggs, "This government is not all that different. That's our main point, actually. You have to look beneath the PR. As rivers always flow downhill, so are the ways of power ever the same. In fact right at hand here on my desk I happen to have a very germane quotation from a decorated war hero, Major Smedly Butler."

Reminding me of Rantor, the fellow rummaged around on his untidy desk and finally produced a something that looked like it had been printed from an online article, which he proceeded to read to me –

> *I spent 33 years and four months in active military service and during that period I spent most of my time as a high class muscle man for Big Business, for Wall Street and the bankers. In short, I was a racketeer, a gangster... I helped make Mexico and especially Tampico safe for American oil interests in 1914. I helped make Haiti and Cuba a decent place for the National City Bank boys to collect revenues in. I helped in the raping of half a dozen Central American republics for the benefit of Wall Street. I helped purify Nicaragua for the*

396

International Banking House of Brown Brothers in 1902-
1912. I brought light to the Dominican Republic for the
American sugar interests in 1916. I helped make Honduras
right for the American fruit companies in 1903. In China in
1927 I helped see to it that Standard Oil went on its way
unmolested.

"These things don't get taught in the schools," said Bevins, "Or reported in the news, not even on public radio or TV. Have you seen that movie, *Wag the Dog?* What passes for news can be wholly fabricated, and at best is often little more than a litany of PR releases. Hasn't it ever struck you as a bit odd, and eerie, Ifford, that ALL the major news sources, print and electronic, so totally agree on just about EVERYTHING? What do you think is the chance of that happening in a country which has truly free, uncontrolled information services?"

"Yes – for an example of a truly free, uncontrolled information venue," Riggs suggested, "Look at the internet today – where you find a plethora of information and research which conflicts with that uniform pablum purveyed by all the big corporate news sources which are the only news presences on TV, radio, and in the mainstream newspapers and news magazines."

"But if you want an example of a planned false flag operation of this government," Bevins continued, "Just consider the 'Operation Northwoods' plot of the U.S. administration back in 1962. The goal was to justify waging war on Cuba, and the scheme involved various scenarios such as hijacking a passenger plane and blaming it on Cuba. That idea came from the Joint Chiefs of Staff - but it was rejected by JFK, or it would now be a part of history, and much studied – except the truth about the identities of the real masterminds."

"And there is now lots of information, Ifford," said Riggs, "Even readily available online - indicating that the – ostensibly so populist - government of this country – those forces controlling it, that is to say – *wanted* to get this country into the two major world wars of the last century – to keep the highly profitable and in other ways useful wars going, by manipulating the working people of the United States into funding the wars, basically – which funding was achieved largely by means of the hidden tax of inflation. These powers – at base, the big banking houses, which are also owners or big shareholders of many other large corporations, including many which profited hugely from the world wars - knew that the people very strongly did *not* want to get involved – but that an outrageous event allegedly perpetrated by the Axis Powers and causing the loss of American lives would achieve the desired result - would get the American people emotionally willing to go to war."

"Indeed," Riggs concurred. "There is documented historical evidence - available in print and online - just do searches on key names or phrases - detailing that the attacks on both Pearl Harbor and the *Lusitania* were known before-hand to be occurring, in the case of the former, or to be highly likely to occur, in the case of the latter, but that they were *allowed* to happen, and U.S. nationals allowed to die in them, in order to generate public outrage and a create plausible pretexts for bringing the United States – that so wealthy nation – into these wars. These so profitable and so useful wars."

"But, your skepticism is understandable, Ifford," Bevins added. "After all, you can't help the information – and dis-information - you've been exposed to under the labels, or guises, so to speak, of 'news,' 'current events,' and 'history.'"

"Yes, my boy," agreed Riggs kindly. "It's entirely natural to trust these august entities - schools, the media, the government itself - which seem so respectable, and like such - honorable men."

"Which trusting gullibility, of course, the powers which are orchestrating these highly profitable atrocities are well aware of, and exploit very skillfully," said Bevins.

With time's winged chariot drawing near, not to mention the baying hounds of hell, I attempted, in that incisive way of the hybrid under pressure, to get us back to the more pressing problem of what to do with Ifford.

"Well! Thank you both for this most interesting view of things. And information. Not merely opinion, but supporting data. Logically coheres, and most fascinating. Really. But ... back to my present situation then ... as I was saying, I don't see any way that I could be safe here - or how I could possibly escape by traveling off-planet under an assumed identity, or in a suitcase or something. It seems that, if I remain here, hiding like a rat in its hole, it is only a matter of time until I am, like a rat, ferreted out. I guess you could say - dramatic though it sounds - that I am throwing myself upon your mercy because you are my last, best hope."

I sat beaming at them in what I hoped came across as a sort of humbly imploring manner, gently but firmly impaling them with the gaze. I put out with all the force of my character - and my desperation - the imploring pet spaniel stare, with subtle overtones, perhaps of being commanding - *in the name of all that is good and innocent, aid this hapless lad!* - as well as supplicating - while they exchanged the usual flurry of meaningful and questioning glances. The thought occurred that at work and at home, if they were a duo in that arena as well, they must rarely need to resort to verbal communication, as they seemed to have a full vocabulary of meaningful glances.

So we sat there silently in the charged atmosphere, communicating wordlessly. It must have looked rather like one of those narrative paintings of the Victorian era, or like a Norman Rockwell poster. This stand-off seemed to go on several beats too long, and my energy began to falter, and my chin to itch and then rather to my horror, to begin to tremble, and my left eyelid to twitch, and my nose, after that walk in the moist chill air, to drip. Altogether, I felt quite the prize idiot. I rather expected to have a comic rather than tragic impact and dreaded to see the faint suppressed smiles and merry glances, harbingers of full-blown hilarity. But I persisted in the supplicating gaze. I did not want to let up on the pressure. It was the only leverage I possessed. Every time they glanced over at old Ifford, I wanted them to be blasted full force with the pathetic - and as I hoped, subtly commanding - spectacle I made. I perhaps looked a bit like a dog gazing so intently at you as you eat that its brow furrows as if in puzzlement or thought. But more pathetic (and less comic) than that, I hoped. Perhaps with subtle suggestions of the blameless fuzzy fledgling fallen from its nest.

I remember reading in my youth a book about the magnetism of the gaze, and about how successful businessmen on earth practiced the compelling gaze for hours before the mirror, and how that was one of the keys to their success. In fact, as a lad, I myself spent considerable time before the bathroom mirror - when no one else was in there, of course - practicing the compelling gaze; but I never did notice that others felt very compelled, or bent to my steely will and purpose, and after a while I gave it up. But now, it seemed the only ace up my sleeve, the only possible leverage I could apply, and so I beamed both imploringly and intensely at them with all the pathos and magnetism, I could muster.

"… reduced to some sort of fizz …"

CHAPTER 33: ONE LAST CHANCE

And he said, yes, I think it can be easily done,
out on Highway 61 …

Bob Dylan

Having had, I imagine, about as much of the mutely imploring gaze as they could stomach for one go-round, Riggs and Bevins decided to have a little colloquy alone together, your narrator being invited to sit in a small adjoining side-room, a sort of kitchenette with a worn black vinyl sofa crammed into it, while they conferred. Of course, as I sat there thumbing rather sightlessly and mechanically through an old

Entities! magazine I found lying on a scarred and rickety end table next to the plastic sofa, I wondered if they were even now alerting the Gestapo to my presence in their offices. Hyper-vigilant though I admittedly am, even when not being pursued by the hounds of the establishment, I doubted that. And I really felt that they were now the only ace I had up my sleeve or in my pocket, the only trick I had remaining, down in the bottom among the dust and lint, the gum wrappers and old bus transfers and ads torn from matchbook covers for home study and body building courses, in that empty gunny sack of gimmicks, hopes, dreams, and long shots. I had no choice but to trust them. I was tired of running and had run out of places to run to.

Finally, I was summoned to return to the office in which I had made my plea for help. It was Riggs who spoke, and he wasted no time in pleasantries (or spontaneous dissertations on the ways of the power elite in general and the international bankers in particular) but got right to the nub of the matter.

"Well, Ifford ... we do have a colleague who is conducting researches in the general area of which you speak. But first - did you make any effort at all to assure that you were not followed here?"

"Yes, sir, I did check behind me several times to see if anyone appeared to be tailing me. It looked as if I were not being followed."

"Well. I am glad that you took such care. We have decided to put you in the hands of our colleague. But you will understand that it would be impossible to include either of your two friends - the girls for whom you expressed concern. If, as you suspect, you are a hunted individual, then time would indeed be of the essence. And we do have at least some reason to credit your tale. You are trusted by those we trust. And it so happens that our friend has been searching for an experimental subject of the -humanoid persuasion. You get my drift. In that general ballpark. She [she?] has seen several of her animal subjects which were placed in her energy field chamber disappear most gratifyingly. But she knows not when or where they ended up. She needs - frankly - a subject with whom she can possibly communicate, no matter how crudely - by means of signals, you know - communicate from the beyond. Her work is experimental - you should know that. She really has no idea what happened to her animal subjects. Theories, of course, but no hard data."

Here a pause ensued, and it appeared to be my turn to hold forth, which I did. The old diffident, pusillanimous, indecisive Ifford was a creature of the past, it seemed. Emerging from the chrysalis was a newer, more forceful entity, who cleared his throat and spoke confidently.

"Sir, I am willing to volunteer as that humanish subject, as I feel I have few options available to me at this juncture. I am willing and indeed actually eager to participate. In fact, it would seem to me that the sooner the better about sums it up. I mean - I do not think it advisable for me to return to Riqi's or to my room. Wouldn't you agree? I would wish to depart pretty much ASAP as these environs seem no longer all that congenial. It appears that the time is ripe to seize the moment. Time and tide wait for no man." Under pressure I resorted to cliché, thinking perhaps it could do no harm to bring in the grand old tradition of Western civilization to buttress my point.

"Yes, I would tend to agree. You understand that we will have to place our proposal before Dr. Perdue. It so happens that we are going to be seeing her at a faculty meeting this afternoon, which is providential as it will provide us with a natural opportunity to have a word with her re this matter. We propose that you merely make yourself comfortable here until we have a chance to speak with her. After the meeting, we will return here and let you know what she says. We expect that she will agree to use you. We will suggest that she conduct the experiment this very evening, given the possible exigency of your situation. The actual procedure as I understand it takes very little time, and she often works late and so will attract little attention by doing so tonight. So - does that meet with your approval, my boy?"

"Oh, yes, Sir. Perfectly. So very kind of you. You don't know what this means to me. Or perhaps you do. At any rate, I shall be forever in your debt. Both of your debts." Gadzooks. I was doing it again. Maundering on.

I was, I will confess, thinking of Glennie and Riqi. You, the perspicacious Reader, might have gleaned that my motives were perhaps not - as motives rarely are - purely altruistic and in no wise self-serving. Yes, I cared for these females, insofar as I am capable of caring - and I still did not know how far that was. But also and additionally: I did not want to go it alone. I wanted company in the wherever and whenever into which I was to be flung, rather like a human cannon ball in one of those old circus acts - only incalculably much farther.

Perhaps that was at base selfish of me. It seemed rather mad to be actually undertaking such a journey. I could not help but wonder how this translation of self across the impalpable but seemingly impenetrable barrier of time was to be effected. I mean, it seemed entirely possible that I was to be simply effervesced, in a manner of speaking. I mean - time/space travel would have to involve some sort of de-materialization, would it not? It would seem inherently to be a procedure, especially at this highly experimental stage, in which the old adage of there being many a slip betwixt cup and lip would most distinctly apply. Did I want them, Glennie and Riqi, to take the risk of being reduced to some sort of fizz or buzz or hum or crackle or blip on some energy-detecting screen before all physical trace of the three of us vanished utterly from the physical realm - or at any rate, the known physical realm? I mean, total annihilation aside - what if it hurt?

But the thorny moral choice was not mine to make. Expediency, as is so often the case, made up our minds for us. I could see the point Riggs was making, and it was a point well taken. I knew before he spoke what he would say, and that it was the right thing to say in the rather bizarre and convoluted situation in which I found myself.

And my mother! How could I have forgotten about her? I had told her, so long ago it seemed, that I would call her again, but I never had. So many good intentions, promises broken. How, I wondered, could one mean so well and yet fail so many, and get into so much hot water, in so short a span of time? It seemed only yesterday that my biggest problem was managing to pull a 'B' in that Earthly Banking mid-term. And Humphrey! My God, Humphrey. He must be running short on food and water. Would anyone remember to take care of him?

I looked up and saw R & B gazing expectantly at me.

"We do understand how you feel, Ifford," said Riggs, seeming to have intuited what, and who, I had been thinking about, " We will try to get word to those you care about as to what has become of you. And perhaps Glennie might be given the choice of following you - or attempting to do so. At some point in the not-distant future, I mean. She being the most trustworthy of the two, given your long association with her."

So, we left it at that. I had many questions. How would my destination be chosen? How great was the chance that I would end up somewhere utterly other than Hollywood and Vine or vicinity in the late 1940s or early 1950s? Would, for that matter, this female professor, this Perdue, allow me to choose my own destination? Did she have any pretense, any hope of being so accurate, of twiddling the dials and selecting any precise space-time destination? And how did she propose to communicate with me once I got wherever it was I did get to? What if I ended up amongst the dinosaurs, or on Jupiter or Mars, or in mediaeval Germany, or Renaissance Italy, or the home planet, or the middle of the Pacific Ocean without so much as a life raft or a spar of wood to cling to? What if I ended up even being some other entity entirely - say, a gibbon, or an opossum, or a duck-billed platypus or - well, say, a true *Homo sapiens*? That was an interesting thought. I made a mental note to bring that one up when I had a chance with this Dr. Perdue, who, if all went well - again - I speak relatively here - would be the midwife effecting my translation into another world. If she was enough of a sorceress so to break the known laws of the Universe in this regard, then perhaps it would be a snap to give me the identity, the ethnicity - broadly speaking - that I had long coveted.

And with this thought firmly in mind, it was a slightly happier, a slightly calmer, a slightly mollified Ifford who was turned once again into that small adjoining room - with its tattered black vinyl sofa, its many small rips patched by some genius of the household with silver duct tape, some of these patches now curling up at the corners and the once-sticky underside now coated with grit of undiscoverable origin, and with its squat refrigerator of a depressing shade of dull grayish-green - who would ever decorate their kitchen in such a drab, funereal color, I wondered - and its sink and inevitable micro-wave oven and a random and rather sad assortment of eating utensils, food, and condiments in the cupboard and fridge. My hosts told to make myself at home, and heat the single can of soup – chicken noodle, it was - or eat a few stale, rubbery miniature marshmallows, which, aside from various condiments of uncertain vintage seemed the only remaining choice - if I felt hungry, until they - they upon whom all my hopes of salvation were now pinned - should return from their faculty meeting.

CHAPTER 34: DISQUIETING DREAM

Trembles to think that his quivering meat
Must finally wince to nothing at all ...

Delmore Schwartz

I must have dozed off on the vinyl sofa; when I opened my eyes with a start, it was twilight outside, and through the one high, rectangular window of the room I saw that the sky was darkening, and that it now offered up a rather glorious jumble of clouds in varying shades of white and gray and deep blue, some of them with delicate pink underbellies, the bare tree branches making dark silhouettes against the lot of them. I wondered if there would be clouds and trees and twilights such as these where I was going.

Going ... that word was perhaps the trigger that brought back into my mind the dream I had been in the midst of when I awoke. It came back to me with great vividness and intensity. In my dream, it was snowing, and the wind was blowing, and it was night, and cold ... but I had to get home. I remember that I slipped once, and fell, on my way to the bridge - some bally bridge, a great huge thing I knew I had to cross, to get home ... and I noticed, then, how very light and dry was the snow. It seemed a - white nothing - a kind of air. On the bridge, I knew – in the way that you just know these things in dreams - it would be bitter cold. There, the wind would be blowing full force; and it was the wind, even here, amongst these tall sheltering buildings - comic-book sky-scrapers of 1940s vintage, is what they appeared to be - it was the wind, which had pushed me - made me fall. (I looked so tiny, all alone walking on the snowy sidewalks, through that desert of empty streets, among all those tall skyscrapers with their tiers of dark windows like so many empty staring eyes). Then one of those shifts of scenes for which dreams are so notorious, and I saw myself, a tiny figure in black silhouette, lifted by a great gust right off the bridge, blown into the blackness like an empty sweater. It gave me a most unpleasant sensation in the pit of my stomach. And I, in the dream, seeing this, remembered at night, and alone, having sat under the bridge, right at water's edge, seeing the water roiling like the backs of great fishes or whales plunging with ferocious effortless energy about the immense blocks of gray concrete from which rose the thick steel underpinnings of the bridge, and lifting my eyes, as if following the gesture of those huge metal girders ... looking up as if on some command, as if scripted ... or as if doing something I had done before ... to see a white - something - drift down, or rather be jerked down, by the powerful gusts of wind that blew about the bridge, to be sucked into the roiling waters as into the mouth of a great, amorphous black creature, or into a vast underworld of shades and shadows - of all things dark. Just so, I feared falling from the bridge - that bridge I had to cross. Its surface crawled with cars, like so many gleaming metallic bugs with headlights for eyes, the small animate toys of, perhaps, some giant metal-clad child. In the dream it was somehow known to me that they - these shiny armored ants - made the bridge from the stuff of their minds - and that it was their belief in their creation which held them to it - like black iron filings to a magnet. But me - their magnetism would not work for me. Like a bit of black plastic held to a magnet, I would slide off. I knew nothing. I had no dreams. I could not cross that bridge. It was utterly silent, as when one presses the mute button on the TV controller. Another scene shift, and I was in a bright room. It was still snowing, the snow up to the rafters now ... thicker, deeper, than sleep. I became aware of a sound that might have been there all along, like a film projector, it was, whirring so loudly, like a bee in a jar held to my ear, as it mindlessly cast its empty square of glistening, glaring luminosity upon the pimpled white wall ... and everyone had gone home - except for me.

That was my dream, and though it had an undeniable beauty, I wished I had not had it. Such an empty feeling. And I realized, with stark, rather sickening clarity, how very alone I had felt, all my life, for as long as I could remember. And the dream, as augury, did not seem to augur well for my - journey. The journey that I hoped I was about to take. What with the white something being sucked into the hungry maw of the black nothingness and all. But in that empty moment, I heard sounds without, the door to my little chamber opened, and Riggs and Bevins (I was very glad it was them and not some SWAT team or other come to haul me in, or even some janitor who might ask the usual questions, and, perhaps, place the usual phone calls) looking pink-cheeked and invigorated from the cold.

CHAPTER 35: PREPARE TO LAUNCH

I don't mind dying;
I just don't want to be there when it happens.

Woody Allen

"Well, Ifford. I hope you were comfortable - not too bored - and not disturbed - in our absence?" Old Riggs, for all his genial affability, his, as I had seen it, clownishness, actually had that, what I believe is called, air of quiet authority about him. Did I just notice this? Or was I investing him with these qualities, now that I had latched onto him as my savior and deliverer? I don't know about the reader, but such questions and thoughts are always popping into my head at the most inopportune moments - moments, you know, when one should be all action and totally immersed in the realm of the actual as opposed to the speculative.

"Fine, Sir - it was fine. Restful. I napped a bit, in fact."

"Good, good. Glad to hear it. Well, Ifford, we will cut right to the chase, as I know you would prefer - and indeed as I should, in your position. Perdue has agreed to take you on - as an experimental subject, you know - and she is available, as we had hoped, this very evening. Had planned to be working late, as she often does. Says it's the only time she can work uninterrupted."

I made the appropriate gladsome sounds. I do not recall exactly what I said. But I burbled gratefully as seemed only the right thing to do. I did not want to appear anything but overjoyed. But truth to tell, dear Reader, fear clutched at my vitals as I heard him speak those words. Once again I felt the hot and icy sensations dashing like quicksilver in my innards. And I felt like saying, thanks but no thanks. I mean, in the abstract, this had seemed the solution, you know, to my thorny knot of problems. Modern science's answer to divine deliverance, the old *Deus ex machina*. But when faced with the actual prospect, one quails. It was so - damned experimental. Not to mention counter-intuitive. Perhaps my face betrayed some of this, for my deliverer - if that was indeed what he was - spoke, his various toad-like features having assembled themselves into a questioning look.

"You do still want to go through with this, Ifford? If not, it is not too late to change your mind, and Lorna would I am sure understand. It is, after all, an experimental situation ..."

"Lorna ...?"

"Dr. Perdue, that is to say. Her given name is Verlorna Aphasia. After her great-grandmother, she tells me, who was as her name suggests a rather silent woman, often lost in thought - but a great doer, as I understand. Our Lorna, as she prefers to be called, is rather like her, a thinker and a doer - but not a great talker. Do not expect her to give any detailed explanations of the underlying principles by which her process - works its wonders."

If in fact it does work, I thought to myself. Looking at it from one angle, this Verlorna wheeze made a great cover story. Who knew where - and to whom - they were taking me. But there I was, once again being either reasonably prudent, *caveat emptor* and all, or paranoid. Who was it who so humorously - the black variety of humor, don't you know - opined that if you're not paranoid you're just not in touch with the realities of our modern situation, or perhaps post-post-modern situation - or as some would call it, predicament? Well, no matter. The time for doubt, for shilly-shallying, seemed well past.

"No doubts, not in the least, Sir. I am determined to go through with it. Frankly, as I have said, I see no other - way out - of these problems. I feel that Fate, for its own imponderable reasons, has rather painted me into a corner."

"Very well then. Florence - those clothes ...?"

Bevins had been carrying a plump tote bag which she now held out to me.

"Janitor's garb. No fake ID card - we couldn't manage that, of course, on such short notice. But with this outfit and a lunch-box, you should make it over there safely."

"You - aren't going to accompany me?" That sounded pathetic as soon as I said it, and I wished I could take it back.

"No. It does not seem advisable - nor, actually, is it necessary. I believe that you know how to find the building in which her laboratory is located. It is the same one in which Torvald has his lab and office. I understand you have been there?"

"Oh, yes."

"Do you think you can find it again? It is only the equivalent of a few blocks due west of here, across campus."

"Towards the setting sun. Or the land of opportunity. Yes. I am sure I can find it again. I was, after all, a student here." I took the bag and pulled out the grayish brown shirt and pants. They had even included a light jacket, and a baseball cap, and a pair of sturdy work boots - and even a rather battered workman's lunch pail, one of those with a humped lid in which fits a thermos. I wondered how they had come up with all this stuff on such short notice.

Riggs and Bevins left me to make the change, which I did. The clothes were large on my slender frame, but luckily the pants were belted. I knew I should freeze on the way over, wearing only that light jacket; but that would have to be borne. I was shivering as it was, I noticed - just from trepidation.

When I emerged from the little kitchenette, Riggs handed me a half-empty pack of cigarettes and a lighter. He explained that it would not hurt for me to pause to light a cigarette, upon leaving the building by a rear service entrance, and to appear to be smoking it on my way to Perdue's office. Also, Bevins came forward with scissors and cut very short the locks of the black wig I was wearing. She also had some pancake make-up of a sort of brownish hue which she patted on my face, after using cold cream and tissues to remove the make-up I had applied at Riqi's, which I had forgotten about. Remembering all the clothing I had borrowed from Riqi, I asked R & B if they could get an anonymous someone to leave them for her to pick up at the counter at The Silver Stud, which they agreed to do.

Then the two urged me off. They told me that Purdue would be expecting me at a certain precise time. The plan was that she and I would just happen to enter the now locked building at the same time and by the same back entrance - the one that was used by the cleaning staff and which she also customarily used, it being near the lot where she parked her car. All I needed to do, they said, was walk around the building at the appointed time - which was but 15 minutes from now - and I should encounter her, as if by chance, and we could enter the building together.

Riggs' parting words to me were a bit of advice: "Good luck, my boy. Godspeed. And, Ifford - if I may offer a bit of advice, from this perspective of hindsight - buy real estate. Buy real property, my boy."

Which Bevins punctuated with an emphatic nod of her head, thrusting into my hand a scribbled note which, when I glanced at it on my way to meet this Lorna Aphasia person, said, *'Invest in real estate ... Catch gold/silver bubble ... Blend in* [As if I needed to be told that!] *.. .buy Elvis memorabilia ... Buy Microsoft stock - early. Retain this list!'* It

410

seemed a motherly send-off. She also for some reason included a paperback copy of Jack Kerouac's *On the Road*. I don't know if it was an attempt at humor, or what. Bevins had never struck me as having much by way of a sense of humor.

CHAPTER 36: CHILLED STEEL

The scrimmage of appetite everywhere ...

Delmore Schwartz

As I made my cautious way over to find Perdue and keep this, my latest - and I hoped ultimate - desperate and furtive assignation, I thought of Glennie and I wondered what she was doing right this minute; I wished I could call her - but I knew I dared not. I thought also of Riqi. I mean - the pathos of it all, don't you know. I imagined her popping out of her cake, with a big smile plastered on her lovely girlish face, gyrating suggestively before lustful strangers, clad only - she, I mean, and not the lustful strangers - in some delightful pink satin and fringe bit of next-to-nothing ... I remembered the honey color of her skin, her hair; her slow smile, both shy and forthright, and the way she held my eyes with hers; I thought of her coming home to find Ifford vanished without a note or a trace. I wanted very badly to believe in her, and above all to see her again. I thought of little Humphrey in his little cage. I must tell Perdue of him - that he needed food and water, and a new master, and needed it ASAP. I thought of my mother. She would think either that I had betrayed her - just cut her loose as too risky to have any further contact with - or that I had come to grief - which perhaps indeed I had, or was about to, in some terrible and final sense of the phrase. I did not know how to get word to her as to what had happened and was about to happen to me.

You know - dear Reader - you know how assiduously I have resisted any information, or interpretation, to the effect that the hands seen and unseen guiding our world are anything but beneficent, and loftily disinterested in personal gain or advancement. Boy Scouts *sans* the uniforms, as it seems they would have us see them. You know that. And yet - the point I am making - this theory, this vile theory of the corruptibility in theory and in fact of those who seek and gain power - of the impurity of their motives, of the impurity of their deeds - this vile theory, that I so loyally rejected as so much nonsense, as so much 'conspiracy theory' ... well: it would seem to have - shall we say, impacted my life. Despite my denial of its validity, it would seem, in the vulgar argot of the streets, to have crept up and bit me in the arse. That is what I was thinking as I walked and shivered in the gathering gloom of these, what I imagined would be my last moments in this particular corner of the time/space continuum that I had latterly called home.

I know it was, presumably, only the home-grown Gestapo that were pursuing me now. But they did so with the full, not to say enthusiastic, cooperation of the authorities here on Earth. I mean - wasn't the United States of legend supposed to be opposing and not assisting this sort of thing? And what about all the surveillance cameras in public places, and these random stops of cars and pedestrians to check the mandatory biometric ID? What of the sweeps and searches through the coffee-houses and bookstores and restaurants and work-places, which occur so often now, and without warning? What about the way all they had to do was call anyone a 'terrorist' and they could just take him off to no one knew where for as long as they wanted, and hold him incommunicado and try him in secret military courts, intern him in a work camp, even execute him - and never even tell his family and friends what had happened to him? What about the 'internal' passports now required to travel from state to state and city to city? I mean - what would the founding fathers have said to all of that? What about the taxation at well over 50% and still climbing? What about the homelessness - which there did not used to be here, except for the alcoholic men who had always been living that marginal type of existence? I mean - were we talking the land of the free and the home of the brave here - or were the sound and the picture simply not matching anymore?

Something popped into my mind that Torvald had said at one of our coffee house rendezvous - he was talking about these two classics of the mid-20th Century political literature - *Brave New World*, which foresaw a future in which the masses are controlled by deception, and by pleasurable escapist drugs, and a chillier number called simply *1984*, in which the masses live in a highly controlled and surveilled totalitarian state, the government holding sway without any good-guy mask, by means of sheer power and terror. Torvald had said that the move in the 20th Century – in Europe and the United States, at any rate - had been first away from rule by force and fear and towards rule by means of deceit, drugs, deception, and trickery; but that once the ruling elite had gotten in their universal citizen disarmament, which they called gun control, the pendulum had begun a rather rapid swing back toward the rule by naked force and terror - chilled steel. I felt that I had come, rather up close and personal, as the saying goes, against the reality of those remarks.

413

For some reason having perhaps to do with my admittedly morbid state of mind, the image came to mind of a pair of white test dummies in an experimental car crash, perhaps staged to test seatbelts or airbags or brakes - or maybe even to test the test dummies. I saw in my mind's eye a black and white film showing, in slow motion, two such dummies crashing stiffly, their faces blanks, featureless masks, against the windshield, the steering wheel and dashboard, and rebounding in slow motion, their dummy arms waving wildly, as the car they were in ploughed soundlessly, amidst the slowly exploding dust and debris of the crash, into the cement wall of a vast low-ceilinged, dimly lit parking garage. It was night, and the place had darkness lurking in all its corners, just dimly broken by pools of stark, yellowish light here and there from widely-spaced overhead fixtures. This parking garage, which seemed to go on forever, was empty save for random bits of debris on the floor, and the occasional parked car, and those fat, cast-cement cylindrical support pillars scattered about as in some contemporary art installation, the now congealed thin oozing of cement from the seams in their molds spiraling up and around them in a graceful repeated motif which was the single bit of beauty, of poetry, in the place. The scene had Kafka written all over it. Bergman couldn't have made it any bleaker if he'd tried. Perhaps I had found my métier. I, test dummy, I thought - living out my life in a windowless black-and-white world of gray concrete, level after level of it, a kind of modern labyrinth in which the echoing stairways and claustrophobic elevators lead only to another identical level, or to a locked door at the end of a long series of stairs. It seemed to me, as I walked, to be indeed, in more ways than one, a stark and pitiless world – what with the double whammy of nature's silent indifference and man's active and enthusiastic inhumanity to man, you know. And my naïve denial of its chill realities had proven no defense against it.

Such were my thoughts as I trudged along. Bleak. I admit it was hard to think clearly. In fact, it was hard to think at all. I was trying only to pretend to smoke that horrid cigarette, but it was making me feel sickish nonetheless; and of the state of my nerves I will not speak. And yet I saw the above with a cold, hard-edged clarity that looked and felt like sharpened, chilled steel. I wondered about all these glorifiers of violence, generation after generation of them – and their love of weapons made of chilled steel. Perhaps I simply lacked the good old testosterone in the proper manly proportions - but I wondered why the worlds had to be this way - ruled by the lovers of chilled steel – and peopled, it sometimes seemed, when it boiled right down to it, and you looked at the sticky residue at the bottom of the pot – if the reader can bear with a mixing of metaphors – by so many animate test dummies. Test dummies are made in molds, aren't they? And the matrix of culture – or culture and genetics - is but a mold - is it not? We alone of the creatures have the capacity to rise above our programming, to choose, to self-determine, to reach for the stars – but by and large, we don't do it.

But I shook off these thoughts, these dark thoughts to which we hybrids are said to be so prone, took another weak drag on my cigarette (not inhaling, of course), and - kept on truckin'.

"Lorna Perdue"

CHAPTER 37: BORROWING A LITTLE TIME

It ain't no use in turnin' on your light, Babe,
I'm on the dark side of the road ...

Bob Dylan

Well, the part about meeting and getting into the building together worked out as planned. The area appeared utterly deserted, and we were unobserved but for the camera by the door - which Dr. Perdue - or

Lorna, as she asked me to call her - said was not monitored 'in real time,' as she put it. Also, I was wearing that baseball cap which cast my face into shadow and obscured my features. And then, there was that silly fake mustache that Bevins had insisted I wear - did I remember to mention that? - ridiculous though it made me feel. I was glad to be able to peel it off once we got into the office and lab of Lorna Perdue.

Verlorna was a small, slim woman of middle age, with rather wiry salt-and-pepper hair pulled back into bun. But all sorts of hairs escaped from this attempt at control, which helped soften the severity of the style and made her look a bit like an Italian grandmother in a TV commercial for pasta sauce. She was not beautiful, by any means, but I rather liked the way she looked. She had skin of an olive tone and was slim, with a narrow face and a slightly pointy chin; she wore functional clothing under her open black woolen coat - a loose-fitting dress that came to mid-calf, in a bumpy, textured cottony fabric of black and beige threads interwoven into a kind of plaid pattern, and dark blackish-gray hose with practical, comfortable-looking shoes which had those high-rise soles that gave her a couple of extra inches of height. Perhaps she was as self-conscious about her small stature as I was about my over-all Andy Warhol bleached-out and thin-as-a-rail look. The thought gave me a sort of comfort. Perhaps we were a bit alike. And I drew comfort from the fact that she wore a dress and was not mannishly dressed, in one of those ghastly pants suits, as so many career females are, in all the worlds, from what one sees on the telly.

 Even I could see that I was grasping at straws. I sorely did need to feel that she was a proper repository for my trust.

Once in the building she indicated that it would be better if I were to take the stairs and meet her at her lab - which was on the second floor - she gave me the number and told me to go use the men's room or something and then to slip into her lab without knocking, which I did.

Her lab was not at all like Torvald's, for which I was glad. His had been almost - creepy - it had been so odd. Very mediaeval, as the reader will recall. Very 'trippy' is what I think Riqi might call it. Simply being there made one feel strange, as though some magic mushroom was just beginning to take effect. Perdue had a nice corner space with an office and then behind it the lab, and the office decor was just ordinary and comfortable, with a houseplant or two, and a poster of some lovely coastline, perhaps in Marin County, photographed in the warm light of late afternoon, and books in shelves on the walls, and a desk with papers on it, and a computer and a phone. It did not, as did Torvald's cave-like nook, make a statement, or create a quasi-theatrical atmosphere.

She got right down to business. There were no forms to fill out and precious little in the way of explanation. I tried to feel her out a bit regarding the theory behind this process we were about to employ. On the walk over, I had started worrying, for one thing, about whether I would have to be accelerated up to the speed of light. I had been thinking about it all and had recalled from some past physics class that according to Einstein, the relativity theory and all that, that as one approached the speed of light, time got slower, somehow. I had read somewhere that to travel backwards in time, one had to go faster than the speed of light. Time goes by more and more slowly, is the idea, as one approaches the magic number and then, as one rounds that curve and is going even faster than light - *voila* - one is regressing temporally. So, I believe, goes the theory. Anyway, as one approached or neared the s.o.l. clip, one aged less, or hardly at all, is what I remember. That part I liked. But also I recalled that the mass of objects approaching the speed of light grew greater - very much greater. Well, for these purposes and in these circs, I would be treated by the inflexible laws of the Universe, with its utterly democratic and impartial approach to matter, as a mere object, I imagined. And this growing vastly larger - well, I didn't like the sound of it. It sounded as if it could hurt - rather badly. I wondered if that was what she had in mind. I did not see how it could be - I mean, here in her office and all. I saw no launching pad.

But one never knew, with these physicists and mathematicians. Who knows what one of them, immersed in highly arcane and advanced realms of thought and possibility, might not be able to pull from some desk drawer or closet in a corner of the lab. A sort of instantly expandable - inflatable, perhaps - mini-launching pad and economy-sized rocket ship, which would purr like an expensive car when fired up, and ascend to the heavens via a silently opening remote-controlled garage door sort of thing concealed behind a curtain or remote-controlled sliding panel on a wall - well, why not? Stranger things have been pulled out of the hat by these scientific fellows. Ingenious, one had to give them that; but they had always struck me, temperamentally, as a rather bloodless lot, had these metaphysicians of the hard sciences; I had never gotten any warm toasty feelings from a single one of them, that I can recall. This Verlorna seemed to be actually among the better - in the sense of, more human - in the sense of humane - of the lot I had encountered so far - for which I felt so grateful that I had to watch myself that I did not start burbling moistly and getting all sentimental on her, clasping her hands in mine, holding her gaze and oozing sincerity and saying I did not know how I was ever going to be able to repay her and so on and so forth - embarrassing the poor woman, as of course it would.

But I was in a sort of jumbled state, because such impulses alternated with quite opposite ones which caused me to detect, or think I had detected, a steely glint in her dark eye and which impelled me towards the door. I guessed that this was the approach-avoidance conflict I had read about in that intro psych class. I was in the throes of it up to the eyeballs and I felt for those poor lab rats that were shocked as they tried to cross that metal grid to get their rat chow and a simple drink of water. The diabolical things these scientists come up with. Just a glorified bunch of sadists is what it makes one think, who as lads got their jollies pulling the wings off flies and tormenting their younger siblings when the parents weren't watching. And that isn't the half of it, from what Glennie has told me. When they devised these experiments for the poor shocked rats, they were just warming up.

Anyway, Lorna was actually a pretty reassuring sort. She had a kind of bedside manner - a nice little smile, really, with crinkly eyes, one of those smiles that came in a flash and left in a flash, just traces lingering in her eyes, and she shone on me a friendly humorous look every now and then as she gave me her explanations. It made me wonder if she had ever been a nurse, or a kindergarten teacher, before taking up advanced experimental physics. (Riggs and Bevins had assured me, before sending me off with lunch pail in hand like some over-grown child off to school, that she actually had quite the reputation, in her field.)

I voiced my speed-of-light concerns, and Perdue told me not to worry. I would not be accelerated; I would not grow great as did Alice when she ate the mushroom, nor regressed to my infancy, or earlier. She used a different method entirely, she told me. The underlying theory was all different. She tried to tell me a bit about it - as I recall, she told me that time and space actually spiral, like slinkies - you know those accordion-like toys that can go down a set of stairs. She also mentioned wormholes. My mind kept wandering. I was wondering what outer space actually looked like, and if wormholes would be claustrophobic, like elevators. She said that she was working with this theory - of time tunnels, and the wormholes, don't you know. There were actually these tunnels, she said, connecting different years, several decades apart. I would emerge through the 'gateway' as she called it, into this precise space but in a previous year. She asked when I wanted to go to, and I told her.

She was fortunately able to offer me 1953. It sounded like a very good year. She said that according to the same theory, space travel was also possible, but that she was working only on the time angle at present and could not accommodate my desire to be in a different space. I would have to make my own way to southern California. Or at least, she did not think she could do both at once - not at the point she had reached so far in her experiments. But since I was in the right country, and only about 1500 miles away from there, and would, if her theory was correct, emerge from the gateway in this same local - she seemed quite sure of that - I should be able to make my way to my chosen destination, in terms of space, if she handled the time aspect of my journey.

Did I mention that Riggs and Bevins had given me some money that I could use? I had in fact a few US gold $20 pieces of an earlier era, which they told me I could take to any coin shop and exchange for paper money. I do not know how they came up with that for me on such short notice and will be everlastingly grateful for it. (For all I knew, they were running some sort of underground time/space railway for political fugitives or some such thing.) I was taking with me only that seed money, so to speak, and the janitor's lunch pail holding the Kerouac paperback - and this journal, of course, which I had gotten in the habit of taking with me everywhere. I didn't even have a comb, a change of underwear, or a toothbrush.

Perdue told me that there was only one thing that she asked of me, and that was to send her a signal, with something about the size of a cell phone that she asked me to take along, called - I think it was - a tachyon pulse emitter. I think that was what the old girl called the thing. It was this signal-sending that the rats or guinea pigs or whatever it was she had sent out as the *avant garde* had been unable to do. All I had to do was remember to press some buttons periodically, in a simple code that would indicate to her the time and locale to which I had been transported.

And then, after this extremely sketchy explanation, she stood up and said, "Well - shall we?" Just like that.

I can tell you, Reader, that old Ifford had a hard time standing, and walking. I was clutching that bally lunch box like it was a mother. It, and this journal, had come to be kind of like a security blanket for me. And I was wearing that light workman's jacket, the manly kind that zips up and has elastic at the waist. And then I was wearing also this pair of black working man's shoes that Riggs and Bevins had somehow dug up for me at the last moment. I think I mentioned these. They were heavy and clunky. But they did make me feel rather virile. And that baseball cap, of course.

Virile or not, however, I felt as if I were walking to an execution chamber. That is exactly how I felt. It took all I could manage to get up, and smile a quavery smile at her - Verlorna. She looked so beautiful at that moment! It flitted through my mind to ask her if she needed a houseboy - someone to wax the floors and water the plants and just do what needed doing around the house - whatever house it was she lived in. But that would have been too undignified. We hybrids do not throw ourselves on the mercy of strangers - any more, that is, than is absolutely necessary.

So. I managed to smile, a bit shakily, and to stand, and to follow her into that lab of hers. And therein I saw what indeed did look like a doorway, or a gateway. And I did approach it. And I did stand where she bade me stand. I was thinking about Glennie. I was thinking about Riqi. I was thinking that they would join me. I had penned messages for them that I asked Riggs and Bevins to try to deliver. Whether they will pass these messages on, or not, I do not know. They have their doubts re Riqi's trustworthiness. I had asked them to use their judgment. They had said they would. I hoped they would include my note to her with her clothes when they left them at The Stud.

Perdue went over and started fiddling with some dials. My heart pounding in my chest, I called to her in what sounded to my own ears a very shaky voice, "Wait! Wait just a minute. One more thing. You must tell Riggs and Bevins to ask Torvald or Rantor to see to it that Humphrey is given food and water and a suitable home found for him. Will you promise to do that? My good friend Glennie would probably take him. He's my hamster - Humphrey, you know? He must be getting low on food and water. He needs attending to."

She glanced up, nodded agreement in a distracted sort of way, murmuring as if to herself, "Humphrey ... OK ..." and went back to her dials and knobs. But my anxiety must have registered, for after a moment she looked up at me briefly and, with one of her crinkly-eyed smiles, said to me, "Don't worry, Ifford ... I'll tell them about Humphrey, and you - you'll be as safe as - money in the bank."

She did look like she knew what she was talking about. But her simile - or would it be a metaphor? - I can never keep them straight - seemed particularly ill-chosen, regarded in light of all that Torvald and Rantor had so recently told me about that sleight-of-hand disappearing act that the central banks allegedly routinely perform, with their inflation/ recession cycles, on the earnings of the working stiffs of the world. In fact, my eyes popped open and I drew in a breath to tell the mad scientist to hold on a minute, just one tiny minute, and explain that last crack of hers. I raised my hand to signal her to stop the proceedings, intending to grill her as to the possible *double entendre* aspects, you know, of that last remark. It all seemed just a wee bit too sinister to be a mere coincidence.

But just then I heard - and felt - a whirring sound. I don't know if the reader has ever felt a whirring sound, but I did, and I won't even try to describe it, as it was pretty much indescribable. But definitely vibrational, you know. It was actually quite relaxing. Feeling it was too late now to go into it with her, I closed my eyes and steeled myself for ... and then I felt a sort of tap on my shoulder. Opening my eyes with a start I saw Perdue standing before me, offering me something - a book.

I forgot to tell you," she said. "I am not absolutely certain I will be able to land you in the exact same strand of probable reality as the one we currently inhabit."

I hummed, placing a question mark at the end. I mean - what was one supposed to say to such an announcement? What would Miss Manners advise? I hadn't the foggiest. Verlorna was telling me she wasn't 'absolutely certain' where she was even jettisoning me off to? Perhaps I was over-reacting, but that seemed a rather serious admission to be casually tossing out at this stage of the proceedings.

"I'm sure - quite sure - it will be a very near relative, so to speak, of this strand. But I thought it might be a good idea for you to take this book along with you. That way you can - well, compare."

I must have stood there gaping. Really, it was all a bit much. Probable reality strands. Were they as many, then, as hairs in a lion's mane? Didn't this add considerable complexity to an already inherently risky business? After a beat or two in which I stood trying to wrap my mind around this latest casually divulged bit of intelligence, Verlorna literally picked up my hand and placed the book in it.

"Well - do take this, then. Perhaps you can find room for it in your lunch box." Rather numbly, I looked down at it. It was a grubby, worn paperback entitled, *A Brief History of the 20th Century,* looking rather as if someone who had loved it very much had been in the habit of fondling it as he or she drifted off into the nightly slumber. We did manage - just - to find room in my lunch box, she cramming it in while I held the lunch box open.

"You can compare and contrast, you know," she said chattily, snapping shut the clasps on the lunch pail as she spoke. I might have been going off for a picnic and a bit of boating on the river, to judge by her casual manner. I wondered in a remote and dazed sort of way if she would be so cool were our present roles reversed. "It could be interesting. And on the inside front cover I've scribbled for you again that simple code by which you can, I hope, message me."

One if by land, two if by sea. I considered bring up my concerns in re that last ambiguous crack of hers about money in the bank, but she was already back at her console, twiddling knobs and pressing buttons with a look of deep concentration on her face, and then that whirring sound resumed, and shifted into sort of a whine, and I ...

Well, Reader, I - let it ride.

CHAPTER 38: FARE-THEE-WELL

What else endures, in all this broken world,
save only dreams.

Dana Burnet

Hello, dear Reader. Hello-ello-ello. I seem to have made it. Either that, or I am dreaming, or Heaven has an office where new arrivals are processed, and they are having a slow day. It seems altogether too pleasant a place - and too deserted - to be one of the waiting rooms of Hell. For it is in a quiet, old-fashioned office that I find myself, lunch pail in hand. Did I mention that in my lunch pail I had stuffed this journal? Perhaps I forgot to mention that. I didn't want to leave it behind. It feels like an old friend - and is the only connection I have or may ever have with Glennie - and all the rest of them.

Well. I made it, by Jove. It felt sort of like I was being whirred in a blender, you know, where there was no up nor down nor right nor left - closest I can come to describing the odd sensations - for a period of indeterminate duration, and then the feeling subsided, and I cautiously opened my eyes and found myself in this very roomy corner office space on this very campus - but it was, in fact, as I managed to ascertain by glancing at a wall calendar conveniently near - in the same old mid-winter month, but of the year ... 1953. How magical and full of possibility that number sounds to me!

For some reason, it is daytime and not night as it was back there in Dr. Perdue's laboratory, which strikes me as being not quite in accord with her theory, as I dimly recall it, but all to the good. And, as luck would further have it - perhaps, just perhaps, old Ifford's luck is changing - I popped into this space - the office of some professor or other, as it appears - at a moment when, luckily, there was no one loitering in the immediate vicinity. The fellow must be out doing research, or teaching a class, or conferencing over coffee with a fresh and dewy student. Suddenly, there I was. And, with considerable verve and presence of mind, considering all I had so recently - if that is the word I want - been through - I walked out casually through the office, in which a single secretary with a matching sweater set of a rich garnet red, and a white Peter Pan collar, a pageboy hairdo, and a nubby tweed dirndl skirt of grayish-brown with pale green flecks - dressed rather like Donna Reed, actually, on that TV show in which she so long starred - was rummaging about in a file cabinet, very intent, and muttering to herself in an annoyed-sounding voice. She did not notice me in my janitor's garb walk quietly past her and out the door ... and along the empty corridor, and down the stairs, and out the massive doors of that massive old building, and out, out into the open air. There is no snow on the ground, and the temperature seems warmer. It seems to be mid-day or thereabouts. (I forgot to look for a clock.) As I stood on the broad stone steps of that building, surveying the students walking on the quad singly and in twos and threes, I could hardly believe my luck. I was where I wanted to be - or perhaps I should say, I was when I wanted to be.

425

I don't know where or when you are reading this ... you, my hypothetical Reader. Or if anyone is reading, or has read, or will ever read this picaresque account of the misadventures of Yours Truly: I, hybrid, inter-galactic malcontent, misfit, and fugitive from injustice. Minus the injustice part, I am sure that would be Squinch's take on me, that or something worse. Whatever. At any rate, I shall no doubt keep writing in this journal. It has become by now a habit with me. Perhaps I shall even get around to submitting it to a publisher or two as a sci-fi manuscript. It possibly might have some commercial value as pulp fiction or whatever. Viewed from a certain angle, it does all sound pretty fantastical, doesn't it? It just goes to show that truth really is stranger than fiction.

R & B told me that if I inquire in bars and coffee shops and similar hang-outs, I should be able to find someone who will employ me and pay me under the table - just any job, for starters, whether as dishwasher or bus boy or whatever - and also some underworld type who can make me a fake Social Security card - the work permit, if that lot are to be believed - with which I can get an above-board job, once I have made my way to southern California ... and commence buying real estate. And collecting Elvis memorabilia.

It is all up to me now. But at least I am here. And the sun is shining - a pallid winter sun in a northern clime, but the sun, nevertheless. It puts me in mind of that song - you probably know the one. Or maybe you don't. I don't think it's been written yet - or perhaps ever will be, in this particular probability strand. But anyway, it has a catchy tune, and it goes like this ... *'I can see clearly now, the rain has gone ... I can see dum de dum de daaaaa ..... I can see clearly now the dum de daa .... gonna be a briight, briight, sun-shiny day ... gonna be a briight, briight sun-shiney day ...'* I never could quite catch all the words. You know how those singer chappies mumble.

Well. I don't mean to get all maudlin on you, dear Reader. That, after all, would be contrary to my upbringing. But it's just that ... well, this is a rather epiphanic moment, isn't it, in the life of old Ifford? A turning point, and all that? Not to mention a veritable *Deus ex machina* ... and I thought those only occurred in made-up stories. But I seem to be rambling. Perhaps hurtling through the time/space continuum does that to a fellow. I mean - there is so much we don't know - isn't there?

But, back to the present - in a manner of speaking, and also, in a manner of speaking, realistically - as for the bright, bright sunshiny day, well - we shall see, shan't we? We shall see. But for now - well, I've got to find a bally place to stay for the night - don't I, dear Reader? And a bite to eat. I wonder if a latte is to be had for love or money in this particular corner of that slippery thing we call reality. Yes. Well. As to that, we shall see. I don't think they have lattes here yet. I shall have to be brave. Or perhaps I can get rich by opening up a chain of espresso shops. Get a jump on the competition. Ifford the entrepreneur. Perhaps I shall change my name to Starbuck. It does have a nice sound. Ifford Clarence Starbuck. More catchy – certainly more euphonious - than Furze. But for now, I must make my way off this campus, and out into what we call the real world - one of them, anyway - and - well, find a place to stay for the night - don't I, dear Reader?

finis

Websites
(Not exhaustive, and in no particular order)

Note: There are many excellent websites (and books) created by true lovers of liberty – and a good deal of 'Pied Piper'/paid piper disinformation masquerading as the work of populist dissidents – so, *caveat lector.*

Just doing a search on subject phrases found in this book will lead one to much information not reported in the MSM.

www.CAFR1.com (information concerning undisclosed investment income on part of local governments)

http:www.apfn/OKCcoverup.htm (suppressed information on the OKC bombing)

legal_reality@earthlink.net (contact for a book on CD - were the Constitution and the federal government ever lawfully created?)

http://www.scholarsfortruth911.org/

http://911blogger.com/

http://www.reopen911.org/

http://www.geocities.com/killtown/

http://www.standdown.net/

http://www.911truth.org/

http://thewebfairy.com/killtown/911links.html

http://www.tvnewslies.org

http://www.prisonplanet.com/911.html

http://stopthelie.com/home.html

http://www.911proof.com/

http://georgewashington.blogspot.com/

http://www.whatreallyhappened.com

http://www.rense.com

www.conspiracyarchive.com

www.givemeliberty.org

http://911research.wtc7.net/

http://www.PatriotsQuestion911.com

www.realityzone.com (the problems with central banks/fiat currencies, and collectivism; general information on covert agendas of government damaging to the public interest)

www.mises.org (information on free market economics)

www.iahf.com

www.teamlaw.org (information on the corporate parallel government)

www. mindcontrolforums.com

http://www.apfn.org/apfn/aids.htm   ('designer' diseases)

http://www.criminalgovernment.com/docs/enemy.html (amended Trading with the Enemy Act and the perpetual 'emergency' – Dr. Gene Shroder)

www.UsofAvUS.com   (information about the 'corporate' government)

Search on 'AIDS Ft. Dietrick', also 'designer diseases.'

Search on 'Codex Alimentarius.'

Search on 'Pan-American Union'

Search on 'gold-fringed flag'

Search on 'invisible contracts'

Suggested Reading

(again, not exhaustive, and in no particular order)

Man should not be in the service of society, society should
be in the service of man. When man is in the service of
society, you have a monster state, and that's what is
threatening the world at this minute.

Joseph Campbell

1. *The Creature from Jekyll Island* by G. Edward Griffin (see also   website)
2. *A Caveat Against Injustice* by Roger Sherman
3. *The Road to Serfdom* by Frederik Hayek
4. *The Fatal Conceit* and other writings by Frederik Hayek
5. *Was Jonestown a CIA Medical Experiment* by Michael Meier
6. *From Constitutional Republic to Corporate State* by Walker Todd
7. *Theory of Money and Credit* by Ludwig von Mises
8. *The Case for Gold* by Ron Paul and Lewis Lerhman
9. *The Mystery of Banking* by Murray Rothbard
10. *America's Great Depression* and others by Murray Rothbard
11. *Wall Street and FDR* by Antony C. Sutton
12. *Wall Street and the Bolshevik Revolution* by Antony C. Sutton
13. T*he Best Enemy Money Can Buy* by Antony C. Sutton
14. *Wall Street and the Rise of Hitler* by Antony C. Sutton
15. *The Franklin Cover-up:Child Abuse, Satanism, and Murder in Nebraska* by John Decamp
16. *The CIA's Control of Candy Jones* by Donald Bain
17. *A Father, a Son, and the CIA* by Harvey Weinstein
18. *Operation Mind Control* by Walter Bowart (both 1978 and a newer expanded self-published edition)
19. *Votescam: The Stealing of America* by Kenneth Collier and James Collier (also – see website)
20. *The Anglo-American Establishment* by Carroll Quigley
21. *Jack the Ripper: The Final Solution* by Steven Knight
22. *The Thirteenth Tribe* by Arthur Koestler
23. *Secrets of the Federal Reserve* by Eustace Mullins
24. *Report from Iron Mountain* by Leonard Lewin
25. *The Real Lincoln* by Thomas J. DiLorenzo
26. *Thanks for the Memories* by Bryce Taylor

27. *Trans-Formation of America* by Cathy O'Brien and Mark Phillips
28. *Spychips: How Major Corporations and Government Plan to Track Your Every Move with RFID* by Katherine Albrecht
29. *An Essay on Trial by Jury* by Lysander Spooner
30. *The Law* by Frederick Bastiat
31. *Mind Control, World Control* and other books by Jim Keith
32. *The Clam Plate Orgy* and other books on subliminal persuasion by Wilson Bryan Key
33. *Compromised* by Terry Reed
34. *The Politics of Heroin* by Alfred McCoy
35. *Don't Blame the People* by Robert Cirino
36. *The Tyranny of Gun Control* by Jacob G. Hornberger
37. *That Every Man Be Armed* by Stephen P. Halbrook
38. *U.S. of A. v U.S.* by Richard Dwight Kegley, TJ Henderson, RCL, and Edward Wahler (see also website)
39. *The Ultimate Evil* by Maury Terry
40. *To Destroy You Is No Loss* by Joan D. Criddle
41. *Journey Into the Whirlwind* by Evgeniia Semenovna Ginzberg
42. *Wild Swans: Three Daughters of China* by Jung Chang
43. *Bitter Winds* and *Troublemaker* by Hongda Wu
44. *The Crazed* by Ha Jin

Not to engage in the pursuit of ideas
is to live like ants instead of like men.

Mortimer Adler

431

The conscious and intelligent manipulation
of the organized habits and opinions of the masses is an
important element in democratic society. Those who who
manipulate this unseen mechanism of society constitute an
invisible government which is the true ruling power of our
country.

Edward Bernays

The ruling class
are the rich, who really command
our industry, our commerce, and our finance.
And these people are so able to manipulate
our democracy that they really
control the democracy.

Walter Cronkhite

Give me control
of a nation's currency,
and I care not who makes the laws.

The founder of the Rothschild banking dynasty

I never wonder to see men wicked,
but I often wonder to see them not ashamed.

Jonathan Swift

In the end
it was all about who got what.

From the film,
Blood Diamond

www.ingramcontent.com/pod-product-compliance
Lightning Source LLC
Chambersburg PA
CBHW030929020726
47498CB00001B/176